## ACCLAIM FOR
## THE PSYCHIC EYE MYSTERY SERIES

"Intuition tells me this book is right on target—I sense a hit!"
—Madelyn Alt, author of *Home for a Spell*

"Abby's inner monologue is always entertaining."
—*Publishers Weekly*

"If you like to mix a bit of witty banter with suspense and a touch of mysticism, this series is for you." —Examiner.com

"The story line captures your attention and doesn't let go until the final pages. . . . Don't miss this one."
—Monsters and Critics

"Abby Cooper is a character I hope will be around for a long time." —Spinetingler Magazine

"Natural pacing and humor." —*Kirkus Reviews*

"It doesn't take a crystal ball to tell it will be well worth reading." —Mysterious Reviews

"An edge-of-your-seat mystery." —Darque Reviews

"A fabulous who-done-it." —The Best Reviews

*continued . . .*

"Readers will understand the meaning of mission impossible when they try to put the novel down."
—Genre Go Round Reviews

"Plenty of surprises and revelations in the exciting story line."
—Gumshoe

"Full of plots, subplots, mystery, and murder, yet it is all handled so deftly."
—The Mystery Reader

"Victoria Laurie has crafted a fantastic tale . . . giving the reader a few real frights and a lot of laughs."
—Fresh Fiction

## ACCLAIM FOR THE *NEW YORK TIMES* BESTSELLING M. J. HOLLIDAY, GHOST HUNTER MYSTERIES

"Victoria Laurie is the queen of paranormal mysteries."
—BookReview.com

"Reminiscent of Buffy the Vampire's bunch, Laurie's enthusiastic, punchy ghost busters make this paranormal series one teens can also enjoy."
—*Publishers Weekly*

"Laurie's new paranormal series lights up the night."
—Elaine Viets, national bestselling author of *Catnapped!*

# DEADLY
# FORECAST

*A Psychic Eye Mystery*

## Victoria Laurie

AN OBSIDIAN MYSTERY

OBSIDIAN
Published by the Penguin Group
Penguin Group (USA) LLC, 375 Hudson Street,
New York, New York 10014

USA I Canada I UK I Ireland I Australia I New Zealand I India I South Africa I China
penguin.com
A Penguin Random House Company

Published by Obsidian, an imprint of New American Library, a division of Penguin
Group (USA) LLC. Previously published in an Obsidian hardcover edition.

First Obsidian Mass Market Printing, June 2014

Copyright © Victoria Laurie, 2013

ISBN 978-0-451-41969-9

Printed in the United States of America
10   9   8   7   6   5   4   3   2   1

For my sister, Sandy,
who is the Cat to my Abby,
minus the bullhorn and bulldozer, of course . . . ☺

# Acknowledgments

I've wanted to get Abby and M.J. together for years. One of the great joys about having multiple series is playing around with the idea of having them team up to solve a mystery together someday. This particular challenge, however, came with its own set of obstacles. Which series to set the story in was the first decision to make, and since M.J. had her roots in *A Vision of Murder*, I thought it only natural to bring her back for another Psychic Eye mystery.

Then I had to decide how to give clear voice to both Abby and M.J., who are each always written in the first person. Sort of by accident I decided to give M.J. a third-person perspective. Timing was also a tough decision—should I bring M.J. in at the beginning? Or allow her to ease into the story a bit later? I chose the former because I've always wanted to try a double-time-line scenario, and this seemed like the perfect vehicle.

Mostly, I wanted to share a little space with my two favorite girls, who've served me so well over the past nine years. And this task truly could not have been accomplished without the support of some very special people. How wonderful that we authors are given the space to acknowledge all the special people who make each book possible.

First, I'd like to give my heartfelt thanks to my fabulous

editor, Mrs. Sandra Harding-Hull, who has in her fan club many a devoted coworker, author, and friend. In a word, Sandy is amazeballs. She makes a wonderful collaborative partner and I'm deeply, deeply grateful to have her as an editor and friend. Sandy, thank you for all your hard work and insight. I'm deeply, deeply grateful.

Next, my schmabulous agent, Jim McCarthy, who has opened this book, skimmed past the first part of these acknowledgments, discovered his name, and is right now reading at breakneck speed to find out what lovely new things I will say about him this time. (Waves) Hi, Jim! Gotcha! ☺ Heh, heh. Truthfully, though, the very best compliment I could possibly pay him is that I know in my bones that there is no other person on EARTH who could be a better agent and advocate for me. Thank God Jim is one of a kind. Thank God he's my agent. Thank God he's delightful, and charming, and witty, and funny, and oh so wise. Thank God I lurves him enough to tell him the truth. Thank God he lurves me enough to listen, and tell me the truth too. Most of all, thank God he and I are still together and strong as ever nine years into the mix.

I also must acknowledge my wonderful team at NAL, from fabulous editorial assistant Elizabeth Bistrow, to publicist Kayleigh Clark, to Sharon Gamboa, and my most favorite copy editor of all time, Michele Alpern. Oh, and of course editorial director Claire Zion. I'm so blessed to have the benefit of each and every one of your talents, and I humbly thank you.

Katie Coppedge, my Webmaster/personal assistant/BFF. Kay-Kay, you are often the brightest ray of sunshine in my day, and I love you sooooo much! Thank you for being such a wonderful person and dear, dear friend.

My sister, Sandy Upham, to whom this book is dedicated. You are so lovely and so amazing. I'm crazy proud of you, and all of my good days begin with a phone call from you. If only the rest of the world knew how hilarious and entertaining we are together! ("Shut up—we're awesome!") ;)

Allow me also to mention the rest of my inner circle, who are seriously the best cheerleading squad on the planet. Nicole Gray, Karen Ditmars, Leanne Tierney, Steve McGrory,

Matt and Mike Morrill, Hilary Laurie, Jackie and Will Barrett, Jo Agnelli, Nora, Bob, Liz, Katie, Mike, and Nick Brosseau, Silas Hudson, Thomas Robinson, Laurie Proux, Drue Rowean, Suzanne Parsons, Betty and Pippa Stocking, John Kwaitkowski, Matt McDougall, Sally Woods, Anne Kimbol, McKenna Jordan, Jennifer Melkonian, Shannon Anderson, Juan Tamayo, Rick Michael, Molly Boyle, Martha Bushko, Juliet Blackwell, Nicole Peeler, and Sophie Littlefield.

Deepest gratitude to each of you for your generous hearts and kindred spirits.

# Chapter One

The first thing I noticed after regaining consciousness was a splitting headache and how uncomfortable I was. My head throbbed, but more than that, my body felt wrapped in iron. With effort I tried to sit up, and so many realizations sprinted into my brain that it made the ache in my head even worse.

The ensuing dump of adrenaline quashed much of the headache, but I was hardly relieved. My fingers found the metal cage wrapped around my torso, and also the wires poking out from a device centered over my heart.

I knew exactly what that device was—I'd seen the havoc it could wreak firsthand, and I also knew I had very little time left to live. Feeling a sob bubble up from the center of my chest, I did my best to quell it—I had to think!

But thinking proved nearly impossible. "Oh, God!" I whispered, as tears filled my eyes. Carefully, and I do mean *carefully*, I moved my fingers along the metal, hunting for a way out. It was then that I realized I was wearing a bundle of cloth that made movement even more cumbersome. Lifting my chin, I looked down at myself. I was wrapped in metal and white silk.

Raising my right arm, I saw the ornate lace of the cuff and I could feel the puffy fabric around my arms, but I could also feel that my shoulders were nearly exposed, and as I turned my head from side to side, I could see that the wedding dress I'd been wrapped in was about four sizes too big.

This wasn't my wedding dress, though, so why would it fit? I knew to whom it belonged, and also who'd dressed me in it and strapped the metal, wires, and timepiece to my chest.

Looking around the room, I was shocked to register where I actually was. As I lay on a large king-sized four-poster bed with soft linens, romantic lighting, and a painting on the wall of the manor home where I was to be married, I knew this had to be the little cottage my sister had told me about. Dutch and I would have come here after the reception and fallen into this bed to begin our life together as man and wife, but instead, I was strapped to a bomb that would likely go off before all the wedding guests had arrived.

And then my breath caught again. Had the countdown already begun? How long had I been out? I swallowed hard and summoned the courage to slowly prop myself up on my elbows, searching out the digital numbers and hoping for time.

"Hello, Banes," said a voice, and my gaze snapped to the other side of the room, where a figure sat speaking into a disposable cell phone. "The clock is now ticking. You have two hours."

And then, as if on cue, there was a little beep from the device strapped to my chest and as I looked down, I could see a digital display come to life. Even though it was upside down, I could tell the countdown had begun. I had two hours to live.

My thoughts railed against the reality of it. How could this have happened to me? And how was it that I hadn't seen it coming?

But as I stared in shock at the digital display counting down the final moments of my life, I realized the clues had been there all along. I'd simply failed to put them together. I'd been focused in another direction entirely, and it'd never occurred to me that I would end up as the target.

My thoughts darted back to when fate had turned against me—a mere two weeks earlier—to the day I'd gotten involved in a case and I'd unwittingly altered everything.

I remembered the start of that day well. It'd been a beautiful fall morning, with temps in the low seventies. My fiancé had brought me breakfast in bed. He'd looked so worried as he set the tray of pancakes down next to me. "How're you feeling?"

"I'm fine," I'd assured him, moving my legs under the covers to show him they were functioning properly. His worry over my health had been the result of a nasty encounter with a murderer in a case I'd solved just a few days earlier involving a missing woman. In the process, I'd gotten pretty beat up, and I'd then taken it very easy for a week, doing little more than resting on the couch and catching up on my sleep.

"Any pain?" Dutch asked.

"No, no real pain," I assured him. "But I am still a little sore from the beating."

Dutch pulled down the comforter to eye my right thigh with concern. It was covered in purple and black bruises. "I'll bring you up an ice pack."

I put a hand on his arm to keep him from leaving me. "Later, cowboy. Right now I just want to look at you."

My fiancé, Dutch Rivers, is about the most gorgeous hunk'a man you've ever seen. He's tall, blond, and muscular, with midnight blue eyes, a firm jaw, and a beautifully straight nose.

He's just as handsome on the inside too. And for whatever reason, he's crazy about me. Which is his only fault, because I'm a handful. Just ask him, and he'll tell you. Heck, just ask *anyone* in my inner circle about how much of a pain in the ass I can be, and they'll likely ask you how much time you have.

Still, for whatever reason, the Dutch and Abby partnership has always worked, and after three and a half years together, we were about to make it official with a walk down the aisle. "Your physical therapist called," Dutch said, scooting onto the bed to help me eat the pancakes. (And by "help" I mean one bite for me, five bites for him. . . .)

"Ugh. I forgot I had an appointment with her today."

"I told her you were canceling."

I eyed him with surprise. "Why?"

"Are you kidding?"

"No. I can make the appointment, sweetie."

"Edgar," he said, using his pet name for me, after famed psychic Edgar Cayce. "There's no way you can go to physical therapy with a leg that looks like that."

You'd think by now Dutch would know better than to tell me what I could and couldn't do. "Oh, please," I said, throwing the covers to the side and easing my legs gingerly out from under them. "It looks way worse than it is. Besides, we're getting married at the end of the month, cowboy. There's no way I'm giving up on the idea of walking down that aisle without my cane."

Several months earlier I'd been in a really bad accident, and my pelvis had been broken in several places. My recovery had been very slow, frustrating, and painful. (But mostly for my friends and family. For me, it'd been that times a hundred.) Still, I was determined to at least gimp my way down the aisle.

Dutch responded to my declaration with a skeptically raised eyebrow.

I glared at him. "Challenge accepted," I said, before carefully planting my feet and standing up. Very slowly I took one small step, mentally crossing my fingers that I wouldn't fall. To my surprise, the step didn't hurt or feel weak; it felt sure and steady. Encouraged, I took another step. Then another. And another. And another. Then one more for good measure.

When I looked behind me, Dutch was sitting straight up and staring at me in shock. "How long have you been able to walk that far without your cane?"

I glanced down at my toes gleefully. I hadn't taken more than three steps on my own since the accident. I'd just doubled my long-distance record. "I haven't been able to do more than three steps until today! Holy freakballs, honey! I can walk!" And then my hip gave out and I fell face-first into the wing chair by the window.

Dutch was at my side in a hot second. "You okay?" he asked, picking me up into his arms.

Embarrassed, I swiped at my hair, which had fallen over my eyes, and tried to play it off. "I meant to do that."

Dutch chuckled. "Sure you did."

"No, really. I did. How else could I get you to sweep me off my feet?"

Dutch leaned forward to give me a kiss, but I stopped him because now that I'd actually walked several steps, I wanted some reassurance. "Honey, do you think I'll really be able to make it down the aisle without the cane?"

"Have you given any thought to an escort?" he asked.

I frowned. I'm not close with my parents, and by that, I mean I don't speak to them and haven't in years, so I'd always planned on walking down the aisle alone at my wedding.

"Abs, I only say that because, if you're determined to leave the cane behind, having someone at your side to lean on would help steady you, and if you choose the right guy, they'll protect you from falling if you trip or one of your hips gives out."

I eyed him with interest. "Who volunteered?"

"Milo, Brice, Dave, and—curiously—Director Gaston."

That got me to smile. "Brice is out," I said right away. "He's Candice's groomsman. And Dave will be so nervous he'll trip over his own two feet and take me down with him. I couldn't walk with Director Gaston, because walking down the aisle with your boss's boss would make *me* so nervous I'd trip for sure."

"So it's Milo?" Dutch asked hopefully.

I frowned again and shook my head. "He's your best man. I can't take him away from you."

"He's willing to do double duty, dollface."

"You five guys have already talked about this, huh?"

"We have."

"Who's your pick?"

"Milo. I trust him to take care of you."

"You really think I should walk with someone?"

Dutch leaned in for his kiss and did his best Humphrey Bogart impression. "I do, I do, I do, sweethot."

In a flash I had the most horrible feeling wash over me in

a strange sort of déjà vu. The sensation was so intense that I actually gasped.

Dutch mistook that for desire and gave me a passionate kiss that normally would have started those belly embers burnin', but instead I stiffened and pushed at him.

He pulled away immediately. "What's wrong?"

I gripped his shirt in my hands and stared intensely into his eyes. The intuitive feeling rippling along my energy suggested that some terrible fate awaited my fiancé. And by terrible, I mean deadly. "Something's wrong."

Dutch held very still. After almost four years together he could read me like a book. "A vision?"

I shook my head. "Not exactly." That terrible feeling of something really, really, *really* bad happening to him wouldn't leave. I continued to stare at him, trying to make sense of the psychic vibe surging between us. I couldn't see what would happen to him, but I knew that some new and awful danger was lurking in the shadows somewhere. And I knew he was defenseless against it. His fate felt so imminently deathly that it set my heart racing in a panic. "What is it?" I whispered, trying to isolate the origins of this threat.

"What's what, doll?" he asked me, his eyes searching my face.

My gaze locked with his, and I almost couldn't form the words. "You're in danger, Dutch."

His brow rose. "Me?"

"Yes," I said, cupping his face and feeling a cold shiver take root at the base of my spine. "And it's connected to your work."

His expression softened. "Comes with the territory," he said, full of that bravado that makes courageous men say and do stupid things.

Dutch works for the FBI, and although his division is more focused on solving cold cases than active ones, it still means that he has to deal with the occasional dicey situation.

But this wasn't just a dicey situation. This was his murder. And the fact that it felt so close and so definite left me reeling and panic-stricken. "Dutch," I said, my eyes welling with tears. "Please don't go to work today."

He looked curiously at me. "Edgar, what is it?"

I opened my mouth but couldn't find the words to fully describe what I was picking up in the ether. It was like a thousand warning bells going off all around us, and I knew with absolute certainty that before the month was out, my fiancé, the person I loved most in the world, would be dead. I choked on a sob and threw my arms around his neck, clinging to him, and willing him to stay next to me where I could try to keep him safe.

Instead, Dutch turned with me still in his arms and sat down on the chair. He hugged me tightly and tried to comfort me. "Aw, babe," he said softly. "Whatever it is, we can figure it out. Tell me what you see and we'll work on it together, okay?"

I shook my head and pulled back to look at him. "It's not anything I can articulate. It's just a knowing."

"What is it you know?"

I wanted to tell him that I saw his death, if only because I wanted him to take me seriously, but try as I might, I couldn't hold in the sobs forming in my throat to speak the truth he needed to hear.

"Dollface," Dutch said softly, kissing my wet cheek before he hugged me tightly again. "If you don't want me to go to work today, I won't go."

I lifted my chin from his shoulder. "Really?"

He nodded. "You'll have to help me figure out what I'm gonna tell Gaston, though," he said, referring to the FBI director. Dutch and his entire department were working a critical case where a suicide bomber had targeted a mall in a city northeast of Austin.

The bomber and an elderly couple had been killed, and the Austin-based bureau was trying very hard to hold on to their jurisdiction because both the Dallas branch and Homeland Security were chomping at the bit to take the case away from Gaston's squad.

Director Gaston was former CIA, and he didn't flinch at much, but the director of Homeland Security and the FBI director in Dallas had teamed up against him at their first official meeting and that was the wrong thing to do to a man like Gaston. He'd since dug in his heels and it was no secret that he was determined to hang on to and solve the case, even if that meant working his men into the ground.

At issue were the intentions of the bomber, who, as it turned out, was a pretty young girl from Austin who'd been attending college at Texas A&M. No one could figure out why she'd suddenly strapped a bomb to her torso and walked into a mall to blow herself and three others up.

The case was a nightmare of unanswered questions, and normally I would've volunteered my services as a professional psychic (I consult with the FBI on a regular basis), but for whatever reason, my crew—those spirit guides tasked with giving me intuitive insight while trying to keep me out of trouble—were insisting that I not get involved.

This was problematic because Gaston told me repeatedly that he could really use my help on the case, and he wasn't necessarily buying the whole "My spirit guides said no" excuse.

I could hardly blame him. It sounded lame to my ears too. And I could only imagine what he'd say when Dutch called him to let him know he wasn't going into the office. "Can't you call Brice and tell him that I have a really bad feeling about your safety?" I asked, hoping Dutch could simply bypass the director and report to his immediate supervisor, Brice Harrison, who was far more reasonable with things like this, mostly because he was a good friend and currently engaged to my best friend, Candice.

Dutch sighed heavily. "If Brice okays it, then he'll have to inform Gaston, and you know that won't fly. Gaston would have his foot up Brice's ass in about three seconds."

I swallowed hard. I might be able to convince Gaston to give Dutch this one day off, but it would come at a price. "Let me try," I said, holding out my hand for Dutch's phone.

He eyed me skeptically. "I can call in my own sick day, Edgar."

"Could he fire you?" I asked, suddenly worried about office politics.

Dutch shrugged. "He could. But he won't. If he fires me, he loses you. He'll probably write me up, though."

I held my hand out again. "Gimme the phone."

Dutch sighed, but he turned sideways to pull his phone out from his back pocket. Just as he was handing it to me, the cell rang.

I jumped, but Dutch took the device back and after quickly looking at the display, he answered with a commanding, "Rivers."

I watched Dutch's face intently, that awful foreboding feeling never wavering. Five seconds into the call his expression hardened. "Dammit! Again? Where?"

And I knew. I knew exactly what'd happened. I closed my eyes and felt hot tears leak out. Tears of panic, sadness, and terrible fear. I wiped clumsily at my cheeks while he finished the call and sat there numbly for a moment. "There's been another bombing," I said.

He nodded, and pocketed the cell. "I have to go in."

I wanted to say something—anything—that would stop him from leaving the house, but I knew there were no such words. Dutch was a cop through and through, and telling him to do nothing when a crisis hit was like asking a bird not to fly.

"I'm coming with you," I told him, and he immediately stiffened.

"No," he said firmly.

"What do you mean, 'no'?"

"I have to go to the crime scene, and there's no way I'm letting you anywhere near that."

I pushed at his chest defiantly. "Are you seriously *kidding* me? I've been to crime scenes before, cowboy. I'm not some wilting flower, you know."

But Dutch was unmoved. "Remember the footage from the last bombing? Remember how that affected you?"

I glared hard at him. The footage from the first bombing had sent me into such hysterics that I'd had to leave the building. "That's some dirty pool, cowboy."

"Abs," Dutch said with a sigh. "If you go with me, you realize Gaston is gonna pull you right into this mess, and you know you can't get involved. Your crew said for you to butt out, and as much as you'd like me to believe they want you out of it because you might misinterpret and cloud the case, I *know* it's because there could be some danger to you."

Son of a beast. He'd figured that out.

"And," he went on, "if you're right and I'm the one with a target on his back, then there's *no way* I want you anywhere near me while I work this case. You're staying put, sweets."

"But I'm worried about you!" And for the record, I was more than worried; I was flat-out terrified.

"I'll be extra careful."

I turned my face away from him, angry that he didn't seem to be taking this seriously.

"Hey," he said, pulling my chin around again so that he could look me in the eyes. "I will be careful, dollface. I promise. I'll even wear a vest and keep the guys close, okay?"

"A vest won't do a damn thing against a bomb."

"Exactly my point and why I don't want you anywhere near this case, Edgar."

I could see that I was fighting a losing battle, so I said nothing more.

"Besides," he went on, trying to lighten the mood, "you have a physical therapy appointment, and probably a lot of other wedding stuff to work on, right?"

I glared defiantly at him. I wouldn't be doing any of that today.

Dutch took my silence for acquiescence and he carefully got up with me still in his arms to set me on the bed to kiss me sweetly before heading to his closet to retrieve his bullet-proof vest and gun holster.

I watched him dress silently, taking him in from head to toe. How could I love someone so completely? There wasn't a part of Dutch that I didn't adore with my whole heart. I couldn't lose him. It'd kill me.

When he was finished getting himself together, he came over to kiss me again. "I'll call you, okay?"

"Every hour," I replied flatly.

He chuckled into my hair. "I'll try," he promised. "And I'll be careful."

With that he left me. The moment he was out of the room, I grabbed a pair of jeans, a sweatshirt, my purse, my phone, and my cane and moved as fast as I could down the stairs. When I reached the landing, Dutch was already backing out of the driveway. I waited until his car had straightened out, then hurried out the door.

The stairs slowed me down a little—as they always do—but I managed to get into my car and start the engine with Dutch's car still in sight at the end of the street. He turned right and I backed out of the drive with a loud squeal of my tires. Zooming down the street, I flew past the stop sign (silently apologizing to the traffic god) and kept Dutch's black Audi in my line of sight while letting it cruise ahead well down the street. I prayed that he didn't look in his rearview mirror, because my blue Mini Cooper was a hard one to miss.

I followed him stealthily to the highway, which made it easier for me to hide behind other cars; then I saw that he was about to turn off onto an adjoining highway. I eased my car over and settled in, putting two cars between us. As we headed north, the traffic started to get considerably more congested. I became aware of a helicopter overhead, then another helicopter and the sound of sirens.

I ignored all of them and kept my focus on Dutch. Very soon the cars in the far right lane slowed to a near stop and began to put their left turn signals on. The blue and red flashing lights mounted to the rear of Dutch's backseat came on, and he took the shoulder. I eased my car over slightly to watch him zip up the road to the next exit, stop at the barricade manned by an Austin patrolman. The cop waved him down the ramp as soon as Dutch flashed his ID.

The minute he cruised out of sight, I also edged onto the shoulder and drove straight toward the cop—who did *not* look happy to see me. "Lady, this exit is closed!" he barked the moment I pulled to a stop and rolled down my window.

Fishing hastily through my purse, I pulled out my own FBI ID and waved it at him. "I'm supposed to meet Director Gaston at the crime scene," I said, hoping he'd been told who the head of the investigation was. "I'm with Special Agent Brice Harrison's team," I added. When in doubt drop all the names you can think of.

The cop scrutinized my ID; then he took in my appearance and seemed to hesitate.

I felt my cheeks flush. I was still in my pajamas. I motioned to the jeans and sweatshirt at my side. "The director told me to get my ass here ASAP," I told him. (Swearing doesn't count when you're trying to worm your way closer to a crime scene you haven't actually been invited to.) "And you've probably heard that the director doesn't like to be kept waiting."

The cop actually broke into a grin. "Yeah, I got a captain like that. Okay, go ahead, but be discreet where you change, okay? I don't want to see you cited for indecent exposure."

I smiled and gave him a two-finger salute, before backing up and weaving around the barricade.

The crime scene wasn't hard to spot—I just had to follow the smoke, which led me to a parking lot filled with smoldering embers. There must have been a dozen cop cars and another dozen or so black sedans lining the street leading to the decimated building. At the front of the scene were three large fire trucks, and behind that, three ambulances and even more cop cars. The fire department was still working to make sure the fire was completely out, while several paramedics remained on hand to help the injured, but it was hard to believe that anyone who'd been inside that building could still be alive.

A crowd of pedestrians had also gathered, most of them with a look of shock on their faces as they huddled close to one another. Several were even crying. The helicopters overhead were a mixture of news crews and police, and a row of news vans lined the street about a block away, many of the assigned reporters out in front of their vehicles reporting live from the scene.

As I made my way down the side street across from the strip mall, I waved my badge to several more patrol officers, and was finally directed to a spot just at the corner. I'd long since lost sight of Dutch's car, but I knew he was somewhere in the mess of first responders.

As I pulled into the space, I breathed a huge sigh of relief, because I was a good distance away from the crime scene, but with an unobstructed view, and even as I turned off the engine, I spotted Dutch making his way toward a cluster of men

I recognized from his office. Gaston was easy to see with his sleek black hair and handsome face. Despite the fact that the director was a taskmaster and often manipulated me into working for him, I liked him. I couldn't exactly tell you why, but he was an honest and earnest man, completely devoted to the job of protecting the innocent and bringing the guilty to justice. I also liked that he didn't suffer fools gladly—a trait I'd been accused of on occasion . . . cough . . . cough.

While keeping my eyes on Dutch, I shimmied into my sweatshirt and discreetly pulled on my jeans. Not an easy feat in a Mini, let me tell you. As I was setting my jammies to the side, I heard a loud rap on the passenger-side window and I think I jumped about a foot. Immediately locating the source, I hid a groan and undid the lock.

"Morning," Brice said, sliding into the seat to offer me one of two cups of coffee he held.

I took the coffee and waited for the lecture.

"Dutch sent me over," he explained. Something I'd already guessed. "He called me from the car and said you were tailing him."

"I'm not going to get in the way, sir," I said, adopting the formal address because he was on duty and, technically, I worked for him.

"I know," he replied, turning his gaze back to the chaotic scene. "And I'm a little torn about that."

I sighed. "You think I could help."

"I know you could help. But Dutch would probably do something stupid and insubordinate if I talked you into joining us."

"And we know where Gaston falls on the subject," I added.

He waved his cup at the throng of people working the scene. "This is only going to make him more insistent, Cooper." Brice rarely called me Abby, and truth be told, I rather liked the way he treated me like one of the guys.

"So what're you saying?"

"I'm saying that when Dutch called me on his way here to ask me to talk some sense into you, my first thought wasn't to order you away from the scene."

I bit my lip, my eyes searching for Dutch and finding him scribbling in his notebook while Gaston spoke to him. "Something's changed, sir."

"What's that?"

"Something around Dutch has changed."

Brice's brow furrowed. "I don't understand."

I sat up straighter and tried to think of how to explain it to him. He didn't have an intuitive bone in his body, so sometimes my predictions—or the way I worded them—confused him. He was a pretty literal guy. "There's been a shift in the ether," I began, watching him only to see his brow furrow even more. "My Spidey sense says that Dutch is in serious danger."

The brow rose sharply. "What kind of danger?"

My gaze drifted back to the scene and I scanned the crowd standing behind the police barricades. "I think he might die," I whispered so softly that Brice asked me to repeat myself.

When I did, he scratched his chin and stared hard at his second-in-command. "How?" he finally asked.

I shook my head and closed my eyes. "I don't know."

"Do you think someone might try to shoot him?"

I considered that, and had to discard it. "I don't think so, sir, but I can't say for sure."

"Is it someone from an old case he worked on?" Brice asked next, clearly trying to help me identify the source of the threat.

I shook my head. "No. The threat feels strongly connected to this case, sir."

"*This* case?" he repeated.

"Yes."

Brice blew out a sigh. "I can't take him off it, Cooper. Gaston would never let me remove my top man, even if the prompt came from you."

I felt my eyes well with tears again, and I turned to my friend, not my boss, and laid a hand on his arm. "I'm so afraid for him, Brice. I don't know how to stop it from happening."

Harrison was quiet for a moment before he said, "I do."

My hopes lifted. "You do?"

"Work the case, Abby," he said bluntly. "If someone connected to this mess is really out to hurt Rivers, you're the only one that'll see it coming in time to stop it."

My crew weighed in immediately and my mind was flooded with a feeling that under no circumstances should I get involved, but then I turned to look at Dutch again and I made up my own mind. "Okay."

Brice seemed surprised. "Yeah?"

I nodded. "You're right. It's the only thing I can do to try to keep him safe."

Brice clinked his coffee cup with mine. "Welcome aboard," he said, but then he sobered a little and added, "Dutch is gonna go ballistic when he hears that I talked you into working the case."

"He will," I agreed.

Then Brice seemed to think of something, because he reached for his cell, and the door handle. "Listen," he said before departing, "sit tight for a few while I figure this out, okay?"

I eyed him quizzically but agreed to stay put, and about a half hour later I knew what Brice had been up to, and I silently thanked the gods for his resourcefulness when a bright yellow Porsche pulled up next to me—my best friend behind the wheel.

# Abby & Dutch's Wedding Day— T-Minus 02:00:00

"That is one sweet car," Gilley Gillespie said, whistling appreciatively, as he and M. J. Holliday walked past a shiny yellow Porsche parked in the lot of the manor home where Abby and Dutch were about to get hitched.

"I think that belongs to Abby's best friend, Candice," M.J. said, digging in her purse to retrieve the wedding invitation in case the doorman asked for it. She remembered meeting Candice the last time she got to hang out with Abby, which was a few years earlier when Abby had needed M.J.'s help ridding an investment property she'd purchased of its spectral squatters. M.J. was a spirit medium and professional ghostbuster. Gilley was her best friend and her partner in their ghostbusting business, and the computer tech on their cable TV show, *Ghoul Getters*.

"How can you tell it's Candice's?" Gilley asked.

"My first clue was the vanity plate," M.J. replied. The tag on the yellow Porsche read CANDYPI.

"Oh," Gil said, craning his neck to take a look. "Yeah, I guess you're right."

M.J. shivered in the cold breeze blowing across the huge lawn of the manor home. It was a pretty awful day for a wedding, she thought moodily, pulling at the wrap around her shoulders. The sky was dark and overcast, and the local weather forecast threatened rain for late afternoon.

Still, there was something else bothering M.J. as they neared the entrance and waited for three people ahead of them to show the doorman their invitations. Something had shifted in the energy around her that morning, and as the time of Abby and Dutch's wedding drew closer, she found herself anxious to get to the manor house and check in with the bride.

"Why are we here two hours before the actual ceremony again?" Gilley asked as they made their way to the interior.

"Because the invite said that guests were welcome to arrive anytime between twelve and two and because I want to see if I can have a private word with Abby," M.J. told him, tucking the invitation back into her purse and looking around at the small crowd already in attendance. "She said she needed my input on a case she's been working, but she never called me to give me the details, and I have the most pressing feeling that she still needs my help with it."

"Ugh," Gil said, pouting next to her. "Only you would take a job during a wedding." M.J. couldn't really blame Gil for being grouchy. After all, she'd dragged him to Austin to be her plus one because her boyfriend, Heath, couldn't make it—he was busy moving his mother into her new condo in Santa Fe. "Hey," M.J. said, nudging her best friend. "Stop pouting, would you?"

Gil leveled his eyes at her. "Girl, you know I love a good wedding, but what I love even more is a good nap, and the fact that you dragged me away from a comfortable—oh look! Food!"

Gil immediately headed in the direction of a small buffet table with artfully arranged hors d'oeuvres, and M.J. breathed a sigh of relief. That'd keep Gil's bouche amused for a little while at least. Hopefully long enough for her to find Abby and make sure she was okay.

After scanning the crowd, M.J. found a face she recognized—Abby's fiancé, Dutch Rivers. He was a great-looking guy whom she'd met only once but it was enough to leave a very favorable impression. He seemed perfectly suited to

Abby, as he was even-keeled and cool under pressure, with a keen insight and a sharp mind. Not much got by him. Also, he clearly adored Abby; that much had been evident when M.J. had seen the two together two and a half years ago, and it was even more evident now, because although Dutch seemed to be engaged in conversation with a few other people around him, M.J. noticed that he kept bouncing slightly on the balls of his feet, and casting quick glances toward the back of the house where the bride was obviously getting ready. He looked as excited and impatient to get things under way as any love-struck groom could.

"Well, hello, handsome," said a voice right next to M.J. She turned her head and saw that Gil had come up beside her again holding a small plate piled high with hors d'oeuvres while he drank in the sight of Dutch across the room. More than weddings and a nap, Gil loved free food and good-looking men. "I thought you were taken?" M.J. kidded, referring to Gilley's new beau.

"I'm taken, not dead, M.J.," Gil replied. "I can look and flirt all I want. I'm just not allowed to touch."

"We can all breathe a little easier now," M.J. said with a laugh. Then she pointed across the room to the object of Gilley's current affection. "That's the groom. Dutch. Remember? We went to dinner with him and Abby before when we helped her with her investment house."

"Sugar, I could never forget a man that gorgeous," Gil replied, popping a small quiche into his mouth.

That anxious, nervous feeling that'd been bothering M.J. all morning cropped up again. "I need to find Abby," she whispered.

"Before the wedding?" Gil said.

"Yeah. I keep feeling like everything's not okay with her."

Gil made a face. "How could things be anything other than perfect for a girl about to marry that tall drink of water?"

M.J. ignored him and moved away in the direction that Dutch seemed to be perpetually focusing on, the back of the manor home. Winding her way through the crowd, she finally came to a corridor that looked promising. "I don't think you're supposed to go back there," Gil said from right behind her, and M.J. jumped. She hadn't realized he'd been following her so closely.

"Do me a favor," she told him. "Stay here and keep a lookout. I just want a quick word with the bride."

Gilley's frown returned. "Are you about to meddle?"

"No, Gil, that's *your* territory. Just keep a lookout. I'll be back in a minute."

M.J. then hurried into the corridor and followed it to a room with the sounds of excited voices. Knocking first, she poked her head in, but found two women wearing jeans and impatient looks. "Oh, sorry!" M.J. said. "I thought the bride might be in here."

"She's not," said one woman, and M.J. noticed she was wrapping up the cord to a curling iron. "And neither is the maid of honor."

"Uh," M.J. said, not quite knowing what they were subtly hinting at. "Are they farther down the hall?"

The other girl, who was shuffling makeup around on the vanity, said, "Nope. The bride's missing and now so is the maid of honor."

A jolt of alarm went through M.J. "Missing?" she repeated. "The bride is *missing*?"

Both women nodded. "We see this thing all the time. The bride gets nervous and tries to bolt right before the ceremony. I just did a wedding three weeks ago where the bride fled to the Bahamas with the best man."

M.J.'s mouth fell open. She couldn't imagine Abby skipping out on Dutch. Those two were as meant to be as any two people she'd ever met. "Does the groom know?" she whispered.

Both women shrugged. "I think only Mrs. Cooper-Masters knows," said the woman with the curling iron. And she and the makeup artist exchanged another knowing look. "Which is why we're hiding in here. No way do I want to be around that bundle of crazy right now."

M.J. nodded and closed the door. She hadn't met Abby's sister, but she'd heard she could be a handful. Still, that feeling of unease heightened up another several notches. Something bad was happening. Really, really bad, and it involved

Abby. Something far more terrible than just Abby skipping out on the wedding was taking place, M.J. could feel it in her bones.

Moving back down the corridor, she found Gilley still popping those hors d'oeuvres and staring at the gathering crowd. "Did you find her?" he asked when she came up next to him.

M.J. wrung her hands. "No. And now I'm worried."

"Maybe she's in one of the other rooms?" Gil suggested. "A house this big has to have a whole wing devoted to dressing rooms."

But M.J. ignored him. She believed the hairstylist and the makeup artist. Abby was missing, and M.J. didn't think she was even on the property. The question was, Should she say something to Dutch? Because it was obvious he didn't yet know that his bride was MIA.

Another wave of unease washed over her, as if in answer to her internal struggle, and M.J. was moving toward Dutch without giving it any more thought.

He was still engaged in conversation with several other guys, one also dressed in a tux and almost as handsome as Dutch, and three others dressed in suits who bore a striking resemblance to the groom.

As she came up next to the small crowd, she knew she'd have to work to get his attention. "Dutch!" she called softly, but he was in the middle of telling a joke and not aware of her presence. "Dutch!" M.J. tried again, a little louder.

This time the man in a tux standing next to Dutch gave him a nudge and motioned toward her. At last Dutch turned to her. "M.J.!" he said, his face lighting up with a happy smile as he leaned in to give her a brief hug. "Abby told me you were coming. Did you need something?"

M.J. opened her mouth to speak, but hesitated. Dutch continued to stare expectantly at her and finally she said, "Do you know where Abby is?"

His expression turned humorously quizzical before he motioned with his chin toward the corridor she'd just come from. "She's getting ready back there. Did you want to poke your head in? I don't think she'd mind if you went back to say hi."

M.J. bit her lip. "I've been back there," she said, moving closer to him to keep her voice low enough that only he and the people around him could hear. "She's not there."

Dutch's face lost all of its humor. "What do you mean, she's not there?"

"I spoke with the hairstylist and the makeup artist. They said that Abby's missing. And so is Candice."

The man next to Dutch leaned forward, his own face suddenly alarmed. "Hold on," he said. "What do you mean they're missing?"

Given the man's reaction, M.J. realized that he must be Candice's fiancé, Brice. "That's all I know, but, Dutch, I have this feeling, this really *bad* feeling. . . ." M.J.'s voice trailed off. She didn't quite know how to explain what she felt. This awful feeling swirling around her was so oppressive it was hard to think.

He was staring at her intensely now. "You're psychic too, right?"

M.J. nodded. "I'm more a medium than a psychic, but every once in a while I get a really strong feeling that something bad is about to happen."

Dutch's posture stiffened even more. "Like now?"

"Yes."

"Dammit," he muttered. Feeling along his pockets and coming up empty, he nudged Brice. "My phone's at the guesthouse. Brice, give me your cell."

Brice pulled out his phone and handed it to Dutch. "Abby's in the contacts list," he said.

Dutch tapped at the screen and placed the phone to his ear. M.J. waited anxiously, but that mounting feeling of something terrible occurring continued to fill her mind with dread. "What's going on?" a voice beside her demanded.

M.J. turned to find Gilley next to her again, his plate now empty of food. "Nothing. Go get some more hors d'oeuvres. I'll be there in a sec."

But Gilley wasn't having it. "Obviously something's up," he insisted. "Seriously, tell me what it is!"

"Voice mail," Dutch said, calling M.J.'s attention back to him. He then tapped at the screen again. "Where's Candice's number, Brice?" he asked impatiently.

His friend took the phone and tapped at it himself. After a minute he spoke into the phone. "Sweetheart, it's me. Call me back as soon as you get this message." He then hung up and began texting, but M.J. couldn't see what he was typing.

Meanwhile Dutch was scanning the crowd. "Has anyone seen Milo?" he asked. "He told me he was going to check on Abby an hour ago and I haven't seen him since."

"The hairstylist said that Cat might know where Abby and Candice are," M.J. confessed. She didn't like ratting on Abby's sister, but this was serious. She just *knew* something bad had happened.

At that moment a petite woman with short blond hair emerged from the kitchen area and began to weave her way through the crowd. She wore a Bluetooth headset, and gripped a large clipboard in both hands as she moved swiftly through the crowd, making a beeline for Dutch.

"Speak of the devil," Dutch muttered. "What's happened?" he asked the moment Cat came close.

"It's probably nothing," Cat replied in that way that told you it clearly wasn't.

"Where's your sister?" Dutch said next, his voice sharp. "Cat, tell me, has something happened to Abby?"

"No!" Cat said a bit too hastily. "I'm sure she's *fine*. It's just . . ."

Dutch's eyes flickered to M.J.'s and that horrible foreboding feeling surged within her with renewed energy. M.J. shook her head to let him know that she knew better. Abby was in trouble.

Dutch then stepped forward and took Cat by the shoulders. "Please tell me," he whispered.

"She's missing."

"She's *missing*?" he repeated. M.J.'s heart began to pound.

"Well, maybe not missing so much as she's left the building and no one seems to know where she is," Cat explained.

"And Candice went with her, right?" Brice asked, his own face a mask of worry.

Cat gulped. "No. Candice went to look for her, along with Milo. I didn't want to worry you, Dutch, but they're not back yet and I don't know what could be keeping them."

Dutch focused again on Cat. "Talk to me," he demanded quietly. "Tell me everything you know and don't leave anything out."

Cat wiped her brow, which was creased with perspiration even though it was chilly out. "Abby ducked out on us somewhere between hair and makeup. The makeup artist was too afraid to tell me until an hour ago. I sent Candice to go find Abby. She took Milo, and now I can't get either of them on the phone."

Dutch lifted Brice's phone out of his hand and dialed. A moment later he said, "Milo, it's me. Call me back on this number as soon as you get this message."

Dutch then hung up and dialed again—and a second later one of the two phones Cat held on top of her clipboard began to vibrate. Dutch reached out and took it from her. When he looked at the display, his face immediately darkened. *"You took her phone, Cat?"*

Cat gulped again. "I had to, Dutch! You know my sister! She's been so crazy over this case your people have been working that she wasn't letting go of it even though this is her wedding day! I needed her to focus on getting ready, not make phone calls all day long!"

Dutch squeezed the phone in his hand so hard his knuckles whitened, but he kept his tone even as he said, "Explain to me what the hell you're talking about, please."

Cat sighed, and wiped again at her brow with trembling fingers. "Abby was trying to call her boss—"

"Me?" Brice interrupted.

Cat nodded. "Yes. Well, at first she was trying to call Mr. Gaston, but I wouldn't let her, because she was sounding like she was going to have all you bureau boys leave the ceremony and go chase down some new lead she'd discovered. I told her it could wait until after she said her vows. I was only thinking of how much she'd regret it if her wedding day was ruined over something that could keep a few hours!"

"So she left," Dutch snapped, his eyes narrowed and angry.

"Yes."

"Did she take the limo?" Brice asked next.

"No. She took her own car."

"*Why* was she driving her own car?" Dutch's voice was starting to rise above the hushed whispers they'd all been speaking in.

"According to Candice, Abby got up early and left her a note that she wanted some alone time, and she took her own car here. Candice was worried about Abby, because she's been acting weird all week, so she took her own car too. Nobody thinks about the effort and money it took me to get the limo to pick the girls up, oh, *nooo*! They're all off driving their own cars all over town while I—"

"Cat!" Dutch barked, putting his hands on her shoulders again. "Focus! About what time did Abby leave here?"

"I don't know!" she cried, and several people nearby turned to stare at their little group. M.J. could feel a sort of ripple of alarm spread through the room.

Dutch's jaw bunched, and M.J. could see he was trying to think through the possible places his bride could be.

Abby's sister put a hand on his arm, attempting to console him. "I know that Abby would never leave you at the altar, Dutch. I'm sure she just needs a little time to get her head together, and she'll come back. You wait—Candice and Milo will talk some sense into her."

It was then that M.J. realized Cat still didn't understand that Abby was in trouble. She was thinking that her sister had turned into a runaway bride.

"She isn't missing because she doesn't want to be here, Cat!" Dutch nearly yelled, and the rest of the room fell silent. "She's missing because something's happened to her! Don't you get it?"

Behind them M.J. heard gasps coming from the crowd, followed by lots of murmuring.

Brice looked around the room and pointed toward a small cluster of guys near the buffet table before waving them over. The three men hurried through the crowd and the minute they got close enough, Brice quietly told them that Abby was missing and that Candice and Milo had been sent to find her, but no one was answering their calls. Meanwhile Dutch was dialing the phone again. "Milo, where the *hell* are you guys?!" For a moment M.J. thought he'd connected with his friend, but Dutch followed that with, "Just call me back, buddy, okay? Right away." That bad feeling coursing through M.J. wouldn't let up. Turning to Cat, she said, "Where did Candice say that she was going to look for Abby?"

Cat blinked. "She didn't."

"And you haven't heard from Candice since she left to go look for Abby?" Dutch pressed.

"No. It's only been an hour, but still, she's not answering her phone."

Brice put a hand on Dutch's shoulder before nodding to the three men who'd joined them. "We'll split up. You and I can go to the condo, Rodriguez and Cox can go to the girls' offices, and Director Gaston, will you check our office?"

"Immediately," he said, already turning to go.

"We should send somebody to check our new place," Dutch said, eyeing the group in front of him as if he were a general gathering his troops.

"Gilley and I can go," M.J. offered.

"You have a car?" Dutch asked.

M.J. nodded. Holding up her own phone, she added, "And GPS. Just give me the address and we'll be on our way."

"Three-three-one Overlook," Dutch told her. "The house was just built, so if it doesn't come up in your GPS, then use our neighbor's address, three-two-seven Overlook. It's not far from here. Just look for the white stucco house with the red clay roof and blue shutters." He then gave her Brice's number and added, "Call the minute you get to the house and let us know if she's there."

"What about us?" said one of the guys who looked close enough to Dutch to be his brother.

Dutch began walking hurriedly toward the door and they all shuffled forward with him. "Mike, if you, Chris, and Paul could stay here and search the grounds, just in case Abby's here somewhere, and call Brice's phone the minute she comes back, that would be great."

Dutch's three brothers nodded and peeled off from their group.

M.J. plugged Brice's number into her phone before grabbing Gilley by the wrist. "Let's go!"

From the driveway everyone separated, rushing toward their separate vehicles. M.J. passed Candice's yellow Porsche again and wondered why Candice hadn't responded to the urgent messages and texts Brice and Cat had left her. Brice's car was next to Candice's and he and Dutch jumped in, pulling out of the space with the engine roaring and the police strobe light in the back of Brice's car coming on. It washed over Candice's car like a bright red wave of alarm.

# Chapter Two

"Morning, Abby," Candice said, smiling at me from inside her Porsche as the strobe lights from the crime scene pulsed off the yellow paint. Seeing her amid the chaos of the crime scene was a sight for sore eyes. That girl always had my back.

"Morning, Cassidy," I said, using the nickname I'd coined for her.

She waved toward the crime scene. "I hear we're gonna consult with the boys on this one."

I felt a slight smile tug at the corners of my mouth. "We are, huh?"

Candice nodded. "My role is less consulting and more bodyguarding, but the pay is the same."

"Oh? And who would you be bodyguarding exactly?"

"You and Dutch," she replied without a hint of apology.

My grin widened. Hers did too and then she pulled her car over to wedge it between a no-parking sign and a fire hydrant. Candice isn't exactly a candidate for the title World's Most Responsible Driver.

She got out and so did I and we met in the middle of the street, where she assessed me critically. "Did you roll out of bed and drive straight here?"

"Yep."

"Huh," she said, looping the lanyard of her FBI ID over her head to nestle it in the folds of her impeccably styled pinstripe suit. "Rumpled is a pretty common look for you these days, you know."

"Shut it, Cassidy," I muttered, nudging her with my elbow.

"I'm just saying, maybe you and I should go shopping sometime soon."

I gritted my teeth and began to head over toward the boys, and Candice fell into step beside me after only one or two more wardrobe suggestions. Dutch's back was to me as we approached, and as if he had his own highly tuned radar, he turned and locked eyes with mine.

I smiled winningly.

His lips pressed together into a thin line.

"Brace yourself," I muttered to Candice, who edged a little closer to me.

Dutch then said something to Brice, standing several feet away, and Harrison pretended not to hear him. Undeterred, Dutch walked over to him and said something while pointing sternly at the two of us.

Harrison turned away from the other agent he'd been talking to and crossed his arms, adopting that hard, unreadable expression that used to drive me crazy. I quickened my pace, because I suspected that Dutch was about to cross a line, and while Brice had some measure of patience for that because Dutch was also his close friend, he'd be less willing to stomach it out here in front of so many witnesses. But Dutch looked mad enough not to care. "Aw, shit!" I muttered (swearing doesn't count when you're about to get your fiancé fired).

Dutch's hands had balled into fists as Brice spoke to him, but whatever he said didn't stop the angry train. In fact, it seemed to make Dutch madder. "I think he's going to hit him!" I said, panting hard and trying to move faster.

"We're too far away," Candice said, and out of the corner of my eye I saw her glance at my cane and my hobbling walk with frustration. She could've spared me the look; no one was more frustrated about my hampered pace than me at that moment.

So I did the only thing I could think of to get Dutch's attention off Brice. I let go of my cane and tried to run. It did the trick. Or trip, as was the case. I fell. Hard. I heard Candice cry out as I went down, and saw her arms flail for me, but she'd been too slow. I hit the pavement on the side of my bad hip—which, with my bad hips, could have been either the right or the left, but in this case, it was the left—and I let out a good long wail . . . and maybe a few expletives . . . (swearing doesn't count when you're trying to stop your fiancé from getting fired by taking one for the team on your bad hip).

The pain was intense, and I squeezed my eyes closed and bit my lip hard enough to taste a little blood. *"Mother Falkland Islands!"* (Sometimes I think that coming up with a clever curse word alternative should win me back one of the quarters from the swear jar.)

After groaning and rolling to my right side, I felt a hand latch onto my wrist, followed by Dutch's clear baritone calling my name. "Abby! Jesus, what happened?"

I opened my eyes to find both him and Brice running toward us. As they got close, Candice glared hard at Dutch. "She was trying to get to you before you did something stupid, and she tripped!" Candice yelled at him.

That was my cue to complain—loudly. "Ow, ow, ow, ow!"

Dutch reached my side, practically shoving a paramedic out of the way, who, I realized belatedly, had come to my rescue too. "Doll?" he asked, bending low to run his hands gently over my arms and legs. "Where does it hurt?"

"My ass!" I told him, even though that was a lie. My hip hurt like a mother Falkland Island.

Dutch blinked. Clearly not the answer he'd expected. "Your rear?" he asked me.

"Yes," I said, gritting my teeth again. "You are a royal pain in my ass, Dutch Rivers! You weren't going to wait for me to explain, and you made me fall!"

My fiancé looked like he had to bite back whatever retort he really, *really* wanted to say to me, and instead he helped me to my feet and yelled at the poor paramedic he'd shoved out of the way to get my cane. "Can you walk?" he asked in a far gentler tone.

I pushed at him as I took my cane from the kindly man trying to hand it to me. "I'm fine!" I snapped.

Now, you should probably know that all this bluster was a ploy I'd used once or twice before with Dutch. (Okay, maybe a few more times than once or twice.) Anyway, I'd managed to figure out that the secret to defusing Dutch's anger was to get mad myself. If I start snapping and throwing a little hissy fit, he becomes all calm and reasonable. In fact, for whatever reason, he often finds my hissy fits funny.

"Why don't you let one of the guys check you out?" Dutch said in a steady, soothing voice. (See? It totally works!)

"I'm fine!" At least I hoped I was. I took one small step, and managed okay.

"Did she hit her head?" Dutch asked Candice.

"I don't know," she said. "I don't think so."

"We can take her to the hospital and have her checked out," said the paramedic.

"I saw her go down," Brice said. "She hit the ground pretty hard. She could have a concussion."

I realized that everybody was so busy discussing my condition that no one was paying attention to me. Well, save for one man looking on from the parking lot with an amused expression.

While they were so distracted by the discussion about what to do with me, I eased away from them and gimped my way over to him. "Abigail," Director Gaston said warmly. "That looked like it hurt."

"Took one for the team," I told him.

He put a hand on my shoulder. "I applaud your timing, but are you all right?"

"A little sore, but I'll live."

"I understand you've decided to join the investigation."

"Yes, sir."

"Your fiancé will come to me to try to have you removed from the case," he replied, that gentle hand on my shoulder never wavering.

I spoke rapidly, aware that the others might be walking up

to us at any moment. "Sir, I think that Dutch may be in danger. And I worry that the danger he's in has something to do with this case."

Gaston's brow rose. "Oh?"

"Yes. I can't explain it other than a feeling that his life could be in jeopardy, and it has something to do with these bombings. Can you please, for me, take him off the case?"

Gaston's brow lowered and as if to make a point, he turned his head and took in the surrounding scene. "Abby, as long as these bombings continue to happen, any one of us could be in real danger. I can't afford to take one of my best investigators off the case, not after this."

I was disappointed but hardly surprised. I knew I'd have a tough time trying to convince Gaston. "Okay, well then, will you make me a promise, sir?"

"What's that?"

"I think Dutch is gonna threaten to do something drastic if I'm not taken off the case. But it's only because he's really mad, so, no matter what he says, or threatens to do, will you please not fire him and keep me on board so that I can try to keep him—make that everyone—safe?"

Gaston squeezed my shoulder and his smile was even more amused. "You have yourself a deal, Abigail."

"Sir!" I heard Dutch call. I turned and saw him hurrying toward us.

"Also," I added quickly before Dutch got within hearing range, "it would really help if you ordered Dutch to wear his vest for a while."

"He's got it on now," Gaston said.

"Yeah, but I want him to wear it all the time. Can you do that?"

"Director," Dutch said, coming the last few feet to stand right next to me. "May I have a word with you?"

"Agent Rivers, Miss Cooper here was just telling me that she will be lending her considerable talents to this investigation, and as I worry about the politics of having her on board with regard to the other agency currently sticking its nose

into our business, I'd like you to stay close to her for the re-
mainder of the investigation. And, as I also worry that she
could become a target if word got out that a talented psychic
was working for us on this one, I'd like you to wear your vest
at all times."

I had to work hard not to break out into a big ol' grin.

For a minute Dutch looked completely taken aback—he
didn't know what to think. And while Gaston had him
slightly off guard, the director took out his cell phone and
said, "That's an order, Agent Rivers. Now, if you'll excuse
me, I have to call Washington and give them a brief of the
scene."

As the director walked away, however, I saw Dutch's
stunned reaction fade and it was replaced by something just
south of furious.

Uh-oh.

"You know, Edgar . . . ," he said, shaking his head angrily.
"You accuse me of not playing fair, but as things go, *that* was
dirty pool."

I started to feel really bad, but in my mind I'd had no
choice. "Dutch . . . I—"

"We'll talk later," he said, cutting me off. At that moment
Candice and Brice came up next to us, and without another
word, Dutch stalked off.

"How mad is he?" Candice asked.

"If we were already married, I think he'd be asking me for
a divorce."

"He'll get over it," Brice said, his gaze moving to the
smoldering rubble. The firemen were starting to coil up their
hoses and Brice lifted his chin toward the fire chief in an
unspoken question.

The chief waved us over. "It's safe, but there are parts that're
still hot. Watch your step," he said, his eyes fixed on me.

"Yes, sir," I said, and moved with Candice and Brice over
to the front of the building, which had a huge hole blown out
about the place where the door would have been.

"It looks like the bomber walked in and didn't waste any
time detonating the bomb," Brice commented.

Broken glass crunched under my feet as I stepped gingerly

into the space. A large hole had also been blown through the ceiling, but otherwise the interior was fairly intact.

What surprised me most, however, was what I saw bolted to the floors. The remains of six barber chairs lined one wall, and toward the back I could clearly see the partially melted remains of two dryer stations.

"A hair salon?" I said.

Candice nodded, a puzzled look on her face as well. "Odd choice of target for a suicide bomber."

"Very," I agreed, continuing to scan the area.

"When did the blast occur?" Candice asked.

"Right after the shop opened," Brice said. "A little after nine a.m."

The last time I'd looked at a clock had been while I was in my car—right before Candice showed up. I remembered it'd been a little before eleven a.m. "They got the fire out fast."

Brice nodded. "The fire station is just around the corner."

I looked again at the scene, and had to tuck in my emotions when I spotted five yellow body bags set to the side ready for the coroner to take them away. "Any idea who they were?" I asked.

Brice read from his notepad. "We believe one of them is the owner of the shop, Rita Watson, and the other four we haven't identified yet, but several calls have come in from the families of two other women who work here, Kelly Longfellow and Grace Williams, as well as a call from the mother of a possible client—Valerie Mendon. Mrs. Mendon had just dropped off her daughter five minutes before the blast."

I bit my lip and fought back against the moisture welling in my eyes. Brice read the facts of the scene without any emotion, which is what his training called for, but stuff like this affected me deeply. All I could think about was that poor mother who would forever blame herself for giving her daughter a ride to the place of her premature death.

Candice subtly laid a hand on my arm and squeezed. I nodded and silently thanked her for the reassuring gesture.

"And the bomber?" I asked when I could talk without losing it.

Brice shook his head and sighed heavily. "There's not much left," he said.

I grimaced. "Do you know anything?"

"We have a witness who was walking by at the time who saw a woman cut through a row of houses, run through the parking lot and into the front door of the salon. He says she had what he thought was a backpack strapped to the front of her torso, and he says that she was moving erratically. He stopped to watch her because he thought she was high on drugs and he might need to call the cops. He says the door barely closed behind the woman when the front of the shop exploded."

"Did he give a description of her?" Candice asked.

"He said he thought she was young, maybe mid- to late twenties, but he's not sure on the hair, height, or anything else."

"So, this is a similar profile to the College Station bomber," I said, remembering the bomber at the mall had also been a young female.

Brice shrugged. "Possibly. I've learned not to rely on eyewitness testimony too much. Anyway, we won't know anything for sure until the coroner gives us a report, but, so far, yes, her MO fits with the other bombing in College Station."

"Which doesn't fit at all with normal psychology," Candice said. I looked at her and she explained, "Men are far more likely to choose a violent means of suicide than women. Guys will use a gun, or jump off a building, or crash their car into a wall. Women typically choose self-poisoning—pills or arsenic and the like."

"Unless they've been brainwashed," Brice said.

Candice turned to him. "You guys really think this is the work of some sort of terrorist group?"

He shrugged. "Two suicide bombings in the space of a couple weeks? Yeah, we're entertaining that theory pretty hard. So is Homeland Security, by the way."

Brice then nodded through the large hole and I saw a bunch of men in dark blue jackets standing just to the side of the building.

But I wasn't buying the terrorist theory. "Where was the witness standing when he saw the girl?" I asked.

"He was on the sidewalk right in front of the shop," Brice said.

"Is he okay?" Candice asked. The sidewalk was on the other side of the parking lot—maybe twenty-five feet away.

Brice flipped the lid closed on his notebook. "He's got a couple of small scratches from flying glass, but he was far enough away not to get hit with the blast."

"Lucky," I muttered.

"Yeah, except for witnessing something he'll never forget, he's a lucky bastard."

Brice wasn't trying to be sarcastic; it was just his manner. We fell silent after that and I could feel the weight of Brice waiting for me to give him my intuitive impressions, but the truth was that I was working up the courage to open my intuition to the scene.

Crime scenes are always an assault on the senses, and this was one of the worst I'd ever been to. My nose was filled with the acrid smell of charred plastic, wood, and other unmentionable things, not to mention that everywhere I looked I could see the destructive violence of the bomb, and my ears couldn't drown out the sound of dozens of first responders still covering the scene. I could only imagine what my sixth sense would encounter when I clicked on my radar.

"You okay?" Candice whispered.

I realized I was breathing a little hard and maybe I was starting to feel a touch cold and clammy too. "It's the smell," I said, bringing my arm up to cover my nose.

Candice wrapped her arm around my waist and guided me out of the shop to a spot in the parking lot about ten feet from what had been the entrance. "Better?" she asked.

I swallowed hard. "A little."

"You don't have to do this," she reminded me, which won her a sharp look from Brice, who had followed us.

Truth be told, I very nearly backed out, but then that feeling of knowing with absolute certainty that Dutch would then be left unprotected and vulnerable settled into the pit of my stomach and it gave me the resolve I needed. "I'm fine," I told her, squaring my shoulders and turning again to the scene.

I stared at it with unfocused eyes for a long time, sorting

through all the energy swirling and tumbling around the area. It took me a while to sort it all out because there was so much emotion clouding the ether. Pushing my radar away from current time, I tried to find my way back to the time of the explosion, but I had to push past a great deal of stuff to get there. There had been the urgent energy of the firefighters who had worked to contain and put out the blaze, the anxiety of onlookers who'd witnessed the explosion or the aftermath, and finally the small thread of energy that was most unsettling, the vibrations of the five women who'd been caught in the explosion.

The second I felt them, I focused hard and followed the thread. And then I had the energy of one woman in particular—and what's more, I actually had a strong psychic connection to her. She seemed to come out of the fog and chaos of the scene to step right in front of me—and although I couldn't see or hear her, I could certainly sense her.

She felt heavy against my energy—and she felt full of panic. I knew in an instant that I'd connected to the grounded spirit of one of the women killed in the explosion, and for a minute I didn't know what to do with her.

I realize that most people think that all psychics are the same, but we're as diverse as specialists in any given field. Under the "psychic" umbrella, there are mediums, healers, energy workers, and folks like me—psychic forecasters who predict the future. While I can sense a grounded spirit just as well as any medium, communicating clearly with one really isn't my forte. The ability to actually "hear" a spirit is called "clairaudience." As a psychic forecaster, my dominant sixth sense is clairvoyance, which simply means that in my mind's eye I "see" images that allow me to predict the future. Alternatively, spirit mediums rely on clairaudience to "hear" spirits and converse with them. They often have some clairvoyance as well, but it's their clairaudience that dominates. Unfortunately, with clairaudience, either you have it or you don't, and I'm more in the "don't" category.

So I wasn't very confident about attempting to communicate with the grounded soul banging on my energy, but this woman was pretty insistent, and I felt such sadness for her that I sucked it up and went for it.

*Hi, my name is Abby,* I mentally told her. *I can try to help you, ma'am.* (Little-known fact: ghosts *can* hear our thoughts if we direct them at the spirit, so there's no real need to speak out loud to them should you ever encounter one.)

What I got back wasn't so much a thread of conversation as it was a wave of emotion. Relief mixed with panic, and confusion, and then that pleading sense to help her, but there were no words exchanged. I was back to my own frustration for lack of clairaudient skill.

But then I had an idea, one that I'd never tried before, and I hoped it'd work. I shut my eyes and envisioned my FBI badge, and I even went so far as to put my hand over it as it dangled from my neck.

That panicked pleading subsided, and I knew she was trying to work out what I was saying. I then envisioned the inside of my office—specifically the room where I conducted my readings. I mentally called up the image of the last client I'd read for and then in my mind I drew a plus sign. *This,* I said in my thoughts while wiggling my badge, *plus this*—I again called up the image of my office—*is what I do.*

With relief I felt her make the connection, and I knew she understood that I was telling her I was an FBI psychic.

Encouraged, I told her to fill my mind with an image for what she did, and immediately I saw a woman with black hair and heavy makeup standing in a pink and green beauty salon, cutting another faceless person's hair. The image was so strong that I swear I smelled that flowery scent of shampoo and hair products right under my nostrils.

*You're a beautician!* I said mentally.

There was a sort of mental nod inside my head, but then that pleading to tell her or show her what'd happened to her returned.

I bit my lip. "Abs?" I heard Candice whisper, and not wanting to interrupt the link I had to the ghost in front of me, I replied to Candice by holding up one finger. The next bit was going to be tricky, because I knew it would shock the dead beautician, but there was no way to avoid it. I took her image of the inside of the salon and on the floor I placed the image of a stick of dynamite with a lit fuse. That was it. Anything else I felt would be too cruel and upsetting for her.

What she did next shocked *me*. She took the stick of dynamite, turned the beautician's chair around to show me a young girl in her early twenties with light brown hair, freckles, and big hazel eyes. I didn't quite know what was happening until the beautician slapped the dynamite stick to the torso of the girl, and then, in the next instant, a ball of flame completely obscured my inner vision. My breath caught and I took a step back and opened my eyes.

Brice and Candice were staring worriedly at me. "I saw her," I said. "The bomber. I know what she looks like."

"You *saw* her?" Brice asked, and I could tell he was mentally trying to work that out. He was neither intuitive nor very imaginative, and it's always hardest for the analytical types to get me and what I do.

"Yes." I had a very clear impression of what the girl looked like. Her sweet face was likely permanently ingrained in my memory.

"Where?" Brice asked. He was looking around like he thought I saw her in person.

"I saw her in my mind's eye, Brice. But I could describe her down to a T if I had to."

Brice blinked several times. I knew he wanted to ask me how I could have possibly seen the bomber in my mind's eye, but he also knew that I was pretty adept at revealing what seemed impossible to expose. "You're sure you saw *her*, Cooper?" was all he asked.

"Positive."

"Could you sit with an artist?" Candice asked, before turning to Brice and adding, "If she can give you an image to offer the press, it might be faster than waiting for DNA to come back."

Brice's gaze flickered to me. "Yeah, we can get an artist for you, but a name would be faster. Any chance you could pull that out of your psychic hat?"

I shook my head. "You know I don't get names."

Brice shrugged. "Worth a shot." He then turned away to make a call and get me the artist.

Meanwhile Candice rubbed my shoulders. "You look cold."

The day had become overcast and had the smell of rain in the air, and the temperature had dropped significantly since that morning. A cold front was blowing through town. "I'm okay," I told her, barely suppressing a shudder.

Candice grinned. "How about we get outta here and go for coffee? Brice won't be able to get anyone to work up a sketch for at least a half hour."

I almost said yes, but then I remembered that Dutch was still on the scene and I had a ghost I couldn't just leave without at least attempting to help. "Naw, I'm good," I told her, before scanning the area for my fiancé. I found him over by Gaston and a guy I didn't recognize in a blue Windbreaker. It looked like they were examining several small pieces of charred metal. I wondered if they were pieces of the bomb.

"You sure, Sundance?" Candice said, pulling my attention back to her.

I bumped her with my shoulder. "I'm okay, Cassidy. There's a grounded spirit here that I'm going to try to help." I pointed to the area right in front of me where the beautician was standing.

"There's a what where now?" Candice asked, her eyes widening.

"A ghost."

Her jaw dropped. "Like . . . a real *live* ghost?"

"She's not exactly alive, Candice, but, yes, there is a real ghost standing right in front of us." Candice took two very big steps back from me. "Don't tell me you're scared of ghosts?" I said.

"Okay. I won't tell you. But I am, Abs. I mean, I think the psychic stuff you do is really cool, but ghosts freak me out."

I rolled my eyes. "Well, this one won't hurt you. She's scared and really upset by what's happened to her."

"Who is she?"

"One of the beauticians from inside the shop."

"Which one?"

That was a good question. I remembered the names Brice had rattled off. Kelly Longfellow, Grace Williams, and the owner, Rita Watson. As I was recalling them, I felt a surge from the woman in front of me as my mind hit on the name

Rita Watson and I knew I had the beauty shop owner in front of me. I closed my eyes and whispered, "Rita, do you understand you've been killed today?"

I was hit with such a wave of sadness that my eyes immediately began to tear. For a long moment I was terribly overcome with emotion, and I had to wipe my eyes several times and take deep breaths before I was able to focus again.

"Abs?" Candice said, once again at my side. "Sweetie! What's the matter?"

I tried to speak and tell her what was happening, but I couldn't, so I just held up one finger for her to wait a moment and reached out again to Rita. *I'm so sorry,* I told her. *I know it must be a shock, Rita, but you didn't survive the blast, and you need to leave this place and cross over to the other side. Do you know how to do that?*

I waited with bated breath, hoping she would know how to cross, because if she didn't, I'd have to call my friend M.J.—a medium and good friend I knew in Boston—for assistance.

Rita took a while to answer me, and through the ether I could feel her struggle and it tore me up inside. I had the distinct impression that she was leaving behind a son, a young man not yet out of high school. *I'll reach out to him,* I promised her.

I felt another twinge of emotion that was like a surge of gratitude. And then I knew that Rita was still resistant to the idea of crossing over. I didn't want her to lose her courage, so I mentally said, *Rita, you'll be so much better able to watch over your son from the other side. If you stay in this realm, you'll be stuck right here in front of this burned-out shop and that's not an existence your son would ever wish for you.*

I think that did the trick because in the next few seconds I could feel a sort of warmth come over me and then I had the impression that Rita's spirit was lifting and becoming lighter. A moment later she was gone, and I opened my eyes to once again find Brice and Candice standing in front of me looking extremely worried. There was also a third person there— Dutch.

"You okay?" he asked. His eyes conveyed that he was both: still pissed off, and just as worried as Candice and Brice. Belatedly I realized I was crying.

I wiped at my checks. "I'm fine. How're you?"

"Peachy."

For the record, his tone suggested anything but.

"Swell," I told him, in a tone that also suggested anything but.

An awkward silence followed and it was finally broken when Brice said, "The sketch artist is on the way and should be here in about twenty minutes. Why don't you ladies head down the street and grab some coffee at Starbucks and I'll send the artist over when she gets here?"

I turned and spied the familiar green and white logo about a block and a half down. It had nice big windows from which I could keep my eye on Dutch. "Okay," I said, motioning for Candice to follow me as I turned on my heel and walked away.

"Abs," I heard Dutch say before I got very far.

I glanced over my shoulder but kept walking. "Yeah?"

"Wait up for me tonight. We need to chat."

Oh, boy. The shih tzu I get myself into sometimes . . .

# Abby & Dutch's Wedding Day— T-Minus 01:40

"Girl . . . *what* have you gotten us into?" Gil asked as M.J. took a corner a little too fast and the tires of the rental car squealed.

"Nothing," she replied impatiently. "Just keep your eye on the map and tell me where to stop."

Gil pointed to his right and a little behind. "That's three-two-seven, so three-three-one should be . . . M.J., slow down, you just passed it!"

M.J. stomped on the brakes and backed up fast. She'd had a strong feeling that they'd be the ones to find Abby, and she'd also had a strong feeling that they should go to Abby's new house, so she hoped her hunch paid off. Once they were in front of the house, she hit the brakes hard again so that they could consider the stately Mediterranean-style home. "White stucco, blue shutters, and clay roof. This is it," she said.

"They live *here*?" Gilley asked, ogling the house.

"Apparently," M.J. said, backing up the rental even more to ease it into the drive, which dipped down a short hill before curving off toward the garage.

"Those FBI boys sure make some coin," Gil muttered.

"Dutch has a side business providing VIP security or something," M.J. said. "Abby told me he does really well from it. I think Milo is his business partner, in fact."

"Milo's a hottie," Gil said. "And so are Dutch and Brice. Have you realized how good-looking everybody at that wedding is?"

M.J. sighed. She seriously missed her own great-looking guy, Heath Whitefeather, who was also a medium and who would've been a whole lot more help than Gil. But then, that was sort of always true.

She had no choice but to ignore the commentary coming out of Gilley's mouth and navigate the driveway as quickly as she could. "Whose cars are those?" Gilley asked as they swerved around to the right of the house where the garage doors were located.

M.J. almost sighed again with relief. There were two cars in the drive. A blue Mini Cooper—which, from Abby's Facebook page, she knew that Abby drove a Mini—and a black Mercedes. "I think we found them, Gil," M.J. said, guessing the black Mercedes was Milo's car.

Pulling the car all the way over to the far right of the other two cars, she was about to cut the engine when something else caught her eye, and she gasped, pointing to the rear door next to the garage where a pair of legs were just visible sticking out of the doorway. "Gil!" she cried. "What's that?"

Gilley leaned forward, and he too sucked in a breath. "It's Milo! And Candice! She's to his side and facedown on the ground!"

M.J. shoved the gearshift into park. She then had to grab Gilley's arm as he was about to jump out of the car and said, "Wait! Let me call first!"

Gilley pulled against her grip. "They're hurt!"

"What if they're not?" she countered. That wave of dread filled her chest like cement. Somehow she *knew* that the worst had not yet happened, and the house itself was giving off a very dangerous vibe that she couldn't quite figure out. "Gil, what if whoever did that to them is still inside?"

Gilley blinked at her, and then let go of the door handle. "Call," he said softly, handing over her phone. "And don't cut the engine. We may need to get outta here fast!"

M.J.'s fingers trembled as she tried to navigate the screens on the phone. She bypassed the idea of calling Dutch, and headed straight for 911.

# Chapter Three

A patrol car with the words "Call 911" stenciled in blue on the side pulled up and parked right outside the window I was staring out of at the Starbucks down the street from the bombing scene.

The sketch artist Brice had called for got out, and juggled her sketchbook and set of pencils as she waved to the officer driving the car, who then left her to go help his fellow brothers in blue.

While I'd waited for her to arrive, I'd kept my eye on Dutch and by that I mean my intuitive third eye as well as my two physical ones. The sense that he was still in terrible danger never wavered, and what's more, I couldn't seem to find the source no matter how hard I intuitively "looked" to find it. It seemed near him and yet at some distance, and that unsettled me more than I can say.

Luckily, the appearance of the sketch artist distracted me, at least temporarily, from my worries. The sketch artist, Linda, was an earthy, soft-spoken woman in her fifties with kind eyes. She sat with me for the next two hours while she and I worked up a pencil sketch that I knew was nearly the spitting image of the face that Rita had shown me in my mind's eye.

After we were done, Candice called Brice, who came down

to the shop to take a look. "I'll get this posted on the five and six o'clock news."

"What're you going to say?" Candice asked, then clarified by adding, "I mean we want to be sensitive to her family, Brice. They may not know she's been killed, and seeing her face in a sketch on the news about a bombing is a seriously shitty way to find out."

"They may not know she's a terrorist either, babe, but we have nothing else to go on right now. Maybe it won't be her family who sees the sketch. Maybe it'll be a neighbor or friend and they'll call us with the girl's name."

My chin lifted at the mention of the word "terrorist." "You really think she's a terrorist?"

Brice studied the sketch and sighed heavily. "I don't know what else to think, Cooper. We have two dead girls, roughly the same age and race, who walked into two places of business and blew themselves and innocent bystanders up. If it's not a terrorist cell orchestrating these hits, who the hell is it?"

Neither Candice nor I could answer him, so Brice headed off to talk with the school of reporters waiting for some kind of a statement from the Feds.

Once he'd left, I turned to Candice and said, "I need an address."

"Whose?"

"Rita Watson's."

"The beauty shop owner?"

I nodded.

"Why?"

"I made her a promise to find her son and make sure he's okay."

Candice looked at me with surprise. *"When?"*

"Today, while I was trying to convince her to cross over."

"You *talked* to her ghost?"

"In a manner of speaking, no pun intended. Anyway, can you get me the address?"

Candice blinked a couple of times, like she was really trying to figure out how I managed to have a conversation with a dead person in plain view of her without ever opening my mouth. "Uh . . . yeah, but, Abs, are you sure you want to try to talk to her kid *today*?"

That took me back a bit. "Do you think he's already been told about his mom's death?" I asked.

"I'm sure an officer was sent to Rita's house to inform the family that the beauty shop had exploded, and that his mother was presently unaccounted for. They'd also likely ask for her toothbrush."

"Her toothbrush?" I asked, then realized why they'd need it. "Oh, yeah, DNA."

What bothered me was the feeling that Rita and her son had no other close family nearby. I felt strongly it was just the two of them in the world, which is what made her passing so tragic. Her young son would be left to fend for himself, and if he wasn't yet out of high school, he could end up in foster care or, even worse, out on the streets. "I don't think I want to wait," I said after considering it. "Her poor kid is probably going to be holding out hope that his mom didn't die in the blast, and waiting for DNA to come back could take weeks."

"You want me to come along?"

I nearly said yes, but then I thought about how the errand would take me away from keeping an eye on my fiancé. "No, thanks, honey. I'm gonna try to get Dutch to go with me."

"You're really worried about him, aren't you?" Candice said. She knew me pretty good.

"I am," I admitted. "It's nothing I can put my finger on, but there's this terrible feeling I have that something bad is going to happen to him."

"How bad?"

I had to swallow hard before answering. "The worst."

Candice's eyes swiveled to the window, and I knew she was searching the crowd for my sweetheart. "He's there," I said, pointing to Dutch, who was talking on his cell and pacing next to his car.

After watching him for a few seconds, Candice said, "Maybe we should all go to Rita's house."

I offered her a half smile. "I'm sure Dutch is gonna *love* being babysat by the two of us."

Candice shrugged. "I can get Brice to go too. We can explain it by suggesting we get something to eat on the way back."

"That could work," I told her.

As it happened, it couldn't work. Brice was ordered back to the office along with Gaston, and Dutch would have been ordered there too if I hadn't suggested to the director that I needed him to accompany me to the Watsons'. "You think there's something there?" Gaston asked me in a way that suggested he was ready to launch an army of FBI boys to her house to search it for clues if I thought it necessary.

"No, sir," I said quickly. "I just want to make sure her son is okay." Gaston hesitated and I knew he was wondering why I needed Dutch along, so I added, "But you never know, there may be something there that gives me more to go on, and if Agent Rivers is along, I'll be able to focus fully."

Gaston nodded and called to Dutch, who came over to us (a bit stiffly, I thought). After giving Dutch his orders, Gaston left us. I watched him walk away and had second thoughts about what I'd asked him to order Dutch to do. My fiancé wasn't exactly giving off the warm fuzzies. "How long are you gonna stay mad at me?" I asked.

"A while."

"Should I mark my calendar for a specific date? Cuz our wedding's right around the corner and I'd hate to walk down the aisle and say 'I do' to a guy who's seriously pissed at me."

Dutch glared at me.

"Nice. That face will look great in the wedding photos."

"Now is not the time to poke the tiger, Edgar," Dutch warned.

"Oh, should I also mark my calendar with a good time to poke the tiger, then?" For effect, I pulled out my cell phone and opened up the calendar app with a wee bit of bravado.

"What the hell's wrong with you?" he growled, taking me firmly by the elbow as he moved toward his car.

"Hey, hey, hey!" I protested, nearly tripping over my feet as he hauled me along. "Crippled person here, big guy!"

Dutch immediately let go. "Sorry," he said, but his tone

suggested he wasn't so much. He then stopped and put his hands on his hips, turning to glare at me again. "Why?" he demanded. "Why did you put yourself in the middle of this when you *know* your crew told you it was dangerous?"

I searched for the right words to say. Words that would tell him how worried I was about his safety, how terrible that feeling of dread was, and how terrified I was about losing him. But all I came up with was, "Because." (Woman of passionate, eloquent speeches, I am not.)

Dutch stood there staring at me and waited me out.

"I'm worried about you," I finally managed.

"I told you I'd be careful. I told you I would call. I even promised to try to call you every hour, *and* I'm wearing my vest."

"I don't know that all of that is enough, Dutch," I said, reaching for his hand, but he pulled it out of my reach with a shake of his head.

"It's almost five," he growled. "And here I am remarkably unscathed."

"I didn't say I knew *when* something bad might happen to you!" I could feel my own anger starting to flare.

Dutch glared at me some more and I glared back. "Abby," he said, "if someone wants to take a shot at me, there isn't anything you can do to stop it."

The anger brewing in the middle of my chest evaporated and a terrible fear took its place. "You don't know that!"

"I do know that. I've been to sniper school, remember? I know how these hit men think. He'll pick a spot somewhere high, somewhere out of sight, and you won't know he's there until after I've been hit."

I physically flinched. The idea was too abhorrent. I closed my eyes against the image of Dutch lying dead in the street, and my heart wanted to break right then and there. "Please don't say stuff like that."

I felt his strong hands on my shoulders and a moment later he was holding me close. "Edgar," he said softly. "If someone really wants me dead, then I don't know what you can do to stop it. By being here you put yourself in danger. Don't you get it? What if you're nearby when he takes his shot? What if he misses me and you get in the way?" And then I heard Dutch's voice crack. "What if he gets you instead?"

I wrapped my arms around him and squeezed hard. I wanted him to stop talking and just hold me.

"This case sucks, dollface, and I want no part of it either, but it's my job, and right now I don't have a choice. But you do. You can walk away and I can be careful, and maybe at the end of the day, the good guys will come out okay."

I wiped at my eyes, which were misting again. "No," I said.

"What?" He hadn't heard me.

I backed up a little from him. "No. If you're here, I'm here. I can't sit at home or in my office and wonder about what could happen to you, Dutch. I'll go insane. And you *don't* know that I won't be able to stop someone from taking a shot at you. I have pretty good radar, and right now it's feeling the ether everywhere around you. The *second* I feel a shift, I'm going to warn you, and maybe that'll be the key to saving your life."

"As long as you're nearby, I'm gonna worry about both of us," Dutch said, still fighting me. "That's gonna get mighty distracting, Abby, and Gaston needs me fully focused."

I hesitated for just a moment before I said, "Gaston needs me focused more than he does you, sweetie."

Dutch's eyes narrowed. I'd dealt him a low blow to be sure, but it was the only way I could get him to listen. "Mean," he said.

I reached for his hand again, and this time he didn't pull it away. "It wasn't intended to be, cowboy. But it *is* the truth. I'm not going anywhere. I'm on this case as long as you are. Period."

Dutch looked like he was about to say something more, but we were interrupted by a man dressed in one of those dark blue Windbreakers who sort of pushed his way into our conversation by yelling, "Rivers, what's this about another eyewitness to the bomber?"

"What the hell are you talking about?" Dutch countered, clearly annoyed by the intrusion. (And maybe me . . .)

The man pointed behind him to a row of reporters speaking into their microphones for the cameras while Brice stood to one side with his arms crossed. "Harrison just gave a sketch of the suspect to the press!" the man nearly shouted. I noticed a vein throbbing at his temple and thought maybe he should take a chill pill before his head exploded.

"So?" Dutch replied, with obvious disdain. I didn't know who this guy was, but it was pretty obvious he didn't play for Gaston's team.

*"So?"* the guy snapped (and, yes, this time he actually shouted). *"So why is this the first I'm hearing about it?"*

Dutch crossed his arms too, his face turning to granite. "Don't know, Willis. Maybe you should take it up with the director."

"If I could find Gaston, I'd take it up with him," Willis growled. That vein in his temple bulged as it continued to throb, and my radar kicked in.

"Do you have a history of high blood pressure in your family?" I suddenly asked. I hadn't meant to—it's just my radar zeroed in on him and it sort of fell out of my mouth.

He swiveled large, surprised eyes at me. *"What?"*

"High blood pressure," I repeated calmly. "It runs in your family, right? On your dad's side more so than your mom's, but there's also heart disease on both sides of your family and you've already been told you've got an issue, haven't you, Mr. Willis?"

*"Agent* Willis," he corrected, his wide eyes narrowing as he turned back to Dutch, pointed at me, and snapped, "What the hell is she talking about?"

Dutch's face remained hard and stoic, but I could tell Willis had just pissed him off royally. "Seems to me she's talking about your ticker, *Agent* Willis. Might want to pay attention to her and get it checked out."

Willis's jaw dropped and he looked dumbly from Dutch back to me.

"You also carry all of your stress in your chest," I told him. "That's not a good place for it. Especially when you have a family history of high blood pressure and heart disease. Of course, it wouldn't be nearly as concerning if you didn't eat so much crap. You've been ignoring your doctor's advice on that front. I think you might be addicted to salt, and it's the worst thing for you. I'd lay off the potato chips, French fries, and deli ham if I were you, sir."

Agent Willis continued to stare at me openmouthed, but he added blinking to the expression.

"Also, that promotion you want isn't going to happen. You'll need to brace yourself for the news that it's going to someone younger and slightly less experienced. It's why I really think you should try to take care of yourself. It's gonna hit you hard."

With that, Agent Willis's head moved slowly to the left and I saw him eye a guy also in a dark blue Windbreaker—at least ten years younger than Willis—who was busy talking to several other agents on Dutch's team.

"Yep," I said. "He's the guy getting promoted. If it's any consolation, he won't like the job as much as he was hoping to."

Willis's attention snapped back to me and there was real anger in his eyes now.

"But that could be because he'll be your supervisor, and I doubt you'll make it easy on him." (Sometimes I have a hard time quitting while I'm ahead.)

"Who *are* you?!" he demanded.

I showed him my badge. "Abby Cooper. FBI civilian consultant."

Willis blinked again and then something seemed to register. "Hold on," he said. "Are you that fortune-teller we heard the bureau hired?"

"I'm the professional intuitive they hired, yes," I said, feeling a little flinty about being called a "fortune-teller."

Willis started to laugh, and it wasn't a nice laugh, and it certainly wasn't kind. "Rivers, are you puttin' me on?" he finally asked.

Dutch responded by offering me his hand. "Come on, Ms. Cooper. We have an interview to get to."

I gave Willis what I hoped was my best "You're a real dickhead" expression and took hold of my fiancé's hand.

"Good luck with that ticker," I told him, in my best "eff you" voice. The humor left him pretty quick.

When we were out of hearing range, I asked, "Who *was* that asshole?"

"That's another quarter," Dutch said, reminding me that the swear jar on our kitchen counter was due a few coins (or $678.75 to be exact . . .).

"Yeah, yeah. But who was he?"

"Homeland Security," Dutch told me. "They've been trying to weasel in on our case for the past couple weeks, and after today we'll be lucky to hold on to it."

"Who decides if it stays with you guys or gets moved over to them?"

"It has to be worked out at the top, between the secretary of Homeland Security and the FBI director."

"Gaston?"

"No, the national director. The problem is that it's not clear who the case should belong to, so we've been asked to join forces and work the case as a team."

I looked back at Willis, his hands on his hips while he glared at our departing forms. "It's going well, this working together, right?"

Dutch actually laughed. "Peachy. Harrison is close to breaking that little guy's neck." Dutch motioned to the younger man I'd pegged for the promotion.

I read the younger guy's energy. "He's hungry and scared he'll blow this opportunity. That's gonna make him a major pain in your—"

"Careful," Dutch warned again.

I scowled at him. The swear police never cut me any slack. (So I made sure to cut myself some extra when I could get away with it.) "The *point* is that I'm sensing he's going to be a thorn in your side."

At that moment the man in question looked up, and like a hawk seeing two juicy mice, he started off in our direction. Dutch wrapped an arm around my waist and we shuffled to his car as quickly as we could, but the Homeland Security agent was closing in fast.

"Where ya goin'?" I heard Candice ask, and I turned my head sharply. She'd come out of nowhere.

"We're headed to Rita's house," I told her, continuing my speedy shuffle.

Candice quickened her pace to come up on my side. "Who're we avoiding?"

"That guy," I said with a nod toward the agent.

Candice brought her arm up and pressed a button on her key fob. Two cars away, her Porsche beeped. "My car's closer," she said.

Dutch and I didn't argue. We simply leaned to the left and made a beeline to her car. She had us in and the engine turned over before the agent really registered what was happening. As Candice pulled out from the curb, I saw him stop and put his hands on his hips. I couldn't help it; I waved at him. Probably not a smart move, but it was deeply satisfying.

We drove in silence while the navigation system gave Candice turn-by-turn directions from the address that Dutch had given her. I had to give my BFF props for driving like a reasonable person, something I suspected she was doing only because there was actually someone in the car who could arrest her for reckless driving.

We arrived at Rita Watson's house, which was already surrounded by police and a small mob of onlookers. "What's going on?" I asked as we pulled over to the curb down the street.

Dutch glowered in his seat. "This isn't us," he said. "It's gotta be HS."

"But Rita didn't have anything to do with the bombs!" I exclaimed. I could just imagine her poor son, having to endure this invasion of privacy after hearing about his mother's death. It was awful.

Dutch opened his car door. "It's part of their protocol, Abs. They'll vet anyone connected to the explosion in case there's a possible connection."

"We have to find Rita's son," I said as he helped me from the backseat. I was a little desperate to find the young man and make sure he was okay.

Dutch and Candice took up either side of me as we moved

forward toward the small but charming home in an older neighborhood that'd probably seen better days. Nearby a dog barked incessantly, and several neighbors stood on their porches or front steps talking to one another or gabbing away on their phones. Most of the onlookers wore eager expressions, almost as if they were gleeful at the chance to witness such fallout from tragic circumstances.

The whole thing made me sick to my stomach, and yet I couldn't help looking at the crowd. Something was drawing me to them, in particular to one young man with curly black hair, pale skin, and red swollen eyes.

Dutch flashed his badge to several people in those familiar blue jackets with "Homeland Security" silk-screened on the back; then he motioned me up the walk, but I hesitated. "Abs?" Candice asked.

I didn't answer her. Instead I shuffled past the front walk and headed toward the young man standing alone and slightly removed from the rest of the crowd. He saw me coming and shifted uncomfortably. I could tell he'd been crying and my heart went out to him. He looked away and moved farther down from the crowd.

"Hey," I said when I was just a few feet away. "You're Rita's son, aren't you?"

The poor kid didn't even acknowledge me. Instead he just stared hard at his front lawn, as if he hadn't heard a word I'd said.

For several seconds I didn't quite know what to say. Rita had asked me to look in on her son and I could feel his terrible sadness and it broke my heart. But approaching him would require delicacy . . . something I'm not especially known for.

"What's your name, honey?" I said to him. His eyes flickered to me, then away.

"No comment," he muttered, and I wondered if he'd already been approached by a reporter.

I could feel Dutch and Candice right behind me, obviously letting me take the lead. "Okay," I told him, "I'll do the talking, and you can just stand there without saying a word. That all right by you?"

He shrugged. "It's a free country."

I wished I knew his name—it'd go a long way to making this easier—and then something weird happened. . . . I *never* get names. . . . Okay, well maybe once or twice a year I may get one, but they sure don't come easy to me. Anyway all of a sudden the name Brody clicked into my head and I knew it was his. "It's Brody, right?" I asked, mentally crossing my fingers.

His eyes flickered to me with a hint of surprise, but then his gaze darted right back to the lawn. Still, I knew I was on the right track.

"You're probably wondering how I knew that," I said.

He glared at the grass.

"I'm not a reporter."

He glared harder.

"I work with the FBI."

Not a flicker of interest.

"But I'm not an agent. I'm a psychic consultant."

His eyes came back to me, and this time they held my gaze. "For real?"

I nodded. "For real." Doubt clouded his expression. I took my phone out of my pocket and tapped at the screen. When I had what I wanted on the display, I showed it to him. "See?" I said. "That's my Web site. I take personal clients along with occasionally helping out the FBI."

Brody took my phone and I said nothing while he skimmed the text. He then handed me back the phone and said, "I get feelings sometimes."

I cocked my head. "You mean, intuitive feelings?"

He nodded sadly and his eyes welled with tears. "This morning I tried to talk my mom into taking the day off. But she said she was booked solid and she couldn't."

His lip quivered and his face seemed to crumple in on itself. I handed Candice my cane and held my arms open wide, and Brody sort of shuffled into my embrace. I hugged him for a long time, trying with all my might to hold in my own tears, but it was pointless. His heartbreak was so raw, and so painful, and so guilt-ridden, that it just tore me apart. "I'm so, so sorry, honey," I said to him. I could feel Dutch place a hand on my back and Candice hedged in to stand shoulder to shoulder with me.

At last, Brody stepped back and we both wiped our eyes. "Do you have any place you can go?" I asked.

Brody nodded toward his house, but he was still too overcome to speak.

"Is anyone going to stay with you?"

He shook his head.

I turned and looked at Dutch. We couldn't let this kid stay in his house by himself after what'd happened to his mom. Plus, Homeland Security was currently trashing his home. I didn't think they'd pick up after themselves either.

"You hungry, son?" Dutch asked gently.

Brody shook his head, but then I heard his stomach gurgle.

I took his hand. "Come on, sweetie. You're coming home with us until we get this all settled."

Brody wavered and he pointed to the cluster of Homeland Security agents currently rifling through his home. "They told me to stay here."

"Leave it to me," Dutch said, and off he went in search of the agent in charge.

Meanwhile Brody looked like he was ready to bolt. I had a feeling all this was just a little too much for the poor guy, and Candice must have noticed it too, because she said, "It'll be a tight fit, but I think the four of us can squeeze into the Porsche." She winked at me and I caught on right away. The mention of a ride in a Porsche might be too tempting for a young man to resist.

"Brody should sit up front," I said. "Dutch and I don't mind cuddling in the back."

Brody looked from Candice to me, and I nodded toward her bright yellow car. His eyes widened. I had to hide a smile. "Try not to drive too fast this time, Candice," I said with a wink back at her.

"It's no fun unless I open her up, Abs," Candice said. "But I'll try to keep it under a hundred, for you guys."

I felt Brody's hand tighten slightly around mine. Good, he was coming along, and then we all heard yelling. I turned to see a man shouting at Dutch, while my fiancé calmly stood in front of him with his arms crossed and a look on his face so hard it could cut diamonds.

"I think we should head to the car right now, actually," Candice said, moving to take up Brody's arm from the other side. We wove our way through the crowd, and luckily no one tried to intercept us. After getting in, we waited anxiously for Dutch, but he didn't seem to be close to ending the argument he was having with HS.

I texted him that we were all in the car, waiting for him; then I watched him glance at the phone and type a reply. Immediately his text hit my phone. It read, *GO!*

From the backseat I put a hand on Candice's shoulder. "Dutch says he'll catch up with us later."

"Awesome," she said, pulling out from the curb and carefully navigating the street full of people, cars, and news vans.

Once we'd turned the corner, she headed straight to the highway and opened the car up to speeds well over ninety. I gripped the side handle and whispered a few light prayers *(Please, oh, please, God, don't let us die!)* and after a little while she slowed down and got off the expressway.

"That was *so* cool!" Brody said. I could feel that his sadness and heartbreak had lifted just a fraction, and was immediately grateful to my best friend for it. Candice drove to the house Dutch and I were renting (in less than a month we'd be moving into our new, permanent home). She then dropped Brody and me off while she went to pick up a pizza.

Dutch called right after I'd gotten Brody settled on the couch with a Coke, some chips, and the remote. "How's he doing?" he asked.

"We just got home. Candice went for pizza and Brody seems to be doing okay so far."

"Do you have a game plan?" he asked me.

"Nope."

"Glad to hear you've thought this through."

"I'll come up with something. Do you want me to send Candice to pick you up?"

"Brice and Gaston are on their way over here. HS didn't inform us that they were searching Rita's place. They're supposed to keep us in the loop about everything they do, and this isn't going over well with Gaston."

I felt out the ether and knew that things were about to get very ugly . . . for Homeland Security. "How late do you think you'll be?" I asked. It was already going on six o'clock and that familiar worry began to seep into my chest about Dutch's safety.

He sighed. "Hopefully I'll be home by nine. Have Candice come back over here to drop off your keys so I can get one of my guys to drive your car home. Meanwhile she can pick up a change of clothes for Brody. And could you try to find out if he's got any relatives that can take him in? He should be with family at a time like this."

I smiled. Underneath that hard exterior, Dutch was such a softy. "I'll work on it, cowboy. Do me one favor, though, in return?"

"What's that?"

"Keep your vest on and get home as soon as you can."

"Done," he said, and at last I could hear the humor in his voice. "Love you, dollface, even though you drive me crazy sometimes."

"Ditto, cowboy."

After hanging up with Dutch, I called Candice and filled her in. She came in the door with a giant pizza about ten minutes later; then she was on her way again back to Rita's house.

I let Brody eat his six slices in silence while he watched HBO. At last he seemed full and without looking at me, he said, "Thanks."

"You're welcome."

After another bit of silence he said, "So, are you really psychic?"

"Yeppers."

"Like . . . how does it work?"

I shrugged. "I don't know that anyone knows *exactly* how it works, but I have a theory. Do you want to hear it?"

Brody inhaled deeply. He looked drained, but still, he clicked the mute button and said, "Yeah. I do."

I waited for him to turn to me and then I started talking, and while I talked, I felt out the ether all around him, looking into his own future. "My theory is that every living thing gives off a unique energy. We create our own electromagnetic current, and like a force field it surrounds us. Some people can see this current, and they call it an aura. To them it's sort of like the northern lights, bands of beautiful colors pulsing with energy.

"Within that aura, I believe that we're carrying all our hopes, thoughts, feelings, wishes, fears, anxieties, and bits of our futures. It's the future part of your aura that psychics like me—future forecasters—can focus on. I send my own electromagnetic current out into the ether and pick through yours, and that's how I gather information. For instance, that's how I know you won something recently. An award or an accolade of some kind, but why you've kept it a secret, I'm not quite sure. Further, there's a bit of money attached to the award, and again, why you've chosen to keep it a secret is beyond me."

Brody was staring at me in astonishment. It took him a minute to find his voice. "I won a scholarship," he said.

I smiled. "I thought it was something like that. You should be very proud of yourself. You're crazy smart."

Brody's gaze dropped to his lap. "I didn't tell Mom."

I bit my lip. "Oh, honey. I'm so sorry."

"I was saving it," he said. "She's been so freaked-out about cash lately, and she really wants me to go to college. Her birthday is in two weeks and I didn't have any cash to get her anything, so I thought I could surprise her with this, but . . ."

Brody's voice trailed off as he realized his mom was never going to make it to her next birthday. His eyes welled up and I reached out my arms and squeezed him tight. "Why didn't I tell her?" he asked me.

I had no answers for him. "I think you were trying to do something really nice, Brody."

He pulled back from me. "Now she'll never know," he said. His forlorn face broke my heart.

I held his hand and said, "I don't think I believe that."

He wiped his nose on his sleeve and eyed me with a puzzled expression. "What?" he asked.

I wavered for a long moment before I said, "Today, when I went to the beauty shop after the . . . after the fire, I felt your mom's spirit. She asked me to check in on you."

Brody's brows knit together and he stared at me hard. I could tell he was trying to determine if I was for real or feeding him a line of bullsh—er . . . baloney.

I held his gaze and felt around in his energy some more. I had the urge to prove to this kid that I was for real and that his mother's spirit had really connected to me. It was the only way I knew to comfort him. "Arizona State, huh?" I asked him as he continued to look at me skeptically.

His eyes widened.

I smiled. "It's a good school, Brody. Except for the fact that it may have a reputation for being a party school. Still, I think that you'll do really well there. But you need to respond soon. There's a deadline, right?"

Brody cleared his throat. "November tenth," he said. "I applied for early admission."

"And there's more money headed your way too," I said, still reading his energy. "You applied for more than this scholarship, if I'm not mistaken." I held up five fingers, looked at my hand, then added one finger from my other hand.

Brody gasped. "You're freaking me out!" he said. But I knew he wasn't really scared. "How're you *doing* that?"

I shrugged. "It's not hard, honey. You definitely have a predilection to the intuitive. I could give you some pointers."

"Can you tell me what my mom said, first?"

I squeezed his arm. "Of course, although I didn't have a chance to talk to her for more than a few minutes."

"Why not?"

Inwardly I winced. We were getting into a delicate area here. "She only hung around long enough to find someone who could hear her and get a message to you."

Brody seemed to accept that, thank God, and motioned for me to continue. "Well, she said that she was worried about you—about who would take care of you now that she's . . . now that she can't look after you."

Brody's gaze dropped back to his lap again. "I guess I can't stay at the house by myself, huh?"

"Don't you have any other family? Your dad, maybe?"

"He's out of the picture," Brody said with no small measure of bitterness. "He dumped my mom the minute she told him she was pregnant."

"Yeah, but that was nearly eighteen years ago," I said gently. "Maybe your dad would feel differently about you now?"

Brody's gaze lifted and his eyes were hard. "Doubt it. He was married when he started dating my mom. He fed her a bunch of shit about how he was divorcing his wife and promised to marry my ma, but the minute I show up, it was all too real for him or something and he just dumped her. He sends her a support check once a month, but that's it."

I felt a little better hearing that there'd be at least a little money continuing to come in for Brody to help pay for his expenses. At seventeen, he'd definitely be allowed by the state to live on his own, but I worried about where he'd stay, because I doubted his dad's child support check was large enough to cover his mom's mortgage payment plus utilities, food, clothing, etc.

"Extended family?" I asked.

Brody shrugged. "My mom's parents are both dead, and she has a sister in Wisconsin, but they got into a fight about seven years ago and they haven't talked since. No way would my mom want me to go live with her."

I searched the ether again and all of a sudden I had the answer. "You've got a buddy you hang out with, right?" I asked. "A kid you help with his homework, right?"

"You mean Greg?"

I nodded only because I figured Brody's first guess was probably the right answer. "His mom's super nice, right?"

Brody nodded. "Greg's dad cut out on him too. Mrs. Dixon and my mom hang out sometimes and talk about raising us without a dad around. They've bonded over it or something."

I smiled. Brody's energy was blooming with new hope and a new home for him. In my mind's eye I saw him packing a suitcase and being received into a small but loving home with his buddy. It filled me with relief. "Does Mrs. Dixon know what happened today?"

Brody took out his phone and handed it to me. There were two dozen voice mails and sixty-three texts on the display. "I had to turn it to silent," he admitted. "I was too choked up to talk to anybody and mostly the only people calling were reporters anyway."

I tapped the contacts tab and scrolled down to the *D*s. "Would you mind if I called Mrs. Dixon?"

Brody leaned back against the cushions and closed his eyes. He looked completely wiped out. "Go for it. I'm just gonna rest my eyes for a sec."

In the time it took for me to dial Mrs. Dixon and briefly speak to her about the possibility of taking Brody in—something she was very glad to do—the poor young man had fallen into a deep sleep.

"Thank you, Mrs. Dixon," I said to her as we were wrapping up the call. "We'll keep Brody here for the night and drop him off to you in the morning."

Dutch came in as I was laying a blanket over our houseguest. "How's he doing?" he asked.

I moved to my fiancé and wrapped my arms around him. "He'll be okay," I said. "It's you I'm worried about."

Dutch kissed the top of my head and hugged me back. "I'm still mad at you, you know."

"I can live with that."

He chuckled. "Oh, I'll bet."

"I just couldn't bear it if anything happened to you, Dutch. It'd kill me."

My fiancé leaned back and tilted my chin up with one finger. "And you think I could handle it any better if something happened to you?"

"I only know that the best chance we have of keeping each other safe is to work together," I told him. The truth was, I didn't know that. The dangerous energy surrounding Dutch was like a moody tempest, shifting and swirling and never quite letting me define its source or direction. But sticking to him like glue and working the case was the only reasonable thing I could do, so I wasn't about to back off.

"Okay, sweethot," he said after gazing into my eyes for a long moment. "It's you and me. Till death do us part."

I shuddered involuntarily, and that horrible feeling of doom seemed to sink all the way into my bones.

"You cold?" Dutch asked, pulling me close for a hug again.

I squeezed him tight. "Very."

# T-Minus 01:20

M.J. trembled as she clung to Gilley's arm while they watched Milo and Candice being loaded into separate ambulances. Nearby, Dutch stood stiff and pale, clearly shaken to the core. A team of firemen was currently suiting up in hazmat gear, ready to enter the house, and two more first responders were lying on the grass sucking oxygen through masks secured around their faces. They'd been the police officers who'd shown up ahead of everyone else after M.J. had called 911, and they'd managed to pull Milo and Candice partially out of the house, but then they'd collapsed on the driveway themselves.

Faced with four unconscious people, M.J. had nearly lost her cool, but she'd held it together long enough to order Gil to make another emergency call to 911 and run to aid the victims.

She'd first reached Candice, whose complexion was a frightening greenish yellow. And it was as she reached Abby's best friend that she felt a wave of dizziness overcome her. M.J. had lifted her chin and noticed the side door of the house still ajar, and something about the small window right above her had also caught her attention. There was duct tape along the perimeter of the window.

As her head swooned, she put it together and immediately

held her breath. Hooking Candice under the arms, she managed to drag her well out onto the lawn. M.J. checked to make sure Candice was breathing and, thankfully, she was. Then she kicked off her heels and tugged free the pashmina she'd been wearing before tying it at the back of her head to cover her nose and mouth. She then dashed back to the three men still lying prone on the drive, holding her breath as she got close. Darting forward, she pulled the door to the house closed before grabbing Milo under each arm, and with great effort, she managed to get him onto the lawn as well.

"M.J.!" Gilley called from inside the car, where she'd ordered him to stay. "They're on their way!"

M.J. had already gotten that from the parade of sirens coming closer and closer, but she was too busy to do anything other than check to make sure Milo was still breathing—which he was—and rush back to the police officers.

Gilley joined her and she couldn't help barking a command at him. "Hold your breath!"

His eyes crossed and he waved his hand in front of his face. "Sweet baby Jesus! What the hell is that?"

*"Hold your breath!"* she yelled again as she bent down to the officer who was now semiconscious.

Gilley puffed out his cheeks and grabbed the man's other arm, and together they got him to his feet and over to the lawn, where he fell to his knees and promptly threw up.

Gil scrunched up his face and looked like he was about to hurl himself, but M.J. didn't have time to deal with him. She dashed back one final time to the remaining officer, who had recovered enough to get to his knees. Wrapping his arm around her shoulders, she managed to get him to the others and then she flopped to the ground herself.

Pulling the wrap down, she crawled over to Candice, whose eyelashes were beginning to flutter, as she let out a small moan. M.J. took off the pashmina and scrunched it into a ball, placing it underneath Candice's head. "Candice?" she asked. "Honey, can you hear me?"

Another moan behind her caused M.J. to look back. Milo had rolled to his side and was struggling to lift his head. "Gilley!" M.J. said. "Help him!"

The sirens grew deafening and M.J. was never happier to see a set of ambulances in her life. These were quickly followed by two fire trucks and four squad cars. A series of black sedans also appeared at the top of the drive and she gave over the care of the four victims to the paramedics, pulling Gilley back to their car to give the emergency workers room.

A swarm of uniformed and plainclothes responders descended on the area, and M.J. felt that familiar terrible sense of doom hit her in the solar plexus again. She saw several people run to the house with guns drawn, and she had to shout at them to stop. "The house is full of gas!"

That's when she caught sight of Dutch, who was pushing his way through the crowd to get to the front door. "Dutch! Wait! Don't go in there!" she cried, but he either didn't hear her or was ignoring her. M.J. turned to a nearby man in a black suit with an air of authority—she remembered Brice had called him Director Gaston—and cried, "Stop him!"

Gaston shouted to two others dressed in formal attire nearby, and they raced to intercept Dutch, who put up a hell of a fight in his desperation to get inside the house.

M.J. didn't know whether Abby was inside, but she suspected that if the bride-to-be was in there, she'd likely be dead from the fumes and beyond their help. "What do we do?" Gilley asked.

M.J. wrapped her shaking hands around his arm and focused on Candice and Milo, who were being loaded onto stretchers. She wondered if they'd be in any condition to talk. "Come with me," she said, moving around the cluster of people over to the front of the large house. Closing her eyes, M.J. reached out with all the power of her sixth sense, searching for any hint of Abby inside the house.

"What're you doing?" Gilley whispered.

"I don't think she's in there," M.J. said, opening her eyes and searching for the groom.

"How can you tell?" Gil asked.

"I don't know how to explain it, Gil, but the house feels empty. And when I try to get a bead on Abby, I feel her energy behind me, not in front of me."

Gil moved to look around M.J., squinting toward the road. "I don't see her."

M.J. sighed. "Not behind me, behind me," she said impatiently, still searching the crowd for Dutch. "She's somewhere to the south, and she's alive, but something really bad has happened to her."

Gil motioned toward the house filled with gas. "Gee, M.J., you *think*?"

M.J. spotted Dutch at last, over at the ambulances, attempting to get close to Milo, who was being wheeled into the bay, but two firemen, Director Gaston, and Brice were holding him back, demanding he let the paramedics tend to Milo and Candice. In her bare feet, M.J. hurried over to him and managed to grab the sleeve of his tuxedo. "She's not here!" she said loudly to get his attention.

Dutch snapped his head to her, then cast a desperate glance at the house and the hazmat team only now approaching it. "How do you know?"

"I just know," she said. She didn't have time to explain it and deep in her bones she could feel that time was running out. "But we have to find her, Dutch. I think she's in serious trouble."

Dutch's eyes darted to the house again, then at Milo and Candice on their stretchers. Finally he turned to her desperately. "Tell me what you need to help find her and I'll get it for you."

# Chapter Four

The morning after the bombing I wanted to help Dutch out by getting his breakfast ready, just to give him another few minutes to sleep. The poor guy was exhausted and I hated that he had several more late nights ahead of him.

Brody was still asleep on our couch when I came downstairs. As quietly as I could, I shuffled around in the kitchen, whipping up half a dozen eggs and frying up some potatoes to spoon into a couple of flour tortillas for some handy breakfast burritos for the three of us.

Of course, I also had to share the eggs with Eggy and Tuttle. "You two are getting a little pudgy, you know," I told them as I set their bowls down. The irony of feeding them an extra breakfast was not lost on me either. "Mommy will have to get Daddy to walk you a little more."

Eggy wolfed down his portion before lifting his muzzle to eye me skeptically.

I wiggled my cane. "You want me to walk you with this thing?" I asked him.

He licked his chops.

"Oh, sure, it'd be fun until you saw a squirrel. Then I'd be in trouble."

Eggy wagged his tail.

I bent down to stroke his graying muzzle. Eggy was almost eight. "Such a good pup."

"Morning," I heard a voice say.

Turning, I spied Dutch in the doorway, already showered, dressed, and ready to bolt to work. I straightened up and looked at him crossly. "I told you I'd get you breakfast so you could sleep in a little longer."

He walked into the kitchen and kissed me on the cheek before lifting one of the burritos. "These look good," he said evasively.

"Honey, it's only six thirty. Why are you already showered and dressed?"

"Couldn't go back to sleep," he said, taking a bite and giving me his best "I'm totally innocent of all crimes you might be ready to accuse me of" look.

"Uh-huh. And the minute my back is turned, were you thinking of slipping outta here and heading to work without me?"

"No," Dutch said.

*Liar, liar, pants on fire . . . ,* the little voice in my head said.

I reached into the pocket of my robe and pulled out both sets of his car keys. "Good. Then you won't mind if I hold on to these until I'm showered and dressed too, hmm?"

Dutch's eyes narrowed. "Nope."

*Liar, liar, pants on fire . . .*

I put two burritos on a plate and handed them to Dutch. "Make sure Brody eats something while I'm getting ready. I promised his friend's mother that we'd drop him off around seven thirty." With that, I headed upstairs.

I was back down only fifteen minutes later. My sixth sense had kicked in right in the middle of a great hot shower and told me Dutch had outsmarted me. Sopping wet, I fished through my robe and found both sets of car keys still in the pocket of my robe and the door to the bathroom still locked, but that nagging feeling of being outwitted persisted.

I pulled my hair back in a ponytail, threw on some black slacks and matching sweater, and rushed downstairs. (Okay, okay, so I threw on some mascara and a little blush too. A girl's gotta have some vanity now and again.)

When I reached the landing, Brody was sitting bleary-eyed on the couch, tucking into a burrito. "Hey, there," I said, looking around the room for any sign of my fiancé.

Brody's mouth was full, so he simply nodded and lifted the burrito up slightly to show me he liked it.

"Is Dutch around?"

I had to wait for my houseguest to chew and swallow. "He left."

My jaw dropped. "What do you mean he left?"

Brody took another bite and pointed to a note on the coffee table. I lifted it and read:

> *Next time you might want to hold on to your own keys too. . . .*
> *By the way, the Audi needs gas.*
>
> *Love you,*
> *D*

I crushed the note in my fist and rushed to the window. "You son of a beast!" I yelled the moment I saw my own car was gone. Turning back to Brody (who was looking at me with big wide eyes), I said, "Was he wearing his vest?"

Brody's brow furrowed.

"His vest!" I nearly shouted. "Was Dutch wearing his vest?"

The young man had to swallow again. "He was wearing a shirt and a tie, Miss Cooper. No vest."

"Dammit!" (Swearing doesn't count when you realize your fiancé has outwitted you *and* forgotten his bulletproof vest.) Just to be sure, I shuffled to the closet and pulled it open. Dutch's vest wasn't there, so at least he'd taken it with him, and for that I was partially grateful. Still, he wasn't wearing it, which meant he wasn't taking me seriously. "Grab your gear," I told Brody, pulling my purse down from the shelf and reaching for the door. I'd have to drop Brody off and rush to the office to try to catch up with Dutch. Of course, he could be off to any one of the many interviews and meetings I knew he'd lined up for the day. It was actually somewhat surprising that he'd come home last night at all, but then, I knew he'd never leave me alone at night with a stranger in the house, even one as seemingly innocent as Brody.

After locking up, I rushed Brody into the car and grumbled through adjusting the seat and the mirrors and right then I heard a ding that made me focus on the dashboard. Dutch must have come home on fumes, because the gas gauge warning light was bright red, indicating that I had less than two miles of fuel left. "Well, that's just craptastic!"

"You okay?" Brody asked.

I glanced at him and realized that I was making the poor kid really nervous. Taking a calm, steadying breath, I said, "Fine. I'm fine."

Brody didn't look convinced.

"We'll need to stop at the gas station on the corner before I drop you at your friend's house."

"Okay."

"Sorry for the outburst," I said, putting the car into gear and beginning to back out of the driveway. "I'm just worried about Dutch."

Brody nodded. "Yeah. He feels a lot like my mom did yesterday."

I stomped on the brakes and turned to him. "What did you say?"

That alarmed expression returned to Brody's face. "Sorry," he said, throwing up his hands in surrender. "I didn't mean anything by that."

I put the car back into park. "I know you didn't," I said, trying to conceal my own surprise and fear. "But it was a really interesting statement. One only a highly intuitive person would make. So, please, explain to me what you were sensing."

Brody's gaze fell to his lap again, and he didn't reply.

I put a hand on his shoulder. "Brody, please? Tell me what you meant."

He shrugged. "I just had this feeling about my mom, you know? Like, I couldn't figure out what it was. It felt like she was gonna be in a car accident or something. I couldn't put my finger on it. Maybe if I had, she'd still be alive."

I bit my lip, and I was about to console Brody when he

added, "Anyway, when Agent Rivers shook my hand and said good-bye this morning, I had that same feeling again."

My pulse quickened and after squeezing his shoulder, I threw the car back into gear and flew out of the drive. Racing down the street to the gas station three blocks away, I put only three gallons in before I was back inside the car and calling Candice. "Morning, Sundance," she said. "Saw your car in the garage but no sign of you at the office. Where are you?"

"On my way," I replied, weaving through the morning traffic. "I just have to drop Brody off at the Dixons'."

"The whose?"

"Brody's friend's mom, Gretchen Dixon, has agreed to take him in. She lives at Lamar and Thirty-eighth, about a block over from his house, so it should only take me twenty minutes or so before I can get to the office."

"Got it. I'll let the troops know."

"Candice?" I said quickly before she could hang up. "Can you tell me if Dutch has made it there yet?"

"He's in with Harrison and Gaston. They're looking for you too."

"Can you patch me through to Gaston?"

There was a chuckle. "You sound a little distracted, honey. You do know you called me on my cell, right? I can't exactly patch you through unless I walk my phone into Brice's office."

I shook my head. I was distracted. Brody's words kept circling in my mind and I was frantic to get to Dutch. "Walk the phone into the meeting, Candice, and hand it to Gaston. Tell him it's urgent."

"Okay, hang on," she said.

A few moments later I heard, "Abigail?"

"Director, I'm so sorry to interrupt your meeting, but I'm running a little late and Agent Rivers left without me this morning."

There was a pause, then, "And I gather that has upset you?"

"That would be putting it mildly. Is he wearing his vest?"

"Not presently."

I blew out a sigh. "Sir, I need a huge favor from you. I need you to keep Agent Rivers in the office until I get there, and then I need to have a private meeting with you and Candice, where I'm going to ask you for another favor."

Again the director paused. "I look forward to it. What time should I expect you?"

"Eight at the latest."

"See you then, Abigail."

After hanging up with the director, I focused on where I was going and managed to get Brody to the Dixons' without a lot of headache. As he was getting out of the car, I stopped him and reached for my purse. Digging through, I pulled out all the cash I had (which was a good chunk, as I'd just been to the bank) and handed it to him. "Here."

"I can't take that," he said.

I shoved it into his coat pocket. "You can, and you will. It goes toward the Brody Watson college fund."

Brody fished into his pocket and pulled out the cash. "No, really, Miss Cooper. My ma would freak out if I took that." In an instant I saw Brody's face change and his eyes watered. "I mean . . . she wouldn't have liked it if I took it."

I pushed the money into his palm and curled his fingers around it, waiting for him to look at me. "Brody," I said, "you're going to be okay. And the reason you're going to be okay is that now you have a very special angel in the form of your mom watching over you. Total strangers will feel compelled to help you out, honey, all because your mom is tapping them on the shoulder and saying, 'Will you please help my son?' Help won't always come in the form of money, but it will always come, and when it does, you must never turn it down."

Brody held my gaze for a long moment, and at last he tucked the cash into his jacket pocket and whispered, "Thanks."

Before he left the car, I also made sure that he had my e-mail address and phone number. I planned to check in on him every once in a while, just to make sure he was doing okay.

When I got to the bureau, I walked straight to Brice's office, where Gaston, Harrison, and Dutch, along with a man in a black suit, were sitting at the small conference table littered with files and crime-scene photos. "Hello, gentlemen," I said, taking the seat that Brice pulled out from the conference table for me.

There was a knock on the door and we all looked up to see Candice there. "Okay if I come in?"

"Yes," I said before the boys could decide otherwise. Dutch pressed his lips together; I knew he would've rather had it be just the fellas.

Candice declined to take the chair Brice offered her, opting to stand with her back to the wall and observe the meeting.

"Thank you for joining us," Gaston said graciously. "This is Agent Valencia from Homeland Security. He's briefing us on the investigations conducted at the Watson, Mendon, Longfellow, and Williams residences."

Mentally I went through those names and recalled that these were the ladies in the shop when the suicide bomber walked in and detonated the device. I nodded and motioned to Agent Valencia to continue. Although I really wanted to talk to Dutch and the director alone, I'd have to wait until this meeting was over.

I also noticed that Dutch wasn't looking at me, and I could tell he was still pretty miffed from the day before. I couldn't exactly blame him except for the fact that I thought he should friggin' understand that I wasn't doing this to be a pain in his asterisk. I was trying to keep him safe.

"As I was saying, Director," Valencia said, eyeing me with part curiosity, part hostility, "we didn't find anything incriminating at the Watson residence last night. No bomb-making material, guns, or manifesto in the house or on the computers, and the kid's Facebook page comes up clean. We're gonna continue to keep tabs on him, though, just to make sure he doesn't have ties to any terrorist groups, but at this point I think the kid's in the clear."

I bristled. "His name is Brody," I said softly.

Valencia paused and looked at me. "Excuse me?"

All eyes swiveled to me. I cleared my throat. "Sorry. It's

just that I've gotten to know Brody Watson, and I can tell you he had nothing to do with this."

Valencia cocked his head. "How long have you known him . . . er . . . who are you again?"

I felt my cheeks flush. I extended my hand. "Abigail Cooper. I'm a civilian profiler here with Director Gaston's team."

Valencia shook my hand firmly (too firmly if you ask me) and said, "I didn't know we had any civilians on this case."

"We've made an exception for Miss Cooper," Gaston said smoothly. Gaston had this way of stating something with such subtle authority that it invited no further debate or discussion. Valencia simply nodded and moved on.

"Anyway, where was I? Oh, yeah, we also came up bust at the Mendon, Longfellow, and Williams residences. Williams and Longfellow lived together in an apartment not far from the beauty shop where they worked, and there wasn't anything in their place that indicated foul play. Mendon was dropped off by her mother for a prebridal hairdo. She was getting married next month."

I bit my lip. Man . . . that hit close to home. "How old was she?" I asked.

"Twenty-seven," Dutch answered, and he moved a photo of the young woman in front of me. She was a beautiful girl with dark red hair and creamy white skin. I had to swallow and blink a lot to hold my emotions in check. There were days I hated this work.

"We don't have a positive ID on any of bodies yet," Harrison said. "We've reached out to each woman's dentist, and we're waiting for them to compare dental records, but we're pretty sure we've identified four of the five women involved."

"What we need is a lead on the bomber," Valencia said. Turning to Gaston, he added, "I know you want to keep this newest eyewitness under wraps, Director, but he or she needs to be vetted by our team."

For a brief instant, the director's eyes flashed a silent warning to me. I understood perfectly and kept my lips zipped. "The eyewitness has already been vetted by our team," Gaston assured Valencia. "We trust that the description of the bomber was accurate."

Valencia wasn't convinced. "Still, Director, our guys need to interview this eyewitness. We need to satisfy our own curiosity about this person's credibility. Until then, we won't be sure they aren't just feeding you some fabricated description of the bomber to throw you bureau boys off track."

I felt my cheeks heat and I dropped my chin to stare at the tabletop. If I didn't hold myself in check, I was gonna blow my cover. Thankfully at that moment there was a knock on the door and Agent Rodriguez—one of our guys—poked his head in. "Sorry, sirs, but there's a call on line three and I think one of you should take it."

"Who is it, Oscar?" Dutch asked.

I felt goose bumps line my arms. I knew even before Rodriguez answered, so I said, "It's the mother of the girl in the sketch."

The room went very still, and everyone looked from me to Agent Rodriguez, who was in turn staring at me in shock. "That's right," he said. "Man, Cooper, that radar of yours gets sharper every day."

Valencia turned to stare at me with squinty, suspicious eyes. "How the hell did you know that?"

"Never mind about that," Brice said, already moving to his desk to take the call. Before he picked up the line, he pointed to Dutch and then to the extra phone on the side cabinet next to our table. Dutch leaned over and pulled the phone close and nodded to Harrison, who then picked up the line, told the caller to hold, and dialed a three-digit number; Dutch's phone lit up. Once Dutch was on the line, Harrison went back to the woman. "Yes, ma'am, this is Special Agent in Charge Brice Harrison. How may I help you?"

I leaned over to try to hear through Dutch's connection, and he politely held the phone a little away from his ear so I could hear.

The woman on the other end was crying. "I need to talk to someone," she said. "My daughter, Michelle, is missing! A neighbor of mine saw a sketch on TV and she thinks it's Michelle. She told me to call this number."

Harrison sat down in his seat and took up a pen and a piece of scrap paper. "Your name, ma'am?"

"Colleen," she said, her voice quavering. "Colleen Padilla."

"Mrs. Padilla, when was the last time you saw your daughter?"

Harrison's voice was smooth and calm, and I knew he'd get as much information out of her as he could without giving away any facts, because once he told her that the woman in the sketch had been killed in the bombing, he'd never get another detail out of her.

"I saw her three days ago. We had breakfast together before her morning class," Mrs. Padilla said.

"Your daughter is a student?"

"Yes, at UT." I could hear the impatience and fear in Mrs. Padilla's voice ratchet up. "Sir, can you please tell me if you know where my daughter is?"

"How old is your daughter, ma'am?" Harrison said, as if she hadn't even asked him a question.

"Twenty-two."

"And where has she been living?" he asked next.

"Agent . . . whatever your name is," Mrs. Padilla snapped. "I'm not answering one more question until you tell me if you know where my daughter is!"

Harrison's gaze flickered to Dutch, and he pointed to the two of us. Dutch nodded. "Mrs. Padilla, I'd like to send some people out to talk to you about your daughter. Can you give me the address of where you are now?"

*"Where is my daughter?"* the woman yelled.

We all pulled back from our phones a little. "I don't know," Harrison said calmly. "But, Mrs. Padilla, I promise to find out if the woman in the sketch is your daughter."

"Why is Michelle in a sketch in the first place?" Mrs. Padilla pressed. "What's happened to the woman you're showing on TV?"

"I promise to have my team explain everything to you, ma'am, but first we need to locate you. Where are you calling from?"

Mrs. Padilla began to cry in earnest now. "I'm at work," she said. "Oh, God! Michelle! What's happened to you?"

It took Harrison another few moments to coax the address

from her, but the second he had it, he handed it over, and Dutch, Candice, and I were in motion, heading toward the door.

"I'll follow," Valencia said.

That stopped us cold. We all looked at Harrison, who in turn looked to Gaston.

Valencia glared at us. "I'm going," he said firmly. For effect he turned to the director and said, "Sir, remind your agents that this is a *joint* investigation until it can be determined that we don't have some homegrown terror cell at work."

Gaston regarded Valencia thoughtfully; then he turned to Harrison. "Mrs. Padilla sounded very upset," he said.

"Very," Harrison agreed.

"I believe this is best handled by as few imposing men in black suits as possible, Agent Valencia."

Valencia's face flushed with anger. Reaching for his cell (no doubt to call someone and raise a little hello Dolly), he said, "I don't care how upset that woman is, Director. If her daughter is a domestic terrorist, then we'll need to talk to her."

Gaston discreetly waved his hand at us, and once again we were all in motion. We booked out of the office and hurried down the aisle when I noticed that Dutch still didn't have his vest on. "Yo, cowboy!" I called to his back. (Both he and Candice could walk a lot faster than my gimpy self.)

Dutch glanced at me over his shoulder, his brow raised in question.

I stopped at his desk and pointed to his Kevlar. "Forgetting something?"

Dutch grumbled under his breath, turned on his heel, grabbed his vest, and said, "Happy?"

"Not until you put it on," I said sweetly.

"Guys," Candice said from the door. "Come on!"

Dutch leveled a look at me before he put his head through the neck hole. "Let's move," he growled.

I didn't waste time standing there giving him a lecture.

I saved that for the car. "Why are you being so reckless?" I demanded once we were all settled into Candice's car. (She got to drive simply because she had the most gas.)

"How am I being reckless?" he snapped. "I'm wearing the damn thing, aren't I?" Dutch swiveled in his seat to show me he was fastening the straps to his vest.

"Yeah, and if I hadn't reminded you about it, you'd have walked right out without it."

He turned away from me and didn't reply. He just filled the car with an intense, cold silence.

I saw Candice look at me in her rearview mirror. Her brows were lifted in that "Yikes!" kind of way.

I rolled my eyes. "I'm just trying to keep you safe, you know."

"So you've told me."

I swallowed hard. Man! He was really starting to hurt my feelings. Pulling open my handbag, I dug through it to pull out the fat coin purse I kept. Opening it, I dumped out a handful of quarters into my palm. "And what's so damn wrong with wanting to keep you safe?" I demanded, throwing a quarter right at him. "Shit, Dutch!" I flipped another quarter at him. "You act like I'm being unreasonable when *all* I've asked you to do is wear your stupid"—insert lots of choice, colorful expletives here and corresponding quarters— "vest!" With that, I turned the coin purse upside down and dumped all the change I had left in his lap. "You think I'm doing it because I like to torture you? No, you asshat! I'm doing it because I freaking love you, although there are days when you make it *really* difficult!"

No one said a word after that for several minutes, but I did notice that Candice was driving even faster than she normally did. Finally, Dutch calmly and methodically gathered up all the coins and turned to me again. "You're right," he said with an apologetic smile. Handing me the quarters, he added, "These are on me."

I crossed my arms and glared at him.

"Peace?" he said, again trying to get me to take the money.

I sighed heavily and held out my hands. And with that, Dutch and I put our quarrel to rest.

Mrs. Padilla worked in a rather nondescript office building right off MoPac Highway in south Austin. We found her crying at her desk surrounded by coworkers who leveled curious and cautious looks at us as we were shown into her office by the receptionist. It appeared by the size and opulence of the space that Mrs. Padilla was pretty high up in the organization—an accounting agency by the tag on the suite door.

As the coworkers cleared out to give us some privacy, I let my eyes take in some detail.

Mrs. Padilla was a heavyset woman, probably in her late fifties, with brassy blond hair, small eyes, and a bit of a bulbous nose. I picked up her alcohol problem right away—it was pretty loud in her ether—and I also took in the mountains of clutter all over the office. There were stacks of paper, plastic bags filled with more paper, binders, and volumes of tax codes strewn all about. I'm a very tidy person by nature, and lots of clutter makes me feel squidgey. This office immediately set my nerves on edge, but I had to put that aside and focus on poor Mrs. Padilla.

We introduced ourselves to her, but I don't think she took in any of our names, and she waved at us to sit, but every available seat had piles of paper on it. "Just put it on the floor," she told us when we looked flummoxed.

Dutch carefully cleared off a seat for me, then began to clear off a seat for Candice, but she shook her head. Obviously trying to hide her own squeamishness at the mess, she said, "I'll stand, thank you."

Mrs. Padilla blinked her eyes at Candice and then she looked around at the disarray of her office, as if seeing its chaotic state for only the first time, and her lip quivered. "I'm sorry," she blubbered, leaking fresh tears. "Michelle has been trying to get me to hire someone to help organize my office for years, but I'm always so busy. It's gotten away from me."

"It's just fine, ma'am," Candice assured her. "You think this is bad, you should see my junk drawer."

Mrs. Padilla caught her breath before a half sob, half chuckle escaped her. And then she seemed to realize she was laughing because she placed a hand over her mouth and squeezed her eyes shut as the crying took full control of her again. Candice moved to her side and rubbed her arm. "It's okay, Mrs. Padilla," she told her. "I know you're worried about your daughter."

At last Mrs. Padilla stopped her sobbing and dabbed at her eyes. Looking up at Candice, she said, "Michelle's dead, isn't she?"

Candice's gaze drifted to Dutch. He cleared his throat. "Mrs. Padilla, we have no evidence of that. But what I'd like to do is see a photograph of your daughter and compare it to the sketch we've compiled."

"This is about that bombing, isn't it?" Mrs. Padilla said, her hand shaking as she pulled her purse out from a bottom drawer. "You think Michelle may have been in that salon, right?"

"We can't be certain until we get some dental records and DNA, ma'am."

Mrs. Padilla paused in the shuffling through her purse and again she squeezed her eyes closed, a look of relief washing over her. "It can't be her," she whispered. "She just had her hair done two weeks ago."

When she opened her eyes again, she looked at us as if expecting us to agree with her. None of us gave her any indication that we either agreed or disagreed. We had to be very careful how we handled her and I knew it. Mrs. Padilla licked her lips nervously and pulled out her cell phone, which was one of those big Droid phones, not quite the size of a tablet, but with an oversized screen nonetheless. She tapped at the device and scrolled through several images, at last coming to a photo she thought we should look at. "This is Michelle."

Even without leaning forward to look at the picture, I knew it was the girl I'd seen in my mind's eye. Dutch pulled out his copy of the sketch and reached for her phone, casting me a very subtle glance as he did so. I dropped my gaze to let him know it was the same girl, but he still did a side-by-side comparison anyway for Mrs. Padilla's sake.

"There's a strong resemblance," he said gently.

Mrs. Padilla balled her fists and put them to her eyes, sobbing near hysterics now.

Candice leaned over the poor woman and hugged her fiercely, and I thanked God she'd come with us. At last Mrs.

Padilla appeared to have cried herself out, and dabbing once again at her eyes, she said, "Ask me what you need to."

Dutch looked at his notes. "You said that you heard from your daughter three days ago. I checked her last known address before we got here, and it's the same one listed to you, but from your response, I'm assuming she no longer lives with you?"

Mrs. Padilla shook her head. "Her best friend has a two-bedroom house near campus and Michelle is staying there for the rest of the semester."

"Where exactly?" Dutch asked.

She gave him the address and Dutch paused so that he could text it to Harrison before asking his next question. I had a feeling Harrison would be working on getting a warrant and send a team out to the girl's house before we were done interviewing Mrs. Padilla.

"What's Michelle studying in school?" Dutch asked.

"She's been working on her PhD in psychology," she said.

"Psychology?" Dutch repeated.

"Yes. Michelle has always been interested in how the human mind works. She's just begun the PhD program and wants to complete it in the next five years. Eventually she wants to open up her own practice."

Dutch tapped his pen on his notes. "When did you realize Michelle was missing?"

"This morning. Her roommate had called my phone yesterday looking for her, but I didn't get the message until after I arrived here around seven a.m." She blushed slightly and added, "It's been a busy week."

"Tell me about Michelle's friends," Dutch said next.

Mrs. Padilla dabbed at her eyes again. She was doing a great job of holding it together long enough to get through this interview. "She doesn't have many. A handful really."

"Why only a handful?"

Michelle's mother sighed. "My daughter isn't a party girl, Agent Rivers," she said. "She's always preferred her own company to most others. She likes to read, and write poetry, and her studies have kept her very busy. She doesn't have much time to socialize."

"Does your daughter work?"

Mrs. Padilla shook her head. "I've been paying her rent, grocery bills, and tuition. Michelle is such a good girl, and she works so hard, I didn't want her to have the added stress of a job while she was working to complete her PhD."

"So these friends of hers," Dutch said, flipping back a page in his notes, "what kind of people are they?"

Mrs. Padilla's brow furrowed. "Normal, twenty-something people," she said.

"Do any of them make you nervous, Mrs. Padilla?" he asked next.

"No. Why would they?"

Dutch shrugged. "You know how young kids are these days. They're occupying Wall Street and demanding to have a say. I'm wondering if Michelle hung around with any rebellious friends. Anyone who might've had a personal grudge against the establishment, or government in general."

Mrs. Padilla seemed taken aback. She blinked several times and stared at the photo of her daughter on her phone, as if she couldn't fathom Michelle being friends with anyone like that. "No," she said. "Michelle's friends are all very much like her: quiet, serious, and studious."

"Does Michelle belong to any political or activist groups?" Dutch asked next.

Mrs. Padilla squinted at him. "Why do you want to know so much about my daughter and her friends, Agent Rivers? Do you think someone she knows could've been responsible for blowing up that shop?"

Dutch let a long pause stretch out before he answered her. "We don't know for certain who's responsible, Mrs. Padilla. That's why we need to ask these questions about your daughter and her associates, to rule in or out any possibility."

Mrs. Padilla's shoulders stiffened. At last she was starting to read between the lines, and she began to look at us each in turn with suspicious eyes. "Michelle is a good girl," she said firmly. "If she was in that shop yesterday, it was by accident."

Dutch didn't react to her statement. Instead he reached into his leather binder and pulled out a photo. Leaning forward, he placed it on Mrs. Padilla's desk. I could see that it was a photo of another girl, about the same age as Michelle, and by the flat, somewhat plastic-looking appearance of her smiling image, I knew that she was also dead. "Have you ever seen this young lady before?" Dutch asked.

Michelle's mother glared at Dutch. She now knew he was the enemy and she was starting to lock up her willingness to cooperate. "Who is this?" she asked by way of answer.

"Her name was Taylor Greene," Dutch said, giving no more explanation than that.

I sent my radar out into the ether, and I could see Michelle and Taylor running on the same parallel lines to each other. It wasn't a visual per se so much as it was a gut feeling that both girls had shared the same fate, but had never known each other.

Mrs. Padilla shook her head. "I've never seen this girl in my life." Dutch glanced subtly at me. I gave a tiny nod—she was telling the truth. "Why?" Mrs. Padilla suddenly asked, picking up the photo to study it more closely. "Was this the girl that set off the bomb?"

Dutch's phone began to vibrate, and distracted by it, he stood up and said, "Excuse me a second."

He walked out and left Candice and me to fill the awkward silence. "Will either of you two please explain to me what the hell is going on?" Mrs. Padilla asked.

"We know very little at this stage," I admitted.

"But you know something about my daughter or else you wouldn't be here," she countered.

I shook my head. "No, ma'am. We only know for certain that the photo of your daughter resembles our sketch of a woman seen at the beauty shop at the time of the explosion."

Mrs. Padilla shook the photo of Taylor Greene at me. "Gail—my neighbor—said she heard on the news that there were five dead, one of whom was the bomber. Was this girl the one responsible?"

I stared her right in the eye. "No, ma'am. That woman was responsible for another bombing. Two weeks ago in College Station."

Mrs. Padilla's face drained of color. "Hold on," she said. "You don't think . . . My Michelle would never . . . She wouldn't have *anything* to do with something like this!"

"Mrs. Padilla," Candice said gently. "We only know three things for certain at this moment: The first is that your daughter hasn't been heard from in three days; the second is that she somewhat resembles our sketch; and the third is that a woman similar to Michelle in age and appearance set off a bomb two weeks ago at another public place. At this moment, we have no idea if your daughter is involved in any way, or even if she was in fact at the beauty shop when it exploded. But you might be able to help us rule your daughter out by providing us with the name of Michelle's dentist."

The older woman swallowed hard. "You need her dental records." It was more statement than question.

Candice nodded somberly.

Mrs. Padilla set down Taylor Greene's photo and picked up her cell phone again. "It's not Michelle," she said, her voice quavering. "I don't know what girl you have in your morgue, but it's not my daughter."

"Let us prove it," Candice said, placing a hand on Mrs. Padilla's shoulder again. "And then, if and when we do prove it's not her, I promise that I won't rest until we find your daughter and bring her home."

Mrs. Padilla stared up hopefully at Candice. "You will?"

"I will."

I looked down at my lap. It's a hard thing to watch a parent trying to deny the obvious truth that her child has been taken violently from this world. I'd seen it too much in my career, and it never got easier.

At that moment Dutch leaned into the doorway and crooked his finger at me. I got up and followed him into the hallway. Holding the front of his phone to his shoulder to cover the microphone, he said, "I need you and Candice to do me a favor."

I arched a skeptical eyebrow.

"Abs," he said, "please?"

"What's the favor?" No way was I committing until I heard what it was. Knowing Dutch, he was probably looking for a way to ditch his babysitting detail.

"I need you two to go check something out while I finish the interview with Mrs. Padilla." (See? Told you so.)

"No."

Dutch sighed (heavily). "This is gonna take me a while, Edgar, and Brice just got the warrant and he's trying to cover two crews on their way to both of Michelle's residences."

"*Both* residences?"

"Michelle's place near UT and her mom's house. We'll want to take a look at both to cover all the bases," he explained. "I need to keep the mother here and talking while he searches the Padilla residence. The minute she hears we've got a search warrant and have entered her home, she'll clam up and we won't get another word out of her."

"She doesn't know anything, Dutch," I said, a bit irritated with him. Hadn't the poor woman already been through enough for one day?

"Maybe she does; maybe she doesn't. How certain are you that the girl in the sketch is Michelle?"

I frowned. "I'm about ninety-nine percent sure."

"See?" he said to me. "Abs, right now we've got two girls under twenty-five setting off bombs in public places. That's way too big of a coincidence not to be linked, which means we probably have a homegrown terrorist cell on our hands, and if we don't move on these leads fast, more people could be in danger. Not to mention the fact that Homeland Security is about to yank this rug right out from under us."

It was my turn to sigh. "What's the favor?"

Dutch handed me a slip of paper. "I need you and Candice to go to this address and interview this guy."

I looked at the paper. "Jed Banes. Who's he?"

"He's an ex-cop from APD. He called in a lead this morning and Rodriguez took the call. Oscar says Banes is claiming that he got a heads-up about the bombs going off a few hours before they actually did."

"Bombs as in plural? He knew about both of them beforehand?" Dutch nodded. "Why the hell didn't he call it in?" (Crap. That was a quarter.) "And who gave him that heads-up?"

"That's what I need you and Candice to find out," Dutch said.

I frowned again. "It's Rodriguez's lead—why not send him?"

"Harrison needs him and the rest of the department at Michelle's two residences. We can't spare him or anybody else right now."

I crossed my arms. I didn't like the idea of leaving Dutch. "Why don't we just send Candice?" I suggested.

Dutch shook his head. "Abs, I need you to see if this guy is legit or not."

"He's an ex-cop, right? Why wouldn't he be legit?"

"Because Rodriguez did a little background check on him before passing the lead to Harrison. Banes was fired a while back and narrowly avoided being brought up on corruption charges. Word is that he was a dirty cop, and this is either an attempt to get back into the force's good graces or he could be involved with the bombings. I need your radar to tell me what his agenda is."

I wavered. I didn't want to leave Dutch, but in my gut I also felt like this lead needed to be vetted—pronto. "You'll stay right here until we get back?"

Dutch held up two fingers. "Scout's honor."

"You quit the Boy Scouts."

Dutch winked at me. "Yeah, but not until after I learned the salute."

I rolled my eyes. "Fine, cowboy, but if you ditch me while we're out chasing this lead, you can plan to sleep in the doghouse tonight."

"Then I better stay here. I quit the Scouts before I learned how to pitch a tent."

"Ha, ha, funny man," I said woodenly as I motioned through the doorway of Mrs. Padilla's office for Candice to come with me.

# T-Minus 01:13

Dutch waved at M.J. to follow him up the hill toward his car at the top of the drive. She grabbed Gilley's arm as she tucked in behind him. No way was she leaving him behind to complain and get in everyone else's way. The chaos surrounding Abby and Dutch's house in the wake of the discovery of Milo and Candice being found unconscious didn't look to M.J. like it would subside anytime soon.

"This is really bad!" Gilley said as he held tightly to M.J.'s hand.

"It is, honey, but we need to keep it together right now, okay?" M.J. said. She was doing her best to focus all her attention on finding Abby. That bubble of panic in her midsection wasn't going away, and her sense of urgency only increased as the minutes ticked by.

As they reached the top of the drive, M.J., Dutch, and Gilley all turned to face the house down below. And that's how they happened to catch the back doors to the ambulance being kicked open before Candice emerged, looking haggard and wobbling fiercely as she attempted to clamber down from the bay. Two paramedics rushed to grab hold of her and restrain her, but Candice pulled back her arm and punched one in the nose before kicking the other solidly in the gut. Both men went tumbling back away from her, and

Candice staggered down onto the drive looking like she was double-dog-daring anybody else to touch her.

"Shit!" Dutch swore, and took off down the hill.

M.J. sighed and looked at Gilley. "Hold these," she said, shoving her heels at him before running after Dutch.

As M.J. ran, she saw that Brice was busy trying to talk to the fire engine captain, while Gaston was pacing on his cell phone, both men as yet unaware of the chaos that Candice was causing.

Dutch reached Candice, and she launched herself at him, catching him by the lapels of his tuxedo. *"Where's Abby?"* she cried, her eyes wild.

"Candice—," Dutch began.

"Is she in there?" she demanded, pointing to the house.

Dutch shook his head. "No. At least we don't think so."

Candice nodded like she'd already guessed as much. "Someone took her," she said, still looking slightly crazed.

Dutch held her by the shoulders as much to steady her as to keep her from swinging at anybody else, M.J. thought. "We're working to find her," he said calmly. "You need to get back inside that ambulance and go to the hospital."

"I'm fine!" Candice told him, trying to shrug out of his grip.

"No, you're not," Dutch told her, gently but firmly.

"Yes, I am!" she insisted. She did look better than when M.J. had pulled her onto the lawn, but not by much.

"Candice," Dutch growled, his patience obviously wearing thin. "Get back in the damn ambulance!"

Candice scrunched up her face defiantly before suddenly leaning over to the side to throw up. M.J. turned away quickly. When the hacking had eased, she risked a quick peek and found Candice panting, but her color was less pale and there was even more fight in her eyes. "I'm not going to any damn hospital until we find Abby, Dutch," she said through gritted teeth.

"She's not going in my ride!" the paramedic who'd been punched said. For emphasis he slammed the ambulance doors shut. "And I'll have her brought up on assault charges!"

Candice bared her teeth at the guy and Dutch had a hard time keeping a firm grip on her.

M.J. stepped up to the paramedic and said, "I'm really sorry about that. The gas must still be affecting her. I think she just needs a minute to get some fresh air and she'll calm down." Behind her, Candice kept on swearing and yelling. "Or not," she added, shrugging an apology at the paramedic, who only shook his head and headed over to help his coworker— who was still doubled over and holding his stomach. With effort the two managed to get into their vehicle and drive away.

"Where the hell are they going?" Dutch snapped.

M.J. turned to him. "They'd rather not take her."

"Ha!" Candice said. "See? I'm *fine*!" With that, she leaned over again and began to retch, and poor Dutch looked like he was seriously about to lose it.

M.J. stepped forward and wrapped an arm around Candice's middle. "I got her," she said, pulling a tissue for Candice out of her purse.

Candice took it and said, "Thanks, Holliday."

"Come on," M.J. coaxed. "If you're going to help us find Abby, then we need to get somewhere where I can focus, away from all this chaos. Dutch's car is at the top of the drive. Can you make it?"

Candice took a few deep breaths. "Yes."

They managed to move slowly back up to the top of the drive and Candice leaned heavily against Dutch's car. He looked like he wanted to argue with her again about going to the hospital, but she held up her hand and said, "I'm fine. Let's talk this through."

"Tell us what happened," Dutch said.

Candice took a deep breath. "Cat sent us out to find Abby. The makeup girl said that she'd ducked out on her sometime around ten thirty, but Cat didn't realize she was missing until about noon. She sent me and Milo to go look for her, and we started with my condo, then our office, then the bureau. As a last resort we came here and found her car in the driveway. The door was open and Abby's purse was on the front seat along with a note. We figured she was inside, so we knocked on the door, and when she didn't answer, we tried the knob and it was open. Milo and I got about three feet when the gas hit us and we went down for the count. I remember falling toward the open door, which is probably why I'm not dead. At least I got a little air, but Milo . . ."

"He's on his way to the hospital," M.J. assured her. "He was breathing and starting to regain consciousness when they took him away."

At that moment one of the men in hazmat suits walked out of the house and waved to Brice. Dutch was about to run to them, but Brice turned, obviously looking for Dutch, and firmly shook his head. Abby wasn't in the house, just as M.J. had suspected. Another man in a hazmat suit came out carrying a large gas canister. M.J. didn't know what gas had been used, but she could tell that it had been meant to knock out anybody who came into the house.

Dutch turned back to focus on Candice. "You mentioned finding a note in Abby's car—what note?"

"It was from you, and it said to meet you at the house if she could get away. It said you had a surprise for her."

Dutch looked like he'd just been struck. "I left that note on her windshield on Wednesday morning. I had our new bed delivered to the house and I wanted to surprise her, but then you guys were dealing with a lot, so I wasn't surprised when she didn't show."

Candice was eyeing Dutch closely. "She never mentioned to me anything about a note or meeting you for a surprise, and I was with her most of this week, Dutch. She would've mentioned it to me if she'd gotten it."

"Then how come you all found it here?" Gilley asked.

But M.J. had already guessed. "Because someone took it off her windshield and kept it until today," she said. "Someone who wanted to lure her here and set a trap for anyone else that came looking for her."

"Who?" said Gilley.

M.J. closed her eyes. A spirit was knocking against her energy with such urgency that it was distracting her. "Dutch?" she asked.

"Yeah?"

"Who's Chase?"

She heard him catch his breath and M.J. opened her eyes to see his stunned expression. "My cousin," he whispered.

"Did Abby know him?"

Candice and Dutch exchanged a meaningful look. "You could say that," he said cryptically.

"He's telling me that he's in debt to the two of you, and he wants to help you. He's pretty frantic about Abby. He says time is running out."

"Can you ask him where she is?" Dutch said, taking a step closer to M.J. She noticed that his hands were shaking.

M.J. closed her eyes. "He says he can see her, but he doesn't know where—"

"Is she hurt?" Candice cut in.

"He says no. But he also says that she's wearing something that's . . ." M.J. paused. Chase wasn't so much speaking to her as he was impressing his thoughts on her. The communication wasn't English; it was more an expression of emotions, images, and feelings, so the translation was a little tricky.

"Wearing something that what? *What?*" Dutch demanded.

M.J. realized she was moving her hand over her chest in a circle. She opened her eyes and said, "I know this is going to sound really weird, but he says that she's wearing a clock on her chest, but not an ordinary clock—it's a bad clock. A very, *very* bad clock."

Candice's jaw fell open and she staggered backward. Turning to Dutch, she gasped, "Oh, God, Dutch! She's wearing a *bomb*!"

# Chapter Five

As Candice drove us over to Banes's house, I kept glancing at the digital clock on the dash. I was nervous about leaving Dutch alone to chase down some weird lead that no one else had time for, and I'd wanted to leave Candice with him, but as my BFF candidly pointed out, no one drives her car but her.

We made it to Banes's residence in only ten minutes and Candice parked in the drive behind an old Buick. We got out and I looked around the scrubby yard, which smelled like dog urine, and up at the house, which was in need of some major upkeep.

A large pecan tree stretched out over the weedy lawn and feebly lifted its limbs to hover over the house. The wind made the limbs moan and rub against the rusty gutters and I could almost sense the fatigue in the old tree. We walked up the dirty walkway, then the front steps, and the smell of cigarette smoke drifted out to us from inside. I made a face as Candice rang the bell, and together we waited for the door to open.

Several seconds ticked by and Candice rang the bell again. "Who the hell is it?" a gravelly voice croaked.

"Candice Fusco and Abigail Cooper with the FBI, Mr. Banes," Candice called.

There was a grunt and then we heard heavy footsteps and a high-pitched creaking sound. The door was yanked open with a squeak and there stood a man with a grayish complexion, three-day-old chin stubble, and eyebrows as big as woolly caterpillars. Protruding from his nose were thin plastic tubes that snaked their way down to a green oxygen tank on wheels at his side. That explained the creaking.

Squinting at us from the doorway, he said, "Got some ID?"

I fished around inside my purse, but Candice was more prepared. She flipped her wrist neatly to unfold the leather case she kept her credentials in. Banes leaned forward to study her ID and I caught a terrible whiff of tar and nicotine. The man smelled like an ashtray.

"PI?" he grumbled. "You're not with the Feds."

Candice delicately tapped the plastic photo ID just under the one he'd been studying.

He made a face. "FBI consultant. What the hell is this? A joke?"

"No, Mr. Banes," Candice said in that way that suggested he might want to take her seriously. "We were sent by Special Agent in Charge Brice Harrison, to talk to you about the lead you called in to Agent Rodriguez."

"Why'd they send you and not the real thing?"

I could sense Candice bristling, but outwardly she kept her cool. "Every available agent is currently working on other leads, sir."

"What other leads?" he said. Banes seemed to me to be the kind of guy who enjoyed being a pain in the ass.

"I'm not at liberty to say."

Banes began to close the door. "You tell your buds at the FBI that when they send the real deal, I'll talk to them about my lead."

Candice put her foot in the door. "Mr. Banes, I can assure you, the next person from the bureau who comes here to speak with you will not be nearly as pleasant as the two of us."

I flipped my hair a little. "Or as cute."

Banes's eyes cut to me and I gave him my most winning smile.

The guy actually chuckled and eased up on the door.

"Since you're already here," he muttered, turning to shuffle back into the interior of the home, wheezing and squeaking as he went.

The house was cluttered and smelled . . . bad. So bad it made me long nostalgically for the fragrance of smelly ashtray coming off just Banes out on the porch. "Have a seat," our host said, waving to a rickety-looking love seat set at a right angle to an even ricketier-looking sofa.

"We're good," Candice said, taking out her iPhone to tap at the screen. "Is it okay if I record this?"

Banes shrugged from his place on the couch. "Makes no difference to me," he said, right before lighting a cigarette.

I eyed his oxygen tank nervously. Then I scanned his energy. In my mind's eye I saw an hourglass with the sands just about out of the top chamber—my classic sign for someone who is terminally ill. A month also came to mind. November. He'd be dead in a few weeks.

"What happened to you?" I heard him say, and it took me a minute to realize he was looking directly at me, or more specifically—my cane.

"She was injured in an undercover assignment," Candice said before I had a chance to reply.

Banes smiled like he thought that was funny. "Playing with the big boys comes at a price, huh, little lady?"

I shrugged. "You should see the other guys."

Banes's bushy brows rose, and he chuckled again. "Yeah, yeah. So ask me what you need to ask me so I can get back to my show."

I swiveled slightly and saw that Banes's old TV was tuned to *Judge Judy*. He'd muted it for our benefit.

Candice tapped her phone to begin recording. "Agent Rodriguez said that in your call you stated that you'd been notified that the bombs were going to go off prior to the explosions. Is that correct?"

Banes nodded. "It was on my answering machine. Thought it was some crackpot the first time, but the second time . . . the second time I knew it was legit."

Banes was looking at something behind me and I swiveled to my right to see a small table with a nicotine-coated telephone and an ancient answering machine. The red light was blinking on it ominously. "May I?" I asked him, edging over to it.

He waved his cigarette at me. "Knock yourself out."

I depressed the play button and a robotic voice echoed out from the speaker. "Hello again, Banes. The clock is ticking. You have two hours."

I felt goose pimples line my arms, but behind me Candice said, "That's it?"

"Yeah," Banes said sharply. "What'd you expect? A full confession?"

Candice ignored that and asked, "Is there another message as well?"

"Naw, I erased it."

"And when did this call come in?" Candice asked, moving over to me to study the answering machine.

Banes gave her a withering look. "Two hours before the bomb at the beauty shop. Man, they don't hire you consultants for your brains, do they?"

"Do you recognize the voice?"

Banes's withering look intensified. "I doubt that guy's own mother would recognize his voice."

Candice pushed the play button and we listened to the recording one more time. She then picked up Banes's phone—which was one of those older push-button numbers with no digital readout screen. "You don't have caller ID?" she asked.

"Nope," Banes said (a bit defensively, I thought).

Candice turned back to him. "Why are you so sure that the caller was alerting you to the bomb?"

Banes rolled his eyes and shook his head. "Are you dense?"

I could feel my fists clench. Old man on oxygen or not, this guy was about to get a thumping if he kept it up.

But Candice could take care of herself. "Oh, come off it, Banes!" she snapped. "You heard the tape. There's nothing there that definitively ties it to the bomb. So some jerk calls you and leaves a cryptic message about clocks ticking and two hours. You only have one recording, and no caller ID for me to identify if the call *actually* came in two hours before the blast. Were you even home when the message was recorded? I mean, how do *you* even know the recording is referring to the bomb?"

"Because I was home!" Banes yelled, then started to cough. We had to wait for him to catch what little breath he had left before he could add, "I didn't pick it up because nobody but telemarketers ever calls me anymore. But I was here when the call came in, and I heard it record."

Candice frowned. She didn't look like she believed him. "What time was that exactly?"

"I already told you!" he hollered. "Two hours before the blast!"

Her frown deepened. "How did you know the blast went off?" she asked.

Banes pointed behind him and to the right, and I realized he had a police scanner on his kitchen countertop. I hadn't noticed it among the clutter.

Candice sighed heavily, and I could tell she suspected he was putting this whole act on just to make himself relevant again. "I see," she said.

"No, you don't," he grumbled. He could read her pretty well.

She shrugged. "Well, even you'll have to admit that this"—she paused and pointed to the answering machine— "isn't much to go on. I mean, all I have is your word, and that's not worth a whole heck of a lot these days, is it?"

What Banes said next would cost me a quarter to repeat, so suffice it to say that he was not really pleased with her comment.

Candice simply stood there and eyed the old crotchety guy with impatience. "What do you want me to do?" she asked him.

"I'm not lying," he growled. "Look up my phone records if you don't believe me! See for yourselves!"

I leaned in and whispered in Candice's ear. "He's telling the truth, and I think the tape is legit."

Candice turned to me with raised brow. "Really?"

I nodded.

She sighed again. I knew she didn't like Banes, and she'd

been hoping the lead wouldn't pan out so that we could get the hello Dolly out of there. "Okay, Mr. Banes, we'll take you up on your offer to look into your phone records, but first, let me ask—why you? I mean . . . did you even know these two girls?"

"What girls?" he asked.

"Taylor Greene and Michelle Padilla. The two girls we suspect as the bombers."

Banes scoffed. "Girls don't blow themselves up, Miss Private Investigator FBI Consultant. Boys do that."

I was starting to hate Dutch for sending us here. This guy was a total pain in the asterisk. But the thing I couldn't shake was that the recording had given me the serious chills. I *knew* that whoever had called Banes had something to do with this case. But why the caller had reached out to this crotchety old geezer, I couldn't fathom.

The police scanner called my attention again. There was something there too.

"In your time on the force, did you ever work a bombing case similar to this one, Mr. Banes?" Candice asked. I gave her big-time brownie points for keeping her cool throughout the interview, 'cause I would've socked this guy in the nose long before now.

"No," he said.

"Anybody you might've arrested in the past like to play with explosive devices?"

"Not that I can think of," Banes said, his attention firmly back on *Judge Judy*.

Candice moved over to stand right in front of the TV. "Okay, then tell me, why would someone call *you* to give an alert that a bomb was about to go off in two hours?"

Banes shrugged. "Ain't that a question for you guys to figure out?"

Candice simply stared at Banes with a look that could've frozen an Eskimo's keister.

Banes rolled his eyes. "I don't know," he said gruffly. "If I did, I would've told your Agent Rodriguez when I talked to him. I don't know who that is on the machine, and I don't know why they called me, okay?"

Candice turned away from Banes and came back over to the answering machine. Pushing the eject button, she took out the tape and held it up. "May I take this to have one of our guys analyze it?"

Banes shrugged like he couldn't care less. "Suit yourself. But put another tape in, would ya?"

Candice and I looked around the small table and Banes told us we could find one in the drawer. I tugged it open and found several cassettes there. Slotting one in, I closed the lid and we headed out with the promise to be in touch soon.

"Wow," I said, once we were back outside.

Candice chuckled. "Right?"

"Dutch is lucky I don't leave him for that charmer."

"I saw him first," Candice mocked. We got in the car and my partner added, "So tell me what you picked up in there."

I blew out a big breath. "What's to tell? The guy's a mean old grouch, who won't see Christmas."

Candice's eyes widened. "He's dying?"

"Of course he's dying," I said. "What? Did you miss the sallow complexion, the hacking cough, the wheezing, or the oxygen tank on wheels next to the lit cigarette?"

Candice squinted toward the house. "Oxygen tanks do like to explode around fire. . . ."

"He's not responsible for the bombs," I told her quickly. "That much was also clear to me in the ether. Everything he told us was true. He doesn't know who Michelle or Taylor are, and he doesn't know why someone would call to alert him to the bombs."

"It could be tied to his past," Candice said. "To someone he arrested and who wants a little revenge."

I shook my head. "So . . . what? A master criminal forces two young women Banes has never met to strap on a bomb and head to the local mall and a beauty shop? How is *that* revenge against a crooked cop and an all-around awful human being like Banes?"

Candice rubbed her eyes tiredly. "Don't know," she said. "But there has to be a connection. Otherwise, why would this mystery person call Banes in the first place?"

I shook my head again. "I have no idea."

Candice put the cassette tape in the little well under her dash and started the engine. "Let's get back to your fiancé and fill him in. I'd feel better if someone could pull Banes's phone records ASAP."

I took my phone out of my purse and called Agent Rodriguez. "Hey," I said when he answered. "It's Abby. Candice and I just met with Banes. Did you happen to pull his phone records before calling the lead in to Agent Rivers?"

"Not yet," he said. "Harrison ordered us all out of the office to comb through the Padilla girl's residence."

"Are you at the best friend's house or Michelle's mom's?" I asked him.

"The friend's place."

"Okay, we'll meet you over there after we pick up Dutch."

There was a pause, then, "Agent Rivers is here, Cooper."

*"WHAT?"* I shouted. *"You put that man on the phone this instant!"*

There was another pause (Rodriguez was probably trying to repair his eardrum) before I heard Oscar say, "Agent Rivers! Cooper would like to talk to you, sir."

Yet another (much longer) pause, then, "Now don't get excited, sweethot—"

*"Don't you dare tell me not to get excited, Roland H. Rivers!"* Next to me, Candice was wincing and leaning all the way over to her left.

"Abigail?" I heard next, and I realized the phone had been passed to Director Gaston.

I was so mad and so startled that I couldn't really speak. "Sir," I said after a moment.

"I personally picked Agent Rivers up from Mrs. Padilla's office. He's been under my protective watch ever since, and he's wearing his vest. Are you on your way?"

I cleared my throat. "Yes, sir. We're en route. We'll be there in . . . ?" I looked at Candice.

She eyed me with a calm smile. "Tell him fifteen minutes."

"In fifteen minutes, sir."

"Now ask him for the address."

I cut Candice an angry look. I might have to murder someone myself by the end of the day.

We arrived at the house Michelle had shared with her best friend almost exactly fifteen minutes later. As she parked next to another fire hydrant, Candice grinned at me in that "told you so" kind of way. I wondered if it annoyed her as much as it did me when I was right about stuff and grinned like that.

We got out and headed toward the small one-story home, painted bright white with lime green shutters. As we came up the walk, I had to watch my step—it was littered with dead crickets, as was the porch. An iron security door was propped open by a folding chair and inside the house was swarming with agents.

I walked inside and felt a chill travel down my spine. I didn't like the energy in the house. My attention had been focused on finding Dutch, but as I walked through the entry and felt that chill, I paused to really take in my surroundings.

The first room we entered was a spacious living room, with the kitchen off to the left. To the right was a half bath and next to that was a hallway, which I assumed led to the girls' rooms.

The place smelled sharply of spices—cloves, ginger, and coriander. I assumed either Michelle or her best friend was a decent cook.

I moved over to the kitchen, separated from the living room by a half wall, and lifted the lid of a large tin set atop the wall. The tin was loaded with small Baggies of various exotic spices. Looking around the kitchen, I saw the sink piled high with dirty dishes and the counters splattered with food stains and crumbs, while a shiny layer of grease coated the stove and the microwave above it. Beside the stove was a garbage can overflowing with trash and I shivered again, barely suppressing the urge to flee the interior.

Instead, I walked behind the half wall and something crunched underfoot. I knew even without looking down that I'd just stepped on a bug, because in the light of the kitchen, I could see that there seemed to be a dead bug in every corner. I shivered anew.

Candice came up next to me. "*How* do people live like this?" she whispered. Candice was an even bigger neat freak than me, and her mouth was turned down in a frown of disgust. "There're dead bugs all over the living room carpet too."

I swallowed hard and turned away from the kitchen. "Well, at least they've tried to take care of the problem," I said, waving my hand at the ones on the counter. "Obviously someone's been out to take care of the critters."

"Yeah, but until you clean the place up, the critters will keep coming back." At that moment I spotted Dutch coming out from the hallway leading to the bedrooms. He wore a similar look of disgust. "Cowboy," I called.

His head snapped in my direction and he crooked his finger at me. We went over to him and he said, "This place is a shithole."

I had once woken up to find Dutch's side of the bed empty and odd sounds coming from the kitchen. When I'd gone to investigate, I'd found him scrubbing a roasting pan that'd been left to soak before we'd headed upstairs for the night. He'd confessed that he'd been unable to sleep knowing the pan was in the sink. It was something his veteran of the navy father had impressed upon him—never leave a kitchen in less than pristine condition.

"I take it the bedrooms are just as bad as out here?"

"Might be worse," he said. "These girls are pigs."

"They're also young and crazy busy," I reminded him. I didn't think I'd been the neatest person in my twenties either. Then again, I was certain I hadn't lived like this.

Dutch nodded, but I think he did so just to move on. "You get anything from in here?" he asked me.

I looked around again, not at the mess but with the eyes of an intuitive. "There's a bad vibe in here."

"What kind of bad vibe?"

I shook my head, moving away from him and over to the living room. There was a sliding glass door mostly covered by venetian blinds. Pulling the cord to open the blinds, I hesitated in front of it. Dutch came over to me. "What?" he asked.

I saw that he was wearing gloves and pointed to the handle. "Try that, would you?"

"It's locked," he remarked, pointing to the small metal lever, which was in the upright position indicating the door was locked.

"Try it anyway," I said, my radar buzzing like crazy. Dutch did and he let out a breath when the door opened easily. Bending down to inspect the catch, Dutch called out, "Cox!"

Another agent came over to us, and Dutch pointed to the handle and the lock. "This has been tampered with. Get the techs to fingerprint the whole door."

Agent Cox nodded and went in search of a fingerprint tech.

I moved away from the door and noticed that Candice was keeping a watchful eye on me. I smiled at her—she always had my back—before moving toward the hallway leading to the bedrooms. I walked slowly and had to move out of the way twice so that agents could get past me. Stopping at the first bedroom, I let my radar extend outward, but I already knew that wasn't the room to investigate.

I then moved on down the hall to the end, stopping in front of the open door that I knew marked Michelle's room.

The bedroom was a mess. Clothes were strewn all over, and whether they were clean or dirty was anyone's guess. The bed was unmade and there was something else, something that gave me the chills. The room had a sense of violence in it. I scrutinized the walls, the ceiling, the closet doors. No blood splatter or marks to indicate that a struggle had gone on here, but I was convinced one had taken place . . . recently.

I was also pretty sure that Dutch and his team simply looked at this space as a young woman's messy bedroom, but not me. "Something happened in here," I said.

"What?" Dutch asked. I'd felt him come along behind me as I navigated my way into Michelle's room.

"There was a struggle. Michelle lost."

"Someone attacked her?" Dutch asked. I looked at him over my shoulder. His gaze was roving all up and down the walls.

"Someone took her."

Dutch put a hand on my shoulder. "You think she's been kidnapped?"

I nodded.

Dutch scratched his head. "Then she's not our bomber?"

"No, she's our bomber," I said. The dental records would take at least twenty-four hours to be matched with the body in the morgue, but I *knew* that Michelle was the girl from the beauty shop.

Dutch sighed. "None of this makes sense."

"Tell me about it." Turning on my heel to go back out into the living room, I found Cox there with the fingerprint tech and the sliding glass door was now covered in gray powder.

"Anything?" Dutch asked Cox when he joined me there.

Cox shook his head. "The door's been tampered with, but other than a broken lock, we got nothin', Agent Rivers."

Candice was inspecting the handle herself and she had a quizzical look on her face. "Which is pretty strange, don't you think?" she said. "There should be a few prints. Some from the two girls at the very least."

My brow rose. "The handle has been wiped clean?"

"The handle and the wall next to the handle," Candice said, waving her hand at the area beside the door handle, which was just one big black smudge.

"Abby thinks there was a struggle in the bedroom."

"What kind of a struggle?" Cox and Candice said together.

"The kind that didn't end well for Michelle," I told them. "I think she was abducted."

Dutch rubbed his face. He looked tired and stressed-out. His phone buzzed and he took it out to look at the display. With a groan he showed it to me. My shoulders slumped. I took his phone and answered it for him. "Hey, Cat," I said, knowing my sister had likely called my own cell a half dozen times before trying Dutch.

"Where are you two?" she demanded.

"I'm fine. You?" I said.

"I didn't ask how you were," she snapped, completely missing my sarcasm. "I asked *where* you were! You guys are twenty minutes late!"

I was tempted to hang up on her. She'd been driving Dutch and me crazy with all this wedding stuff. Cat was our unofficial wedding planner. Unofficial only in our minds, however.

My sister was taking the role very officially. "We're at a crime scene," I told her. "And we can't break free."

*"What?"* she exclaimed. "Abby! You do know you're getting married in two weeks, right? I can't keep rescheduling these appointments!"

"What're we late for now?" Dutch asked.

"I have no idea."

"I have the caterer, the cake baker, *and* the photographer here! You have to come!" Cat shouted. "And where is Candice? She was supposed to be at her final fitting appointment ten minutes ago too!"

I turned to Dutch. "Cat has the—"

"I heard," Dutch said, waving at me to give him the phone. "We'll be there in twenty minutes, Cat."

"You want to leave?" I asked him when he'd hung up. "Now?"

Dutch looked around at his team. "There's nothing here," he said. "We've searched through everything, and there's no bomb-making equipment, no incriminating notes, printouts, or books, and there's nothing on Michelle's computer except the usual college-girl stuff. I'll have the techs go over her room to try to find any sign of a struggle, but for now, there're no leads here, and I could seriously use a break from this."

I eyed him doubtfully. "Do you think Gaston's gonna let us go?"

"Go where?" asked a voice behind me.

I jumped a little and turned to see the director standing right behind me. "Dutch and I have an appointment for our wedding to go to, sir."

"Ah, well, you shouldn't miss it. Go on, you two, we can handle this."

"Thank you, sir. I'll keep my phone on," Dutch promised. "Call if you need us back."

Gaston nodded and said, "Take the afternoon, Rivers. We'll handle it from here today."

Candice led the way out of the house and I was still pretty surprised that the director had let us go so easily. "That was nice of him," I said as we piled into Candice's car.

"He knows he's going to have to give you two up to the

wedding soon anyway," Candice said. "I mean, it's not like he can ask you to postpone the nuptials."

Dutch snickered like he thought that was funny. "I'm surprised he hasn't asked us to do just that."

Candice laughed. "Me too."

But I looked out the window, trying to hide my disappointment that the director hadn't asked. If he had, I knew I'd have taken him up on the offer, and that troubled me more than I could say. . . .

# T-Minus 01:05:48

Standing next to his car at the top of the hill, Dutch looked so pale and shaky that M.J. worried he might be ready to faint. Instinctively she moved closer to him and placed a steadying arm under his. "Stay with me," she told him. "Breathe, okay?"

"How did this happen?" he muttered. And then he lifted his chin and searched M.J.'s face pleadingly. "Can you tell me where she is?"

M.J. bit her lip. She knew what the answer would be, and yet she asked his dead cousin anyway. *Chase,* she said, *can you see where Abby is?*

His answer came without pause. "He says he can see her, but he doesn't know where she is. For the moment he thinks she's alive."

Dutch staggered backward to lean heavily against the car. "How much time do we have?" he asked.

M.J. asked, but Chase didn't know. Dutch then shouted down the hill to someone named Rodriguez, and he came running up to them. "Who's monitoring Banes's phones?" he snapped.

Rodriguez blinked. "At the moment, no one, sir."

Dutch put his hands on Rodriguez's lapels. "I need you to

find out if a call has come in to his line, Rodriguez. Do it. Do it right now!"

The poor FBI agent paled, and held up his phone. "Yes, sir. Right away."

They waited anxiously while Rodriguez talked on his phone with his back to them. At last he turned around, his expression grave. "A call came in approximately fifty-five minutes ago, sir. It was from an unlisted number. Sounds like it was another one of those disposable cells."

Dutch closed his eyes and M.J. knew he was battling mightily to keep it together so that he could think. She didn't know what was going on until Candice said, "That means we have only one hour to find Abby before the bomb goes off."

Dutch's eyes flew open. "How the hell do we find her? Jesus, Candice! How do we get to her in time?"

Candice was silent, and M.J. knew she was trying to think quickly, but she'd already been through a lot that afternoon herself.

"This has something to do with the big case Abby wanted me to help you with, right?" M.J. asked them.

Dutch pulled his gaze away from Candice to focus on M.J. "Yes. So far, three other women have been abducted, forced to carry a bomb to a public location, and the bombs were then detonated, either remotely or by the device running out of time. The sick son of a bitch orchestrating this always puts two hours on the clock. And he always calls an ex-cop to warn him that the clock has been activated."

"Then I think the place to start is at the beginning," M.J. said. "Tell me everything as quickly as you can. Bring me up to speed and maybe I can use the info to fish out a clue about where Abby is."

Candice and Dutch exchanged a look before Candice pointed shakily to the blue Mini Cooper at the bottom of the drive. "My valise is in the trunk of Abby's car. I've got copies of everything in it."

Gilley handed M.J. back her shoes. "You stay," he said to Candice. "I'll get it."

No sooner had Gil taken off to retrieve the files than Dutch began to debrief M.J. He spoke quickly and efficiently, and midway through his speech when Candice was rifling through her valise pulling up files and photos, M.J. suddenly had another spirit enter the picture. Holding up her hand, she said, "Who's Brody?"

Dutch blinked. "He's a kid loosely connected to this case."

M.J. shut her eyes to concentrate. "I don't know if you guys will know this, but is there an older female connected to him—someone from the other side—with the first initial *R*? Like Roseanne, or Reanne?"

"Rita," Candice said.

M.J. opened her eyes and saw that Candice had pulled up a photo of the deceased woman's driver's license. "And her middle name was Anne!"

M.J. nodded. "I have to talk to Brody," she said. "Now!"

# Chapter Six

I was on the phone with Brody, checking in with him to make sure he was doing okay, when Candice pulled up to the curb in front of Cat's office building and parked so Dutch and I could get out before she headed off to her own appointment. "How's he doing?" Candice asked as she put the car into park.

"Hanging in there. I think he'll have a whole lot of bad days until the sharpness of his grief fades a little."

Dutch was still gabbing away on his phone in the back-seat.

The whole way over, he'd been filling Brice in on what we'd found—and hadn't found—at Michelle's place. He'd also let Brice know that I'd picked up on a possible abduction, and about the tampered lock on the sliding glass door.

Hanging up, he said, "Brice is coming over tonight after he wraps up searching the Padilla residence."

"Did his team find anything?" I asked.

"Nope. Total bust." Then turning to Candice, he said, "Care to come over for dinner with your fiancé?"

I saw Candice's gaze slide to me. "Who's cooking?"

I cut her a dirty look. For the record the only thing I know how to cook is an omelet. But it's a mean omelet, all the same.

"I thought we'd spring for takeout," he suggested.

"Perfect. Call me when you guys are done here and I'll come pick you up." With that, Dutch and I got out and headed in even though I was in no mood to deal with my sister. In fact I was in no mood to deal with any of this wedding stuff, period. "You okay?" Dutch asked as we loaded into the elevator.

"Fine."

"Did you know that's the most commonly told lie there is?"

I looked up at him. He was grinning down at me. "Huh?"

"The most often told lie is 'I'm fine' when asked how a person's doing," Dutch explained.

I rolled my eyes. "Well, I really am fine."

"Liar, liar, pants on fire," Dutch sang, but he reached for my hand and lifted it to give me a sweet kiss all the same.

I gave in to a smile. He had this wonderful way of making things feel okay even when they weren't. "Please don't ditch me or leave a place you've promised me you'll stay put at again," I said to him.

He wrapped an arm around me and squeezed. I felt the bulk of his bulletproof vest and was glad for it. "Okay, Edgar," he said. "We'll work this case together until the wedding, and then, if it's not solved, we're cuttin' out and going on our honeymoon. Deal?"

"We could just cut out early and elope," I said.

Dutch laughed. He thought I was kidding. The doors parted and I lost the opportunity to convince him, because standing in the hallway was Cat's assistant, Jenny.

Jenny is a petite little thing, much like my sister, but unlike my sister, Jenny doesn't dress to impress. She goes for a more efficient librarian look, with her black, brown, or gray business suits, brunette hair pulled back into a tight bun, and oversized round glasses constantly sliding down her perky nose. Still, she is a very pretty girl, and that's impossible to hide, with her high cheekbones, deep-set eyes, and heart-shaped face.

I don't exactly know what Jenny's last name is, but I suspect it's Makeanote. (You'll see why in a minute.)

"Welcome, Miss Cooper, Mr. Rivers," she said, and then she caught herself and blushed a little. "Sorry, *Agent* Rivers."

Dutch smiled politely to show her no harm, no foul, and Jenny's blush deepened.

I hid my own smile. Jenny had a crush on Dutch, and I felt for her, because he is truly a beautiful mountain of a man that I rather like climbing. I squeezed his hand and edged closer to him, just to make it clear to Jenny that this cowboy was taken.

Jenny dropped her gaze to the clipboard she held. She'd picked up on my body language. After clearing her throat, she said, "Miss Cooper, your sister is waiting for you in the conference room. If you'll follow me, please." With that, Jenny turned on her heel and we followed along obediently.

Cat's offices are a grand affair, taking up the entire floor of the posh professional building. The joke is that it's staffed by a total of nine people, so most of the individual offices we passed were empty. The place had that somewhat haunted ghost town feel to it. I knew that in the next several months Cat would be hiring more and more staff to fill the spaces, but in the meantime I privately thought it a somewhat depressing place to work.

We arrived at the conference room—a space I was familiar with, having been brought here against my will just a few weeks earlier—and it was much the same as last time, with the conference table covered in food, party favors, fabrics, and photos. I got woozy just looking at it.

"There you are!" my sister exclaimed, untangling herself from several different-colored fabrics to come hug me fiercely.

"Hey, honey," I said. "Sorry. We got tied up."

"It's fine," she assured me, letting go to hug Dutch. "I'm just glad you two are here now."

I had to hide another smile, because Cat's embrace had obviously caught Dutch off guard, and I had observed that he never quite knew how to respond. Cat's five feet two in heels, and Dutch is well over six feet, so when they hug, it's more like she grabs him around the waist and he tries to hold his groin out of the way, while patting her awkwardly on the back. It's a bit like watching a bear hug a bunny.

At last she released him, but snuck a wink at me, and I knew she was in on the joke. I had to press my lips firmly together to keep from chuckling. "Shall we get started?" she said, moving over to the table, where three people were already seated. I didn't recognize a single one of them. Before introducing them, Cat said, "Jenny, make a note to call the florist and ask if the centerpiece sample I requested can be sent over by tomorrow. I want to make a final decision no later than then."

I'd never heard my sister mention Jenny's name without adding a "Make a note. . . ." (Hence why I always mentally referred to her as Jenny Makeanote.)

Next my sister turned to the people already seated. "Alfie, this is my sister and her fiancé. Abby, Dutch, this is your photographer, Alfie Lockwood."

We nodded to the lanky dark-haired man, wearing a crisp white shirt and a lazy smile.

Cat was already introducing the other two in attendance. "This is Esperanza Alvarez, your caterer, and Bridget Monroe, your cake baker."

I nodded to each of them in turn and Dutch and I took our seats. "Now," Cat said, her eyes bright with enthusiasm, "first, a few odds and ends to tidy up, and then we'll make our final decisions with Alfie, Esperanza, and Bridget."

I stifled a sigh. This was likely going to take a while.

"First, we've received one hundred and sixty RSVPs to make our wedding-guest tally three hundred and eight so far."

I blinked. Three hundred and eight? I looked at Dutch, and he looked at me. We wore identical expressions of confusion and shock. "Hold on," I said. "*How* many people did you invite to this wedding, Cat?"

It was her turn to blink. "Well, I sent out well over two hundred invitations, Abby, and all the invites are for plus ones, which is where the numbers really add up."

My mouth fell open. Did Dutch and I even *know* two hundred people? I mean, I could count my close friends on my fingers . . . of one hand.

Cat waved dismissively at our shocked expressions. "Don't worry; Dutch and I talked about it and I'm taking care of most of the wedding expenses as my gift to you two."

I felt my brow break out in a cold sweat and I turned narrowed eyes on Dutch, who was making a point not to look at me. "I'll explain later," he whispered.

But I was completely flustered. I hadn't wanted a big wedding. In fact, I'd specifically told Cat that I'd wanted to keep this thing small. My sister had the invitations piled up to the side of her. The stack was crazy high. Who the hell was coming to this thing anyway? (Swearing doesn't count when you've just discovered your sister has invited the entire state of Texas to your very private affair.)

"The cutoff date to receive the RSVPs is tomorrow," she continued, "so I think we'll be safe by planning on about three hundred and twenty, to three hundred and forty guests."

I saw the caterer, baker, and photographer make a note. The sweat on my brow began to slide down my temples, and I felt a bit dizzy.

"Next," said Cat, "we'll need to finalize a few other details about the actual ceremony. Now, at precisely three o'clock Abby will emerge from her horse-drawn carriage—"

"My horse-drawn . . . what?"

Cat didn't even look up from her day planner. "Your carriage. We talked about this." (For the record, we had so *not* talked about it.) "You're arriving in a carriage pulled by six white stallions . . . or maybe geldings. From what I hear stallions tend to get a bit unruly when they're all tethered together. Jenny Makeanote, we'll want geldings, not stallions."

"But, Ms. Cooper-Masters," Jenny said, "the stable only had two white geldings available, remember? We'll have to go with at least four stallions if you want all the horses to be male."

"Oh, that's right. Well, stallions make such a romantic statement, don't you think?" Jenny nodded. Dutch and I both shook our heads vehemently, but Cat wasn't looking at us. "Right, we'll go with two geldings and four stallions and keep our fingers crossed that the horses behave. Anyway, where was I? Oh, yes, so once the carriage arrives, Abby will step out with the aid of the best man, Milo, who will then walk her past the swan pools—"

"Swans? There are swans?" I asked. Was it getting really hot in here?

"Swan *pools*," Cat corrected, reading the notes in her planner. "I've ordered a dozen each black and white swans to swim in the two pools on either side of your walkway." Cat then turned to her assistant. "Jenny Makeanote, I want you to check in with the swan handler to ensure that he's trained them not to pull off their little bow ties and veils from one another. I don't want any swan squabbles breaking out. Oh, also, make sure they stick to their pools—we don't want them getting out and chasing our bride down the aisle!" My sister laughed lightly, but I could tell either there'd been a discussion where she'd been warned about this, or she'd seen it firsthand.

A quick glance to my right showed me that Dutch was attempting to say something, but Cat carried on as if there weren't two horrified people sitting at her conference table. "Now as Abby comes down the aisle, she'll be serenaded by the Austin Women's Chorus, which reminds me . . . Jenny Makeanote, I'll need to make sure those bleachers can hold all one hundred and fifty singers." Jenny scribbled dutifully on her pad, and I could feel my heart pounding in my ears.

Looking for another ally, my gaze shifted to the photographer, the caterer, and the wedding cake baker, but they were all nodding agreeably and I knew then that Dutch and I were the fourth and fifth persons in this tub, about to go rub-a-dub-glug.

"And as Abby climbs the stairs to the platform where Dutch will be standing, I've hired two little people to dress up like Cupid and sit above the happy couple in the branches of the oak trees shading the dais. The Cupids will be sprinkling the bride and groom with a gentle dusting of white rose petals throughout the ceremony. Jenny Makeanote, I'll need to know exactly how many bags of rose petals to pack among the branches and also check on the status of the safety harnesses we ordered to make sure that the little people don't fall down on top of the bride and groom during the ceremony."

At this point I started to look around the room for cameras,

convinced I was being punked, but my sister remained stead-
fastly serious. "Once Abby is handed off to Dutch, they'll
listen to the short sermon given by the minister, and then they
will each recite the vows they've written for each other."

"Vows we've . . . what?" I said. (What happened to just
saying, "I do"?)

"Jenny Makeanote," my sister carried on as if I hadn't
even spoken, "we'll need to outfit Abby and Dutch with microphones so that all the guests can hear them. Oh, oh, oh!
Which reminds me of something else—I'll need you to check
on the rigging for Eggy and Tuttle, and make sure they get
some training with the replica of the horse drawn carriage."

"The . . . the . . . replica? What?" The world was spinning.
Not just a little. A lot. I clutched the table and tried to hold
on, but it was getting really hard.

Cat was writing something down in her planner. "The
replica of the carriage," she said absently. "Remember? We
talked about this. Neither one of your nephews wanted to be
the ring bearer, so I thought it'd be cute to have Eggy and
Tuttle bring the rings to you on a tiny carriage. We'll need to
borrow the puppies to train them to trot the rings down the
aisle on command. Oh, and, Jenny Makeanote, the swan handler shouldn't allow the swans to snap or honk at the dogs."

I found myself shaking my head, willing for Cat to stop,
but she ignored me and continued. "Anyway, after the bride
and groom kiss, we'll unleash the butterflies."

I was almost too afraid to ask. "Butterflies?"

Cat finally lifted her excited eyes to me. "Yes! I'm having
two thousand morpho butterflies shipped in from South
America. They're the big sapphire and black ones you might've
seen in pictures . . . you know, the really big ones?" Cat held
up her hand and splayed her fingers to imitate their size.
"Anyway, the moment they're released, the butterfly handler
suggests that you and Dutch hold very still. He says they'll
probably swarm you two at first, so wait until most of them
flutter off before you try to make your way down the stairs."

I got up from the table so fast my chair bounced against
the wall. "Abs?" Dutch said.

I looked around the room wildly. "I . . . I . . . I . . ."

"What's the matter?" Cat was saying, but her voice sounded very far away and the world was continuing to spin and spin and spin.

With effort I turned and staggered to the door, leaning heavily on my cane as I went. Once I got out into the corridor, I simply kept walking. Dutch caught up with me easily. "Edgar? Honey, you okay?"

"Did you know about this?" I snapped, my breathing still coming in hard little pants. "Did you know about swarming butterflies, and doggy-drawn carriages, and . . . and . . . this *circus* that's going to be our wedding?"

Dutch didn't answer me. Instead he put a hand on my arm, but I shook it off. I needed air. Lots of air, and there didn't seem to be anything breathable in here. Once I made it to the main door of Cat's offices, I pushed through and paused only a moment to find the stairwell—no way was I enclosing my panicky self in an elevator.

The stairs were tricky with my weakened hips, but I managed to make it down the three flights and push through the emergency doors . . . which set off the alarm.

A security guard came around the corner a few moments after Dutch and I made it outside. Dutch apologized and waved his badge and the guy backed off. Meanwhile I shuffled over to a retaining wall and held on to it while I focused solely on taking deep breaths.

"I didn't know about all of it," he said once I stood back from the wall and could focus angrily on him again. "And I've tried to rein her in, but your sister doesn't understand the word no, as I'm sure you're aware."

"And what was that about her picking up the tab?" I demanded.

Dutch grimaced. A few weeks earlier we'd flipped a coin to see who would work with Cat on the wedding and who would work with our foreman, Dave, to finish the house. Dutch had lost and ended up with Cat. I was now regretting using my radar to cheat on the coin toss. "The house ended up costing us more than expected, Abs," he said. "We went way over budget, so when your sister generously offered to pick up most of the expenses, I said sure. I didn't realize that she'd use that as an opportunity to go nuts with the plans."

I stared openmouthed at my fiancé. "It's *Cat*, Dutch. How *did* you expect her to react?"

He could only shake his head and look chagrined.

I felt myself softening as I gazed up at my beautiful fiancé, whom I loved more than anyone or anything in the world, and my eyes misted. "I can't do it," I whispered. I'd carried around the most terrible feeling about our wedding day, and now I knew why. "It's too big, Dutch. Too insane. I can't do it."

Dutch opened his arms and folded me into them. "Okay," he said at last.

I felt a wave of relief wash over me. "Thank you," I said, so grateful that he understood. We would cancel the wedding. He and I would get married quietly, privately. I closed my eyes, imagining a beautiful white beach with aquamarine waters, and Dutch and I marrying each other under the setting sun.

Dutch kissed the top of my head and said, "Call Candice. Have her come pick you up and take you out for a cocktail. I'll head back inside and finish up with Cat, and get her to chill out on some of these ideas."

I stiffened. "What?"

Dutch backed away from me, but still held on to my hands. "No butterflies, or horse-drawn carriages. And I'll put my foot down about Eggy and Tuttle. Milo can hand us the rings. I'm not sure what to do about the guests, though, babe. You must have given your sister a big list or she's inviting some of her own friends, because I only gave her about forty people."

I blinked and nodded dully, while a dark foreboding ate away at my insides. Dutch didn't want to cancel the circus. He just wanted to help me get through it.

"How will you get home?" I asked, already pulling away from him.

"I'll call Brice, or have Cat's driver drop me off." He smiled at me and squeezed my hand. "Hey," he said. I looked up at him, trying to convey all that I was feeling, but Dutch was never much of a mind reader. "Don't worry, honey. We'll get through the ceremony in one piece and then spend the rest of our lives together away from the circus."

I nodded, but felt a cold shiver snake its way slowly up my backbone.

I waited for Candice on a marble bench out in front of the office building. I sat there dully, wondering what the hell I'd gotten myself into and how the hell I was going to get out of it. (Swearing doesn't count when you only think the words in your head.)

As I was waiting, my phone went off. I looked at the display and my brow shot up. "Hello?" I said, taking the call.

"Abby?" a familiar voice replied. "Hey, girl! Long time no talk to!"

"M.J.!" I said, mustering some enthusiasm, because I genuinely liked the woman on the other end of the line. M. J. Holliday is a seriously talented psychic medium who'd once helped me out with a haunted house I'd been renovating. We'd kept in touch over the years, and I now considered her a true friend. "I saw you on TV the other night!"

"Yeah, Gilley has finally made it to the big time," she joked, referring to her best friend and business partner, Gilley Gillespie.

"How is Gil?"

"He's good, he's good," she said. "Still shrieking at the first sign of a ghost, though, as I'm sure you saw in that episode. But he's also part of the reason I'm calling. We got back to the States just a day ago, and I found your wedding invitation in the mail, and of course I'd love to come, but my boyfriend, Heath, can't make it, so is it all right if I bring Gilley as my plus one?"

I blinked . . . something I'd been doing a lot lately. I didn't realize that I'd invited M.J. to the wedding. . . . And then it hit me. I'd never given my sister a list of invitees—it was one of those things that I'd meant to do, but hadn't gotten around to, and one day she'd simply said not to worry about it, that she'd already taken care of it. But if Dutch had only given her forty names to work with, how the heck had she gotten M.J.'s info? "That's fine, M.J.," I told her, trying to cover my surprise. "I'd love to see you and Gil."

"Awesome," M.J. said. "I don't have time to get the RSVP to you before tomorrow's deadline, so would you put me and Gil down as a definite yes?"

"Of course."

"Great. And I think we'll stay a few days after the wedding. I've always wanted to check out Austin."

At that moment a crazy idea hit me. I thought about Rita Watson and my encounter with her at the beauty shop. I wondered if M.J. might be able to make contact with her and get a few more details for our case. What I didn't know was if it was a good idea to get M.J. involved in something as awful as this bombing case. Not everyone had the stomach for this kind of thing, and it'd taken me a few years to be able to handle the grisly crime scenes. "M.J.," I said, just as Candice pulled up to the curb. "Can we talk in the next few days? I'm working a case that I think I might need your expertise with. At the very least I'd like to talk to you about it, and if you're game, I'd like to introduce you to my bosses. I think you might be just the person for the job."

There was a bit of a pause and then M.J. said, "You can talk to me about anything, Abby. If I can help you out, I'd be happy to. And if you want me to come out there early, I can do that too."

I smiled as I pulled open the car door to Candice's Porsche. "Thanks, honey. I really appreciate it, and I can't wait to see you guys at the wedding. I'll be in touch soon."

Once I'd hung up, Candice looked at me expectantly, but I held up a finger and the next call I made was to my sister. "Are you all right?" she asked by way of hello.

"Fine," I said, because I didn't want to get into why I'd abruptly left her offices. I'd let Dutch do what he could to rein her in. "Listen, I have a question about the guest list. Dutch says he only gave you the names of about forty people, and I didn't give you any names at all, but I just heard from M. J. Holliday that she and her plus one are coming, so my question to you is, where did you get her info to send her the invitation?"

"Jenny Makeanote, M. J. Holliday and her plus one are a yes," Cat said. I tapped my knee impatiently, waiting for her to focus on me again. "I got her info from your phone," she said at last.

I looked quizzically up at the office building to the third floor where I knew Cat was still inside her conference room. "My phone?" I repeated . . . and then I remembered. Cat had stolen my phone a few weeks earlier, and it'd been right after that that she'd stopped bothering me about giving her a guest list to work with. My brow broke out in a cold sweat again. "How many people from my phone did you invite?" I asked.

"All of them."

My jaw dropped. "What do you mean, *all* of them?"

"All your contacts, Abby. I mean, it's not like you have enough close friends in your life to make up a decent guest list. So, I just went with all of the contacts you had in your phone with listed mailing addresses."

I was speechless. Utterly speechless. And it was a good thing that I wasn't up on that third floor because I was fairly certain I would have resorted to violence. Instead I pulled my phone away from my ear and clicked over to my list of contacts. "Oh . . . my . . . God . . . ," I whispered. "My dentist is in here. . . . My *gynecologist* is in here! The AC guy . . . the vet . . . guys from Dave's crew . . ."

I could hear Cat's tiny tin voice echoing out from the earphone, but I simply clicked back to the call and hung up on her.

"Problems?" Candice asked. She was still in idle, waiting for me to fill her in.

"Yes."

"Care to share?"

"Yes," I replied, but didn't elaborate.

"Soon?"

"Over cocktails."

"Oooo. Them's some big problems, then, pardner." With a light chuckle, Candice put the car into gear and sped out of the drive.

"You don't know the half of it," I muttered.

Candice drove straight to our favorite happy hour retreat

and I ordered a prickly pear margarita almost before getting completely settled into the booth. Candice thoughtfully ordered a plate of nachos to soak up some of the alcohol she knew I'd be throwing down, and one prickly pear for herself.

What I love about Candice is that she's very good at reading me. Most people can't—I seem to surprise them with my thoughts, observations, and insights. But Candice just goes with the flow, never really questioning or second-guessing me. She brings great balance to the equation too; I can be pretty emotive (some might even say childish), but Candice never seems put off by my outbursts or reactions. In fact, I would say she often finds them humorous. And that is probably what says the most about why she's such a great friend; she accepts me for me, without judgment, criticism, or back-stabbing. She's a kindred spirit, and she has my back through thick and thin. All women should be so lucky to have a BFF like that. In fact, if you ask me, all women should be as genuine, supportive, and accepting of one another . . . period.

As I sat there pouting into my prickly pear margarita, ranting about Cat, Candice didn't once interrupt my little pity party. She simply picked at the nachos, nodded kindly, and waited out the storm. At last I fell silent and Candice said, "So what are you going to do?"

"Bail," I said with a smirk to hide the truth of how badly I wanted out of Cat's Cirque du Ceremony.

"Why can't you just stand up to her?" Candice offered.

I leveled a look at her. "Why can't *you* stand up to her? You know you hate that bridesmaid's dress she's got you wearing."

Candice stirred her drink with her straw. "Point taken."

I sighed heavily. No one stood up to Cat because Cat simply refused to hear it. Oh, she'd nod, and say, "Yes, yes, I understand," and then you'd be run over by six white stallions and a runaway carriage driven by a mad little person in a pink cupid's outfit.

"So, Sundance, what're you going to do?" Candice repeated, motioning to our server for another round.

I waited for her to look at me, and I said, "I don't know, and I also don't know that I can go through with it, Cassidy."

"What does *that* mean?"

I shook my head and looked away. "Do Dutch and I *really* have to get married to be happy? I mean, we've been so good together for three and a half years as just boyfriend and girlfriend. Why isn't that enough?"

Candice didn't say anything and I finally lifted my gaze back to her. She was staring at me intently. "You made a promise, Abs," she said, reaching out to squeeze my wrist. "Dutch proposed and you accepted, and he's counting on you to keep your end of the deal. If you start talking seriously about bailing on him now, he'll be crushed."

I felt my shoulders sag. "Dammit," I muttered.

Candice let go of my wrist and reached into her pocket. Pulling out a quarter, she pushed it toward me and said, "That one's on me."

We arrived at my place about an hour later. Dutch still wasn't home, but Brice was in the driveway, talking earnestly into his phone. Candice and I sent him a little wave as we headed up the stairs, and he came inside just a short time later. "We brought dinner," Candice said, giving him a sweet peck before handing him an ice-cold beer.

Brice took it gratefully. "Where's Dutch?"

"He's still with Cat," I said, reading the text my fiancé had just sent me. "But he says they're wrapping it up and he'll be home in twenty minutes."

"Should we wait for him?" Brice asked as I handed him a plate filled with pasta from the restaurant.

"Naw. It's almost eight. Go on. Eat. We'll be there in a minute."

Brice took his food and Candice and I continued to plate and serve the pasta for ourselves and put one in the oven for Dutch. He arrived home about fifteen minutes later looking haggard and worn-out.

"How'd it go?" Candice asked him (when I didn't).

Dutch took the beer she offered him and sucked the whole thing down. He then wiped his mouth with the back of his hand and sat down heavily in the chair next to me. "I want a divorce."

I couldn't help it. I laughed. "We're not married yet, cow-boy."

"Fine. When we *are* married, I want to go on record that I get to divorce your sister."

I smirked. "Only if I get to divorce her first."

Candice handed Dutch another beer from the bucket keeping the six-pack cool. "Can I get in on that action?"

"Sure!" Dutch and I sang together.

"I've never met her," Brice said.

"Trust us," I told him. "When we get to the dress rehearsals, you'll want to divorce her too."

We all toasted to divorcing Cat before I asked Dutch, "So where do we stand?"

"I got her to agree to take out the carriage and the horses."

I waited for more, but Dutch only nursed his beer and stared dumbly at the table. "Annnnnd?"

He shook his head. "That's all she'd agree to nix, and it was only after I told her that a team of runaway stallions might wreak havoc on guests and venue alike."

"So the little people cupids?" I asked.

"In."

"Swans?"

"In."

"Swarming butterflies?"

"In."

"Eggy and Tuttle ring bearers?"

Dutch sighed and rubbed his face with his hand. "In. But no miniature carriage. They'll waddle down with the rings on pillows strapped to their backs. And Cat wants you and me to learn the Hustle and exit the podium dancing. I say if we survive to that point that we just make a run for it."

Brice laughed like he thought we were joking, and we all turned to stare at him. He sobered pretty quickly. *"Seriously?"* he asked.

We nodded as one.

Brice gulped. "She sent me an e-mail the other day that she wants to meet with the groomsmen individually next week."

I tipped my beer at him. "Good luck, buddy. You're gonna need it."

We toasted to divorcing Cat again before we got down to more serious business. "Fill us in on your meeting with the ex-cop," Brice said.

"He's telling the truth," I began. "The guy's not anybody that I'd put my trust in, but as far as I can tell, he's not lying. He did receive two calls, but the message the caller left him was pretty cryptic. Still, I think there is some validity to the fact that there's a link between the call and the explosions. What that link is, I couldn't tell you, but my radar says it's there."

"There's no caller ID," Candice added, "but you guys can probably get his permission or a warrant to search Banes's phone records."

"I'll call him tomorrow and get the paperwork started for a warrant and wiretap. If there's another one of these coming, I want to be prepared."

I shuddered, and I didn't express the terrible feeling I had that we'd see another one of these. "You cold?" Dutch asked me, reaching for my hand under the table.

"I'm okay," I assured him, but I knew he knew different.

"You're fine," he said, and I looked at him to see him wink.

I rolled my eyes. "Yes. I'm fine. Pinkie swear."

Dutch got up and went to the couch to bring back an afghan and drape it over my shoulders. "Don't want you getting sick before the big day," he said.

Sick? Why hadn't I thought of that?! My eyes flashed to Candice, and I knew she read my expression. She shook her head subtly, and mouthed, "No!"

I scowled at her as Dutch took his seat again. "Did you get anything more out of Mrs. Padilla?" I asked him.

He picked at the label on his beer bottle. "Nothing other than the name of Michelle's dentist. I got his office to send over Michelle's last dental X-ray and the coroner's going to have the results to us by tomorrow."

"How was Mrs. Padilla when you left her?" I pressed, concerned over the poor woman.

Dutch sighed like he carried the whole world on his shoulders. "Not good," he admitted. "I think it was starting to sink in that her daughter could've been in the salon at the time of the explosion."

Candice's gaze dropped to the table. "Wait till it's confirmed that her daughter was the one wearing the bomb."

We were all quiet for a bit until Brice said, "I'm interested in this lead you came up with at Michelle Padilla's house. You think the sliding glass door was tampered with?"

Dutch nodded. "Looks that way. The catch was jimmied so that the lock could be set without its actually locking the door. If the girls didn't frequently go out on the back patio, they'd never know. We also found no prints on the door handle itself."

Brice's brow furrowed. "None?"

"Nada," Dutch said. "Which means the door had to have been wiped down. There were prints everywhere else from the girls and at least ten unknowns, but the handle was clean, so whoever tampered with the lock also wiped it down."

"So what's your theory, Cooper?" Brice asked me.

I shrugged. "I'm not sure. But if I had to guess, I'd say that Michelle Padilla and Taylor Greene didn't volunteer for bomb duty. And if that's the case, then we've got a serious *mother* of a problem on our hands. Way bigger than just two suicide bombers blowing themselves up. We could have a serial killer who's just warming up with these two. The destruction, fear, and panic he could cause . . ."

My voice trailed off, and in the room you could hear a pin drop.

# T-Minus 00:53:15

The interior of the car was so quiet that M.J. could hear the sound of Gilley's heavy breathing next to her. She eyed him as he clutched the armrest when Dutch took a turn way too fast for it to be safe. Somehow, they managed to keep from rolling, and once around the turn, they were racing forward again. Gil leaned over when the car had straightened out and whispered, "I think I'm gonna be sick!"

M.J. squeezed Gilley's hand. "Don't you dare!"

"Can he let me out?" Gil asked, and M.J. noticed that Gilley was looking a bit like Candice had when she'd first emerged from the back of the ambulance.

"No! Just take deeper breaths and focus on something pleasant."

Gil stared hard at her. "You're kidding, right?"

"It's that house!" Candice suddenly called from the front seat. M.J. looked to where she was pointing and saw a modest-sized redbrick house with black shutters and matching door.

Dutch stomped on the brakes and everyone in the car pitched forward. He was out of the Audi almost before it'd come to a complete stop and running for the front door. He began pounding on it even as M.J. was trying to get herself untangled from the seat belt.

At last she managed to free herself from the car at the same time that two young men appeared in the doorway. Dutch grabbed the boy with black wavy hair and pulled him roughly outside, only to throw him up against the wall of the house and yell, *"Where is she, you son of a bitch?"*

*"Stop!"* M.J. shouted. "Dutch, stop! He didn't take her!"

Dutch continued to hold the young man up against the wall, but at least he wasn't throwing punches at the poor frightened boy. Candice reached Dutch first and pulled on his arm to get him to back off, but he was resisting her. "Dutch, let him go!" she demanded. "Let Brody go!"

M.J. ran over and both she and Candice finally got Dutch to release Brody and take a step back. "What the hell, man?" Brody yelled fiercely once he was free, but M.J. could see the real fear in his eyes.

"Where's Abby?" Dutch demanded. "If you hurt her, Brody, I'll kill you! Do you understand me? I'll *kill* you!"

Brody flattened himself against the brick again, and he looked truly scared. M.J. stepped in between Dutch and Brody and put her hands on the groom's chest. "Dutch, please! You have to let me figure this out, okay? Let me talk to him—"

"There's no time!" he roared, and she could tell he was really close to losing it.

"There is," she told him, only half believing it. "Please, trust me on this, okay?"

Dutch was breathing hard through his nose, and his fists were clenched, but at last he gave one reluctant nod and stepped back. M.J. turned to Brody and said, "You all right?" The young man was literally shaking with fear, and his buddy—who'd appeared in the doorway with him—had gone back inside and slammed the door. M.J. could hear him on the phone calling the police.

*"Brody*, are you all right?" M.J. repeated when he didn't answer her. His gaze was locked on Dutch. Still the boy said nothing, so M.J. plowed ahead. "Brody, listen to me; I'm a spirit medium. I talk to dead people. And a little while ago, right after we discovered that Abby was missing, a woman named Rita pushed her way into my energy and insisted that we come talk to you. Did you know this woman?"

Brody's gaze shifted to her and his eyes narrowed, but he made no further comment.

"She feels very motherly toward you," M.J. went on, feeling Rita's energy surround her, and M.J. also felt the intense and sudden urge to give Brody a fierce hug. She needed Brody to acknowledge the link before getting more information from Rita.

But instead the glint of anger in Brody's eyes intensified. "Is this a joke?"

Candice stepped up to M.J.'s side. "Brody's mother was killed in an explosion two weeks ago. Her name was Rita."

M.J. let out a sigh of relief. Dead people almost always demanded to be recognized before they got to their message, and she felt a sort of release of pressure in her mind once Rita was identified. "I didn't know, I swear," she told Brody when he continued to glare at her suspiciously. But then he appeared to take in their formal attire, and something seemed to click for him.

"Wait . . . isn't today the wedding?" he asked.

"Yes," said Candice. "And Abby's missing. We think she's been abducted. Possibly by the same person responsible for abducting Michelle Padilla. The woman who wore the bomb into your mom's shop."

Brody's face drained of color. "The lady that killed my mom?" he asked meekly.

"Yes," Candice told him, and M.J. noticed for the first time that Candice's hands were shaking. She was scared to death for Abby, but trying very hard to remain calm while they talked to Brody.

At that moment Rita began communicating with M.J. in earnest. "Brody," she said, "I think you may know something that can help us. Your mom says that something happened at her shop that's connected to all this. She's talking about a fight that took place where she worked. I think your mom and another person got into it—"

"My mom never hurt a fly," he said defensively.

M.J. took a deep breath and closed her eyes. Listening to the dead required patience and interpretation, because it wasn't like they spoke to her in full sentences. It was more like trying to hear someone talk to her through a wall—she'd be able to catch about every third or fourth word. But there was another tool at her disposal; the dead could impart feelings, emotions, and imagery to M.J., and she felt Rita do this now. "Brody," she said, "your mom needs you to listen carefully to me. She says she told you about an argument that took place at a . . . a hair salon, I think that's what she's showing me."

"Rita owned a salon," Candice interjected softly.

M.J. nodded. That was a piece of the puzzle she'd been trying to figure out. "Your mom wasn't the first owner of the shop, though, right?"

M.J. opened her eyes to see Brody sort of nod at her. She knew then that she was on the right track. "Before your mom took over the shop, was it called something different? Something with an . . . *M*?"

Brody gasped. "Yeah. My mom bought it from the lady who taught her how to cut hair. Her name was Margo. The salon was originally called Margo's."

"Okay, how long ago did your mom buy the shop?"

Brody shrugged, and in the distance M.J. could hear the sound of sirens approaching. "Almost two years ago."

"Did your mom and Margo keep in touch after she bought the shop?" M.J. asked.

Brody shrugged again. "Yeah, I think so but not, like, every day."

The sirens were getting closer, and M.J. could feel Dutch's impatience and mounting anxiety. Focusing intently on Brody, she said, "Honey, your mom is insisting that there was a fight or an argument or *something* that occurred involving Margo. She thinks there's a link between that and how she died."

But Brody was shaking his head. "My mom got along with everybody," he insisted. "She was really nice, I swear. And everybody liked her. She and Margo were tight, I swear. My mom wasn't in a fight with her."

M.J. could now feel Rita's frustration. The dead woman wasn't wrong—there had been some sort of argument involving Margo—the former owner—and Rita, and M.J. was certain that she'd mentioned this to her son, but either he'd forgotten it or he wasn't letting on because he didn't want them to think badly about Rita. "Brody," M.J. tried again. "This is a matter of life and death. If you don't help us figure this out, Abby could die. Please, *think*!"

But just then two police cars roared up the street, screeched to a halt, and out jumped two officers, guns drawn. "Hands behind your heads!" one shouted. "Now!"

# Chapter Seven

"Now, Edgar," Dutch called impatiently up the stairs to me. "You're gonna make us late."

I groaned. Dutch hated to be late, especially to work, but I was struggling to get it in gear the day after meeting with my sister for Cirque du Ceremony, because he and I had been up late talking over the case with Brice and Candice. During the rest of that discussion, I'd reaffirmed my belief that Michelle hadn't committed suicide. I believed she'd been forced to wear the bomb, and some sick fecker had blown her and three other women up. I also felt strongly that the two girls forced to wear the bombs—Taylor Greene and Michelle Padilla—had some sort of connection to each other, but I couldn't think how. They were different ages, had lived in different places, went to different schools, and had never worked in the same places.

Still, in my gut I knew there was a connection between them; the other thing that I knew in my gut was that whatever that connection was, it was the key to figuring this case out and catching the mastermind behind the bombings. I felt deep in my bones that I had to figure out the connection between the girls, and soon, if I was going to prevent another explosion and more lives lost—and make no mistake, I knew we were dealing with a psycho intent on murdering more people.

"Coming. I'm coming," I called down to Dutch, angling to get my boots on. Just then I heard the doorbell ring. It wasn't even eight thirty, so I hurried to the top of the stairs and saw that our landlord had come over.

"Hey, Bruce," Dutch said in that way that suggested he was annoyed by our landlord's sudden appearance.

I could hardly blame him. I didn't like Bruce either, but my reasons weren't necessarily super specific.

Bruce was a pretty forgettable-looking guy in his early thirties, with mousy brown hair that always seemed to be in need of a cut, and about forty extra pounds on him.

He owned a bunch of rental properties around Austin and carried himself like he thought he was a big deal.

I think my distaste for him was that he had this air of arrogance and entitlement about him that just turned me off. Also, if you pressed me, I'd tell you that there was an element to his energy that I simply didn't trust. It wasn't anything I could put my finger on, but I'd always suspected Bruce was up to no good.

"I wanted to catch you two before you left for work," he said to Dutch, not yet realizing that I was spying on him from the top of the stairs. "I've got someone who wants to move in on the first, so I'll need you guys to move out on the thirtieth. That'll give me a day to clean the place and get it ready for the new tenants."

I frowned. It was just like that oily SOB to want us out a day before our lease was actually up. Dutch and I had planned all along to be out by the day of our wedding, putting our stuff into storage right before the nuptials and coming back from our honeymoon with only a week or two to live in a hotel until our house was ready.

I wanted Dutch to tell Bruce to chill out, that we had the house until the thirty-first, but Dutch was looking at his watch and I knew he was calculating to the minute how fast he'd need to drive to still make it to the office on time. "Fine, Bruce," he was saying.

"Will we get a day of rent back?" I asked, taking a step down toward them.

Both men snapped their heads up in my direction. "Huh?" Bruce asked. Sharp he is not.

"If you want us out on the thirtieth, then we'll need a day of rent back, because, officially, our month-to-month lease isn't up until midnight on the thirty-first." I said all this while making my way carefully down the stairs.

When I got to the landing I saw that Bruce's eyes had narrowed, and I knew he didn't like what I was telling him. His energy rippled with irritation and greed. "Yeah, I guess," he said. "But if you stay over a minute past the thirtieth, I'll charge you for the full month at the same rate that I've given to the new tenants, and it's a lot higher than I charged you. Rents are going up all over town, you know."

I rolled my eyes, and I could see Dutch stiffen a little. Bruce got under both our skins. "We'll be out in time, Bruce," Dutch told him in that tone that suggested the discussion was at an end.

"Good," Bruce said, and just continued to stand there.

I turned to Dutch and said, "You ready, sweetie? We've got to go right now or we'll be late."

Bruce sort of backed up as we made a show of getting our stuff together, but I knew he was trying to get a look at the house. He'd be the kind of landlord to nickel and dime us about the deposit after we moved out too. Thank God I'd had the intuitive sense to take detailed pictures of every room in the house before we'd moved in.

"I'll have to charge you if you leave any stuff behind," Bruce said as Dutch sort of corralled him out the door. "The last tenants left some garbage in the garage and I had to keep their whole deposit."

"I'll bet," I told him. Dutch squeezed my hand as he helped me down the stairs to the drive.

Bruce gave me one of those really forced smiles that actually says, "I think you're a bitch," and I gave one in return that said something that would've cost me a quarter to describe.

Once we were in our car and Bruce was safely off down the street, Dutch said, "If I'd known he was such a douche bag when we were looking at rentals, I would've gone with a different house."

That got me to chuckle. "Well, at least we won't have much longer to deal with him. We'll need to move up the schedule with the movers too."

"I'll handle it," Dutch said, focusing on getting through our sub without getting a ticket for speeding.

A bit later when we arrived at the office (only three minutes late), the mood was somber—tense even. The agents walked around quietly and cast worried glances my way, as if I might blurt out something like, "There'll be another explosion today, guys."

Just as I put my purse in the drawer of the small cubicle that was permanently assigned to me, Brice poked his head out of his office and called me in. On my way past Dutch's glass-enclosed office I saw him looking at Harrison curiously, but Brice made no effort to call Dutch in too.

Once I got inside, Brice shut the door and motioned for me to have a seat. "I was up all night thinking about this case," he said.

He didn't really have to admit it—the dark circles under his eyes and the sag to his shoulders let me know he'd gotten little to no sleep.

"What's happened?" I asked, sensing that something in the ether had shifted since the night before.

"Gaston has been called to Washington. A small terrorist group in Yemen is taking credit for the bombings."

"Bolshevik!"

Brice blinked at me. "Bolshevik?"

I held up an apologetic hand. "My substitute for bull poop."

My boss shook his head. "We gotta get you another hobby, Cooper."

"Sorry, sir."

"Anyway, I agree with you, and so does the director. We don't believe this group is sophisticated enough to have contacts here in the U.S. Still, Homeland is making a power play to take this case away from us and they're using the claim as the grounds to do so."

I sat forward. "How can they justify that?"

"The coroner identified Michelle Padilla through her dental records and also confirmed that she was the bomber. The *shevik* hit the fan when HS discovered we'd searched both her residences without coordinating with them."

"But they did the same thing to us when they searched the Watson residence," I protested.

Brice nodded. "I know, but that's not how it's being played out in Washington. In D.C. there's the suggestion that we're trying to stonewall their efforts to cooperate in the investigation and help identify the terrorist cell responsible."

"Terrorist cell," I scoffed. "This is one guy, abducting two women and forcing them to wear a bomb for his own sick agenda. It has nothing to do with foreign terrorists. And given the targets, I doubt highly this has anything to do with a grudge against the government."

Brice nodded. "We agree. And that's exactly what Gaston's going to argue in Washington. But this is gonna come down to politics, Cooper, and it looks like we'll lose."

"What does that mean, exactly?" I asked.

Brice fiddled with his pen, rolling it over his fingers nimbly, looping it under his palm, then back up to roll it across his hand again. "It means that by five o'clock today we'll have to hand over everything we have on this to HS. We'll be officially taken off any further investigation, and told to go back to resolving cold cases."

I squinted at Harrison, reading his energy; I already saw his game plan. "Does Gaston know you're going to keep me on the case?"

He grinned. "He's the one who told me to do it," he said. "But you're gonna have to be subtle, Cooper. And I do mean subtle. You get a tip, keep it on the down-low and proceed cautiously until you have something solid."

"Okay," I said, and then I noticed that he cast a nervous look at the window overlooking Dutch's glass-enclosed office.

"What?" I asked.

"I'm not sure what to do about Rivers," he said.

Sensing an opportunity, I leaned forward and said, "Reassign him. Put him on desk duty until the wedding."

Brice eyed me skeptically. "I would, Cooper, if I thought he'd follow that order."

I sighed, glancing toward Dutch typing away on his computer. "He is a stubborn son of a beast, isn't he?"

"I think there might be a compromise I can work out with him," Brice said. "He put in a vacation request right before the salon bombing. He asked for next week off. I think when your sister moved the date of the wedding, Rivers got the dates confused and he meant to ask for the week after next off. I'm going to grant the vacation request, although I know Gaston's not gonna like it."

"Wait," I said. "Does that then mean you aren't going to give him the week of our honeymoon off?"

Brice waved his hand dismissively. "No, he'll have that off too. Don't worry. He's got the vacation time available, so it isn't an issue. The point is that once the paperwork goes through, Rivers won't have a choice in the matter. He'll officially be on vacation, and I can order him out of the office if I want to. That means you'll only have a few days left in the week to worry about him, and after that, he's not allowed to butt in on the case. I'll assign the two of you to work together the rest of this week, so that you can keep an eye on each other."

I was confused. "But does that mean you want me off the case next week too?"

"As a freelancer, that's entirely up to you, but I'd prefer if you'd stay on as long as you can."

"I'll stay on, sir, but the tricky part is going to be keeping Dutch from babysitting me while he's on vacation. His family is coming in for the wedding early next week, so hopefully they'll be able to distract him. And he's on wedding detail with my sister, so I think she might have enough to keep him out of our hair next week too."

"Great. For now, just go on as if you don't know anything. I'll give Rivers the heads-up about granting his vacation time at the end of the day on Friday."

Brice fell silent then, and I could tell he had more to say. "There's something else, isn't there?" I asked.

He offered me a half grin and pulled a file out of the stack he had on the corner of his desk. "Homeland is going to be focused mainly on Michelle Padilla and her connection to this terrorist cell in Yemen, because she's the hottest lead they have. While they're working on her and all her associations, I'd like you guys to revisit Taylor Greene. You say there's a connection between the two women, and I believe you. Find it and start with Greene."

I felt myself stiffen. Taylor Greene had walked into a shopping mall in College Station—a city to the northeast of Austin—and she'd blown herself and two other people up. There was footage of the incident captured on a security camera with an amazingly good lens. I'd seen the footage, and I'd tossed my cookies as a result. The last thing in the world I ever wanted to do again was look at that footage, and Brice knew that, but still, he had to ask me, and I knew it wasn't his fault. Reaching forward, I took the file without a word. I then got up and turned toward the door, but eyed him over my shoulder before leaving. "Candice?"

The grin came back. "She's with you guys, but try to keep her out of trouble, Cooper, would you? I've got a crush on that lady."

I smiled back at him and saluted. I then poked my head into Dutch's office and told him that Brice wanted to see him. Then I went to my desk to call Candice.

When she picked up the call, I learned that she was just a few minutes away; she'd stopped to get the office some coffee from our favorite café. I told her to meet us in the conference room and after leaving Dutch a note on his desk about where I was, I headed in with my laptop and the file on Taylor Greene.

Taking out the DVD of the security footage from the pocket of the blue folder, I took a deep breath before inserting it into the drive.

The footage was in black and white, but very clear. The mall was new and it'd no doubt been outfitted with some of the better security cameras available. The footage contained a digital display of the time in the corner—11:55 was when it began, just before noon. The shot looked down on the people in the mall, which was sparsely crowded that day, thank

God. Within the shot was an elderly couple, holding hands as they walked the perimeter of the mall, a mother and her toddler son, and a salesclerk organizing a rack of dresses just inside of a clothing store.

And then from the bottom of the screen a woman appeared wearing what looked like a backpack strapped to the front of her chest. She moved jerkily, her frame bent and arms crossed over her chest. I knew this woman to be Taylor Greene.

The nearest person to her was the mother of the toddler, who took one look at Taylor before grabbing the little tot and swinging him up on her hip. She then took off like a rocket, dropping her parcels as she made a mad dash toward the mall door. But the older couple moved directly toward Taylor, and I bit my lip and felt my eyes glisten. I knew what was coming.

I paused the footage, wiping my eyes and taking a few deep breaths, and then I hit play again. Just as the elderly woman reached Taylor, there was a flash and then . . . well . . . you simply don't want to know.

I closed the lid of the laptop, folded my arms onto the table, and laid my head on top. For a long time I just sat there, hating what I'd seen, hating the sick son of a bitch who'd orchestrated it, hating that there was this sweet, trusting elderly couple just out for a stroll at their local mall who would never see their grandchildren again.

I hated that there'd been a shop clerk who'd also been lost in the explosion, and that a mother and her young son had been rushed to the hospital with severe burns that would scar them for life. And I hated that Taylor Greene had been forced to wear that bomb and walk into that mall, all the while knowing that her life hung by a thread.

Taylor's face had been obscured from the angle of the camera, but I'd seen the elder woman's reaction to the young girl—she'd stepped forward out of concern, the way you would attempt to comfort someone who's very upset.

The mother with the toddler had been a different story. She'd seen Taylor at a different angle, and I had no doubt that she'd gotten a good look at the bomb strapped to Taylor's chest. Or maybe, just maybe Taylor had warned her. There was no audio with the footage, so it was hard to tell. That prompted me to lift my head and jot down a note to myself. I'd want to interview that mother.

Taking a deep breath, I opened the lid of the laptop and replayed the footage again, stopping just before the flash. Had anyone else noticed Taylor and the bomb? I squinted at the store clerk. Just before the bomb went off, she'd looked up, a long dress in her hands, her mouth falling open. She'd seen it too.

The door to the conference room opened and I jerked. "Hey, Sundance," Candice said with a grin. "Little jumpy this morning?"

I swiveled the laptop around so that she could see. "This is the footage of the first explosion at the mall," I told her while she unloaded coffees from a cardboard tray.

"That the same footage that got you so upset a few weeks ago?"

"Yep."

Candice pulled the laptop to her side of the table and sat down to watch it. "Sweet Jesus," she whispered, and I knew she'd gotten to the end.

She put a hand to her mouth and shut the lid of the computer, staring at me with wide eyes.

I held the large coffee cup close, thankful for its warmth. "I know," I told her. "It's bad."

The door opened again and in came Dutch, and he took one look at us and said, "What's happened?"

"We watched the footage from the mall," I told him.

He sighed heavily and came around to sit next to me. "You okay?" he asked, taking up my hand.

I leaned my head onto his shoulder. "For the most part."

"Candice?" he asked next. "You okay?"

She looked at him almost blankly. "I'm a hell of a lot better than that poor old couple."

"It's rough, I know," he told her, then turned back to me. "Did you pick up anything?"

"I want to talk to that mother," I said. "The one with the toddler who made it out alive."

"She was in rough shape," Dutch said, and I knew he'd already had an interview with her.

"What'd she say happened?" I asked.

He reached out for the third coffee on the table and took a careful sip. "She didn't remember much. Cox and I met with her while she was still in the hospital, and mostly she was out of it from the pain meds. She was also too worried about her son to really focus on our questions."

"I think we should go back and talk to her," I said. Then I asked, "Did anyone else in the store survive?"

Dutch nodded. "The owner, Carly Threadgill, was the woman you saw in the footage. She died in the blast, but one of her employees in the back survived and made it out of the store."

I reached for the laptop again and pulled it close. I rewound the footage to the clerk right before the blast, my radar buzzing. Something was familiar, but I couldn't figure out what.

"What is it?" Candice asked me.

"I'm not sure," I said. "But there's something about that store. There's a clue there."

"We can go to the mall if you want," Dutch offered.

I nodded. "Yeah. That's a good idea. Maybe there's something in the ether that'll point me to this nagging feeling that there's something that connects Taylor and Michelle."

"Rodriguez is trying to find that connection right now," Dutch said. "He's going through all the girls' contacts again, trying to see if they know any of the same people. Taylor Greene was originally from Austin, and the girls were a few years apart in age, so it's possible."

I rubbed my eyes and looked again at the frozen image of the store; what the heck was it that kept *bing*ing my energy?

"But you guys never found a connection between any subversive group and Taylor, right?" Candice asked.

"Not a one," Dutch said. "By all accounts, Taylor was a wallflower. She was a B/C student at Texas A&M, and if she had any close friends, we couldn't find them."

That surprised me. "No friends?"

He shook his head. "She lived with another girl—her

name's in the file—and I don't think they got along. When we asked about Greene's personal contacts, the roommate told us she didn't have any. We interviewed several classmates and they pretty much confirmed what the roommate said—Taylor kept to herself."

"What about any social media accounts?" Candice asked.

Dutch scratched his cheek. "We couldn't find any accounts registered to her. Her computer came up missing when we searched her apartment, so it's possible that she had an account registered in a different name, but there's no real way to track it without her hard drive."

"Her computer came up missing?" I asked.

"She took it with her to class," Dutch said. "She could have dumped it, lost it, or it could've been stolen. Hell, her roommate could've hocked it for Taylor's portion of the rent money once she realized her roommate was dead. All we know for sure is that it's not among her possessions."

"This roommate sounds like a stone-cold bitch," Candice remarked.

Dutch shrugged. "She didn't like Taylor—that much was clear. But I'm not sure it was entirely one-sided. Everyone we interviewed who knew Taylor said she wasn't very outgoing. Most people we talked to thought she was aloof and stuck-up."

"When was the last time Taylor was seen before entering the mall?" I asked, curious about the timeline the day of the bombing.

Dutch pointed to the file. "Her roommate remembers seeing Taylor the night before when she came back from an evening class, but she doesn't know if Taylor was out of the apartment when the roommate left for class the following morning. She says she only remembers that Taylor's bedroom door was shut—but I guess it was usually shut, so we have no timeline for the abduction other than the first time any security camera captures her is at the mall right before noon."

"And it's where she was in between that we really need to know," Candice said.

"What about her car?" I asked.

"Found in the mall's parking lot. We dusted for prints, and the odd thing was that it came back completely clean. Not a print on it either inside or out."

"Any cameras in the parking lot that would give you a view of the car?" Candice asked.

"It was parked in the very back of the lot out of range of the exterior cameras, which are all set over the entrances of the mall. We canvassed the area, but no one remembers seeing Taylor wandering through the parking lot with a bomb strapped to her chest. She could have easily driven herself to the mall, parked at the back, rubbed down the car, and avoided pedestrians as she made her way to the mall's entrance. Traffic there was pretty light that day, so it's possible that she could have gotten away with it undetected."

I turned my attention away from the file I was thumbing through and focused on Candice and Dutch. "Can I ask you two a favor?"

They looked at me curiously and nodded.

"From here on out can we operate under the assumption that both Taylor and Michelle were as innocent as the other victims in the explosions? I'm telling you that no one coerced or brainwashed these two girls into strapping on a bomb and targeting a public place in an act of terrorism. My radar says they were abducted and forced to wear the explosives."

"We're dealing with an unsub here," Candice said, using bureau jargon for "unidentified subject."

"Yes," I told her. "And I think that we're only dealing with one person here. A male unsub with psychopathic tendencies who's got some sort of sick agenda he's working through. There's a reason the girls were sent where they were. I don't believe the locations were chosen at random, and I believe they have meaning to this guy. It's a puzzle that we have to figure out."

"But how could he force these girls to go anywhere with a bomb strapped to their chests?" Candice asked. "If it were me, I'd lunge for the unsub and not let go until he defused the bomb."

I felt my mouth quirk, because only Candice would think

of something so smart in a situation like that. Dutch was the one who answered her, though. "The explosives expert who analyzed the parts that remained of Taylor Greene's bomb suspects that the bomb went off five minutes early. He says that, given the clock on the footage from the mall, and what he was able to tell from the only piece of the digital display on the bomb that was intact, that the bomb was supposed to detonate at noon, not eleven fifty-five. He theorized that the bomb could have been wired to receive a signal from a remote control detonator."

My jaw dropped. "The unsub set off the bomb early?"

Dutch nodded. "He could have abducted and restrained Taylor, strapped the bomb to her chest, and told her to head to the mall. He might've promised her that once she got there, he'd defuse the bomb remotely, but if she tried anything tricky, like if she asked anyone for help or went to the police, he'd set off the bomb."

I bit my lip. "So, when that elderly couple reached out to Taylor, he saw that as her trying to get help?"

Dutch shrugged. "Maybe. Or maybe he's just a sick son of a bitch and he set it off just because he could."

Candice tapped the table with her fingers. "If there really was a detonator, then it also suggests that he was watching her."

Dutch nodded. "We've looked and relooked at every piece of footage both inside and outside that mall. No one jumps out at us as anyone who was watching Taylor except the mother with the toddler and the elderly couple.

"The thing we're still trying to understand," Dutch continued, "is why the girls were instructed to go to the mall and the beauty shop in the first place. I mean, I can see the mall—this unsub might've wanted to kill as many people as possible—but a beauty shop? I can think of a lot of other places that would give him more bang for his buck."

Candice and I both stared aghast at him. "Bang for his buck?" Candice repeated. "Seriously, Dutch?"

He held up a hand in apology. "No pun intended, ladies, I swear."

"Horrible pun aside," I said, "I think the oddity of choosing to detonate a bomb at a beauty shop cinches the fact that he has an agenda. Dutch is right; there're a dozen other places I can think of—like a crowded office building, or the university, or the capitol building—where this guy would probably have killed a whole lot more people and made an even bigger statement. No, there's something personal here, some message this guy is trying to send."

"So we need to figure out what the message is before this unsub moves on to another girl and another location."

I stood up. "Exactly. And we start with that mother who was injured in the bombing. Then I want to interview Taylor's parents. I just can't let go of the idea that this guy knew both girls, and maybe by probing a little we'll find the connection."

We filed out of the conference room, nodding to Brice in his glass office on our way out, but I stopped at Rodriguez's desk. "Cooper," he said cordially. "What can I do for you?"

Agent Oscar Rodriguez was a favorite of mine. He'd been hard to win over when we'd first met, but since I'd proved myself to him, he'd been my most loyal work buddy, next to Dutch and Brice of course. "Oscar, have you had a chance to look up the phone records on our friend Jed Banes?"

He swiveled slightly to the left side of his desk and retrieved a short printout of numbers. "I did. Banes cooperated and we got these on a rush. Turns out the number that came into his machine was exactly two hours before the beauty shop explosion. There was another number that came in on the day of the mall bombing, but that was an hour and fifty-five minutes before. Not exactly two hours."

I had several questions in light of that information. "So the calls came in from two separate locations?"

Rodriguez shrugged. "Hard to say. The numbers are linked to disposable cell phones—they can't be traced. We're trying to triangulate the towers where the signal might have bounced off of, but that could take a while."

"How long's 'a while'?"

"A week . . . maybe longer. It's not like in the movies where you can just pull up a number and trace it to a location that has cameras on every corner."

I nodded and asked my next question. "So, we know that the first bomb was likely remotely detonated five minutes early, but what we don't know is, why?"

"Does it really matter?" Rodriguez asked me in return.

I thought about that. "I don't know," I admitted. "But what I do know is that this unsub has to have been watching Taylor for him to actively detonate the bomb. He's got to be somewhere on the footage, Oscar."

He shook his head and sighed. "I've been all over it, Cooper. There's just no one driving around the parking lot or walking near Taylor that's keeping an eye on her."

But my radar wasn't letting go of it. "Could it have been one of the mall employees?" I asked. I knew I was reaching here, but I was convinced the unsub had been nearby when the bomb went off.

Oscar swept a hand through his thick black hair. "We ran all the employees through our databases and there's nothing worse than petty theft and a DUI on the record of any mall employee."

"Yeah, but were any of them *looking* toward Taylor when she entered the mall?"

"Not that I could see," he said. I wondered if Oscar was so tired that he maybe hadn't looked especially close at the footage of the surrounding shops from the mall cameras.

"Will you look one more time?" I asked him. He frowned at me, so I added a smile.

"Fine," he groaned. "I'll look one more time. But you owe me a coffee or a doughnut or something, Cooper."

"You got it, Oscar. We're headed out to the mall at College Station right now to look around, and we probably won't be back till late, so can I bring you breakfast tomorrow?"

"Sure," he said with a lopsided grin. "I'll text you my order in the morning."

I squeezed him around the shoulders and hurried to catch up with Dutch and Candice.

Two hours and twenty minutes later we were wandering around the charred-out ruins of the mall—which was mostly still closed—when I paused at the spot that had been ground zero.

I can't fully describe how terrible the ether was in that roughly five-foot square space, but suffice it to say that I felt like hurling the entire time I stood at its center. There was this wrenching sense of terror, mixed with what I can only describe as a horrible, sudden, and violent expansion of energy—the actual explosion.

I'd felt something similar many years earlier when I'd done a stint for the *Detroit Free Press* one Halloween where they'd asked me to walk around to a few local haunts with a reporter and tell her what I was feeling. We'd entered a library, which supposedly had a librarian that just didn't know when to quit (she is still shelving books there forty years after her death), and while I hadn't picked up on her, there were some artifacts on display from a World War II retrospective. I'd stood next to a glass case that housed a set of personal items from a young soldier who'd been killed when his own grenade had malfunctioned and blown up in his hand. I remembered the weird feeling of being engulfed by a ball of fire and feeling nothing but confusion and shock.

This was similar to what Taylor Greene had experienced in the moment the bomb had detonated. It'd been too quick for her brain to even register, but those moments leading up to the bomb going off . . . those had been the worst kind of panic and dread imaginable. I felt firmly that she knew she was about to die. I also felt firmly that she'd had nothing to do with detonating the bomb. It'd gone off remotely, just like I suspected.

"Hey, Abs," Candice called.

I looked up and saw that she was just inside the store where Taylor had been heading on that fateful day.

"Yeah?"

"Take a look at this."

With my cane I carefully navigated my way over to her and as my foot stepped on a slippery bit of ash and paper, I was surprised that I didn't fall.

"Careful," Dutch said, reaching out to steady me.

"I'm okay," I told him. The truth was that I wasn't nearly as unsteady on my feet as I had been even a week ago. I couldn't readily explain it, but I suspected an incident I'd had at the end of the last case I'd worked had inadvertently helped the nerves that controlled the muscles in my legs regroup and function better.

When I stood next to Candice, she pointed and I followed her finger. The fire had caused a great deal of damage to the shop where the store owner had been killed, but some of the things in the back were still recognizable. And then I felt a sort of "ping!" go off in my mind and I realized why something about this place had felt so familiar.

"It's a bridal store," I said, as a trickle of unease crept up my spine.

"Yeah," Candice said. "Weird, huh?"

I had the urge to turn around and look at Dutch. He was using his foot to shuffle aside some of the debris on the floor. I felt that trickle of unease strengthen. That fear I had for his safety bloomed big and large in my mind.

I shifted my gaze to Candice. There was danger around her too—but it was more subtle, as if it was farther away . . . as if she could avoid it.

And then I wondered quite seriously about my own safety. If there was so much foreboding energy swirling around Dutch and Candice, might it also be swirling around me?

There was no clear way to tell—one of the great drawbacks about being psychic is that it's a skill that can only be projected outward. In other words, I'm able to clearly see other people's futures, but looking at my own can be a bit nebulous. It's like living in a world without reflection; I can easily describe what someone else looks like, but what my own countenance holds is a mystery without a mirror.

Turning back to the mall, I scanned the area, suddenly unnerved and wary. At the end of the long hallway was a huge plastic curtain. No one but police and the Feds were allowed through to where we stood, and beyond the sheeting, I didn't know whether someone was currently watching us, but I was pretty creeped out and shuddered again.

"You okay, Sundance?" Candice asked.

I jerked at the sound of her voice. "Yeah. I'm fine. Let's get out of here, though, okay?"

Candice stared at me with a puzzled expression. She knew

I wasn't "fine," but she didn't press it. Instead she helped me cover my rattled nerves for Dutch.

"Hey," she called to him. "Abby's ready for lunch. What say we get something to eat and then go interview our first witness?"

Dutch nodded without even looking my way, and I sent Candice a grateful smile. "Thanks," I whispered.

"Of course," she said easily. Then, as if reading my mind she added, "This place gives me the creeps too."

I didn't eat much at lunch, even though Dutch had opted to take us to a burger joint. I'm not a huge fan of the hamburger, but any place that serves them almost always has some other form of junk food that I find quite appetizing. Still, I was too worried about the feeling I'd gotten in the mall to do more than pick at the meal.

Candice covered for me again by keeping the conversation light and focused on a neutral topic. "So when's the new house ready for move in?"

Dutch raised his brow and turned his head pointedly to me. "That's Abby's detail."

"Aw, crap!" I said. I was supposed to call Dave, our handyman/construction manager/adoptive uncle the day before. Pulling out my phone, I dialed quickly and he picked up on the third ring.

"Yo!" he said by way of greeting.

"It's me. I'm sorry I forgot to call you yesterday."

"No worries, Abster. Your house is almost ready."

I cocked a skeptical eyebrow. Dave's "almost" could mean "Tomorrow," or "In a week," or even "Maybe in a month or two."

"Can you give me a date?" I asked, already shaking my head and making a face for Dutch and Candice. Dave would never commit to something so specific. "We have to be out of our house by the thirtieth, so I need to know how long Dutch and I will be homeless after we come back from our honeymoon."

"How's next Tuesday work for you?"

I nearly dropped the phone. "Wait . . . what?"

Dave chuckled. "Tuesday. We should be able to do the final walk-through on Monday, and you guys can close on the house Tuesday morning if that works for you."

I looked at my watch—not that I had a calendar there or anything, but I was so surprised that it was more a reflex. "For reals, Dave?"

"What's he say?" Dutch asked.

"For reals," Dave told me. "The guys have been putting in extra time since they all got invited to your wedding. That's their gift, by the way. To give you two a completed house two weeks early."

Mentally, I threw around some expletives like a drunken sailor. I'd forgotten about the wedding invites. "Awesome," I squeaked.

"Oh, which reminds me—I need your landscaper and that bug guy to come back," Dave added.

I'd hired a great landscape architect to take care of the front garden beds and trees, which I thought had looked a little sparse for the gorgeous home. The man I'd hired, Tom Hester, had been a sheer genius and he'd transformed the yard into something truly lush and magazine-cover worthy. "You need Tom to come back?" I asked, already sensing that something had happened. "What'd you do?"

"It wasn't me!" Dave said quickly. "One of the guys smunched a few of your flowers with the Bobcat. He's really sorry, and we'll pay for them to be replaced."

I put my hand over my eyes. There had been several large turquoise clay pots artfully placed in every bed. If the flowers had been smunched, that meant that at least one of the pots was damaged too.

"Where?"

"The bed on the left side of the house. And some of the middle bed too. Also, maybe some of those clay pots you had out there got broken."

"Dave!"

"Abs, he's really sorry! It was his first time driving the Bobcat and it kinda got away from him."

"Dude!" I yelled. "What the hell?"

Dave was silent for a minute. "You can tell Dutch that I'll pay the quarter for that one. We deserved it."

I pinched the bridge of my nose and took a deep breath. "You better not tell me who did it," I warned him. "If I know, I'm gonna disinvite him to the wedding."

"He feels so bad he won't show," Dave assured. "Probably."

I blew out a sigh. "Okay, and you said you needed the bug guy too? Are the scorpions back?" Inwardly I shuddered and thought that if those creepy-crawlies had come back, I was *not* moving into that house.

"No scorpions," Dave said. "But all that rain we got last week brought out a whole bunch of crickets, and a few got into your house. Unless you want to listen to chirping all night, I think you should have the bug man come back out and give it a good spray."

"Fine," I told him, lifting my eyes to Dutch, who was still staring at me with raised, expectant brows. "But you're sure we can close next Tuesday? That's only five days away, you know, and if I call the title company to set up the closing, it's a huge pain in the ass . . . ter . . . isk to get it rescheduled."

"Tuesday?" Dutch mouthed.

I nodded as Dave said, "Go ahead and schedule it. We'll be ready."

I hung up with Dave and promptly called the title company. They were happy to fit us in for Tuesday morning. I then called my landscaper, who was not happy to hear that his hard work had been ruined, but he looked at his book and said he could swing by the next day to assess the damage and offer me a quote to fix it.

In parting he let me know how pleased he was to have been invited to my wedding. I had to force myself to speak in pleasant tones and tell him that we were looking forward to seeing him there.

When I hung up, I glared at Dutch—like it was his fault.

"Is there anyone she didn't invite?" he asked me, ignoring my stony countenance.

"We're about to find out," I muttered as I dialed Russ, the bug guy.

"Hey, Miss Cooper!" he said jovially.

"Hey, Russ," I said. "Listen, I just heard from my builder. Seems like the house has a few loose crickets inside. Can you take care of that?"

"Does tonight at six work? I'm on that side of town this afternoon."

I looked at my watch. "Well, I'm up in College Station working a case right now, so that might be a little tight, but if I can't make it, then I'll have Dave, my construction manager, meet you."

"Cool," he said. And then he hesitated and I knew that he was probably dancing around the wedding invite. After clearing his throat a couple of times, he said, "Thanks a lot for inviting me to your wedding, Miss Cooper."

He sounded so sweetly grateful that I immediately felt bad for not wanting him to attend. "Are you coming, Russ?"

"I think so, yeah," he said. "But is it okay if it's only me?"

I sensed that Russ—a rather husky, baby-faced man who killed bugs for a living and preferred Jim Butcher novels to social interaction—might have trouble finding a date on short notice. "Of course it's okay. Come. You'll have a great time, and I'm pretty sure there'll be other single people there too, so not to worry."

I could sense that he was both a little embarrassed and maybe happy that I'd told him there would be other people there without a plus one. "Cool," he said. "Thanks so much, and I'll see you tonight."

After I hung up with Russ, I felt a little better. Dealing with the everyday headaches of my personal life helped to ground me, and remind me that although I was working a horrendously awful case, my life went on. Belatedly I noticed that Dutch and Candice had already finished eating, and my Reuben sandwich with a side of sweet potato fries was mostly untouched.

I took a few quick bites, knowing we were pressed for time, and motioned for us to get going. "You sure you don't want a to-go box?" Candice asked. (Somewhat mockingly, I thought. Her lunch had been heavy on produce—light on saturated fats.)

"I'm sure," I told her, eyeing my watch and noting the time again. It was nearly one o'clock. "We've got people to interview and only a few hours to do it in before I have to get back."

With that, Dutch paid the bill and we were on our way.

# T-Minus 00:46:45

*"Down on the ground! Hands behind your heads!"* shouted the cop holding the gun on everyone gathered outside the redbrick house where Brody Watson was staying.

M.J. dropped immediately to her knees, shoving her hands high in the air. "Don't shoot!" she heard Gilley cry. "I'm innocent! *I'm innocent!*"

"I don't care if you're Mother Teresa! Get down on the motherfu—"

"I'm down!" Gilley shrieked, falling face-first to the ground. "I'm down!"

M.J. lowered herself the rest of the way to the pavement, lacing her fingers behind her head. She then turned her head to the side and saw that Dutch was still standing, but at least he had his hands raised above his head.

*"I said get down!"* the cop screamed, pointing his gun directly at Dutch.

"I'm a federal officer!" Dutch yelled back, refusing to drop.

"Like I said, I don't care if you're Mother Teresa! Get down on the ground! *Now!*"

M.J. kept her gaze on Dutch and she trembled. They were wasting precious time here and his resisting the officer's command was only wasting more time. At last, however,

Dutch got down on both knees, but he refused to prostrate himself like the rest of them. That seemed to really frustrate both officers. Ignoring everyone else, they marched over to Dutch and shoved him violently. He dropped easily the rest of the way to the ground, but in a move almost too quick to catch he rolled over, kicked the gun out of the hand of the first officer, grabbed the pistol of the other, and twisted the hand holding it in such a way that he managed to pull it free.

It all happened so fast that M.J. could hardly believe it. In another lightning-fast move, Dutch was on his feet and pointing the weapon at both the officers. "Down on your knees!" he commanded. The stunned cops immediately complied, throwing their own hands up in the air and kneeling down on the ground. Dutch then moved in to the side of one officer and pulled up on a set of handcuffs from his belt. He tossed these next to Candice. "Cuff him!" he ordered.

"Shit," Candice muttered as she climbed to her feet, picked up the gun that'd been kicked to the side along with the handcuffs. "Can we talk about this?" she asked Dutch, who looked so angry that M.J. didn't want to make a false move.

"Later," he growled. "Cuff him, Candice, or I'll do it myself." Reluctantly Candice secured the first cop's hands while Dutch grabbed a set of zip ties off the belt of the other cop and tossed one of these to Candice. "And now the other one."

"Dutch—," she began.

*"Do it!"*

Candice moved behind the second cop and secured his hands too. The minute the two officers were restrained, Dutch undid each of their utility belts and tossed them over his shoulder. Then he grabbed Brody by the collar and motioned with his gun for M.J., Candice, and Gilley to follow him.

M.J. exchanged a look with Candice and whispered, "Did this just go from really bad to WTF?"

"Just do as he says," Candice whispered back. "We'll get it sorted out later."

Dutch shoved Brody into the front seat, and Candice got

in next to the poor kid. M.J. pulled Gilley up off the ground and said, "Get in the car, Gil."

"I'd rather stay here," he said meekly.

M.J. looked over at the cops, who were each wearing murderous looks on their faces. "No, you wouldn't," she told him. "And we don't have time to argue about it. Get in the car right now."

With that, they slipped into the backseat and Dutch started the engine, roaring away from the curb with squealing tires.

All M.J. could think about as the smell of burning rubber filled the air was the many laws they'd just broken—from assaulting an officer to kidnapping. . . . They were in some serious trouble now. And their only way out lay in finding Abby.

M.J. didn't want to go to jail—she'd been there once before and she frankly hadn't cared for it. So she leaned forward and said, "Brody, I know you're scared, but you and I need to work together. I've still got your mother with me, and she keeps insisting that there was some sort of argument involving this Margo woman. Please, if you want Dutch to let you go . . . if you want to see Abby alive again . . . please, think."

Brody, who'd been sitting stiffly in his seat, eyed her in the rearview mirror and she could see his fear, his anger, but then . . . something else. Some tiny spark had lit up in his eyes and he said, "You know what? There was something. . . ."

# Chapter Eight

Our knock was answered by a woman with no spark left in her dull, sad eyes. The mother with the toddler in the video from the mall was named Janice McCaffrey, and she lived in a large stone and brick home in a newer subdivision not far from the Texas A&M campus. She answered the door dressed in flannel pj's and a big terry cloth robe. I would be lying if I didn't say that the poor woman looked like hell. "Yes?" she croaked. She'd obviously been crying, and there were bandages on both her arms. A streak of toothpaste at the corner of her mouth told me she hadn't even bothered to look in the mirror while brushing her teeth. I wondered if she'd actually just rolled out of bed, or hadn't moved much since doing so earlier in the day.

Dutch introduced us, holding up his badge for her to study. Her eyes moved slowly from him, to the badge, to the bulletproof vest he wore, to Candice, back to the vest, over to me, and back to his badge again. I had a feeling she hadn't really registered any of it. "Did you find out why?" she asked him once he'd finished speaking. "Why that girl tried to blow us up?"

That caught Dutch off guard. He opened his mouth, but sort of turned to me, like, "What the hell should I say to

that?" (Swearing doesn't count when you're simply inter-
preting your fiancé's expression.)

"Mrs. McCaffrey," I said, stepping forward. "Can we come
in for a few minutes?"

She ran her tongue over her lips nervously and tugged at
the collar of her bathrobe. "I wasn't expecting visitors," she
said.

I suspected that the inside of her house was probably
much like her—unkempt and in need of a good scrub.

"We won't stay long," I assured her. When she still hesitated, I added, "Please? It's really important."

She gave a curt nod and opened the door just enough for
us to enter. The minute we were through the entry, I could see
that my suspicions were correct; the place looked like a small
tornado had been through it.

There were clothes, dirty dishes, toys, and even some garbage littering the place. A small scruffy dog came ambling
out of the kitchen area to sniff moodily at our feet. I waited
until he stopped inspecting my shoes to move over to a cane
chair in the corner of the living room.

Dutch and Candice looked around for a place to sit, but
there was very little available unless they wanted to brush
aside the dirty clothes or garbage. After a quick exchange of
looks, they each took up an at-ease stance on either side of me.

Meanwhile, Janice shuffled over to the one spot on the
couch that was clear of clutter and plopped down with a
heavy sigh. "You're here about the mall, right?"

"Yes," I said, motioning to Dutch and Candice that I
wanted to take the lead with Janice. "I know it's painful, but
can you tell me exactly what you remember about that day?"

Janice squeezed her eyes shut and clenched her fists. Her
energy also reacted to the memory of that day, shrinking
against her physical body, as if it was acting protectively. I
knew then that this poor woman was suffering terribly.

With her eyes still closed, Janice said, "I was taking Jack
to the mall to buy some new sneakers. He's been growing so
fast and his shoes were getting too tight. It was a really pretty
day, and I thought we'd get him some sneakers, then have

lunch in the food court. Jack loves that food court. . . ." Her voice trailed off for a moment before she finally opened her eyes and continued. "We were heading there from the shoe store when I saw this girl push her way through the doors into the mall. It was weird, I mean, I don't know what made me look in her direction, but I saw the doors open, and I saw her come into the mall, and the way she moved . . . it was just . . . off, you know?"

I nodded, because I'd noticed the same thing from the security footage.

"So, I had my eyes on her," Janice continued. "And all of a sudden I felt the hairs on the back of my neck stand up on end, and I had goose pimples on my arms. It was really weird. I knew in my gut that something was really wrong." At this point Janice looked directly at me. "You ever have one of those feelings?"

"All the time."

She nodded. "Maybe it was a mother's instinct, or woman's intuition, but I knew there was something really dangerous about that girl. And I had Jack by the hand, and he was sort of pulling on me, but I was still focused on that girl, and then she said something. . . ." Again her voice trailed off.

"What?" I prompted. "What'd she say, Janice?"

The young mother shook her head. "I wish I could remember. Isn't that funny? I can remember everything else about that moment—how that girl looked, so frightened and pale, and I can remember the song playing on the mall's sound system, and I can remember the smells of the food court not far away and the color of the tile floor under my feet—but the exact words that girl said to me, I just can't remember."

She was staring at me with the most haunted eyes, and they began to fill with tears, which slid down her cheeks. "Isn't it terrible?" Janice asked me. "This girl knows she's about to speak her last words to someone, and she chooses me, and I can't even remember what she said."

"You were terrified," I told her, struggling against the urge to get up and comfort her. If I did that, I knew we'd have to stop the interview, and I needed to help her get through the rest of it. "It's completely understandable, Janice. No one could possibly fault you in that moment for not remembering. You had your son to protect."

Janice wiped her eyes and nodded grudgingly. "Yeah. Some protective mother I am. Jack's going to have scars for the rest of his life."

"And he'll have a life because of you," I told her.

She shrugged, unable to let herself off the hook. "If only we hadn't gone to the mall that day," she said. "I had this feeling that morning that I should order his shoes online, but I really needed a break from hanging out here at the house. I lost my job last month, so I've been home alone with Jack and the walls felt like they were closing in."

"Where's your son now?" I asked, realizing I hadn't heard any noise that might sound like a toddler in the house.

"He's with my mother-in-law," she said, her mouth turning down slightly. "My husband said it was for the best. He and Jack moved back to his mom's house last week. He said it'll give me time to sort this all out."

I bit my lip. I saw my symbol for divorce hovering in the ether. I looked around the house again. In my mind's eye I could see it filled with moving boxes. And poor Janice was a long way away from being able to support herself again. She'd been horribly traumatized, and I doubted she'd be able to get through an interview much less show up for work and be productive.

I really wanted to help her, but I had to focus on that day at the mall first. "Janice, what happened right after the girl in the mall spoke to you?"

She blinked at me with blank eyes for a moment before she said, "Oh, well . . . I guess I ran out of there."

Dutch caught my eye. He wanted me to push her a little.

"You ran out of the mall," I repeated. Janice nodded. "So she said something to you that made you run out of the mall?"

Janice's brow furrowed. "Maybe . . . or I saw the bomb."

"You saw the bomb?"

Janice didn't answer. She was staring at the floor.

"Could you describe it?" I asked.

Again, Janice didn't answer. She seemed lost in thought.

I waited a bit and then tried again. "Janice, you said you saw the bomb. What did it look like?"

She shook her head and snapped her eyes up to me. "I remember!" she exclaimed. "The girl, she said, 'It's not me!'"

I cocked my head. "It's not me?"

"Yes! *That's* what she said! And then she moved her arms to the side and I saw that bomb and I grabbed Jack's hand, lifted him onto my hip, and ran like hell. 'It's not me.' God, I've been trying to remember that for weeks."

Janice appeared so relieved, but then her expression clouded over again. "I wonder what the hell she meant by that," she said.

"Maybe that the bomb wasn't her doing," I said.

Janice's expression turned stricken. "Oh, my God," she whispered. "You think?"

Dutch caught my eye again. *Be careful,* he mouthed.

"We can't be sure," I told her. "But that is a curious thing to say before the bomb you're wearing goes off."

Janice went back to staring at the floor again.

"Janice," I said, hoping I hadn't lost her attention for good this time. "Do you know where the girl might have been heading?"

"The mall," she said listlessly.

"Yes," I agreed, "but I remember seeing the footage from the mall security camera, and it didn't look like she was headed to the center of the mall, which is where I would've gone if my intention was to kill a great many people. She appeared to be heading toward one of the stores, and I was wondering since you were there that day and saw her enter the mall if maybe you got the same feeling?"

Janice's gaze snapped to me again. "You know," she said, "that's really been bugging me. I had that exact same feeling too, but I just didn't know what it meant or who to tell."

"What store do you think she was aiming for?"

"That bridal store," Janice told me. "Carly's Bridal Boutique. I got my bridesmaids' dresses there when I got married."

"Do you know why the girl with the bomb would have aimed for that store?"

Janice grunted derisively. "Maybe because Carly was a real bitch?"

Dutch shifted his stance slightly. I could tell he didn't think this line of questioning was important, but my radar had pinged on Janice's last statement. "Can you elaborate on that?" I asked her.

Janice sat back against the cushions. I could tell this was exhausting for her. "Carly owned that boutique since I was in high school. Her daughter and I even graduated together and we were pretty good friends too. But when I was planning my wedding, one of my bridesmaids and I had a falling-out, and I asked Carly if I could return the dress, which hadn't even been altered yet, and she said no, and she insisted that all sales were final. I would've gotten someone else to wear it and gone with my original plan to have five bridesmaids, but the friend I had a falling-out with was a size two—no way could any of my other friends fit that size. And I heard she was like that with a lot of other customers too." I wondered if Janice knew that Carly had been killed in the blast. I held back mentioning it because Janice was in such a fragile state that I didn't want to risk further upsetting her.

About then I saw Candice subtly point to her watch, and I knew we were going to run short on time if we stayed much longer with Janice. We had other people to talk to before we got back on the road, and I stood up, knowing I'd gotten something from the conversation, but I didn't quite know what. I then dug through my purse and pulled out two cards. The first was my business card, and I offered it to her and said, "I'd really like to give you a free reading, Janice. I think you've got a few challenges coming up on top of all that you're dealing with right now, and I'd like to offer you some insight about how to handle it."

She eyed my card with a mixture of surprise and wariness. I hadn't told her I was a psychic.

"Think about it," I told her gently before pointing to the other card. "That's the name of a really great therapist I know. I've sent him a ton of clients and he's awesome, patient, and an incredibly understanding guy. If you can't physically go to him, he'll be happy to conduct your sessions over Skype. And he can even talk you through how to set that up if need be."

She studied that card with a bit more enthusiasm and far less wariness. "Thanks," she said. "I've been thinking about trying to find someone. I know I look bad." Janice then gazed around at the piles of mess in her living room. "And all this looks bad," she added.

"Then call him first. And when you're ready, think about calling me."

With that, we left her.

We arrived at Taylor Greene's apartment about twenty minutes later. Taylor and her roommate shared a bland-looking apartment just off campus.

We had no idea if Taylor's roommate would be home, but luck was with us and a mousy-looking brunette greeted our knock with a cautious, "Yeah?"

Dutch flashed his badge and introduced the three of us, then reminded her that he'd spoken with her on the day after the mall bombing. "Oh, yeah," she said, reaching up to twirl her hair nervously. "I remember."

I saw Dutch's gaze flicker to his notes. "Can we come in and talk, Amber?"

Her eyes narrowed and as nervous as she was at the sight of Dutch showing up at her door flashing his badge and wearing his Kevlar, I knew she was a little ticked off about something. She hesitated in the partially opened doorway for a moment before she said, "The last time I let you guys in, you tore this place apart. I'm still waiting for you people to reimburse me for the couch."

"Did you submit form E-four-seven-six?" he asked.

I turned my head to glare at him. There was no form E476. This was just what the bureau boys told people who got uppity while their homes were being torn apart during the execution of a search warrant. Dutch ignored me, and Amber said, "I couldn't find that stupid form! I looked all over your Web site and it never came up. If you ask me, there is no stupid form, and you guys are making it up."

"I'll mail you one," Dutch assured her.

She looked at him doubtfully. Amber wasn't stupid.

I peeked through the door and could see a portion of said couch. It had a large blanket over it, but underneath I could tell there were lumps from the stuffing coming through the tears that I knew the bureau boys had put there.

Reaching nimbly into Dutch's back pocket, I lifted out his wallet before he could stop me. Opening it quickly, I withdrew about three hundred in twenties and held them up for our witness to see. "Let us come in and we'll reimburse you off the books, Amber. We really need to talk to you."

Amber opened the door wider but stood in the way, holding out her hand for the cash. I placed it in her palm and she stepped to the side. We filed in and I looked around.

The place was fairly Spartan, but neat. Well, as neat as it could be after being ransacked by the Feds. The lumpy couch was set against the shortest wall in the room, and against the long wall was a smallish flat-screen TV. There was a cheap patio chair in the corner next to the TV and one of those tall floor lamps that looked like it could tip over at the slightest breeze. A sliding glass door, partially hidden by a set of venetian blinds, led out onto the balcony, and I noticed that Candice immediately moved to the far left side of the blinds. With her jacket covering her hand, she tugged on the door. It slid open easily.

The three of us exchanged a knowing look.

"How did that get open?" Amber asked, a note of alarm in her voice.

Candice didn't answer; instead she pulled on the cord next to the door and slid the blinds all the way open. We saw that Amber or Taylor had put one of those long wooden security poles in the ridge of the inner pane, but the pole had been moved to just outside the metal frame, allowing the door to easily open.

Candice then bent down and examined the clasp. "It's been tampered with," she said.

Meanwhile Amber was standing slack-jawed in the middle of the room. I could tell that she was freaked-out to discover that her back door had been monkeyed with.

Dutch moved to the door, nudging it open with his knee before stepping out onto the balcony. I followed him and peered down over the side of the railing. The apartment was on the second floor, so there was a fifteen-foot drop to the ground, but a huge live oak tree crowded against the outside wall. Dutch pointed to a low-hanging branch, then to another one within half an arm's length of the balcony. "It wouldn't take a lot of effort to climb this tree and sneak onto the balcony."

"Which is why we always keep it locked," Amber said. She was standing next to Candice in the doorway. "Taylor caught a creepy-looking guy out on our balcony last June, and that's when we got that security pole."

"There was a guy on your balcony in June?" I repeated.

Amber nodded. "Yeah. A Peeping Tom. He'd been seen looking into a bunch of apartments here in the complex. The police finally caught him in August."

"Do you remember his name?" Dutch asked, already documenting it in his notebook.

Amber shook her head. "No. But I have the case number on the fridge. Taylor was going to go testify at his trial."

"Mind if I get that from you?" Dutch asked, and he and Amber moved back into the apartment. Candice came out onto the balcony and looked at the tree herself.

"Did you notice this apartment is the last one in the row?" she asked me. "It's by the stairwell too. If someone wanted to climb that tree and get in here to abduct Taylor, he could've done it without risk of being seen. He also could've gotten her keys from that dish," she said, pointing back into the apartment to a dish I hadn't noticed sitting on the kitchen counter with a set of car keys in it, "then pulled her car up to there"—she then pointed to a lone parking slot mostly hidden by the mighty oak—"and put Taylor into the car without calling attention to themselves."

"Yeah, all that's true, but he would've had to have had access to the apartment prior to the abduction to rig it for entry later."

Candice drummed her fingers on the top of the balcony railing for a minute. "Had to be someone that either Taylor or Amber would've trusted," she said.

"And someone that Michelle and her roommate would've also known and trusted," I pointed out.

"A college boy?" Candice asked.

I shook my head. "This seems a bit too sophisticated for a college boy, don't you think?"

Candice turned around to face me and crossed her arms. "College Station is a hike from Austin," she said. "That's been bugging me. What's the link between here and there? And why was Taylor headed to a bridal boutique of all places? A mall could be crowded, but just before noon on a Wednesday morning? Not likely."

"That's been bugging me too," I said. "This feels personal, but I can't figure out how the two events are linked other than to involve two girls of similar age who were abducted, strapped to a bomb, and forced to walk into a public place before said bombs were detonated."

At that Dutch poked his head out of the door and motioned for us to come back inside. We filed in and stood against the wall with the TV while Dutch bent down and used a set of tongs he must've swiped from the kitchen to set the security pole back in place. "Do me a favor, Amber," he said. "Don't touch that pole or the door until I get my tech here to swipe for fingerprints, okay?"

Amber was looking at us with wide frightened eyes. I could tell that the revelation that her sliding glass door had been tampered with was starting to put several puzzle pieces into place and she was close to wigging out. "It never did make sense to me," she said, as if she'd been having an internal monologue with herself. "I mean, Taylor had issues, but I knew she'd never do something so crazy on her own."

"How long did you know Taylor?" I asked.

"We'd been roommates for about nine months," Amber said, shuffling from foot to foot. "Not quite a year."

"You said you thought Taylor had issues—can you tell me what you mean by that?"

"She was a little bitch," Amber said. I was a bit taken

aback by the brutally blunt description. "She was," Amber insisted. "If Taylor didn't get her way, or if she felt like you got the better end of a deal, she'd find a way to get even with you."

"Can you give us an example?" I asked.

Amber shrugged. "This one time I got home from class early, before Taylor, who usually beat me here. We have only the one TV, and Taylor always wanted to watch her lame network show, but my favorite show on HBO is on Wednesday nights, so that night I already had the TV on when she came in, and she knew that I'd beaten her to the punch. She didn't say a word to me; she just went into her room and shut the door. The next week it happened again—I got home before Taylor—and when I went to flip the channel, I found out that she'd canceled HBO. I called to complain, and not only had she taken the cable account out of our joint names, but she'd put it solely into hers with a new password. I had to send them a stupid copy of her death certificate to get it put back into my name so I could get HBO back."

"Huh," I said. What could I say? Lots of college-age roommates had personality clashes. Was the HBO thing so terrible to label Taylor a bitch?

"There was a lot of other stuff too," Amber said, probably sensing that she hadn't convinced me of Taylor's bad side.

"Like what?"

"I don't know. She was just mean to people. Rude. She'd point out your flaws and make fun of you to your face. Nobody liked her. I mean, she had like . . . *no* friends. When we first moved in together, I tried to introduce her to some of my friends, but Taylor was a total bitch to them, and none of my friends wanted to hang out here if she was going to be here too."

"What about guys?" I asked. "Did Taylor have a boyfriend?"

Amber laughed derisively. "No guy could stand her longer than one date. Like I said, she was a real bitch, and she was crazy needy and possessive. She'd go out with a new guy and start texting him nonstop right after he dropped her off, about how she already missed him and couldn't wait to see him again and why hadn't he called her yet? That would be the end of that relationship.

"If she saw one of the guys she'd been out with on a date with someone else, she'd do something psycho like walk right up to them and pretend that she'd just caught him cheating on her. Pretty soon every guy on campus knew not to ask her out."

"I'm assuming you guys didn't get along so well either," I said.

Amber scoffed. "You got that right. I was just waiting for the lease to be up in December so I could get the hell away from her too."

"What about Taylor's family?" I asked. "Was she close to them?"

Amber shook her head. "Nope. After her sister died, nobody wanted anything to do with her."

"What happened to her sister?"

"She died in a fire. It happened about a year or so ago, I think. I tried to get her to talk about it, you know. I was trying to be nice and draw her out a little. I thought that maybe she was such a bitch to everybody because she was really sad about her sister."

"Was she?" I asked. "Sad about her sister?"

Amber shook her head. "Nope. At least not that she ever showed me. It was sort of the opposite, actually. She seemed glad to be rid of her."

"For real?" I pressed. Could Taylor really have been as awful a person as Amber was painting her? I wanted to doubt it.

"I swear I'm not making this up," Amber assured me—and the fact that my inner lie detector hadn't gone off once since Amber had been talking meanly about Taylor sort of confirmed it for me. "She called her sister a big fat loser," Amber continued. "Taylor said her sister had only dated one guy in her life, and he was an even bigger loser than she was. She used to joke that she thought that the two of them were both still virgins."

"Did they both die in the fire?" I asked. My radar was pinging. Something about the subject of Taylor's sister was calling me to take a deeper look.

"You mean Mimi and her boyfriend?" When I nodded, Amber said, "I don't think so, but I don't know for sure."

I socked away the info on Taylor's sister and pressed on. "So, she wasn't close with her sister, but was there maybe anyone else in her family that she got along with?"

Amber shook her head. "Taylor's mom died of bladder cancer last winter after being sick for a long time. I told Taylor she should apply for special hardship to get a passing grade in all her classes, but she acted like it was no big deal. She said her mom had suffered and was now out of her misery. She acted like her mom was an old dog they had to put down or something. It was weird."

"And her dad?" I pressed. *Someone* had to have been there for the girl.

Amber shook her head again. "Taylor and her dad never spoke. I lived with her for almost a year and I never heard her on the phone with him. All I knew about her family was that her parents split up while Taylor was still in high school. She and her sister stayed in Austin with her mom, and her dad moved overseas to take a job in some war zone, I think."

My brow furrowed and I looked to Dutch. He nodded. "Mr. Greene works for Halliburton. He was stationed in Iraq for several years, but recently he's been reassigned to Dubai."

"That's why Homeland is so interested in making this a terrorist case," I guessed. "They think there might be a connection to Taylor's dad."

He shrugged, but I could tell he knew it to be true.

Turning back to Amber, I said, "When was the last time Taylor saw her father? I mean, I know they didn't speak while she was here, but if he's been overseas for a few years, do you know if they ever got together for visits?"

"She told me that the last time she saw her dad was when she was seventeen. She said he didn't even come home for her sister's funeral, and I sure as hell didn't see him at Taylor's funeral."

"How do you know?" Candice asked. "He could have been in the crowd and you just didn't know it was her dad."

Amber laughed. "Crowd? Lady, I was the *only* person at her funeral. There wasn't even a wake. Just me and a priest next to a hole in the ground where her remains were put. It was pathetic."

"Wow," I whispered. "Really? Nobody else came?"

"I'm not lying," Amber said defensively. "I only went because I felt sorry for her, but if you ask me, more people were relieved she was gone than were sad that she'd died."

We fell silent for a minute after that. It was a lot to take in, and the fact that Amber had so many nasty things to say about Taylor put a whole new light on the investigation. If she really was that mean, she likely had made her fair share of enemies, but who would go to such lengths to exact their revenge, and once they had it and Taylor had been killed— why strap a bomb to Michelle Padilla?

As if reading my mind, Dutch pulled out a photo of Michelle from the inside of a blue folder he'd brought with him and said, "Amber, does this girl look familiar to you?"

Amber squinted at it, then shook her head. "No. But she does look a little like Taylor, doesn't she?"

I blinked and then I saw it too. From the photo I'd seen in Taylor's file, the two girls had looked a bit alike. I stared meaningfully at Dutch. This was no act of terrorism. This was personal. Someone wanted to punish Taylor, even after she was dead, but for the life of me, I couldn't figure out what the bridal boutique and the hair salon had to do with any of this.

Candice then asked Amber about anyone who might've had access to their apartment in the days before the mall bombing. Amber shrugged. "I had a party here the weekend before the mall thing, but Taylor sulked in her room the whole night."

"How many people were here?" I asked.

"I don't know, maybe twenty or thirty? You know how it is—you invite a couple of people and they invite a couple of people and before you know it, you're in a room with at least a few strangers."

"Did anybody go out on the balcony?" I asked.

"Sure," she said. "It was totally crowded all night."

"And do you remember locking it and setting the pole back in place afterward?"

Amber stared at the sliding glass door for a moment. "Yeah, I do. I've always been nervous about that tree and

Taylor saying she saw a Peeping Tom out there on the balcony. I'm positive I locked it and put the security pole in the slot before I left the apartment the next day."

"Did anybody else come in here? Maybe a maintenance man, or a delivery person?"

Again Amber shrugged. "If they did, then I didn't know about it. Usually if there's any maintenance work to be done, we get a note taped to our door, but Taylor almost always got home before me, so she would've been the one to get the note if there was one."

Dutch jotted something down in his notebook again, and I suspected he was going to check with the apartment manager to see if there had been any interior maintenance work performed in the days prior to the mall bombing.

After that, Dutch had a few more routine questions for Amber and I took the opportunity to head back out onto the balcony one more time. Something was bugging me about it, but I couldn't put my finger on it.

Candice popped her head out and said, "Dutch is ready to go, honey."

I'd been shuffling the dead leaves and debris around and with a sigh I lifted my head and said, "Yeah, okay."

"Something wrong?"

I shook my head. "Nope. It's just that—"

At that moment Dutch's head appeared over Candice's shoulder. "I've got something for you," he said, raising a box high so I could see it.

"What's that?" I asked.

"Some of Taylor's personal effects. Pictures and stuff that we didn't pick up from the first search."

That did interest me. I could sometimes get a vibe off personal items. I moved to the door and Candice and Dutch stepped out of the way, and then the three of us made our way toward the front entrance, thanking Amber for her time. She nodded as if to say, "Yeah, but don't come back."

After that, we piled back into Dutch's car and made our way to the highway, where we immediately got tied up in traffic. I looked at my watch and knew I'd never make it to the new house in time to meet the exterminator. I called Dave and asked him if he wouldn't mind staying a little late.

"Aw, Abs, I've got plans with the old lady tonight," he said irritably.

Dave's "old lady" is his wife, whose actual name I still don't know even after four years of working with him. I had yet to meet her in fact. All those times when our paths should have crossed had been interrupted by something or other. It'd become this joke of sorts between Dave and me, but come my wedding day, the joke would be over because I was determined to meet this mysterious woman. "It shouldn't take too long," I told him. If I knew Dave at all (which I did), his plans involved some sort of happy hour special, and by staying late to meet the bug guy, he'd have to pay full price for his beer and munchies once he made it to the bar. "Come on, Dave, please?"

"Yeah, okay," he said grudgingly. "But you owe me a free beer and a plate of wings."

"Put it on my tab," I told him.

After hanging up with him I rooted around in Taylor's box. Not much was there: some pictures, cards, and kitschy little items. I sorted through the pictures. Most of them were of Taylor alone and standing in front of something of interest— a football stadium, the Grand Canyon, the steps of her high school with her diploma. Only two were photos of her family. One obviously taken when she was young, about eleven, and next to her was a girl maybe fourteen or fifteen, and behind them was a slight man in his late forties and a woman in her late thirties or early forties. *Must be her sister and her mom and dad,* I thought. I also noticed the flat plastic look of the mother and sister along with Taylor. This is how dead people often appear to me in photographs. Their image takes on a slight distortion and it becomes flat and almost waxy. The dad in the photo was the only "normal-looking" one. I felt a keen sense of sadness for the man. Even if he hadn't come home to attend his daughters' funerals, I knew he had to care about them. Maybe he just had a hard time showing it.

The last picture I looked at had been pushed to the bottom

of the box, and it was curious for two reasons. The first was that it wasn't of Taylor. It was of her sister. The second reason it stood out to me was that Taylor's sister had been posing in that sort of couple's pose with a man only a few inches taller than her, hugging her from behind, and both of their faces had been mostly obscured by a felt-tipped pen. Mimi Greene had blacked-out teeth and a big dorky bow on the top of her head, and the man she was standing next to had had his countenance almost completely obscured by a drawn-in pair of glasses, thick mustache, clown nose, blacked-out teeth, and giant clown hat. Next to the image was the word *Losers!*

"Nice," I said with a frown.

"What's that?" Dutch asked from the front seat. I showed him the picture. "Maybe Amber wasn't kidding when she described Taylor," he remarked.

I stared at the photo a bit longer. My radar kept pinging off it. "You know," I said, "I'd like to find out more about Taylor's sister. Do you have anything on her, Dutch?"

He glanced at me over his shoulder. "I'm sure I could come up with something, given a name and a last known address. Why?"

"Call it a gut feeling." *A bad gut feeling,* I thought. And with that, I tucked the photo back into the box and vowed to follow up on it the next day.

# T-Minus 00:40:32

"M.J.!" Gilley squeaked, tugging on her arm as Dutch's car sped away from the two handcuffed police officers. "I have a *really* bad feeling about this!"

"Quiet, Gil," she replied, trying to hold Brody's attention, but it was too late. His eyes had just lifted to the rear window and when M.J. looked behind her, she could see the cops were already on their feet and being helped by Brody's friend. They'd be after them in a minute.

"And I have to pee!" Gilley squeaked as Dutch's black sedan squealed round the corner.

"Quiet!" Dutch barked. M.J. could see the tension on his face in the rearview mirror. Next to him Brody sat stiffly. The kid was scared. It was wafting off him in waves.

But then he blinked and seemed to focus. "The fight you're talking about wasn't between my mom and Margo," he said to M.J. "It was about some guy who came into the shop right after my mom bought it, and he said she owed him some money, but my mom said that he needed to go see Margo about it. He didn't believe that she'd just bought the shop, and he scared my mom so bad that she called Margo and told her to watch out for this guy 'cause he was, like, crazy or something."

"Who was this man?" M.J. asked. Brody's mom was filling her mind with the sense that this was the man that they needed to find in order to save Abby.

Brody shrugged. "I don't know. But I do know where Margo's new shop is, if you want to go ask her. It's not far from here."

"It'd be faster if we called," Candice said.

Brody turned in his seat. "I'm really sorry, but I don't know the name of it. I just remember Mom taking me there when it opened. It's not far from here, I swear."

"Point the way, kid," Dutch said, punching the accelerator even before Brody could give him the first set of instructions.

M.J. eyed the clock on the dash. Already they'd lost three whole minutes. She had a terrible feeling that they weren't going to find Abby in time, and, by the same token, she couldn't imagine what would happen if they did. Could they remove the bomb before it exploded? How the hell were they going to save her with only thirty-some-odd minutes left?

Candice seemed to be thinking the same thing, because when M.J. looked over at her, she could see her lids closed and her lips moving. She was praying. And then her eyes snapped open and she had her phone out again. "Brice?" she said above the squealing of tires as they took another turn too tight. "Listen to me. I don't have a lot of time to explain. I'm with Dutch. Abby's only got thirty-seven minutes left. We're on our way to get a name, and we think it could be the name of the bastard we've been hunting for. When I call it in, you'll need to put every resource you have available to finding this son of a bitch." At that moment the sound of sirens somewhere behind them lit up the tense quiet of the car. "Oh, and call off the police before Dutch hurts somebody, okay?"

# Chapter Nine

"You okay?" Rodriguez asked as I handed him the bag containing his breakfast burritos. "You look like you're ready to hurt somebody."

I pushed a smile onto my face and tried to relax the stiff set to my shoulders. "Yeah, yeah," I said to him. "It was crazy crowded at the restaurant, traffic was awful, and I'm late getting to my office. I've got a full list of clients today."

Oscar was nice enough to look chagrined. "Sorry, Cooper," he said, opening the bag to peer inside. "If I'd known you weren't coming in today, I wouldn't have sent you my breakfast order."

"It's cool," I assured him. "A deal's a deal. Speaking of which, did you take another look at that footage?"

Oscar pulled out one of his burritos from the bag and nodded. "Take a look at this," he said. Scooting his chair over to his computer monitor, he clicked the mouse and set a section of security footage in action. I peered at the screen, but all I saw was a little bit of light mall traffic and the fuzzy image of a guy tending to the plants in the mall's atrium.

Then the footage ended. "That's it?" I asked.

Oscar rewound the footage a little and magnified the view of the guy tending the plants. "See him?" he said.

"Yeah," I said squinting. It was hard to make out anything other than a guy in what looked like a green or brown shirt and shorts spraying plants with a mister.

"This camera sits at the mall's atrium, which has a good view of the south entrance. But this guy isn't a mall employee or a contractor. I checked, and the management says that the crew that comes in to take care of the plants does it every Monday at eight a.m., and the crew is mostly female. This guy isn't on their roster."

I sucked in a small breath. "*That's* our unsub!"

Oscar nodded. "Now watch what happens right here," he said. Oscar closed the window of that footage and opened another. From a different and even more obscured view we watched the guy among the plants pause, set down his mister, and look toward the mall's south entrance. The clock in the bottom of the screen indicated that the bomb would detonate in ten seconds, but for all of that ten seconds the unsub just stood there and looked toward the south entrance. Then there was a bit of movement with his arm, and all of a sudden the camera shook and bits of small debris scuttled past the lens. Everyone in the mall shops began running out, but the plant guy simply bent down to retrieve his mister and hurried away with the rest of the crowd.

"That's *definitely* him, Oscar," I said, suppressing a shudder. "Did you catch that move with his hand? He did set off the bomb remotely." Oscar nodded.

I squinted at the frozen image of the unsub moving into the crowd. He'd been so cold as he'd looked on toward the south entrance. I knew he'd seen the older couple approach Taylor, and he'd just set off the bomb anyway. "Is there a way to get a better view of him?"

Oscar frowned. "I've pored over all the tapes, Cooper, and these are the two best images of this guy we have. It's like he knew where the cameras were and kept just out of view the whole time he was in the mall."

"What about enhancing the footage to get a close-up?"

"I've sent that first section to the photo tech at the D.C. lab, but he's already e-mailed me this morning to tell me he doesn't think he'll be able to get much more than we already have. The guy's too far away and there aren't enough pixels to work with."

I sighed. "Yeah, okay. Listen, show this to Dutch and Candice when they come in, would you?"

Oscar looked around. "I'm surprised they're not with you."

"Candice is babysitting Dutch for the day," I told him. "They're both ecstatic about it."

Oscar laughed. "I'll bet. Okay, Cooper, thanks again for breakfast and have a good day with your clients."

The rest of day was a long one for me. I had clients booked through the afternoon, and I had to meet the landscaper at the new house that evening to go over what could be done to fix the destruction from the wayward Bobcat.

Plus there were a whole lot of other things that needed to get done before Dutch and I could move into our house the following Tuesday. Namely, packing. By some miracle Dutch was able to find a moving company who could come out that weekend to load up the portable storage units, but that would need to be monitored, and I knew he'd never get the time off work to do it, so it would fall to me.

If I took the time to tend to all these things, I'd have to leave Dutch's side, and that bothered me no end. Candice came to my rescue when she said she promised to stick to him like glue.

Around four thirty that evening I met Tom, my landscape architect, at the top of the driveway where he'd parked.

Tom's a fairly nondescript man of about thirty-five. He was an airline pilot for a few years until an auto accident caused him a case of sciatica that wouldn't allow him to sit longer than a few hours at a time. Unable to fly commercially anymore, he dove into his second passion, landscape architecture. He had a smooth, nonconfrontational quality about him, but even for me he was often hard to read. When he saw the damage to the clay pots (three of them had been all but demolished, and the beds of carefully planted flowers had been mushed beyond recognition), his tone never conveyed that he was ticked off.

*My* tone, however, was a completely different story.

Shortly after arriving, we watched Dave's truck pull up and hesitate next to us. I saw him mouth, "Uh-oh," then hide it quickly. He then headed to the bottom of the drive and Tom and I came down after him on foot. At least Dave had sense enough not to try to duck us by doing a quick U-turn and hightailing it out of there. "Abby!" he said brightly.

"Dave," I replied. (This is the part where my angry tone comes into play.)

He cleared his throat and rocked on his heels. "Thought you two were coming by later."

"Nope." I glared hard at Dave. As foreman he was supposed to make sure accidents like the one in my front garden didn't happen.

"I don't know if I can get three more urns like those," Tom said, pointing to the broken clay pots. "I mean, they came imported from Peru."

"Could you find something close?" I asked.

Tom nodded, looking at his watch. "Yeah. If I leave here in the next twenty minutes, I can swing by Miguel's on my way home and see what'll work. It'll be a little pricey, though."

"How much?" Dave asked, squirming in his boots.

"Four to six hundred," Tom said, and Dave looked relieved until Tom added, "Apiece."

Dave's face fell into a hard frown. "Yeah, okay. Roberto can work it off in overtime. I'll front the money for him until he's even."

Angry as I'd been, I suddenly felt bad. I mean, it was an accident after all. "Keep it at or below three hundred apiece, Tom," I said. "We can use the remaining urn as a centerpiece and cascade some smaller ones around it."

Dave shot me a grateful smile and Tom nodded like he approved of the game plan. We walked over toward the front door, talking about how to rebuild the look we wanted, and I couldn't help but make the suggestion that Tom not put the urns in place until after Dave's team was completely finished. "If you want to pick 'em up tomorrow, Tom, you can store them in the garage," Dave offered. "We'll be out of here by

Saturday night if you want to have your crew here to put them in place first thing Monday morning."

Tom nodded. "That'll work," he said.

Dave then moved over to a can of paint set oddly on the front step, and lifted it to retrieve a key. I stared at him curiously, and he blushed a little when he caught my eye, but he didn't explain. Instead he handed the key to Tom and said, "If I'm not here, just let yourself in and hit the button in the garage for the door. You can leave the key under that can of paint if I'm not here when you're through."

"Got it," Tom said, pocketing the key, and with a salute to me he was off to walk back up the drive toward his truck.

"Wanna take a peek inside?" Dave asked when Tom had moved away.

"Sure," I said, following him to the front door, where Dave fumbled through the keys on his key ring trying to find the one that fit our door. "Should we call Tom back?" I asked after much jangling.

"Naw," Dave said, "I've got one on here somewhere."

I waited patiently through more flipping and twirling of the keys until Dave finally came up with the one that unlocked the door. We went inside at last, Dave holding the door for me, and I nearly came up short when I saw the gorgeous interior. "Whoa!" I said. The last time I'd been in the house had been when the dark wood floors were just being laid. Now the house looked finished, pristine, and oh-so gorgeous. It also smelled of fresh paint, new carpet, and something else I couldn't quite identify.

Curiously, Dave squatted down next to the wall and ran his hand about six inches above the molding.

"What?" I asked him.

Dave stood with a satisfied look on his face. "Your guy was out here last night spraying the walls and it was leaving a yellow residue. He promised it'd evaporate and wouldn't leave a stain."

It took me a minute to remember that I'd had Russ come by the night before to spray for crickets, or as I liked to call them—scorpion snack food.

I listened and didn't hear any chirping, so Russ must have been as successful with the crickets as he was with the scorpions.

"Come on," Dave said, waving to me to follow him into the interior. "You gotta see the kitchen."

Three hours later Dutch found me packing up our own kitchen. The moment I saw him walk through the door and tug at the Velcro that locked his Kevlar vest in place, I knew that Candice had done her job of protecting my fiancé very well, because he headed straight for the scotch and suggested that I might want to get a new, less annoying best friend, because she was driving him crazy.

"Did you have any luck on the case today?" I asked, tucking a paper-covered platter into a box.

"None," he said irritably. "I called the management on Taylor's apartment and the reason the complex is under new management is because the old manager kept no records. At all. On anything. The new manager is still trying to get organized, and he's got no idea if Taylor and Amber's apartment was visited by the maintenance crew in the days before the bomb. I managed to track down one of the maintenance guys at the complex, and he tells me he's so overworked he can't remember the apartments he visited yesterday, let alone last month."

"But you ran a background check on him all the same, right?" I asked.

Dutch nodded. "He checks out. No priors, no history of violence, or substance abuse. He's worked for the complex for six years without any record of complaint to the local authorities."

"What about this Peeping Tom Amber was telling us about?"

"Sherman Knocks. He's got a solid alibi," Dutch told me. "He's currently serving time for a parole violation, and he's been locked up for the past three months."

"How about Taylor's sister? Did you get anything on her?"

Dutch rubbed his face tiredly and poured another two fingers into his scotch glass. "Mary Greene. She went by the nickname Mimi. That's about all I have on her," he said.

"Candice has been digging into her personal life, but I managed to find out that she worked at a Jamba Juice in the few months before she died. Her manager remembers her as sweet but shy. A little sad, she said. That was about all she could tell me. She wished she could've gotten to know her better, but Jamba Juice is a pretty busy place, or so she says. Not a lot of time for chitchat between the employees."

I frowned. "That's it?"

"That's it," he said.

"Did the manager remember the name of the guy that Mimi was going out with before she died?"

Dutch blinked. "I didn't ask her," he said. "Was I supposed to ask about him?"

I smiled. I didn't think I'd given Dutch any specifics beyond digging into the girl's past. "No, don't worry about it, cowboy. I'll call the manager when I get back on the case. Which Jamba Juice is it?"

"The one in south Austin, near Mimi's last known address at an apartment off Seventy-one and Bee Cave."

I scoured my internal map of Austin to locate the intersection. "Hey, that's not far from Rita's beauty shop, right?"

Dutch shrugged. "It's about a mile give or take," he said. "You thinking there's a connection between Mimi and the salon?"

My skin felt tingly, like I'd hit on something, but I couldn't quite figure out what. And the truth was that my radar was running on empty after a long day of clients and obligations. I sighed tiredly. "Maybe. Maybe not. But I'm feeling like we should learn more about Mimi. I can't shake the feeling that she's connected to all this." Then I thought of something else. "Did you get ahold of the girls' father?"

Dutch sighed. "No. Homeland has officially taken over the case, and they've got him locked up."

"They put him in *jail*?"

Dutch smiled at me. "No, doll, they've instructed him not to talk to anyone but them while they root around in his past to see if there's any connection between him and this terrorist group in Yemen. I can't make contact with Greene without raising all kinds of red flags."

"Well, that sucks," I grumbled.

"We'll just have to work around it," Dutch replied as he lifted up a container of Bubble Wrap. "Meanwhile I better help you pack."

I sighed again. "I've been working on this kitchen for the past two hours and I feel like I've hardly made a dent."

Dutch chuckled and reached out to wrap me in his arms. His shirt was still damp from wearing the Kevlar all day. "Thanks for keeping your vest on," I told him.

"I'm getting used to it," he said, rocking with me in a slow dance around the kitchen. Just then his foot clunked against my cane, which had been propped against a chair. Looking down at it, he asked, "How're the hips?"

I smiled up at him. "I barely used it today. I swear I'm more balanced than I've been in months."

"You think you can make it down the aisle without Fast Freddy?" Fast Freddy was Dutch's pet name for my cane.

"Maybe," I told him. "But tell Milo to do some extra workouts with that left arm. I'll probably be leaning hard on him."

"Speaking of which, you think we can get this house packed, moved into the new digs, *and* get hitched in one week?"

"Do we have a choice?"

"We could always postpone it," he said. My heart lifted. He was willing to postpone the wedding? "I mean, we don't *have* to move into the new digs right away."

My hopes sank back down. He'd meant postpone the move.

"Yeah, but, honey, Bruce said we had to be out by the thirtieth," I reminded him.

Dutch sighed. "You'll have to do a lot of this on your own," he told me. "I'm gonna be stuck at the office all weekend."

I squeezed my arms around him tightly. What he didn't know yet was that as of Monday he'd officially be on vacation and under orders to butt out. "Please don't go anywhere other than the office. If I have to be here, I'll go crazy if I know you're out in the field."

He kissed me on the top of the head and said, "I promise to stick close to home, babe. Maybe Gaston will give me a break. It's not like we're making progress on this. Maybe I can work some of the leads from home this weekend and help you out too."

I looked up at him again. "Have I told you lately that I lurve you?"

He grinned. "You better, Mrs. Rivers."

I felt my eyes bug and the breath catch in my throat. "Wha . . . what?"

"Oh, sorry. Maybe I should save the Mrs. Rivers until after the ceremony. Speaking of which, you should do some research on filing for a legal name change."

Was he serious? Since when had I agreed to change my name to his? Had we talked about this? And if we hadn't, why hadn't we? "Uh . . . Dutch?"

"Hmm?" he said, still dancing with me and holding me close to nuzzle against my neck.

"About the Mrs. Rivers thing . . ."

"Which reminds me, I need to put in the paperwork to get you a new badge. Don't let me forget to do it on Monday, okay?"

I felt my heartbeat quicken. Oh, God . . . he was serious. I stopped dancing and stepped back. For a moment I couldn't figure out how to tell him, and he eyed me curiously. "You okay?"

I wrung my hands and stammered some words, still trying to begin. "I . . . uh . . . see, the thing is . . . it's not like I don't . . ."

Dutch reached out and put a hand on my upper arm. "Edgar, what is it?"

I squared my shoulders and looked him directly in the eye. "I don't want to be Mrs. Rivers."

To say that Dutch looked stunned would be an understatement. In truth, he looked like I'd just slapped him in the face. Hard. "Ah," he said, letting that hand fall to his own side.

I took a deep breath, about to explain that while I couldn't wait to marry him, I'd been Abby Cooper for so long that I hardly knew how to be anything different. Plus, profession-ally it wasn't a great idea for me to change my name, not with so many clients now scattered in two separate states. But before I could say any of that, Dutch had backed away from me, and without another word he turned, picked up his keys, and left the house.

I was so shocked by his abrupt departure that I just stood there, slack-jawed, for several seconds. I then moved to the front door, half expecting him to be on the front steps waiting for me to come after him, but all I saw was his empty space in the driveway and taillights already winding their way down the street.

With tears in my eyes I went to my phone and called him immediately, only to hear the sound of ringing coming from the kitchen. Walking there, I found his phone on the counter next to the barely touched glass of scotch. And then I saw his Kevlar draped across the back of one of the chairs in the living room and my heart skipped a beat. "Dammit!" I swore. And I was so angry with myself I didn't even vow to pay the swear jar later.

Instead I grabbed his vest and his phone and my own keys and headed out the door as fast as my hobbly legs would carry me. I drove in the direction Dutch had gone, but once I hit the top of the sub, I had no idea which way he'd gone. I flipped on my radar and turned right. I followed my intuition all the way to downtown, but where he'd gone within the confines of the city I couldn't figure out. He could've checked his car into any one of the parking garages and gone into any one of the bars on Sixth Street or Congress Avenue. There had to be at least fifty to choose from.

By this time I was crying like a little girl. I'd hurt Dutch's feelings and I had no idea how to make that up to him. He almost never registered such emotion. He almost always met my angry or thoughtless words with stoic calm. In the nearly four years I'd been with him, I'd never seen him react that way. And I'd had no idea that taking his name meant so much to him. But when I thought about it, should it? I mean, wasn't that a bit old-fashioned and also wasn't that a bit presumptu-ous?

Still, that look he'd given me. That hurt, wounded, rejected look haunted me, and I kept driving the streets searching and searching for him.

Finally I made it back home, hoping against hope that he'd come back too, but the driveway was empty and all the lights were still on from when I'd dashed out of the house.

Carefully I climbed up the steps—I'd left Fast Freddy at home—and as I turned the key, I heard a phone ringing. Quickly I pushed my way inside, nearly tripping over Tuttle, who rushed to greet me, and I scooped her up as I grabbed for my phone, which I'd also stupidly left behind. "Hello? Hello?" I gasped. I hadn't even looked at the ID on the screen—I was so anxious to hear from Dutch.

"Abs?"

Dammit. Screw-the-swear-jar take two. "Hey, Candice," I said, choking back a sob.

"Wanna talk about it?"

I wiped my eyes and slumped down on the couch. "Not really."

"Okay," she said. "No worries. Just wanted you to know that I took Dutch's car keys away from him the moment he and Brice broke open the scotch."

I sat forward. "He's there?"

"Oh, yeah," she said, and not in a way that suggested she was particularly happy about it. Belatedly I remembered that Candice had told me she had planned a special date night out with her fiancé to help him relax after so many weeks of working so hard.

"What'd Dutch say?" I asked meekly.

"He says that you just told him you didn't want to marry him."

*"What?!"*

"His words, Abs, not mine."

"Where the hell did he get *that* idea?!" (Okay, so at some point maybe I really would owe the swear jar a quarter or two.)

"According to him . . . from you."

"I never said that!"

"Then what did you say?" she asked, all patience and solicitude.

"I merely told him that I didn't want to be Mrs. Rivers!" The moment it was out of my mouth, I *knew* what I'd done.

There was a pause, then, "Ah. I see how he could be confused."

"Oh, *shit*, Candice!"

"I'm sure it'll be fine," she said in that way that suggested it might not be.

Getting up, I hobbled into the kitchen and dug for my wallet.

"Abs?" she asked. "You still there?"

I tugged open the zipper on my change purse, then thought better of it and pulled out all the money I had there, from all six clients that day. "Yeah," I told her, moving over to shove the bills into the swear jar. "But I need to go. I've got some credit to work off."

The next morning Dutch crept through the door at just before six. He looked haggard and hungover. I probably wasn't looking much better. I'd stayed up the entire night packing and trying to think of a way to make it up to him. Around four a.m., after I'd run out of things to shove into a moving box, I thought I knew. Since then I'd been waiting with foot-tapping impatience for him to come home.

Dutch paused in the doorway and his eye lit on me as I sat on the ottoman I'd pushed a few feet in front of the door. With a nervous smile I held up a velvet blue box wrapped in a silver bow that I'd had tucked away in my sock drawer for the past few weeks. I'd been saving the gift for our wedding night, but right now I needed a Hail Mary, and the gift was a good one.

As Dutch continued to stand there half in the door, half out, I leaned forward and said, "Dutch Rivers, will you please marry me?"

For several seconds his eyes flickered between me and the box, his face expressionless. My heart started to pound. What if he said no?

Into the horrible silence I tried to insert some levity. "I'd get all the way down on bended knee, but I don't know that I could do it without falling over."

Dutch just stared at me.

"You know, 'cause of my hips," I said, clearing my throat as heat began to rise up from my neck and spread across my face.

Stare.

My arm was starting to tire and my back hurt from leaning forward and holding the box aloft, and the awkwardness of the situation was getting to me. "How about those Longhorns?"

Stare.

I opened my mouth to start singing the theme to *Jeopardy!* when Dutch at last spoke. "Why the change of heart?"

I let the hand holding the box drop back to my lap. "Cowboy, I swear to God, it's not what you think."

He eyed me skeptically.

"Seriously!" I insisted, unable now to even tell him that it'd merely been a poor choice of words to let him know that I didn't want to change my last name.

"So now you *do* want to get married?"

I stood. Keeping it simple might be best. "Yes, Dutch. I do. With all my heart I do."

"You're sure?"

I stepped forward to him. "More than ever," I whispered, offering him the box again, praying with everything I had that he'd accept it.

He hesitated only another second or two before he reached up and took my wrist, pulling me close to wrap me in his arms. "Thank Christ," he said softly. "For a minute there I thought we were gonna have to tell your sister the wedding was off."

I laughed and cried at the same time. "I love you, cowboy. Don't ever forget it, and don't ever doubt it, okay?"

"What's in the box?" he asked after a moment.

I leaned back and took up his hand to place it in his palm. "I was saving it for our wedding night, but now that I think about it, it'd probably go better with your tuxedo."

Dutch kissed me and moved us to the couch, where he

undid the bow and opened the lid. Whistling, he gently lifted out the two-tone Submariner Rolex with deep blue outer rim, and gold face inset with sapphires and diamonds. And, although it looked new, the truth was that it was preowned—no way could I have afforded it otherwise. Even so, the gorgeous timepiece had cost more than my first car. And my second. Combined. It'd taken me months to save up for it, and it'd still put a sizable dent in my savings.

"Edgar . . . ," he whispered. "This is gorgeous." I smiled slyly. Dutch was a great admirer of timepieces. He had several antique watches in a small leather box upstairs, and the Tag Heuer I'd given him on Valentine's Day many moons ago was one he wore daily. "But, doll," he added, "this must've cost a fortune."

My smile widened. "Now you know why I've been skimping on the swear jar."

Dutch chuckled, looping one arm around my neck to bring me close for a kiss. "How about we forget that damn thing and just let you be you?"

I turned my head to look over to the dining room table. The large pickle jar was the only packable object in the house that I hadn't thrown into a box, and it was now crammed with bills. Squirming slightly out of his hold, I sat back and said, "Can we please put that into our wedding vows?"

"Done," he said, slipping on his new watch and marveling at its splendor. "Thanks, sweethot," he added in his best Humphrey Bogart lisp. "And, yes, by the way."

"Hmm?"

"Yes. I'll marry you." And he sealed that promise with a kiss.

By eight o'clock we'd finished reconsummating our reengagement, and as the house was pretty much completely packed, Dutch made us both breakfast while I waited on the movers to come and stack our things into the two storage pods they were bringing along. "What needs to stay here?" Dutch called from the kitchen while he whisked a bowl of eggs. I'd left him precious little to cook with, but he seemed to be managing.

"I think just our bed from upstairs and maybe two of the kitchen chairs and those TV trays," I told him. "I mean, we're only here until Tuesday morning, and we can get by with just that."

Dutch paused his whisking. "No couch?"

"Honey, everything needs to go in the pod. We can have the movers bring down our bed and set it up in here along with the TV from up there, which I think will fit just fine in your car."

"What about the bed?"

"I thought I'd rope Dave into helping us move it to the new house after the closing on Tuesday, seeing as he's feeling guilty at the moment for the damage done to the landscaping."

Dutch came out into the living room, wiping his hands on a towel. He surveyed the space and said, "Yeah, okay. Have 'em bring down the bed. But I'm not sure about moving it to the new house."

"Why not?"

"The mattress is lumpy. And frankly I never did like that bed frame."

Dutch's bedroom furniture was a bit dated, but we lived with it because I'd only brought a queen-sized bed along when we'd moved in together and merged furniture. He had the king. "Well, we can worry about that later," I said, moving to the door because I heard a large truck coming to a halt outside our house. "For now let's just worry about moving and getting hitched."

Dutch turned to go back into the kitchen. "And solving a case," he added.

I sighed. I'd forgotten about that. "Yeah. That too."

Much of the rest of my exhaustive day was spent overseeing the movers as they carefully loaded almost all of our belongings into the two pods, which were then loaded onto a truck and carted off somewhere to be stored until Tuesday. Dutch took the pups to the pet spa/boarding kennel, where they wouldn't get underfoot, and he and I agreed to keep them there until after we'd moved in. They'd of course have to go back to the spa only three days later right before the wedding (I'd put my foot down about not including them in the ceremony—no way was I going to risk having them attacked by swans), and I hoped that Eggy and Tuttle weren't going to be sad about spending so much time away from us.

Dutch worked from home for only part of the morning, and then he got called into the office. Gaston was back from Washington and wanted a briefing. I jotted a few notes of my impressions for Dutch to give to Gaston and figured he'd be back soon, as we hadn't really gathered much in the way of leads.

While the movers took a lunch break, I called Candice. "Just thinking of you," she sang by way of hello. "Wondering if I should buy those expensive Christian Louboutin pumps we saw at Neiman Marcus for the wedding."

I rolled my eyes. "The wedding was never off," I told her. "It was just a big misunderstanding."

"Mmmhmmm," she said in that way that made me think she didn't believe me one hundred percent.

"It was," I insisted. "I just don't want to be Mrs. Dutch Rivers, you know?"

There was a pause, then, "Maybe I should wait until Friday morning to head to the mall."

I sighed. Why was it so hard for everyone to understand me lately? "The *name*, Candice. I'm not sure I want to use the name. I've been Ms. Abby Cooper for so long that Mrs. Rivers sounds like I'd be playing an impostor. Plus, Dutch's mom is Mrs. Rivers, and I can't compete with that."

"Oh, I get it," Candice assured me. "And if you had explained it to him like that, I wouldn't be cleaning up after the two drunkards who made a mess of my living room last night."

"Dutch bolted before I had the chance to explain."

"But you've talked to him about it and he understands now, right?"

I hesitated. "Sort of."

"You didn't tell him what you meant, did you?"

"I can save that argument for later."

"So . . . I probably shouldn't put away the spare pillow and blanket, huh?"

"You're not helping." I'm not so charming when I haven't slept.

Candice laughed lightly. "Okay, okay, Abs. I'll lay off. What's going on besides all that?"

"Dutch is headed to the office to brief Gaston on our progress. I'm surprised you didn't get a call to go in."

"I gave my notes to Brice. He left a half hour ago."

"Yeah, I gave Dutch my notes too. They were pretty short. Dutch told me you were working on Mimi Greene's background. Did you get anywhere?"

Candice sighed. "The girl was a ghost," she said. "Just like her sister. I couldn't find any social media accounts in her name and the best I could do was pull up some news articles about the fire she was killed in."

"Was it bad?"

"It was. She was killed in a gas explosion."

My brow shot up. "An *explosion*?"

Candice chuckled. "I thought you'd hit on that. Yeah, according to the article there was a suspected gas leak in her apartment that went off around eleven in the morning. Eleven eleven on the eleventh, to be exact."

"That's weird," I said, and felt the smallest ping to my radar.

"Right? Freaky coincidence."

I don't believe in coincidences, but I kept that to myself. "Was anyone else killed?" I asked.

"No, thank God. The apartments around her were mostly empty at the time with all the tenants having left for work. Mimi was the only fatality. Still, I want to talk to the arson investigator, because it's a bit too close for comfort, don't you think? Both daughters dying in explosions."

"Totally. Keep me posted on that, would you?"

"Of course." And with a hint of humor in her voice she added, "And you keep me posted about buying those Louboutins."

I rolled my eyes. I was surrounded by comedians. "Go ahead and get them, Cassidy."

"Yeah?"

It was my turn to chuckle. "Yeah. If I turn into a runaway bride, you can always return them, you know."

We both laughed, but deep down something about what I'd just said greatly troubled me—as if I'd hit on something that contained a grain of truth.

"Girl, if I break down and buy a six-hundred-dollar pair of shoes, I'm keeping 'em, so you'd better get married, or I'll come find you and drag you back to the altar, you hear?"

I laughed again, but that sinking foreboding remained.

# T-Minus 00:34:15

"We can find her, Dutch," Candice said for probably the tenth time since they'd decided to head to Margo's. M.J. thought she was trying to reassure herself as much as she was trying to reassure Abby's fiancé. "We'll get to her in time. We will."

M.J. couldn't help but check the clock on the dash of Dutch's car every ten seconds or so. As fast as they were darting in and out of traffic, they weren't going nearly fast enough, she thought. At last Brody shouted, "There!" and M.J. saw that he was pointing to a storefront for a beauty supply store. Dutch stomped on the brake and everyone in the car jolted forward. Gilley thunked his head on the back of Dutch's seat and he let out a small wail. "Owww!"

But Dutch didn't look back, because he was already out of the car and hurrying to the front of the store. Brody, M.J., and Candice scrambled after him and the four of them entered the space with heads pivoting back and forth, looking for anyone who might work there.

"Can I help you?" a woman with straw-colored hair and makeup that made her look like a cheap prostitute asked.

"Are you Margo?" M.J. asked. The woman shook her head. "We need to see Margo," she told the woman, who only stared at her blankly. *"Right now!"* M.J. yelled. The tension was starting to get to her too.

The woman jumped at the outburst but she didn't immediately offer up any more information. Candice then moved to the register and grabbed hold of the woman's shoulders. *"Where is Margo?"*

The woman let out a terrified squeak, but no words came out of her mouth, and M.J. knew she'd be useless for at least another minute or two. So she focused all her intuitive powers on finding Margo within the confines of the walls, but try as she might, nothing came back to her, and she knew that the five people gathered at the front of the small store were the only ones there. "She's not here," M.J. said just as the clerk was trying to form words. "Where is she?"

"She's coming in late," the clerk blurted out at last. "What do you want with her?"

"Call her," Dutch said, his voice low and dangerous. "Now."

The woman's face had already drained of color and she was shaking so badly that M.J. feared she might crumple into a heap and be of no use to them. Stepping forward, she said, "Let her go, Candice. Let me try."

Candice looked ready to punch the woman, but she did let go of her and stepped back. "Ma'am," M.J. said in her most reasonable tone. "This is literally a matter of life and death. We need you to call your boss for us, okay? We think that Margo may be a witness to a kidnapping, and we need to speak with her right away."

The clerk's eyes were huge and M.J. heard her gulp audibly. "Are you the police?"

"Yes," said Dutch, his fists clenching and unclenching with impatience.

"Can I see your badge?" the woman said next. M.J. felt her chest tighten. She knew Dutch didn't have his badge on him.

"No," Dutch replied, his brow darkening to a dangerous degree. "Now make the goddamn—"

"Ma'am!" M.J. interrupted, regaining the clerk's attention. "Please! You have to believe us. This is a matter of life and death! Please call your boss for us, okay? We just want to talk with her over the phone. Then we'll be on our way. I promise."

Still, the clerk hesitated.

"Please!" M.J. begged.

At last the clerk's eyes shifted to the phone on the counter and she moved there warily. Lifting the receiver, she dialed a number and they all waited those tense few seconds to see if anyone would answer the ring. M.J. knew immediately that they weren't going to be successful, because the clerk held up the phone and said, "Voice mail."

Candice snatched the phone and practically shouted into it. "Margo! This is Candice Fusco! I'm with the FBI working on your friend Rita Watson's murder. It is *vitally* important that you contact us *immediately*! My number is . . ."

After leaving her number, Candice hung up and they all stood there for several seconds waiting for the phone to ring. M.J. truly didn't know what else to do, but then Dutch said to the clerk, "What's your name?"

"Ellen," she said, and under Dutch's commanding stare she added, "Rhodes. Ellen Rhodes."

"Ellen, do you know where Margo lives?"

The clerk's eyes got buggy again. "Uh . . . ," she said. "No. No, I don't." She was completely unconvincing.

Dutch's brow furrowed to the danger zone again and he took out of his pocket a pair of the handcuffs he'd pulled off the utility belt of the cop he'd tied up with a zip tie back at the house they'd just left. "We can't," Candice said sharply, moving to intercept him. "Dutch, we can't!"

Dutch's gaze drifted meaningfully to the round clock above the clerk's head. "What choice do we have, Candice? She'll die if we don't . . ." His words drifted off and M.J. knew in that moment that he would go to any length to get to Abby in time, even if it involved breaking every law on the books.

Nudging Candice to the side when she refused to move, Dutch reached out to grab Ellen and she squealed, jerking away to blurt out, "Margo lives two blocks down! The red house! I don't know the address, but she's in the red house on the right side at the corner next to the stop sign!"

Without a word Dutch pocketed the handcuffs, turned, and ran toward the exit. M.J. didn't waste time apologizing to the clerk; she, Brody, and Candice headed out the door after him.

# Chapter Ten

"Someone's at the door," Dutch mumbled in my ear early Sunday morning. He and I were curled up with each other in bed, which had been moved to the living room not far from the door. The TV was propped up on Dutch's suitcase and other than that, the house was essentially bare and freezing. A cold snap had hit during the night and our down comforter had been diligently packed by yours truly, leaving us only a thin summer blanket for warmth. Coming fully awake, I then heard three loud raps against our front door. "Mmmph," Dutch muttered, curling himself closer around me and shivering a little. "Who the hell is that at this hour?"

My teeth chattered against his neck. "Don't know. Don't care."

The doorbell rang.

"Who is it?" Dutch called, his voice rich with a huskiness that I found super sexy. (Maybe that's why I'm always a little more frisky in the mornings?)

"It's Candice," my BFF replied. "You guys still sleeping?"

"Yes!" we both yelled back.

"I have coffee!" she sang.

I lifted my head with interest. I was really cold and coffee could go a long way to warming up my bones. "Open the door, would you, cowboy?"

"She's your friend."

"Yes, and she's just brought *you* coffee."

"And bagels!" Candice said through the door.

Dutch lifted one lid and cocked an eyebrow. "You're closer," he said.

"Yes, but I have less on."

Dutch lifted the bedsheet and took a peek. "You're wearing a tank top and shorts. How exactly is that less?" Dutch was wearing his usual bedtime attire—pajama bottoms and sex appeal.

"Less material overall," I told him.

"Hey, guys? It's cold out here!"

"If I get up, I'm taking the blanket with me," Dutch said.

I put my arms out and tucked the blanket around me. "Don't you dare."

"Do you want coffee or not?" Candice called through the door.

"Can't you just dart out, flip the lock, and run back to bed?" I asked Dutch.

There was a clicking sound and the door swung open to reveal Candice, eyeing us with irritation as she tried to balance a set of keys, a tray full of coffee cups, and a bag from the bagel shop. *"Really?"* she growled, coming in and kicking the door closed behind her.

"Morning!" Dutch and I sang.

Candice sent us a sharp look and her bootheels echoed loudly across the floor on her way to the kitchen. "It's freezing in here," she said, dropping our much coveted coffee on the counter before heading to the thermostat in the hallway. I looked at Dutch and waved toward the kitchen. "Go get the coffee!"

"Why me?"

"You're closer!"

"She's *your* friend."

"Who has just brought *you* coffee!"

Candice stopped fiddling with the thermostat and came to stand in the doorway of the kitchen, hands on hips and looking at us with marked disapproval. "You two are pathetic— you know that?"

"We're cold," I said, shivering anew.

Candice frowned and looked around on the floor, tossing me my hoodie and Dutch his shirt. We both donned them quickly and thanked her, but neither of us moved to get out of bed. With a roll of her eyes Candice brought over our coffees. "Thank you, thank you, thank you!" I said, relishing the warmth of the coffee and the click of the furnace coming on.

Candice then went into the kitchen to retrieve one of the chairs there and came out to sit down with her own coffee and a really delicious-looking bagel. I wasn't about to ask her to bring me one (okay, so it did cross my mind, but then, I didn't think I should push it), and with a bit of a groan I got out of bed and hurried to the kitchen, bringing back the bag for Dutch and me to share.

"What brings you by, Candice?" Dutch asked casually.

"Abby asked me to get some dish on the explosion at Mary's."

Dutch ran a hand through his bedhead and blinked tiredly. "What explosion at whose?"

"Mimi, aka Mary Greene," Candice said.

I swallowed a bite of the bagel and said, "I'm assuming you found something good?"

"Well, I started looking into Mary's death. Guess how she really died."

I made a face. Sensing a trick of some kind, I flipped on my radar and tuned in. I sensed smoke and heat and something explosive. The same as we'd been told. "According to my radar, she died in an explosion caused by a gas leak."

"You're only half-right," Candice said. "There was a fire, and an explosion, but that's only the method. Mimi was the cause. She committed suicide."

I gasped. "Wait . . . what?"

Dutch sat forward. "The coroner's report indicated accidental death, Candice. I saw it for myself."

"Would that coroner be Dr. Nelson Eppley, who retired early six months ago due to illness?"

Dutch shrugged. "I don't know."

Candice pulled out a manila folder from her purse, and opened it to sort through the papers it contained. "I'm familiar with this particular coroner, Dutch, because I was approached about four months ago by a woman who swore that the coroner's report on her brother's death was incorrect. Eppley labeled it an accident, but she was convinced her brother committed suicide. She wanted me to dig into the coroner's record because she needed to know the truth. She suspected that her brother had gone to the extreme of taking his own life as a direct result of a drug he'd been prescribed to help him quit smoking, a drug now off the market due to its mood-altering properties in some patients, and if I could show her that her brother's death was the result of a depression brought on by this drug—a suicide—then she could move forward with a civil suit against the pharmaceutical company."

"What'd you find?" I asked.

Candice pulled out several more sheets of paper. "Dr. Nelson Eppley is a pretty troubled guy. His illness landed him a few weeks in a mental health facility, shortly after which he put in for early retirement. He now spends most of his days at a local community garden pulling up weeds and tending to the plants. I tried talking to him on a few occasions just to get the feel of the man, but he avoids casual conversation with strangers, and mostly I found him to be a painfully shy, very sad, and perhaps even paranoid man. For my client's sake, I did a little digging. I discovered that Eppley's eldest son committed suicide at the tender age of sixteen. Three years later, so did his wife. Thereafter, literally in the first week after his return to work after a short leave of absence following his wife's death, Eppley began labeling suspected suicides 'accidents.' Any case where there was no suicide note or witness, he'd write up as an accidental death. He labeled several hangings accidental autoerotic asphyxiation, several jumps from high places accidental falls, and then of course, my client's brother was tagged an accidental shooting probably while the victim was cleaning his gun, which completely contradicts the evidence left at the scene and written up in the police report."

"But why?" I asked. "Why would Eppley do that?"

Candice smiled sadly. "Who would know the devastating

aftermath of living with a loved one's suicide better than this man? I believe he was attempting to spare the families the anguish of dealing with the kind of terrible loss and unanswered questions he was all too familiar with."

"You're positive it's the same coroner?" Dutch asked.

"Yep."

"But how can you be sure Mimi's death wasn't an accident? How can you be sure she intended to cause the explosion?" I asked.

Candice produced one last piece of paper and handed it to Dutch. I leaned forward and saw that it was a report from the arson inspector. I skimmed it over Dutch's shoulder, my eyes widening as the facts of the investigation became clear. "All four burners on the gas stove were set to high?" I asked.

"Yep. Mimi plugged up the pilot lights, turned up the gas, filled the apartment with gas, lit a match, then . . ."

"Kaboom," Dutch said.

Candice nodded.

I sat back, stunned. "That's a pretty dramatic way to kill yourself."

"It is," Candice agreed.

I pointed to the report still in Dutch's hand. "Why didn't the arson investigator or the police fight the coroner's report? I mean, clearly Eppley got it wrong."

Candice shrugged. "Those guys have far bigger cases to worry about, Abs. Plus, unless the family or an insurance company is willing to make a stink about it, no one really cares that a death gets labeled an accident or a suicide."

"Are we certain that foul play from another source isn't suspected?" Dutch asked.

"You mean like maybe Mimi was murdered?"

Dutch nodded.

"We're certain. Page two of that report goes into detail about what was found at the scene. A large box of charred matches was discovered under the victim's body."

A chill went through me. "It can't be a coincidence that Mimi blew herself up and a year later her sister gets strapped to a bomb and also dies in an explosion. Someone wanted to mimic her death."

Candice lifted her coffee toward me. "My thoughts exactly."

My brain was spinning with possibilities. "Do you think her family knew?"

"That Mimi killed herself?"

I nodded.

"Yes. They definitely knew. The arson investigator told me over the phone yesterday that he had a long conversation with Mr. Greene when he called from overseas, and that Mrs. Greene—Mimi's mother—had requested a copy of his report. What happened to that copy I'm not sure of, but I'll bet that Taylor was aware that her sister killed herself."

My radar hummed. "The question we need to ask is, who else knew what the arson investigator's report said?"

Dutch frowned and wiggled the paper. "It's a public record, Abs. Anyone could have gotten a copy of it."

Candice said, "I also wondered who else might know if Mimi committed suicide, so I called her manager back at Jamba Juice late yesterday, and Debbie, the manager, had no idea that Mimi had taken her own life, but she did confess that she wasn't surprised that the girl had committed suicide. She reiterated that Mimi appeared very sad in the days before the fire. She also told me that the rest of the store employees knew only what was reported in the news, that Mimi had died in an accidental fire caused by a gas leak."

"Well, someone made a point of obtaining a copy of that report," I said. "And hated Taylor enough to torture her by rubbing Mimi's death in her face for two hours before killing her."

We all fell silent for a bit before Dutch said to Candice, "Have you shared all this with Brice?"

Candice grinned. "Of course. He's taking over the file now that you're on vacation. He told me and Abby to pick up the lead as soon as she's done packing up the place."

Dutch's eyes bulged. "He said what about me?"

I winced. Apparently Brice hadn't gotten around to explaining to Dutch that he was officially on vacation. "He granted your request," I said lightly. Dutch turned to stare hard at me and I gave him my biggest winning smile. He grumbled something that, prior to our agreement from the day before, would've cost me a few quarters to repeat. He then hopped out of bed to take his cell to the study. We heard the slam of a door and his raised voice about fifteen seconds later.

Shuffling out of bed myself, I grabbed a pair of jeans, my shoes, and my purse and motioned to Candice that we needed to skedaddle. I was just closing the door on her car when I heard Dutch yell for me from inside the house. "Go!" I told her, and she peeled out of the driveway like a good sidekick.

"How is it that your fiancé doesn't know he's on vacation?" Candice asked me.

"Because *your* fiancé is a big fat chicken." Candice cut me a look and I held up a hand in apology. "Dutch put in a vacation request for the honeymoon, but he got the dates wrong. Brice knew about the error, and granted him the time without bringing it to Dutch's attention as a way to get him off the case as a favor to me. You know how the bureau is about their paperwork—once it goes through, it's set in stone, so Dutch knows he's officially off the case, and I'm assuming he's officially pissed about it."

Candice frowned. "Brice," she muttered. "I love that man, but sometimes he works too hard to avoid conflict and it ends up biting him in the ass."

I agreed, but I couldn't exactly tell her that. We were both a bit too protective of our men. Then Candice said, "But wait. If Dutch is officially on vacation now, does that mean you two have to skip the honeymoon?"

"Naw. Brice is making sure Dutch has that time off too."

"Good. I'd hate to see you miss out on the tropics. Or Europe. Or wherever the hell you two are going on your honeymoon. Which reminds me, are you guys ever going to let me in on where that is?"

"I wish we knew."

Candice gave me a quizzical look. "Come again?"

We hadn't exactly been honest with Candice about who was paying for our honeymoon, which had in fact been arranged by a certain CIA agent who owed us both a ginormous favor. The fact that Agent Frost was withholding the location until the last minute was simply his way of saying,

"I may owe you this favor, but I'm still in control of when I give it to you and where you'll go."

I tried to recover my blunder with Candice quickly. "Dutch's family arranged our honeymoon as a wedding gift. We won't know where we're going until the wedding."

Candice's eyes narrowed. Her lie detector was almost as well honed as mine. "Ah. I see," she said flatly.

My phone rang and with a relieved sigh that I'd been saved by the bell, I answered it. "Hey, cowboy."

"How long did you know?"

"Brice told me on Thursday. I thought he was going to tell you then too."

"You're *not* working this case without me, Edgar."

I felt my temper flare. "Says who?"

"Abigail," Dutch growled. He only used my full name when he was seriously mad.

Candice grabbed the phone from my hand. "Hey, Dutch. Listen, the leads that Abby and I are gonna work this week are all softballs. We're simply going to talk to Mimi's friends and coworkers. We'll save all the heavy lifting for your squad."

I heard some squawking from the other end of the line, but Candice's expression never wavered beyond calm, cool, and determined. "I'll look after her," she promised. "Nothing's going to happen to her, okay? I swear. She won't leave my sight for a second, and you know I never leave home without my Glock."

I felt a sudden sinking feeling in the pit of my stomach. It was all I could do to ignore it.

Candice continued to reassure Dutch and at last she held the phone against her chest and turned to me. "Dutch wants to know if you'll come with him to the airport at three o'clock to pick up his mother and Aunt Viv."

The sinking feeling got worse. "Three o'clock?" I said. "Uh . . ."

Candice rolled her eyes and put the phone back to her ear. "Abby says she has a manicure/pedicure appointment at three. She says she'll need pretty hands and feet to get married. You know how she is."

Candice then listened for a minute before putting the phone back to her chest. "He wants to know if you can meet up with them after your manicure."

My eyes widened and my brain fought for a plausible excuse.

Candice got back on the phone. "She'd love to, just as soon as her nails are dry. She'll text you when she's ready."

I breathed out a sigh when Candice hung up. "So, what's the deal?" she asked after handing me back the phone.

"What deal?"

"You don't like Dutch's family?"

Dutch's mom and aunt were lovely women, but they tended to overwhelm me with questions about Dutch, his work, his health, and how well I was taking care of him. (Little did they know he tended to take care of me *way* more than I took care of him.)

I shook my head. "No, it's not that. It's just, well, Dutch's mom and his aunt Viv are like two separate forces of nature and when you bring them together, it's like trying to ride out a hurricane. It's impossible to have an opinion around them that they didn't grant you. Plus, when we went to visit his family over the Labor Day weekend, Dutch finally admitted to the whole family that he and I aren't interested in having kids."

"Don't tell me," Candice said, "that was met as a personal challenge by his mom and aunt to convert your thinking."

"You have no idea," I told her.

"Yeah, Brice and I are trying to brace ourselves for a similar conversation with his parents. I think it's going to be especially hard, as he's the only boy in the family."

"What is it with parents practically insisting their kids have kids?" I asked. "I mean, some people just aren't kid people."

Candice smiled. "I think that the urge to be a grandparent is pretty fierce."

"Yeah, but Dutch's mom is already a grandparent three times over. Two of his brothers already have kids."

Candice shrugged. "I think that if you're already a grandma, you can never have enough. I know my grandmother loved me, but I also know that it was hard on her to have only one grandchild to dote on when all her friends had at least a half dozen to spoil and brag about."

Candice's grandmother had been a wonderfully colorful woman of French origin who'd left Candice quite a bit of money and property when she passed on. And thinking of my own grandmother and her love for me and all my cousins also helped to put things into perspective. Still, Dutch and I were of the same mind on the subject of kids. We loved them, as long as they were someone else's. They just weren't for us.

A few minutes later we pulled into the parking lot of our office building and headed in. For most of the day Candice worked the phones trying to find anyone who might've known Mary Greene. She even contacted a few classmates from Mary's graduating high school class, but no one seemed to remember her, which was quite sad, I thought.

Meanwhile I went over the case notes until my vision began to blur. I wanted something to jump out at me—for a lead to shout out from the pages and say, "Follow me!"—but all I kept getting was the intuitive feeling that I needed to dig deeper into Mimi's past. We were doing that, but nothing new was coming to light.

Around four Dutch began texting me—where was I? Was I ready to join him, his mom, and his aunt? Could I please come join him? Could I please come join him right now? Could I please come join him yesterday?

By five o'clock the texts were sounding a bit too desperate, so I finally had Candice drive me home so I could change, then joined my fiancé and his mother and aunt for dinner. The minute I arrived at the restaurant, I knew I should've faked an illness. "Abby, honey!" Dutch's mother called loudly across the restaurant as I stepped through the doors. "It's about time you got here! Come sit between me and Viv!"

Pushing a huge smile onto my lips, I obliged. But before I could sit down, Mrs. Rivers had stood up and was squishing me in a big hug. Dutch's mom is a formidable woman, three inches taller than me and with considerably more girth around the middle. "Oh, Abby!" she cried. "It's *so* good to see you! How are you getting on?" she asked, at last releasing me and allowing her gaze to drop to my cane.

"Much better, Dottie. Thank you for asking. I think I'll even be able to make it down the aisle without the cane."

"You poor brave thing!" Mrs. Rivers cried again, clutching me to her breast.

The minute she let me go so that I could sit down, his aunt started in. "So! When do we get to meet your parents, Abby?"

I felt the smile freeze onto my face and my gaze flickered to Dutch. He coughed loudly and said, "Aunt Viv, what looks good tonight? I hear they have a great porterhouse steak here."

"One minute, Roland. I'm asking Abby about her parents." Turning back to me, she repeated, "When will Claire and Sam Cooper be getting in?"

I took a sip of water. I was positive that Dutch had privately told both his mother and his aunt about my situation, so his aunt's question had caught me off guard.

I was raised in a terribly volatile household. My mother had serious mental issues and my father had been a high-functioning alcoholic for as long as I could remember. My earliest memory is of my mother beating me with a wooden spoon. I think I was three. My father had done little more than ignore me my whole life. It'd been an awful childhood. I'd left home at seventeen and I hadn't spoken a single word to my parents in several years now.

I'd also never shared much of what I'd gone through as a child with Dutch. It isn't that I didn't trust him enough to share that history with him; it's simply that I'd been conditioned my whole life to keep silent. It's part of that terrible shame that comes with being a child of abuse—you learn to shut up and bury all those haunting memories just to cope in a world that can't really fathom the idea of a mother throwing her four-year-old down a flight of stairs in a fit of anger. What made it perhaps even worse was that our family was upper middle class and everyone in our social circle pretended not to notice the bruises on the sad little girl who preferred hiding in closets to going outside to play.

Later, when I was out on my own and had the freedom to talk about it, I'd quickly learned how unreceptive the world was to my stories of abuse. Every person I'd ever told about my childhood had looked at me with incredulity at first, and then their eyes had brimmed with something even more hurtful than a physical blow. They'd stared back at me in doubt.

The awful part is that I can actually understand that reaction. To anyone raised by a loving mother, it's unfathomable and uncomfortable to believe that a woman could be so cruel to her own child. So I learned to make it easy on close friends and boyfriends who would inquire about my parents. I would simply say that we didn't talk much these days, or that we weren't a very close family.

Still, I was aware that Dutch knew the truth, because shortly after he and I had moved in together, my sister had come for a visit and while I was tied up with clients one Saturday afternoon, Cat had taken him out to lunch. They'd been gone until the early evening and when they got home, Dutch had come through the door looking stricken. He'd immediately taken me into his arms and hugged me tightly, and I could feel him struggle to hold it together. In alarm I'd looked at Cat and she'd simply said, "I told him, Abby. About Claire and Sam. All of it."

Dutch had never spoken a word about it, for which I was immensely grateful, but there were times when people would ask about my family—where they lived and such—and I'd see his jaw clench and his eyes darken. . . . The way they were now, right across from me at the dinner table.

Viv was also staring at me expectantly, but before I could answer her question, Dutch snapped, "Viv. Don't."

She looked at him sharply and for a moment there was some tension at the table until Mrs. Rivers put a gentle hand over Aunt Viv's and leaned over to say to me, "Dutch took us by the new house today. Such a beautiful home! And so many bedrooms to fill! You'll have guest rooms galore unless you two decide after you've been together for a year or two to fill it with the happy sounds of a little one."

My forced smile ratcheted up another notch, and I saw Dutch signal to the waiter. "We'd like a bottle of wine," he said. "As soon as you can, please."

\*     \*     \*

Later that night after we'd dropped his mom and Viv off at their hotel and made it through our own front door, Dutch apologized. "I told them both not to ask about your folks," he said.

"It's fine, sweetie."

"I can't believe she said that to you," he muttered irritably.

I turned to him after flicking on the light switch and put my arms around him. "It's enough that you get it, cowboy. I promise."

He squeezed me tight. "Are you really ready to marry into this family?"

My radar hummed. There was still something dark swirling in the ether, hovering so close I felt I could almost touch it. It came around every time Dutch mentioned the two of us getting married, and try as I might to shoo it away, it kept coming back. I felt a horrible foreboding, and something close to certainty that no matter how much I wanted it— Dutch and I weren't going to walk down the aisle together. His life still felt in danger, and that elusive threat was so close to him I felt I could taste it, but try as I might, I couldn't identify it. A tremor curled up my spine and I shivered.

"Abs?" Dutch asked, and I realized he had stepped away from me and was holding me at arm's length with concern in his eyes.

I blinked. "What?"

"What?" he repeated. "Honey, I just asked you if you were ready to marry me."

I shook my head to clear it. "Oh! Yes. Of course I am."

Dutch stared at me for several seconds and I saw the concern fade to hurt. "You sure?" His eyes were pinned to mine, forcing me to look at him.

I didn't look away. "I am."

"Then what's up?"

I bit my lip. "I don't know. It just feels like . . ."

"Like what?" I was quiet, letting my gaze drop to the floor while I tried to put what I was feeling into words, and Dutch reached up to lift my chin with his fingers. "Babe . . . please, talk to me."

I pushed myself back into his arms and as I did so, a horrible realization hit me. It was so terrible that my breath caught and I squeezed him tight and closed my eyes. "It's nothing!" I whispered a bit desperately.

Dutch sighed. "Dollface . . . this can't be nothing."

"Please, Dutch!" I couldn't talk about it. I couldn't even say another word because the thing in the ether that I'd just touched on, the thing that couldn't possibly be true, was that the threat to Dutch's life wasn't coming from an unknown source. It was coming from me.

The next morning I was out of the house well before sunrise. I had an almost mounting panic fueling me to put some distance between Dutch and me. I couldn't explain it, but intuitively I knew he was in danger and I was somehow the cause.

The only person who might understand was Candice, and I went searching for her. I found her in the basement gym of her condo building, working out with a set of kettlebells that looked like cannonballs while Brice ran on the treadmill. Seeing me, she immediately put down the kettlebell and grabbed her towel. "What's happened?"

I glanced at Brice. He was running at a really good clip with his iPod earbuds in his ears and he hadn't even noticed my entrance. "I need to talk to you," I told Candice.

"Tell me what's wrong," she said, taking my arm to lead me out of the area so we wouldn't be disturbed by the noisy sounds of the gym.

"Nothing has happened per se."

"Sundance," she said skeptically, "it's five forty-five on a Monday morning. You don't get out of bed at this hour for anything less than an act of God. *Something* must've happened."

"I have a bad feeling . . . ," I began.

Candice nodded, waiting me out.

"It's about me and Dutch."

"An argument?"

"No. Nothing like that. I can't put my finger on it, Candice, but I think I need to spend a little time away from him."

Candice's brow lifted. "Away from him? Don't you think

that's gonna be a little difficult with the wedding coming up this weekend?"

"Yes. Yes, I do. Which is why I need to stay with you. If that's okay?"

Candice stared at me for a full minute, and I could sense that she might be thinking the wrong thing about Dutch and me. "It's not what you think," I said. "I just don't know that I'm good for him to be around right now, and I have to figure out why."

"Of course you can stay with us," she said. "As long as you're okay with sleeping on the couch?"

"I am."

"What're you going to say to Dutch?"

I sighed. "I'm not sure yet. I might use the old 'groom shouldn't see the bride before the wedding' excuse."

"Your wedding's not for five days, honey. Don't you think that's a long time for Dutch to go without seeing you?"

"Well, I was also hoping that I could hang out with you today and tell Dutch that we're doing wedding stuff and working the case."

"Don't you have your final walk-through with Dave at the new house today?" Candice asked.

"Yeah, but Dutch can do that on his own."

"Won't he think that's weird?"

I rubbed my face tiredly. "I don't know, Candice. If he does, he does. He'll get over it."

"Hey, Cooper!" a male voice said behind me.

I jumped. "Good morning," I said, turning to him. I could feel my face flush. Seeing my boss all sweaty and in clingy workout gear tended to make me uncomfortable.

Brice mopped his face with a towel. "What brings you by so early?"

"Abby's going to be staying with us for a few days," Candice said quickly.

Brice's eyes widened and he looked from me to Candice, who in return narrowed her eyes at him as if saying, "Don't ask why or protest. . . ."

"That's great!" he said, nodding and pushing up the wattage of his smile.

We all stood around for a few seconds in an uncomfortable silence before Brice cleared his throat and said, "I better get upstairs for a shower. See you two later?"

Candice leaned forward and gave him a kiss. "We'll be up in a few. Don't take all the hot water, okay?"

He grinned at her and waved good-bye to me. Once he'd left, I said, "I'm really sorry. I know I'll be cramping your style, but I don't know what else to do."

Candice reached into the small wristband around her forearm and pulled up a key. "Here," she said. "Make yourself at home. I'm gonna finish my workout and I'll be up in half an hour."

I pushed the key back. No way did I want to be alone with Brice while he showered. What if he walked out naked thinking he was alone? "I'm gonna go up to the coffee shop and think about what I'm going to say to Dutch. Then I'll probably head to the office. Meet you there later?"

Candice's expression was both sympathetic and filled with concern. "I'll meet you at the café in forty-five minutes. We can figure this out together, okay?"

I felt my throat tighten with unbidden emotion. Candice was such a great friend. She always seemed to know what to say, and she'd always had my back whenever I'd needed her. It meant the world to me. "Thanks, Cassidy."

She reached out and squeezed my arm. "Hang in there, honey. It'll all turn out okay."

I was filled again with that same jolt of foreboding that'd been haunting me for days, and I knew, deep down, that it wouldn't be okay, but no way was I going to say that out loud. "Sure," I said anyway, my voice hollow and flat to my own ears. "Of course it will. See you soon."

With that, I turned away before the tears took over and Candice saw the tidal wave of fear in my eyes.

# T-Minus 00:28:15

Gilley's misty eyes were filled with fear as he sat frozen next to M.J. while Dutch's car raced down the street. M.J. reached out to squeeze his hand because she knew that he wasn't so good in situations like this, but then, who was?

Dutch gunned the motor all the way down the street, then screeched to a halt in front of the red house on the corner. Shoving the car hard into park, he bolted out and toward the front door with Candice hot on his heels.

M.J. told Gilley to stay put before pushing her way out of the car too. She and Brody ran side by side to the door just as it was opened by a red-haired woman with pale skin and ice-blue eyes. "I'm on the phone with the police!" she yelled the minute the door was opened. M.J. could see her house phone at her ear. Ellen, the store clerk, had obviously called to warn her that trouble was on the way.

"I am the police," Dutch barked, snatching the phone and throwing it across the lawn. When the woman—who was obviously Margo—took a step back and attempted to shut the door, Dutch jammed his foot in the doorway and shoved it open.

"Mrs. Dudek!" Brody called from behind M.J. "It's me! Brody Watson! Rita's son."

Margo's gaze darted to Brody and when she saw him, she

stopped struggling with the door and leaned forward. "Brody?" she gasped. "Honey, is that you?"

"Yes, ma'am," Brody said.

"Oh, sweetie," Margo said, her eyes filling with tears. "I've been crying and crying about your mom."

"That's why we're here," Brody said, and Margo seemed to once again become aware of the four people on her doorstep.

"What's going on?" she said, recovering herself and quickly turning defensive.

"Mrs. Dudek," M.J. said, stepping forward with her palms raised to show her they meant no harm. "Please, can we speak with you? It's literally a matter of life and death."

"Who're you?" Margo demanded, taking another step back as if she thought she might be in danger again.

"My name is M. J. Holliday, and I'm a psychic medium. As you know, your friend Rita was murdered by someone wanting to cause many people harm, and we"—M.J. pointed to everyone on the front lawn—"believe that one of our friends has been taken hostage by this same person and she's in imminent danger."

Margo's lids blinked rapidly. M.J. knew that was a lot to take in, so to cut to the chase she reached out to Rita for some proof. "Rita's spirit sent us to you," she said calmly, her hands still raised.

"Her spirit?" Margo repeated. "What the hell are you talking about?"

"Mrs. Dudek," Brody said. "Please? Just listen, okay?"

Margo frowned, but she nodded too, so M.J. continued. "To prove to you that Rita's spirit really did send us, she's asking me to mention the leopard print."

Margo's expression became incredulous. "The *what*?"

"I think she's referring to a specific conversation you two had not too long ago. She's telling me you two were here, having coffee. You have a room in the back of this house with a bay window that looks out onto a water feature, right?"

Margo's jaw fell open. "My kitchen nook has a bay window and it looks out onto a small fountain."

M.J. nodded. "Rita says that she came here to have coffee

and to seek your advice about something. She says you told her to wear the leopard print, and she says your advice worked."

"Oh . . . my . . . God . . . ," Margo gasped, shaking her head at the same time. And then her eyes flickered to Brody. "That's not something she ever would've shared with you, Brody, but this one time your mom was really interested in the UPS delivery guy, and she wanted him to ask her out, so I told her to wear something sexy, like a leopard print bra, and when he came into her shop, she needed to just lean forward and show him the goods. He'd ask her out for sure."

"You mean Gary?" Brody asked. "The guy she dated last year who worked for UPS?"

Margo nodded. "I'd forgotten all about that," she said. Suddenly her face flushed red and she began to sweat. Her breathing quickened too, and it became clear that she was having a hard time dealing with the sudden realization that her dear friend was talking to her from the beyond.

"M.J.," Dutch said low, his fists clenched with impatience.

"We need your help, Margo," M.J. said urgently. "Rita needs to ask you about a man who came into her salon. Someone who confronted her, thinking she was you."

Margo's eyes fluttered with confusion. Her face became even more flushed and she was panting hard and waving a hand in front of her face. M.J. was worried that Margo was starting to hyperventilate. Behind them she could also hear the sound of sirens, and she knew the police were on their way to the house. "Margo!" M.J. said sharply, hoping to snap her out of the panic attack she was clearly in the throes of. "I need you to focus! Rita told you about a man who came to the salon looking for you. A man she might've gotten into an argument with."

The sirens grew closer, and out of the corner of her eye M.J. saw Dutch glance nervously down the street. "We need to go . . . ," he whispered.

"I don't know what she means," Margo said, still fanning away at her face.

Brody pushed his way to M.J.'s side. "Mrs. Dudek, I remember my mom called you on the phone about that guy who came to the salon right after she bought it from you. He scared her. Remember?"

The sirens drew closer still, and M.J. sensed there were a lot of them. What was worse, they also seemed to be closing in on them from opposite directions. "A guy who scared her?" Margo repeated, her flushed face starting to drain of color and the sweat on her brow beginning to drip down her face, and all the while her labored breathing got heavier and heavier.

The sirens were closer still and Dutch put a hand on M.J.'s elbow. "We'll have to bring her," he whispered.

Next to her Candice was typing furiously on her phone, and M.J. knew that their situation was getting desperate, because Margo didn't look like she would come either quickly or quietly. "Margo," M.J. tried, one last time. "Rita is insisting that you know this man. She says you can tell us his name. Please! We've *got* to have his name!"

Margo wobbled on her feet, and several arms reached out to steady her, but it was too late. The woman was hyperventilating and with two more panicked breaths her eyes rolled up and she swooned. Dutch caught her, and as she was a big woman, he struggled to keep her upright. "Dammit!" he swore. The sirens sounded like they were only a few streets away now.

"Get her to the car!" Candice urged, trying to pick up Margo's feet, but the woman's body was limp and heavy, and the two of them couldn't even manage to get her out of the doorway and down the two steps by the time six patrol cars screamed to a stop in front of the house. Within seconds they were surrounded by uniformed police, guns drawn and demands for them all to get down on the ground.

M.J. felt a jolt of terror at all those guns pointed at her, and her eyes locked on Gilley, hunched down in the car and looking like a frightened puppy. He tended to panic first, follow instructions second.

"I'm a Fed!" Dutch shouted, as calls from the cops for them to get on the ground continued to echo around them.

"Get down on the ground now!" an officer with a face like a bulldog shouted.

Dutch was still holding on to Margo, while everyone else was slowly following the cops' instructions. "Dutch, set her down!" Candice told him.

"I'M A FED!" Dutch shouted, still refusing to let go of Margo and defiantly ignoring the cops slowly closing in on him.

"Set her down and get on the ground!" another cop shouted.

"Dutch!" Candice pleaded.

M.J. was on her knees, her hands behind her head while her heart thumped hard in her chest. She was staring at Dutch, willing him to cooperate, when she saw Margo's eyelids flutter and her lips move. M.J. was close enough to hear her mutter something—it sounded like a name.

"GET DOWN!" the bulldog-faced cop shouted so loud they all winced.

At last Dutch carefully set Margo down right next to M.J., and as he stepped back and began to raise his arms, the cop behind him fired and Dutch's body seized before collapsing to the ground in a heap.

A moment later a swarm of police moved in to completely encircle them.

# Chapter Eleven

"Abby?" the coffee shop barista called loudly.

At the sound of my name I pushed my way through the swarm of people waiting for their drinks in the busy café, happy to get my coffee and get out of the crowd of bodies. I took my coffee gratefully, then edged through the throng again to a table in the corner with my coat over the chair. I'd gotten lucky—the table was next to the heat vents.

It was still chilly from the cold front that'd moved in the day before, but once I was tucked into the corner of the café, it was really quite pleasant. As I sat waiting for Candice, I tried to think of a way to tell Dutch that I was going to stay at Candice's overnight. I thought I knew what to say so he wouldn't be hurt or suspicious, but the next few days might prove trickier. At some point he was gonna figure out that I was avoiding him.

And the following few days were bound to come with questions about my evasiveness. We had our closing, the move, the rehearsal dinner, and I was positive Cat would want at least one final meeting with the two of us. (My voice mail was full of such requests, in fact.) But the danger I sensed swirling around Dutch whenever I was close made it clear to me that I couldn't be near him, and I didn't know how to explain it in a way that he wouldn't worry, and wouldn't try to talk me out of staying away. He was stubborn enough to come find me and stick close, simply to protect me.

I took a sip of the coffee and stared out at the dark streets. It was just a little after six a.m. Dutch wouldn't be up for another half hour or so. I'd slipped out while he was sawing some pretty good logs. Even though I'd only been gone an hour, I already missed him.

With a frown I pulled out my phone and sent him a text.

> Morning! Couldn't sleep so I'm hanging out with Candice. Working on the case with her. And before you ask, she's sticking to me like glue, so not to worry.

> May run late, so can you do the final walk-through with Dave?

> Love you!

To my surprise, Dutch texted me right back.

> You okay, dollface?

Did the man know me, or what?

I assured him I was fine, just nervous about the wedding and was trying to take my mind off things by focusing on something else. I think he bought it, because he replied with a simple

> I've got the final walk-through covered.
> Love you.

And that was the end of it.

"This seat taken?" Candice asked.

I jumped. "Sorry. I didn't see you come in or I would've ordered your coffee."

Candice waved to the group of customers at the collection counter. "I just ordered. It'll be up in a bit."

Sitting down, Candice folded her hands on the tabletop and looked me in the eye. "Tell me."

I sighed and shook my head. "I wish I could articulate it. . . ."

"Try."

"You know I've had this really bad feeling about Dutch being in danger, right?"

"I do."

"And you also know that I've been unable to figure out where it's coming from, other than that it's connected to the bombing case."

"Yes."

"Well, last night I was able to pinpoint the source of the danger."

Candice's brow furrowed and she eyed me closely. "Where's the source?"

My eyes misted and I felt my lower lip quiver. I pointed to myself. "Right here."

Candice studied me for about ten seconds before she sat back and blew out a breath. "What does that even mean, Abby?"

"I have no idea. But I'm a danger to Dutch, and until I figure out why, I can't be around him."

The barista called Candice's name, but she didn't turn away or get up to retrieve her coffee. Instead she continued to study me intently and at last she said, "Then I think we need to solve this case fast, 'cause it's going to be a challenge to marry the two of you off if you're hiding under the bed at my place and he's waiting at the altar."

I grinned in spite of myself. "Get your coffee, smart-ass."

Candice and I spent the next few minutes talking through a game plan. We both agreed that we would be most effective if we stuck together and worked the case away from the bureau boys. Once we'd finalized our plans, we headed to our shared offices and got to work. Candice moved the furniture in her suite to the side and we began to lay out the case on the floor with index cards and photos of all the players. We started with Mary's suicide, moved to Taylor's bombing, and piece by piece we put together a theory. "The sisters are the key," I said. "We find out what the bomber's motive really is, and we'll solve this case."

"Well, in simple terms, the killer wanted to mentally torture and then murder Taylor."

"Yes, but the why is the essence of this whole thing, Candice. It matters *why* he wanted to mentally torture and murder her."

"We heard from Amber that Taylor wasn't well liked around campus. Maybe she ticked somebody off enough for him to want her to suffer and die."

I thought about that for a bit. I didn't know if I agreed or disagreed with that theory, and my intuition wasn't definitive about giving me a yea or nay on it. I decided to try to throw a wrench into Candice's thinking by saying, "Then why follow it with a second bombing in Austin? College Station is a hike from here. Why take the risk and make the effort unless there's something else here we're overlooking?"

Candice frowned. "Good point. But you know the other thing that bothers me is, why call Jed Banes?"

"Our killer wants to get caught," I theorized. "So he called a cop."

"Yeah, but he didn't call a cop," Candice countered. "He called a retired and somewhat disgraced former cop."

"You're thinking the killer intentionally picked Banes, knowing his history?"

"Or," Candice said, "maybe he knew Banes in another way. Maybe he wants Banes to suffer a little too. Maybe he's playing with Banes and getting a little revenge to boot."

"You think it was someone Banes arrested?"

"Or double-crossed," Candice said. "Banes was a crooked cop. Maybe that crookedness extended to his criminal associates."

My brow rose. "That's a possibility, but I have two issues

with that theory: The first is that Banes doesn't seem to care so much that young women are being targeted and forced to carry out mass murders—in fact, that old geezer doesn't seem to care about much at all—and second, how does Banes connect back to Taylor and Michelle? I mean, neither of them has a criminal record—and it's not likely that either would've ever met Banes, so what's the connection?"

"Our killer," Candice said simply. "He's playing some sort of cat-and-mouse game, and using Banes is part of that game. What I'm saying is that Banes may not be connected to the girls at all, but he's being used as a convenience and maybe to settle a different score."

"Two birds, one stone," I said.

"Yep."

I tapped my lip with my forefinger. "Okay, so we think that the killer had some sort of personal connection to Taylor—someone who knew her well enough to know that her sister blew herself up—but that still leaves the biggest question of all, which is, why choose a different city and a beauty salon of all places as your second target? I mean, why is he still carrying this out? He got his revenge on Taylor— she's dead—so why keep going?"

"Maybe he's a sick fecker and he enjoyed it a little too much the first go-around," Candice said with a sigh.

My radar didn't agree with that theory, though. "No," I said. "It's more complicated than that. He's got an agenda here. He's not just having some sick twisted fun; he's trying to tell us something. It's a puzzle with pieces that need to be put together in order to see his overall message."

"Message?" she repeated. "What message other than that he hates women?"

I looked at Candice. "Why do you say that?"

"Well, look at who he straps to a bomb. Look at where he sends them—to a dress shop and a beauty shop. He's specifically targeting women, Abs."

I couldn't help feeling that I was missing something super obvious, and try as I might to make the theory of the angry misogynist work, my radar wasn't buying it. "Yeah, but if he just wanted to kill a bunch of women, there are so many better targets than a shop at a mall. I mean, you saw how close Janice McCaffrey and her son came to getting killed—and what about the old couple who were also murdered? You saw the footage that Oscar pulled up. The unsub waited until the older couple was close to Taylor to detonate the bomb. So, does this guy also hate children and old people?"

Candice sighed again. "I don't know, Abby," she said. "But I think you're right that there's a bigger message here."

For a minute we were both silent, looking at the index cards and photos of the victims on the floor. My eye kept going back to Michelle Padilla. I felt a huge question mark form in my head. Why her? "I don't think Michelle was random," I said when Candice started shuffling the index cards in frustration.

"Hmm?"

"Michelle Padilla. I don't think she was picked randomly. The killer had to have had access to her house at some point, right? We know that from the sliding glass door, so he knew her. Maybe the two were even intimate at some point."

Candice bent to sift through several files crammed into a Bankers Box on the floor. "According to both Michelle's mother and her roommate, Michelle wasn't seeing anyone at the time of the explosion at the salon, and she hadn't been seeing anyone in the past couple of months. Plus, her last boyfriend is currently in Europe as an exchange student. He's been out of the country for the past nine weeks, Abs."

"Yeah, but what if Michelle was secretly seeing someone else, and she just didn't tell anybody about it?"

Candice held up the file and flipped her thumb against several dozen pages. "This is a printout of Michelle's e-mails and texts. There's no exchange between her and anyone who might be considered a romantic interest."

"There's a connection, Candice," I said, bending down to pick up Taylor's photo and Michelle's . . . but then, my intuition sparked and I set down Taylor's photo and picked up Mimi's. With a small gasp I said, "Or maybe . . . the connection isn't between Taylor and Michelle. Maybe the connection is between Michelle and Mimi. . . ."

Looking up, I saw the surprise on Candice's face. "Michelle . . . Mimi . . . two similar-sounding names."

I nodded, a small surge of excitement running through me. "Candice, maybe this isn't about Taylor at all. Maybe this is actually about Mimi."

Candice came over to lift the driver's license photo of Mimi out of my hands. "You think someone drove her to suicide?"

"Possibly. But more important, I think there's a connection between Mimi and Michelle—and I think it's more than just that their names sounded a little alike."

"We should go have another talk with Mrs. Padilla," Candice said. "And this time we'll bring Mimi's photo along."

"Good idea. Maybe we should also find Mimi's manager at Jamba Juice and talk to her again. Hopefully, either she or one of the store employees will recognize Michelle. Also, I want to go back to our friend Jed Banes and pick his brain a little. I think he knows something that'll help us link all of this together."

Candice smirked. "Anything else you want to fit into that packed schedule for today, Sundance?"

I grinned back at her. "At some point I'm going to have to call my sister and fend off a final prewedding meeting. I won't be successful, and she'll rein me into her office and cover me in swarming butterflies, swan feathers, and taffeta. I'm not gonna go in alone, and I can't go with Dutch."

"You want *me* to go with you?" Candice asked (like I'd just asked her to come with me into the center ring of lions, tigers, and bears).

"Please?" I begged her. Candice began to shake her head. *"Pleeeeeeeeeease?"*

Candice glared hard at me before picking up her purse and the photos we'd need for our interviews. "You. So. Owe me."

"Yes, yes, I'll buy the margaritas!" I told her with a grateful smile.

"Oh, you owe me way more than that," she groused.

I gulped. Candice would expect a favor of some kind, and it was likely to be a big one. "What were you thinking?"

"Get me out of that purple people-eater your sister is hell-bent on making me wear at your wedding."

Candice's bridesmaid's dress was a bit of a disaster . . . in the way one might consider Katrina a "bit" of a disaster. The dress was a purple velvet number with a heart-shaped bodice, big poufy sleeves, and a short, clingy skirt. The whole thing managed to transform my elegant and sophisticated best friend into a girl who could possibly be rented by the hour.

The odd thing was that Cat normally had excellent taste—and I wondered if the wedding had just become such a spectacle that it'd all gotten away from her a little. (Or a lot.) I also thought that since the dress came with a designer label, Cat hadn't bothered to really look at it. It was more likely that the garment was the right color, which had trumped fit and style.

"I promise, you will not have to wear that god-awful dress," I vowed, crazy relieved that I actually already had a solution. "In fact, wait here a sec, would you?"

I moved into my own small suite and retrieved a garment bag from the closet. Bringing it back to Candice, I handed it to her with a triumphant smile. "I was gonna save this for the margarita and nacho night we were planning as my bachelorette party, but right now might be better."

Candice took the bag warily. Still she unzipped it and pulled out the dress I really wanted her to wear, an aubergine-colored chiffon gown, with thin shoulder straps, a deep V-neck, and a loosely belted waist. It was elegant and feminine and I knew it would show off Candice's well-toned arms and beautiful skin. "Oh, Abs," Candice whispered, pulling it all the way out of the bag to hold it up high and get a better look. "It's *gorgeous*!"

My grin was ear to ear. "I hadn't planned on telling Cat," I confessed. "I figured you'd just show up in it on Saturday and we'd lose the other one in a tragic Dumpster accident," I added with a wink.

Candice's eyes filled with tears and she hugged the dress to her and looked at me with gratitude and a bit of mischief.

"It's perfect, and I thank you. But the margaritas are still on you!"

About an hour later we arrived at Colleen Padilla's home. Candice had called Michelle's mother from the car to ask for an early-morning meeting. She agreed and we arrived at just before eight thirty.

Colleen met us at the door, dressed in black and looking incredibly sad. My heart went out to her. Once inside the stately home she led us to the dining room, which was set up as if to receive company, and I realized that we might have come at the most inappropriate of times. "The funeral is to-day," she said, gazing at the table laden with flowers, plates, Sterno warmers, and silver flatware. "We're having the wake here."

"I'm so sorry that we've come at such a bad time," I apologized.

"No, no," Mrs. Padilla said. "It's fine. Are you closer to finding out who did this to my daughter?"

I had to give the woman credit; no way would she ever believe that Michelle had purposely killed herself and four others. "We're narrowing in on some leads," I said. "The reason we wanted to see you, ma'am, is that we know you said that—to your knowledge—Michelle had never met Taylor Greene, but I'm wondering if perhaps Michelle had ever met this girl?"

Next to me Candice pulled out a photo of Mimi and handed it to Mrs. Padilla.

"Oh!" she said right away. "That's Mimi!"

I sucked in a breath. I'd hoped that Mrs. Padilla might recognize the photo, but I'd never thought she'd identify Mimi so quickly. "Yes," I said, recovering myself. "How did you know her?"

Mrs. Padilla blushed a little and she continued to stare at Mimi's photo. "Michelle felt so terrible about what happened to Mimi," she said. "Her suicide hit my daughter very hard and it haunted her for months."

My radar buzzed with energy while Candice said, "You're telling us your daughter *knew* Mary Greene?"

"Mimi Greene," Mrs. Padilla corrected. "And, yes, I'm afraid Michelle knew her quite well."

"They were friends?" I asked.

Mrs. Padilla handed the photo back to Candice. "No. Michelle counseled her for a time when she was interning at ACC's health clinic."

"Austin Community College?" Candice clarified.

"Yes. Michelle interned there for six months before continuing her studies at UT. She wasn't supposed to counsel students who were deeply troubled, but the psychiatrist in charge was the one who matched Michelle with students who came to the clinic for mental health support, and before she realized it, Michelle was in way over her head. The clinic was swamped, you see, and she was only one of two interns."

"How did Michelle know that Mimi's death was a suicide?" I asked.

Mrs. Padilla tugged at the pearls around her neck. "The arson investigator came to the house shortly after we saw in the paper that Mimi had died in a fire. He asked a lot of questions about Mimi's mental state, and Michelle admitted that Mimi was a very troubled young girl. She'd even asked Dr. Wiseman to sit in on the session she'd scheduled with Mimi on the day she died. Mimi never showed up for the session. She killed herself earlier that morning. It was so tragic. My daughter was crushed and she felt responsible. She even considered giving up counseling because of it."

"It wasn't her fault," I said, knowing it to be true. Mimi Greene was certainly a victim of circumstance—seeking help at a facility unprepared for the burden of so many troubled and stressed-out students—but Michelle was hardly to blame for that.

"I agree," Mrs. Padilla said. "Which is what I was eventually able to convince her of." And then she seemed to realize that we wouldn't be inquiring about Mimi if there wasn't some connection between her and the case involving Michelle. "Why are you asking me about Mimi?" she asked us.

"Just following a lead, Mrs. Padilla," Candice said evasively, before deftly changing the subject. "Do you know if

Michelle told anyone else about Mimi? That the fire hadn't been an accident but a suicide?"

"Oh, no," Mrs. Padilla said, as if she was shocked by the idea of her daughter spreading such gossip. "Michelle was very ethical. She would never talk about a patient's personal issues. Not even to me. And the only reason I knew about Mimi in the first place was that I was here when the fire marshal came to get Michelle's statement."

My radar buzzed again and I asked, "Did Michelle share with the fire marshal the reason Mimi came looking for counseling in the first place?"

Mrs. Padilla sighed tiredly and scratched her forehead. "I believe it was boy trouble. The same as most girls that age."

I leaned forward, remembering the box of photos from Taylor Greene's apartment and the one picture in particular marked with all that black felt-tip pen graffiti. "Boy trouble?" I asked Mrs. Padilla. "Michelle said that Mimi had a boyfriend?"

Mrs. Padilla nodded. "Yes, but I think they broke up. I seem to recall that Mimi's sister got in the middle of things and it led to a breakup, which sent poor Mimi into a downward spiral."

The hair rose on the back of my neck. "Do you recall this boyfriend's name?" I asked.

Mrs. Padilla frowned. "No. I'm not sure it was even mentioned. But I do remember Michelle commenting that the man Mimi was seeing was quite a few years older than her, and she wondered if that hadn't also been an issue or a factor in the breakup."

"Is there *anything* about him specifically that you can remember?" I pressed. "Like where Mimi might have met him, or even where he worked?"

Again Mrs. Padilla scratched lightly at her forehead. "He owned his own business," she said. "I knew that because Michelle said that Mimi had convinced herself that she would never find anyone better than this older man, who to her was so worldly and accomplished for owning his own company."

"Is there anything else you can tell us from that meeting, or afterward, that might be important?" Candice asked.

Mrs. Padilla closed her eyes, taking in a deep breath; she let it out slowly and said, "No, ladies. I believe that is the entire gist of that meeting. The fire marshal was very nice, and sympathetic to how upsetting the news of Mimi's suicide was to my daughter. But that's really it."

We thanked Mrs. Padilla for her time and headed back to the car. "Holy freakballs!" I said the moment the door was closed. We *finally* had a direct link between the girls.

"And now we can prove that this was no act of terrorism," Candice said, already dialing her phone. Holding it up to her ear, she waited several seconds before saying, "Hey, baby, it's me. Call me back right away, okay? Love you."

"Brice?" I asked once she hung up.

Candice nodded and eyed the clock on the dash. "He might be in a meeting. Our choices are to head to the bureau or to keep following this thread and see what we come up with."

"Let's keep going," I said. "What time does Jamba Juice open?"

Candice put the car into gear and pulled away from the curb. "They should be open now—hey, buckle your seat belt, would you?"

I realized that I'd been so excited by our discovery that Michelle and Mimi knew each other that I'd forgotten basic safety precautions.

"Sorry."

"And by the way," Candice added, zipping down the street at a steady clip, "where's Fast Freddy?"

I looked to my right in the car well where my feet rested and where I always stored my cane, but it wasn't there. "Ohmigod! I've been walking around without my cane!"

Candice grinned. "I noticed it when we left the office, but I was wondering how long it'd take you to realize it."

But I wasn't so happy. "We have to go to the office and get it!" I insisted, feeling no confidence about my ability to get along without it.

Candice laughed. "Girl, you've been managing just fine without it for the past half hour. Why would you think you still need it?"

"I just do!"

"The office is on the opposite side of town from Jamba Juice. You really want to waste an hour?"

"Yes."

Candice rolled her eyes. "Fine. But at some point you're gonna have to realize that you don't need it anymore."

"I can realize it on Saturday. Between now and then I get to hang on to Fast Freddy."

# T-Minus 00:25:48

M.J. had been holding on to the desperate hope that they could get to Abby in time to rescue her from the bomb right up until the cop with the bulldog face had shot Dutch in the back with a Taser gun.

Once he fell to the ground and M.J. heard the thump from his head striking the pavement, she knew Abby's chances were nil.

And the scene only got worse as Dutch's rigid body seized and jerked beside a dazed Margo. Candice jumped to her feet and rushed to his side, while Brody knelt on his knees and screamed at the cop who'd just shot Dutch.

*"Get down on the ground!"* the cops kept shouting at all of them, but most of their attention remained on Candice and Brody.

"Candice! Brody!" M.J. cried, fearing at any moment the cops might shoot them too. "Please! Just get down!"

For several tense seconds it looked as if things might escalate even further, but finally Brody bent forward and lay down on his stomach with his hands behind his head, and then Candice followed suit. M.J. felt sick as she lay on the wet grass and looked again at Dutch's twitching body. His eyes were closed and she knew the fall had knocked him out. M.J. felt a burst of anger toward the cop who'd Tased him when he'd been cooperating. Still, she had to keep it together because Abby's life hung in the balance, and up until they heard about an explosion, she wasn't going to give up fighting to save Abby.

So she held very still and kept her hands laced together over the top of her head. Cooperating didn't stop the adrenaline-fueled cop from jamming his knee into her back and roughly yanking her hands into a set of cuffs. Somewhere nearby she heard Gilley cry out, "Hey! Careful! I bruise like a peach!"

At last the police had everyone handcuffed, and one by one they were each pulled to their feet. Candice looked as if she were ready to spit fire, and Brody was arguing with the cop who had hold of him—but the officer clearly wasn't listening to the young man.

Margo was the only one who hadn't been put into handcuffs, and she was being looked after by another policeman who was helping her sit up. "Margo!" M.J. yelled. She'd be the only person who might be able to stop all this. "Tell them!" she begged the woman. "Tell them we meant you no harm!"

Margo was still pretty dazed, however, and she could only stare blankly at M.J.

In desperation M.J. looked around and saw Candice also arguing with one of the cops. ". . . then make the call! Ask for Special Agent in Charge Brice Harrison!"

But he wasn't listening to her either. Instead he pushed her up onto the top step of the porch and went over to where several other cops were bunched together, no doubt talking about who would ride in which car.

M.J. was also roughly pulled over to sit down next to Candice and then Brody joined them as well, while Gilley was left to sit on the sidewalk, and Dutch was left lying on the ground, his hands cuffed behind his back. *"Dammit!"* Candice swore. "Dammit, dammit, dammit!"

"What can we do?" M.J. asked desperately.

Candice's eyes filled with angry tears. "I wish I knew. We only had about thirty minutes to get to Abby when they showed up. Now I just don't know what we can do."

At that moment, three dark sedans came roaring down the street, screeching to a stop next to the police cars. Out jumped several men in formal suits and tuxes, all of them flashing bright bronze badges and guns.

The cops were caught by surprise, and in an instant several of them had their own guns drawn too. Then the shouting began, and the posturing. A very large officer stepped forward, his hand firmly on the hilt of his holstered gun, and from the small crowd of dark suits a man M.J. recognized also stepped forward.

"Brice!" Candice shouted, getting to her feet. Brice's eyes flickered to his fiancée and her cuffed hands. Then they moved to Dutch lying prone on the ground, clearly unconscious, and a look of anger so intense flashed across his face that M.J. could only brace for what was going to happen now.

# Chapter Twelve

"What now?" Candice complained as we hit another patch of backed-up traffic. So far our progress across town and back had been hampered by construction and a fender bender.

In hindsight I realized that it was a stupid idea to head back to the office to grab my cane. Something which, on the ride from the office to Jamba Juice, Candice made sure I felt a little guilty for. The projected hour delay had now turned into an hour and a half with all the traffic backups. Feeling bad, I switched on my radar, which had a pretty good navigation feature when I needed it. "I'm feeling like if you get off at the next exit and take the frontage road all the way down to Thirty-eighth, we can cut across to MoPac," I suggested.

Candice frowned but inched her way forward to the exit, and sure enough, my suggestion paid off when not twenty minutes later we arrived in south Austin without further traffic delays.

By now, however, it was a quarter after ten and Candice and I still had a lot of ground to cover if I wanted to get to everybody on my list and chase down some of the new leads that Mrs. Padilla had provided for us.

After Candice parked in a slot at the Jamba Juice, I got out to hobble after her, leaning heavily on Fast Freddy, more for effect than for anything else. Candice's sideways grin told me she wasn't buying it for a Fast Freddy second.

"It's mind over matter," she told me, eyeing the cane pointedly. "The minute you realize you don't need a crutch anymore, you'll be free."

"Can we just get inside and talk to the manager?" I grumbled. I didn't want to talk about my cane anymore.

Candice held the door open for me and we found the place a bit of a mess. The counters were cluttered with straw wrappers, spilled Jamba Juice, and there was a pretty good crowd waiting for drinks—rather unusual for a weekday after rush hour.

Pushing our way to the counter, we inquired after the manager, and the girl behind the counter looked at us like she was seriously annoyed. "She's not here," she snapped, ringing up a sale and giving the patron some change. "And Ryan and I have been slammed all morning and I haven't even had a chance to go to the back to try to call her."

I leaned in to see a rather harried male crew member struggling to make smoothies as fast as his shaking hands could.

"Do you know when she'll be in?" Candice asked.

"No," said the girl. "Debbie's normally here by eight, but she must be at a meeting or something."

Candice set her card on the counter. "Please have her call me at her earliest convenience," she said.

The girl nodded, but she didn't even look at the card—too distracted by the woman in front of her ordering something called a Pumpkin Smash.

We left the store and headed back to the car. "What's next?" Candice asked me.

"Did Brice call you back?"

Candice checked her phone. "Not yet. How about we swing by their office and see what's up?"

"Sounds like a plan."

We cruised over to the FBI offices and headed inside. The minute we were through the door, I came up short. The man I was working so hard to avoid was right there surrounded by the bureau boys and three other men who were definitely cut from the same cloth as my fiancé.

"The Rivers clan has descended," Candice whispered.

"I wasn't expecting his brothers to come into town until Thursday," I said, slightly stunned at the sight of them all elbowing Dutch, and joking around with the rest of the bureau boys.

Mike—Dutch's oldest brother—turned and spotted Candice and me still standing by the door. "Abs!" he shouted, and came running toward me. I braced for impact and before I knew it, I was swept up in a huge bear hug and carried into the room to be handed off one by one to Dutch's two other brothers, Chris and Paul. "You keeping this little guy in line?" Chris asked me, ruffling Dutch's hair. He was only eleven months older than Dutch, but he treated him like his baby brother.

"Doing my best," I told him, pushing up that same practiced forced smile onto my face that'd been getting such a workout of late and counting the seconds until I could run out of there. (Okay, well, maybe hobble as fast as Fast Freddy would let me.)

"I'll bet you are!" Paul said—by far the most boisterous of the bunch, he swept me up for another impromptu hug.

Dutch held up his arms and moved close to me. My radar *bing*ed with warnings for his safety the second he did, something that was getting harder and harder to ignore. "Hey, hey, hey," he told his brothers. "Guys, give her some air, would you?"

"Aww, cut us some slack, Rolo," Paul said, using Dutch's real name—or rather his real name's nickname. "You can't blame us for wanting to hug this gorgeous babe, can you?"

And with that, Paul handed me back over to Mike. I endured it all, because that's what Rivers women did. They never complained at being tossed around like a football between the brothers, and I'd learned that eventually they'd tire of the sport and set me down again.

Dutch must have read my mind because he intercepted the next pass and gently lowered me to the ground to wind a protective arm across my shoulders. "Hey, sweetie," he said, bending down to give me a quick peck. "The clan surprised me by showing up at the house this morning. They heard it's moving day tomorrow and they came in early to help us get settled."

"Awesome!" I said, hoping I sounded totally on board with that. (Okay, so I was mostly hoping the Rivers clan didn't break my furniture.)

"Thought I'd show them around the office before we head over for the final walk-through with Dave," Dutch continued.

"Fantastic!" I said, all head nods and grins. I had to remind myself not to get caught doing the crazy eyes. "Say, have you seen Brice?"

Over Dutch's shoulder I saw Candice in Brice's office, but no sign of the boss man.

"He's with Gaston at the Homeland offices."

"Do you know when he'll be back?" I pressed.

Dutch eyed me quizzically. "You guys find something?"

The last thing I needed was for Dutch to get reinvolved with the case, so I fibbed a little (or a lot). "Naw. Not a thing. But he asked us to keep him updated, so that's what we're doing."

"Okay," he said, distracted by his brothers again because they were now jostling and ribbing one another. "Did you free up some time to come with me to do the walk-through at the house?"

"Uh . . . ," I said, thinking fast. "Cat called and she wants to meet with us." (Thank goodness we didn't have a pickle jar for big fat fibs.)

Dutch's eyes shot back to me. "You told her we're busy, right?"

"Well, she sort of caught me at a weak moment, sweetie. So I thought you and the Rivers clan could head over to the new house and take care of the walk-through, and I'll handle Cat on my own."

Dutch snorted. "You sure you're up for it?"

"Candice is coming with me."

"How'd you manage that?"

"I bribed her."

"You promised her the money in the swear jar, didn't you?"

I laughed. "Yeah, something like that."

"Okay. Well, how about we meet back at the house around six and we'll all head to dinner together?"

I gulped as my radar kept pinging, *Warning, warning, warning!* "Yeah, sure!" I said, though I had no intention of meeting up with him later. Even being near him in one of the safest places in the whole city made me nervous. "I'll call you later and get the scoop on where to meet up."

"Perfect," Dutch said, leaning in for another sweet peck. He then hugged me and whispered, "Love you, dollface."

My throat tightened and I found it hard to swallow. "I love you too," I managed after a moment. "So much."

And then he was letting me go, and he and his brothers were sweeping out of the office and I had the coldest chill come over me. I shivered against it.

"You ready to roll?" Candice said, nudging my elbow.

I jumped. "Uh, yeah. Where're we headed?"

"I thought we'd feed you, then stop by Jed Banes's."

Normally I'm all over being fed, but today I wasn't very hungry. "Sure."

Candice led the way out of the office, and we both waved to the bureau boys as we left. Once we were headed down to the parking garage, I said, "I gather Brice is at the Homeland offices with Gaston."

"Yep," Candice replied. "Cox told me. They turn their phones off when they're in meetings, but not their laptops. I sent Brice an e-mail to call us the minute he can break away."

"What do you think they're meeting about?"

"This case."

I cut her a look. "Duh."

Candice smiled as she unlocked the doors to her car and we got in. "Brice mentioned something to me last night that the Homeland boys are starting to doubt the whole terrorist-cell theory. That group in Yemen isn't sophisticated enough to pull this off, and they can't find a single member of the group who might've gotten into the States and set up a cell here. Still, they'll argue to hold on to the jurisdiction, but they don't have the local investigating skills that our guys do, so I'm fairly certain that Gaston and Brice will argue to get the case back."

"And we've got the key to getting it back for them if we can just get word to Brice."

"Yep."

I sighed and glanced at Candice's phone, which she'd put in the little cubby under the dash. "I wish he'd call."

"He will, Abs. Not to worry. Now, where'd you like to go for lunch?"

I shrugged. "You pick."

She turned her head to look at me quizzically. "Hey, are you feeling okay?"

"Yeah." Candice cocked an eyebrow. "I've just got a lot on my mind."

"There's a new food truck on South Congress. Supposedly they have the best chicken sandwich and fries in Austin."

That perked me a teensy bit. "I'm game."

We ate at a picnic table in relative silence. The day was cold and overcast, so we ate quickly and got back in the car to head over to Jed Banes's place. On the way Candice glanced a few times up at the darkening clouds. "Have you seen the forecast for the week?"

"No, why? Is it bad?"

"There's a pretty big storm cell that's moving in from the northwest. They say it's going to be here through the weekend."

I leaned forward to look up at the moody sky. "You mean it's gonna look like this the whole week?"

"'Fraid so, Sundance."

"Craptastic," I groused. "Fecking craptastic."

"Maybe it'll clear up and be nice on Saturday."

"I don't have that kind of luck."

Candice smirked. "Way to look on the bright side."

We arrived at Jed Banes's residence, which was no more homey than the last time we'd seen it, although there were perhaps a few more leaves on the sidewalk, and he hadn't picked up his Sunday paper from the day before. Candice rang the doorbell and we waited to hear sounds of movement from inside, but nothing but the TV blaring came to our ears. Candice then gave the door three hard knocks. We waited some more, but nothing.

"Maybe he's not home," she said, but I was starting to get a prickly feeling at the base of my neck. I leaned over to my right and took a peek through the window, as the blinds were open. The fact that it was overcast outside made it easier to see into the interior. A light was on across the room, and it was illuminating Jed's ugly green sofa. A brown afghan was strewn over the right half of it and something about its shape caught my attention. Shuffling a little farther to the right, I cupped my hand around my eyes and really peered in.

"See him?" Candice asked me.

I stood up fast. "Kick the door in!"

Candice just stared at me in alarm.

*"Kick it in!"*

Candice snapped out of her surprise and backed away from the door. Raising her booted foot, she kicked hard and fast and the door shot inward. We both rushed forward and saw Jed Banes on the couch, bent double at the waist and slightly sideways, his face a sickening shade of grayish blue. "Jesus!" Candice said, rushing to his right side to feel for a pulse.

In the meantime I was digging through my purse, trying to find my phone. At last I had my hands on it, but when I pulled it free, my fingers were shaking so hard I found it almost impossible to dial. "He's unconscious but still alive!" Candice said, and gently she eased him down to the floor, placing the oxygen mask by the side of the sofa over his face and cranking up the dial.

I finally had the emergency dispatcher on the line and begged for an ambulance, but I got thrown when the dispatcher asked me for an address. I had to head back outside and look at the number on the side of the house, but I couldn't remember what street we were on. "Hamlet Street!" Candice shouted from inside when I called to her.

We waited the anxious four minutes for the ambulance to

arrive, and Banes's condition hadn't improved since Candice put on the oxygen, but at least he hadn't died on us. We then had to fill out a report for the police when they arrived, and there were lots of questions regarding our presence there in the first place and why we'd kicked in the door. Candice flashed her PI license and I flashed my FBI consultant's badge, but that did little good to dissuade the suspicious cop from perhaps thinking we were clever would-be robbers posing as a PI and an FBI consultant. (I didn't say he was the sharpest tool in the shed.)

I finally made a call to Agent Rodriguez at the bureau and he vouched for us, which got us off the hook and on our way a mere hour and a half later.

Once we were back in the car, Candice looked smartly at me and said, "What trouble can we get into next?"

"Well, the day is still fairly young, so I'm thinking plenty."

"You wanna head over to the hospital?"

I checked the ether on Jed Banes. His energy looked very bad, and I thought back to my first encounter with him—that he wouldn't live through November. Maybe he wouldn't even make it through the end of October. "I'm thinking we should let the doctors do their thing, Candice. We can check on his condition later, but I'm not sensing that he'll come back out of the hospital now that he's gone in."

"What do you think happened?" she asked me.

My radar *bing*ed. "Stroke," I said. "I think he had a stroke."

Candice's mouth turned down distastefully. "All that chain-smoking finally caught up with him."

"Yep," I said. If smokers could sense what I could when I sent my radar out to assess their health, they'd never pick up another cigarette.

"Okay, so the hospital is out for now. Where do you want to go instead?" she asked me.

I sighed heavily. "At some point we do have to face the music and go meet with my sister."

Candice's shoulders tensed.

"*Or* we could head back to Jamba Juice and see if Debbie is back from her meeting."

"Jamba Juice it is!" Candice sang, steering the car into the left turn lane and relaxing her shoulders.

We arrived back at the smoothie store and were both relieved to find the parking lot mostly empty. Heading inside, we found a different clerk behind the counter. Her name tag read HALEY. "What can we get started for you today?" she asked us brightly.

"Actually, we're here to speak to Debbie," I said. "Is she around?"

Haley's perky little mouth turned down in a frown. "No, sorry. I think she's at a meeting."

Candice tapped her finger on the counter. "Do you know if she'll be back today?"

"No, sorry," Haley said.

Candice and I exchanged a frustrated look. We were really striking out today, and the only person left on my list of must-sees was my sister. Turning back to Haley, I said, "Can I have one of those Pumpkin Smashes?"

Candice rolled her eyes, but she was also smiling. "I'll take a Berry Bitten smoothie," she said when I nudged her.

Haley rang us up and then moved over to make our drinks. While she filled the prep cups with fruit, flavoring, and tons of empty calories, I chatted her up a bit. I asked her how long she'd worked there. Did she like it? Was she in school?

I discovered that Haley was working her way through the nursing program at ACC, and at that point Candice picked her head up from her phone and asked, "Did you know Mimi Greene?"

Haley's mouth turned down into that sad frown again. "Yeah," she said. "Mimi was so sweet. I still can't believe she's gone."

Candice and I exchanged another look. This one said, "Jackpot!"

"So . . . you two were friends," I said, less question than statement.

Haley nodded and handed me my pumpkin-flavored frozen-smoothie concoction that looked and smelled like heaven. "We were friends. I really liked her."

"Did you guys hang out much?" Candice asked.

Haley cocked her head at Candice, suddenly suspicious. "Why are you asking about her?"

"We're investigating her death," I said, keeping it simple because it wasn't far from the truth and I didn't want to scare Haley off with a lot of talk about bombs and killers and such. I also flashed her my FBI ID to show her that my questions were legit.

"She died in a fire," Haley told me, her eyes widening a little at the plastic badge in my hand.

"Do you know how the fire started?"

Haley shrugged. "I heard it was an accident. Her stove got left on or something."

"Did Mimi talk to you about her personal life?" I asked next.

Haley handed Candice her drink and said, "What do you mean?"

"Well, we heard she had a boyfriend who dumped her. Do you know anything about that?"

Haley's brow rose. "You mean Buzz?"

I nodded eagerly, hoping she'd elaborate.

"Buzz didn't dump her," Haley said.

"Really?" Candice said. "I thought he did."

Haley shook her head. "No. Mimi dumped him."

"Do you know why?" I asked.

Haley shrugged again. "I think she got scared. Her sister, Taylor, kept telling her that Buzz was a loser, and that she could do better, but I'm not sure that Mimi really believed it. But then he got so serious so fast, and I think that freaked her out. So she broke it off with him, and then she really regretted it."

My radar hummed with urgency. Haley was finally giving us the information we'd been searching for. "How serious was he?" I asked, working to keep my voice casual.

"Well, he proposed," Haley said. "And Mimi told me that he wanted to get married right away. Mimi accepted the proposal, and they started going crazy planning the wedding. I think they had the whole thing set up in, like, a week. It was crazy fast."

"So what happened?"

Haley bit her lip. "Her sister happened. Mimi wanted Taylor to be her bridesmaid and went up north to pick out a dress with her, but while she was visiting her sister, Taylor started playing with her head. Mimi came back home with a lot of new doubts about Buzz.

"And then she was even more on the fence because our manager Debbie offered her a promotion. Debbie really liked Mimi, and she wanted to train her as an assistant manager here so she could make enough money to pay for her tuition and stay in school. But Mimi told me that Buzz wanted her to quit her job and the nursing program. He was older than her and he said that he wanted her to get pregnant right away. Can you believe it? Like there are guys that actually want their wives to be all barefoot and pregnant in this day and age."

Candice and I exchanged a look. Mimi had gotten herself involved with a control freak.

"Anyway," Haley continued, "it was all a little too much for Mimi, I think, and she just couldn't go through with it. She told me that on the day of the wedding she just didn't show up."

I blinked. "She left him at the altar?"

Haley nodded sadly. "Sort of. Mimi told me that she'd asked her sister to go to the church and tell Buzz, but then she found out that her sister never left College Station. Taylor just let Buzz wait there for, like, two hours or something until it was pretty obvious nobody from Mimi's side of the family was going to show up."

I felt a jolt of electricity go through me, and Candice and I exchanged meaningful looks. Buzz had waited two hours for his bride to show up. The clock on the bombs was set to two hours, and old Jed Banes always got a call two hours before the bombs went off.

"Did she and Buzz talk much after the wedding was called off?" I asked Haley, wondering if maybe Buzz had had a hand in Mimi's suicide after all.

Haley shook her head. "Only once, and that wasn't even face-to-face," she said. "Mimi heard what her sister had done and she sent Buzz a really long e-mail trying to explain, but she felt so bad that she couldn't bring herself to call him or take any of his calls when he tried to phone her."

Something in the back of my mind was trying to surface, but I was too focused on Haley to pay it much attention. Still, it nagged at me, like a fly buzzing against the TV screen. "When was this?" I asked.

"Last year. Right around this time, actually. And then Mimi died in that fire a month later."

A chill ran up my spine. "Haley, did you ever meet Buzz?"

"Oh, sure!" she said. "He used to come in here all the time."

"But he hasn't been in lately?" Candice pressed.

"No. Not since Mimi broke up with him." Haley opened her mouth to say something else, but she hesitated.

"What?" I asked her.

"Well, you might think this is weird, but there were a few times when I swore that I saw Buzz sitting in his car in the parking lot."

"When was this?" I asked.

"Not long after Mimi died. It was only a few times, but it sort of gave me the creeps."

"But Buzz knew you, and he knew you were friends with Mimi?"

"Yeah," she said. "She and I used to study together. We had a lot of the same classes."

The hairs on the back of my neck were standing on end, and I glanced at Candice, who was also looking at Haley in alarm. I knew what she was thinking. People close to Mimi were being abducted and forced to wear bombs for the last two hours of their shortened lives.

"What?" Haley said, and I could tell we were starting to make her nervous.

"Nothing," I assured her. "We're just surprised because we didn't think that Mimi had any friends."

Haley hung her head a little. "Yeah. I was pretty much her only friend. Mimi was really shy."

"Do you happen to remember Buzz's last name?" I asked next.

Haley shook her head. "No. Mimi just called him Buzz, which wasn't even his real name."

I cocked my head. "Come again?"

"Buzz is his nickname. I know she probably told me his real name once, but I don't remember what it was. Anyway, she just always called him Buzz."

Candice walked subtly out of the shop and I could see her dial her phone and lift it to her ear. I knew she'd be calling Brice.

To put Haley at ease, I sat down at the table nearest the counter and changed the subject, asking her what her favorite smoothie flavor was.

We made chitchat until Candice returned. She sat down and gave me one curt headshake, and I knew she hadn't been able to get ahold of Brice. Some customers came in at that point and Haley went to wait on them, which gave Candice and me a minute to talk.

"We should be worried about her, shouldn't we?" Candice asked me as she eyed Haley at the cash register.

My radar was sending all sorts of alarm bells about the girl's safety. My skin tingled with urgency about the danger I knew she was in. "We definitely should be worried," I told Candice. "My gut says Buzz is our unsub, and it also says that Haley is quite possibly his next target."

"He'll set off another bomb?" Candice said, studying my face as if she was looking for answers there.

I nodded reluctantly. "He's not done, Candice. Of that I'm positive. And, if he wanted to grab another victim to wear the next bomb, Mimi's only friend would be his likely choice."

"Okay," Candice said. "We'll stay put and keep an eye on her until we can get ahold of Brice."

We then sat in the shop the rest of the afternoon, Candice eyeing her phone almost constantly and Haley waiting on the slow trickle of customers coming in for their smoothie fixes.

Finally at four thirty Brice called, and Candice headed outside to fill him in on the important stuff. When she came back in, she said, "He's on the way. I told him what you said, and he doesn't want to take any chances. He'll bring Haley in for her own protection."

I relaxed a fraction. "Good. I'm glad."

Candice looked over at Haley, who was busy wiping down the counter and occasionally casting suspicious glances our way. "Poor kid," she said. "She doesn't even know what she's about to get into."

"Well, I'd feel bad if I didn't think we were probably saving her life," I said.

"True that," Candice agreed.

My phone rang then and I groaned. It was Dutch. "Hey, doll," he said, his voice happy and relaxed. "Just wanted to let you know that we're all gathering at your favorite restaurant—Second Bar and Kitchen."

I bit my lip. Here went nothing. "Yeah, about that . . ."

"What's up?"

"Candice and I are working a lead."

"What lead?"

"I'd rather not tell you."

There was a pause, then, "Why not?"

"Because I don't want you to get sucked back into this."

"Like you've just been sucked back in?"

"Yes."

Dutch seemed to take that in. "Okay," he said at last. "How solid is this lead?"

"Crazy solid."

"You close to solving it?"

"We are."

"Are you thinking you'll wrap it up by tonight?"

I traced small circles with my finger on the tabletop. "No. I think it might take me the rest of the week."

"Aw, come on, Edgar . . . ," Dutch grumbled, clearly annoyed.

"I promise, sweetie, the minute Brice and his team grab this unsub, I'll be home."

"Hold on," Dutch said, his voice going hard. "Now you're not coming home?"

Crap on a cracker. I hadn't meant to say it like that. "I thought I'd stay at Candice's until this thing is over. That way Candice can keep an eye on me and protect me like she promised you she would." (I threw that one in there in the hopes that Dutch might soften a bit.)

It didn't work. My fiancé didn't say a word, and I could sense the anger and hurt coming through the phone.

"Plus," I added, trying again to make light of it, "it's bad luck to see the bride before the wedding."

Dutch was silent for so long that I thought he'd hung up, but just as I was about to ask if he was still there, I heard, "Do what you gotta do, Edgar." And then he really did hang up.

# T-Minus 00:19:23

It was hard for M.J. to tell who threw the first punch. It all happened so fast and the events of that afternoon had been so tense that her brain was slow to process everything happening around her.

She remembered that Brice and the officer built like a bulldog had approached each other angrily, and the second that Brice had seen Dutch lying unconscious on the ground with his hands bound in cuffs, Brice's face had turned from angry to furious. He'd barreled into the cop with his chest, yelling at the top of his lungs, and in the next second the two were exchanging blows. The rest turned into an all-out brawl between the police and men in dark suits—it was like a Friday night hockey game without the Zamboni.

Caught in the middle of it was Gilley, who was trapped on the sidewalk next to the fighting men, and as both teams descended on each other, Gilley got lost in the shuffle. M.J. could hear him, however—his howler monkey shriek told her that he was in serious trouble.

Getting to her feet, M.J. ran toward him, weaving and dodging between the fighting men. "Gilley!" she cried, trying to reach him before he got trampled. *"Gilley!"*

His shriek continued until it was abruptly silenced, and that nearly brought M.J. up short, but she had to keep moving herself lest she be flattened by the shoving and fighting men all around her.

She wove around a group of four who all had hold of one another so tightly that no one could raise a fist to punch, and as she rounded them, she suddenly found herself in the clear. And she also came face-to-face with Director Gaston.

He had hold of Gilley and was helping him into the street, away from the fight. His eyes locked with M.J. and he nodded at her to come with him. They got to one of the parked sedans and the director let go of Gil and reached through the open window to retrieve a bullhorn. Holding it above his head, he hit a button and the air was filled with a piercing horn.

It mostly did the trick; several of the brawlers broke apart, although they continued to yell at one another. The director hit the button again, and this time he held it there until everyone but Brice and the bulldog broke apart. Gaston nodded to one of his men who happened to be standing near Brice, and he went in and pushed the two apart, albeit not before getting a sock to the shoulder from the cop.

Candice and Brody appeared at M.J.'s side, and Candice said, "Director Gaston! Thank God! We believe Abby's been taken by the bomber. That woman over there," she added, nodding toward Margo, "knows his name, sir. We were about to get it from her when these sons of bitches showed up, and they Tased Dutch!"

Gaston's face was expressionless, but there was perhaps a flicker of anger in his eyes. "Is he conscious?" he asked just as Brice limped over. M.J. saw that his right eye was swollen and his lip was bloody.

"He's coming to now," Candice said. "Sir, we have to get to Abby! I think we've got less than twenty minutes before the bomb detonates!"

Gaston was in motion in a second and even though he wasn't a tall man, he walked with such authority that every person present seemed to stand up a little straighter. M.J., Gilley, Candice, Brice, and Brody all tucked in next to him and hovered protectively around him as he bent to check on Dutch. "Get them out of these damn cuffs!" Brice barked to one of the officers, and after a hard glare from Gaston, the officer quickly moved to Candice's back and began to unlock her cuffs. M.J. turned toward the officer when he moved to undo hers, and just then they heard a siren. Looking over her shoulder, M.J. saw that yet another squad car had arrived on the scene. It screeched to a stop and out stepped a man in uniform with enough stars on his lapels to be its own constellation.

"Director!" he shouted, running over to them.

The director barely acknowledged him. "Chief," he growled, as he helped Dutch, who was struggling to sit up.

M.J. realized that the chief of police had just arrived and she could see every cop in the vicinity turn suddenly fidgety and nervous. "What the *hell* is going on here?" the chief demanded.

Immediately hands were raised and fingers were being pointed, along with accusations and barely veiled threats from both the cops and the Feds.

Gaston silenced much of that by standing up and glaring hard at every man present. He then took the chief by the arm and moved with him a little away to speak with him.

Meanwhile M.J. bent down and with Candice's help managed to keep Dutch on his feet. Overhead the sound of a low-flying helicopter made it impossible for M.J. to hear what the FBI director and the chief of police were saying, but one glance told her that the chief was receiving a pretty good dressing-down. She wouldn't be surprised if he ended up losing a star in his constellation over it.

As the helicopter flew wide, she heard another voice shout something that turned her blood cold. One of the officers came running over to the chief and the inspector. A call had just come in, he explained. A woman wearing what a witness described as a wedding dress and a bomb was currently running along Highway 71.

Next to her, Dutch's head snapped to attention and with effort he squared his shoulders and took a wobbly step forward. "Abby!" he gasped. "Jesus! We have to get to her!"

Director Gaston looked from Dutch to Candice to Brice and then his eye traveled to the helicopter. Turning to the chief, he said, "We'll need to borrow your bird, Art."

# Chapter Thirteen

I stared out the window of the Jamba Juice at a flock of birds picking at the remnants of a muffin tossed there by a careless customer. Candice and I had waited for Brice to show, and then we'd also stayed while Brice gently questioned Haley for nearly three hours. The interview produced little more information than we'd already managed to ferret out of her, but at the end of it, we were convinced that whoever this Buzz guy was, he was our killer.

Haley was then told that the safest place for her would be in FBI custody, and the poor thing was scared enough to agree to go with Agents Cox and Rodriguez as they escorted her home to gather some things before they took her to a safe house.

"Think she'll be okay?" Candice asked me, and I pulled my attention away from the window to look over at my BFF, who in turn was staring at Haley being helped into her coat by Agent Cox. I felt a pang in my heart as I watched the young woman. She'd looked so pale and frightened when Brice had told her about Michelle and Taylor.

"She'll be in good hands with Cox and Rodriguez," I said.

Candice sighed. "Yeah, and now that we have a solid lead, I doubt it'll be long before we figure out who this Buzz guy is."

But I wasn't so sure. I was troubled by how elusive his energy felt—and as close as I knew we were to figuring out who he was, I had the unsettling feeling that we weren't quite close enough.

"I called the manager," Brice said, interrupting my troubled thoughts. I looked over my shoulder to see that he'd come out from the back, where Haley's coworker—who'd relieved her at five—told Brice he could find Debbie's phone number.

"Did she have anything to add?"

Brice shook his head. "Got voice mail."

"She's been in a meeting all day," Candice told him.

"We need to talk to her in case she remembers Buzz's full name," Brice said.

"Taylor's dad probably knows," I suggested.

Brice frowned and shook his head. "I called the team in Dubai overseeing Greene. They patched me through to him, and he had no idea Mimi was even seeing someone before she killed herself. He admitted that he didn't have a close relationship with either of his daughters, and Taylor never mentioned this boyfriend of her sister's to him either. He has no clue who he could be."

"Dammit!" I swore. Candice and Brice both looked at me expectantly. "Oh, whatever, you guys! This situation calls for an expletive or two. Plus, Dutch has let me off the swear-jar hook."

"Good thing," Candice said. "You were likely to go broke otherwise."

I made a face at her and then focused on Brice. "How'd it go with Homeland? Did you get the case back?"

Brice sighed. "No. Mostly we argued all day about it and we couldn't get them to agree to let go of the case."

"Maybe filling them in about what you learned from Haley will help sway it our way," Candice suggested.

Brice rubbed his eyes. He looked tired enough to drop where he stood. "Gaston's called for another meeting with them tomorrow. We'll send a car over to the manager's place tonight and see if we can interview her, and if she doesn't know who Buzz is, then we'll lay out our hand to Homeland tomorrow and hopefully it'll be enough for us to win the case back."

Candice looped her arm through Brice's. "In the meantime, how about we take you out for dinner?"

Brice's brow lifted. "That sounds like a great idea. Should we call Rivers and have him join us?"

Candice looked to me, and I bit my lip. I couldn't be around him until we'd nabbed this Buzz guy and the case was solved. "Uh . . . Dutch's family is in town, babe, so I think he'll be tied up with them," Candice said, reading my body language well.

Brice looked curiously at me but he didn't press it and we all pretended like it was a perfectly natural thing for me to be hanging out with the two of them four days before my wedding. Then we went off to dinner and a much deserved night's rest.

The next morning I woke up on Candice's couch feeling grumpy and sore. I'm a light sleeper by nature, and Candice's couch—although perfectly comfortable to sit on—couldn't hold a candle to a real bed.

I got up while it was still dark out and checked the time. It was five a.m. I knew that the two workout fiends would be up at any moment, and I didn't want them to have to fish around in the dark while they tried not to disturb me, so I turned on a few lights and got the coffee going.

While I futzed in the kitchen, I couldn't ignore the most unsettling feeling that washed over me. I felt so strongly that I'd missed something—something important—and there were going to be major repercussions for that. "Morning," Candice said just as the coffee was done brewing.

"Hey."

"Sleep okay?"

"Great," I lied.

"Brice is still asleep and he's been working so hard I thought it'd be good to let him catch some z's. He can run tomorrow."

"You headed downstairs?"

"Yeah. Wanna come?"

I started to make my "Are you kidding me?" face but then thought better of it. "You know what? I do. I can try walking on the treadmill."

"Without your cane?" she asked. I nodded. "Good for you, Sundance. You'll do great on Saturday, honey. Milo's got you if you have any balance issues, but if you can walk even twenty yards on the treadmill without needing to hold on, you'll do perfect at the ceremony."

"It's the stairs from the terrace to the aisle that worry me," I said, moving back over to the couch to put on some shoes.

"Again, you'll have Milo there to help guide you down. And we can fit in some work on the stair-climber if you want. And maybe we can also talk to Cat and have her build you a ramp instead of stairs."

I slapped my forehead. "Cat!"

Candice eyed me sharply. "You did call her last night, right?"

"I forgot!" I said, a bit panicked as I looked for my phone. Oh, my sister was likely to be furious, because I'd promised— as in pinkie swore—that I'd meet with her by the end of the day yesterday, but all of that had gone out the window when we'd encountered Haley at Jamba Juice.

I finally unearthed my phone from between the seat cushions and, sure enough, there were six new voice messages— all from my sister . . . my very *angry* sister. I looked at the time again. It was now 5:05 a.m. If I called and woke her up, would that make it worse?

I settled for sending her a text . . . a very *apologetic* text, and told her that I would call her at eight a.m. Come hell or high water, I would contact her at that time.

After that, Candice and I went downstairs and she put me through my paces. An hour and a half later we found Brice cooking us some pancakes and looking much better rested. "Your phone rang a couple of times, Cooper," he told me the minute we got in the door.

I looked skyward and playfully shook my fist. "Of all the sisters in all the world . . . you had to give me Cat!"

"Better call her," Candice advised. "Get it over with."

I took a piece of bacon off the plate that Brice had prepared and moved to the couch. But when I looked at my phone, I noticed that the calls weren't from my sister—they were from Dutch.

I listened to my voice mails and immediately felt even guiltier. "Hey, dollface, it's me. I didn't hear from you last night. You okay?"

Next message. "Abs, if you're up, call me."

Next message. "Edgar, we have the closing at nine a.m. and I need to make sure you know how to get there. Call me as soon as you get this."

I was about to call Dutch back when I heard a buzz and saw Brice reach for his phone. "Harrison," he said crisply. "Oh, hey, Rivers . . . Yeah, she's here. You want to talk to her?"

I stood up, ready to take the phone, but Brice wasn't handing it over. Instead he'd grabbed a pen and notepad, jotted something on it, and said, "Okay, buddy. I'll pass on the message. Congrats on the new home."

With that, he hung up, ripped the note off the pad, and handed it to me. "That's the address to the title company. Dutch said you don't have to be there at nine. He's arranged for you to go in whenever it's convenient for you and sign. He says as long as he's bringing the cashier's check, they'll give him the keys so he can start moving in."

I took the note and felt my lower lip quiver. I knew Dutch wasn't trying to be mean; in fact, it was much more likely that he was simply being thoughtful and allowing me some extra time to get over to the title company. But given the energy in the ether that continued to haunt me like a bad storm on the horizon, I knew that I would wait until later in the morning to go over to the title company and sign the documents. It was a terrible thing to want nothing more than to be close to my fiancé, and yet feel like I couldn't get far enough away.

Hiding my face by turning back toward the couch, I asked, "Have you mentioned anything about our new lead to him, Brice?"

"To Rivers?" he asked.

"Yeah."

"No. He's on vacation . . . which is where you should be, Cooper."

I glanced up at him, and found him staring at me pointedly.

Candice subtly laid a hand on his arm and he turned back to the pancakes, letting the subject drop, but I knew that while he was willing to tolerate my presence here without a hint of complaint, he didn't exactly approve of what I was doing to Dutch by keeping my distance from him.

After breakfast I excused myself and headed to the shower to get ready. When I came out, Brice had left for the office and Candice had left me a note that she had a nine a.m. appointment with her masseuse, and she'd be back at ten thirty to head with me over to Cat's if I wanted.

I called Cat and got her voice mail. I wondered if she was now ducking my calls, but I left her a message—heavy on the apologies—and then headed out of the condo.

I drove to the address Dutch had given to Brice and parked in the back of the parking lot. At eight fifty I saw his Audi pull in and park, and he and his brother Chris walked into the building together.

I thought it was sweet that Chris was going with him, but that still didn't stop me from crying a little in the car. I told myself over and over that I was being ridiculous, but every time I went to get out of the car, that horrible foreboding feeling swept over me, and I couldn't make myself go into the building while he was there.

At last Dutch and Chris emerged, Chris slapping Dutch on the back affectionately, and in Dutch's hands was a set of shiny keys. I knew that he and his brothers would get right to work moving our things into the new house.

I waited a little bit before I got out of the car and headed inside to sign the documents too. The process took only twenty minutes, and I was told that my fiancé had all the keys. I assured the closer that I would get one from him.

Getting back in my car, I sat there numbly for a bit, my mind a jumble of worries and disjointed thoughts. Amid that tangle was something out of place and rather odd—my mind kept flashing to the memory of the keys in Dutch's hand.

Sometimes I'll see something that will seem completely random, but my intuitive brain will seize on it—as if saying, "There's a clue there! Focus!"

But focusing was next to impossible; I was a mess of feelings, fears, and forebodings. My phone rang as I fought internally with myself, and I was almost relieved to hear Cat's voice on the other end. "*What* happened to you yesterday?"

Cat always did have a way of getting right to the point. "I'm so sorry! We had a huge development in this case I've been working, Cat, and I lost all sense of time."

"Was your phone malfunctioning too?"

I sighed. "No. I honestly just forgot."

Cat made a sound like she didn't believe me. "You *forgot*? Abby, you're getting married in *four* days! Four days!"

"Yes, yes, yes, honey, I know. I'm really sorry, and I have the whole rest of today free. I'm yours from right now until midnight if you want me."

"Aren't you moving today?"

"Dutch and his brothers are handling it," I said, hoping she didn't press me on that.

Cat was silent for a moment, and I knew she was trying to get over her frustration with me. At last she said, "Can you be here at eleven thirty?"

"I can! Absolutely. See you in exactly one hour."

With that, I hung up and sent Candice a text, asking her to meet me at Cat's in an hour. She didn't text me back, which meant either she was ducking me, or she'd be there and didn't feel the need to answer. With a little time to kill, I began to head back toward the rental house. I'd left most of my things there the day before, because I hadn't wanted to wake Dutch when I'd snuck out of the house. As I drove, the moody sky turned even gloomier, and a slight drizzle began to fall, perfectly fitting my melancholy mood. So much seemed to be hanging over my head oppressively, and no matter how hard I worked to figure out why I was so unsettled, the answer seemed only to taunt me by scuttling even farther away.

But what bothered me most of all was the feeling that I'd be walking down the aisle in four days and in my heart of hearts, I didn't want to do it. I couldn't pinpoint why, but every time I imagined myself in my gown, walking down those steps toward my fiancé with all those witnesses, I felt almost nauseated with anxiety.

But I loved Dutch more than anyone in the world, and he wanted to marry me in front of his family and all of our friends (and my contacts list). I'd said yes to him when I accepted the beautiful emerald ring on my left ring finger, and my sister had planned and paid for the whole affair, so there was no going back on it now. Still, I felt that so much of my life was out of my control at the moment, and traditionally, when things get sticky, I tend to run. Or divert my attention by focusing on something else, like this case.

And that was the other terribly troubling thing—all the oppressive, dreadful energy of the bombing case felt like it was growing tentacles, snaking its way into my life and ruining all that should be giving me great joy. I had an eerie premonition that my nuptials would somehow be wrecked by this case, and all I could think was that perhaps the next incident might take place on the day of the wedding. A cold shudder zipped down my spine, but also, something else. A connection, loose and gossamer thin, formed in my mind, and I wondered . . .

Next to me a car honked and I jerked. I'd been drifting a little into the other lane. Shaking myself out of my dark thoughts, I focused on getting to the rental house in one piece. I pulled into the driveway and stared up at the house, which had been such a happy home. I'd liked living there, even though it wasn't nearly as grand and luxurious as our new house promised to be.

I headed inside as the gray clouds overhead thickened even more and the drizzle turned to rain. Once inside I flipped on the lights and saw that the bed was unmade, the sheets wound into knots. It appeared that Dutch had had a restless night too.

I sat down on the bed and hugged his pillow, smelling his essence and missing him so terribly that I shed a few tears. After ten minutes of pity party and knowing Cat wouldn't forgive me if I was late, I pulled myself together and gathered all my things, pausing in the doorway to say good-bye to a house that had been good to us, even if it'd been only temporarily.

After putting all my things in the car, I had a thought and went back inside. Digging through my purse, I pulled out a pen and an old receipt and scribbled a love note to Dutch, leaving it on his pillow after straightening out the bed. He wouldn't be sleeping here tonight, I knew, but he'd come back for the bed and his things at some point during the day.

As I turned back toward the door again, it opened unexpectedly and there stood our landlord. "Do you knock?" I asked sharply before I could catch myself.

He eyed me with surprise and irritation. "Sorry," he said in a way that clearly said he wasn't. He then held out a check to me. "I saw your car and came to give you this."

I took the check and looked at it. It was enough for one day's worth of rent. "Thanks," I said, then eyed him expectantly. I wanted him to leave, but he was looking at the bed and the otherwise empty living room with interest. "You guys almost out?" he asked, and I knew he was thinking he could get a cleaning crew in here earlier.

I sighed. "We agreed on the thirtieth, Bruce."

"Yeah, but if you're already mostly moved out . . . ," he said.

I glared at him. I wasn't in the mood to be patient or cordial. "I have to go," I said to him, and held my arm out toward the door. "If you don't mind?"

Bruce rolled his eyes and turned away from me. "Make sure your fiancé gets that check," he said, like he fully expected me to use the money to go on a shopping spree at the dollar store and not tell Dutch about it.

I ignored him and headed down the stairs on his heels, putting the pressure on him to get a move on. As he got in his car, he scoffed at me. Clearly we weren't ever going to be buddies, but he did leave, which made me happy.

Still, as I pulled out of the drive on my way over to Cat's offices, I had an icky feeling that Bruce was going to go back into the house after I'd gone just to see what was still inside. "Bastard," I muttered, knowing I couldn't wait around to catch him in the act. Cat would kill me if I was even a minute late.

Twenty minutes later I pulled into a parking space in the front lot of Cat's building, letting out a sigh of relief. Candice's Porsche was neatly tucked into a slot a few spaces down. As I got out of the car, she appeared at my side, startling me. "I thought you'd be inside," I told her.

"Oh, no," she said. "I'm not heading into the lion's den alone, Sundance."

I grimaced. Cat was going to be difficult. Even more difficult than normal, because I knew she'd still be mad for my having blown her off the day before. "I should've bought her a gift or something," I said.

"A peace offering?" Candice asked.

"Yeah." I looked at my watch; it was eleven twenty-five. "No time for shopping. I'll just have to win her over with my perky personality."

Candice eyed me doubtfully. I frowned at her and we went inside. Jenny Makeanote met us at the elevator. "Good morning, Ms. Cooper. Oh, and hello, Ms. Fusco. Mrs. Cooper-Masters has been detained in a meeting, but she asked me to show you to the conference room and she'll join you as soon as her meeting is over."

"Awesome!" I said, already practicing the perky.

Jenny Makeanote squinted oddly at me, then proceeded to lead us through the large suite. I noticed a few more people in residence since last I was there—maybe Cat had been on a hiring jag.

Jenny opened the door to the conference room, and we were shown in. The place looked just like it had the other day, save for a dress rack in the corner with a garment bag I recognized. "She picked up my dress?" I asked.

"Yes, ma'am. Mrs. Cooper-Masters had me collect it on Saturday. She'd like for you to try it on and make sure it fits. If we have to call the seamstress, I'll need at least an hour's notice."

Once the door was closed, I moved immediately to the garment bag and unzipped it, sighing with satisfaction at the sight of the beautiful dress. I'd had it modeled after the one worn by Carolyn Bessette Kennedy at her wedding to John Kennedy Jr., because I'd always loved the simple elegance of the bias-cut, silk slip dress.

Candice whistled appreciatively while I took it out of the garment bag. "It's *so* you, Sundance," she said, when I held it up against myself.

I smiled before tucking in to the restroom to try it on. Thankfully, it fit like a glove (probably because I hadn't had lunch yet), and I came out to parade myself in front of Candice. "Beautiful, honey," she said, her hand over her heart. I was touched to see a slight mist in her eyes.

After I'd changed into my regular clothes again, Jenny Makeanote came back into the conference room, carrying a tray of salads and refreshments. "Mrs. Cooper-Masters apologizes," she said. "Her meeting is taking much longer than expected. She's asked me to bring you lunch and see if there's anything else you'll need."

"We're fine," Candice assured her as I looked over the salads (hunting for something more substantive, like potato chips).

As she was leaving, my phone buzzed with an incoming text at the same time Candice's phone gave a small chirp. I felt a jolt of anxiety go through me, and Candice and I both snatched our phones and took a look.

The text was from Agent Rodriguez, and it was alarming to say the least. Little Haley Nolan had apparently slipped her protection detail, and on top of that, Oscar noted that he'd seen a blip on the phone logs for Jed Banes. A call had come in about an hour and a half earlier from an unknown—and untraceable—number. He was in the process of sending one of the agents over to retrieve the tape in Banes's answering machine.

"Shit," Candice whispered.

I eyed my watch. It was twelve thirty. "I've got a bad feeling about this, Candice."

She grabbed her purse. "I'm heading over there to see if there's anything I can do."

I grabbed my purse too. "I'm coming with you."

That's when we saw Jenny Makeanote still standing in the

doorway. "What? No! Ms. Cooper, you can't leave!" she said, looking a bit desperate.

We both ignored her and marched toward the door. Jenny spread her arms and legs, trying to prevent us from leaving. Candice stopped right in front of her and glared hard, and that was enough to get Jenny to gulp loudly and step aside. As we passed her, I called over my shoulder, "Tell Cat I'm dealing with an emergency at work, and I'll try to come back later."

"She'll be very upset!" Jenny said (a bit shriekishly, I thought).

"She'll get over it," I muttered, trying to get my legs to move faster to keep up with Candice.

We drove separately to the bureau, which meant that Candice (the speed racer) got there a few minutes ahead of me. When I got upstairs and through the door, the first thing I saw was Oscar, sitting in his chair with his head down and the phone pressed to his ear. Cox stood nearby looking like he'd been kicked in the gut, and Brice was in his office pacing angrily with a phone pressed to his ear.

Candice was in with him, and I knew better than to go in there, so I sidled up to Cox and asked, "Any word?"

He nudged his chin toward Rodriguez. "Oscar's on the phone with her parents. They haven't seen her."

"What the hell happened?"

Cox shrugged and sighed at the same time. "She went into the bathroom to take a shower and after a half hour of the water running, we got nervous and knocked on the door. No answer led us to break it down, and that's when we found the bathroom window open."

"Why would she run?" I asked.

Cox rubbed his face tiredly. "My guess is that she got scared, and took off to a boyfriend's or something."

"She's got a boyfriend?"

Cox nodded again to Rodriguez. "That's what we're trying to find out."

I eyed my watch. It was five minutes to one. "Any word on the answering machine?"

Cox pointed over his shoulder. "Brice has been trying to

get a judge to sign a search warrant to retrieve it for the past twenty minutes. With Banes still alive and in a coma, he's not having the best luck with it."

"We're almost out of time," I growled. "We need to know if the call on Banes's machine is another warning."

"You're preaching to the choir," Cox told me. "But if it is another warning, there's not much we can do about it in the four minutes we've got left."

Rodriguez hung up the phone, his face hard as granite. "Her parents haven't seen or heard from her," he said. "But they did say that Haley's been dating a guy who lives on campus at UT."

"They give you a name?" Cox asked.

"Bill Reid. I'm calling campus police to have them check his dorm room."

Rodriguez picked up the phone and began dialing when Brice poked his head out of his office, waving a paper in the air. "I've got the warrant and I've e-mailed it to Donovan at Banes's house. Cox, I'll need you to pick up the original and meet Donovan with it in case someone calls the police on us."

"On it," Cox said, grabbing his coat and hurrying out of the room.

I looked at my watch again. It was one o'clock. All around me the remaining agents in the room seemed to sense the hour, and a hush fell over the room. Only Rodriguez's strained voice remained at full volume as he explained whom he was looking for, and where he hoped they'd find her.

Five more tense minutes went by, and then several phones rang, including Brice's. I watched him through the window as he grabbed up the phone. I then watched the color drain from his face, and I knew. I knew we were too late. Another bomb had gone off.

We drove to the crime scene in Brice's sedan. All we'd heard was that there'd been some kind of explosion at a small strip mall on the south side of town. Through the window I could see a rise of thick black smoke as we drew close. The area was also swarming with police, fire, and rescue trucks, not to mention news vans from every local station and a few from the national ones too.

Brice waved his badge at several police officers to gain us access to the area closest to the detonation. Brice parked on the street and we got out and followed him over to a cluster of police and men in dark suits—no doubt Homeland Security had been alerted and gotten there too.

Gaston appeared as if out of nowhere, and he and Brice broke away from Candice and me to talk privately. Rodriguez came up beside me. He looked terrible. "It's not your fault," I told him, but I might have saved my words. He stared hard at the smoldering remains of a storefront like he hadn't even heard me.

Nearby I saw a man with a camera clicking away, and something about him struck me. The press were always kept at a safe distance, so how the heck did he get through the barricades and up so close? "Hey!" I yelled, moving toward him full of piss and vinegar. "Who the hell let you in here?"

The man blanched and backed away from me. "Sorry!" he said, but I also noticed he took a few more shots of the scene.

"Yo!" I yelled loudly. "Stop taking pictures or I'll have you brought up on obstruction charges!" I had no authority to bring anyone up on any such charges, but I was angry and he was a convenient scapegoat.

He took another step back, and that's when I noticed that Candice had come around him from the back, and laid a firm hand on his arm. Nimbly lifting his camera out of his hands, she said, "The lady asked you a question, buddy. Who let you in here?"

By now I was in front of the guy. He was a slight man with a face like a rat and a thick brown mustache. "Nobody let me in here," he said angrily, trying to take back his camera. "I own that shop."

My gaze lifted to the storefront at the end of the row. It was a photography studio. "Well, you should have evacuated with the rest of the tenants!" Candice snapped. She was being a little rough on him too.

"Can I have my camera back?" he asked meekly.

"Nope," Candice told him, waving to one of the crime-scene techs. "We're keeping it as evidence. You'll get it back when we're through investigating."

The guy puffed his chest up. "You can't do that!"

Candice handed the camera over to the CSI. "Wanna bet?" she said, before instructing the tech to log the camera into evidence. She then took the photographer by the collar and pulled him over to a nearby cop. "This suspicious character was taking photos of the scene," she said. "I'd like you to hold him in your custody until we can question him."

"Yes, ma'am," he said.

Fully alarmed now, the photographer began to struggle with the cop. Bad idea. He was quickly twisted into a choke hold and stuffed into the back of a cop car.

"Doofus," Candice growled as she came back to me.

"We really should check him out," I said. "I mean, who sticks around after an explosion next door to take photos?"

Candice thumbed over her shoulder. "That idiot. But, yeah, I agree. That is a little suspicious."

We walked over to Rodriguez, who was pacing back and forth with his phone once again pressed to his ear, a strange expression on his face. "You're sure?" he asked the caller. Then, he wiped his brow and let out a breath. "Yeah, that's her. Where is she now?"

Candice and I waited a bit impatiently for him to disconnect. "They have her," he said, wiping his brow again.

"Who?" we both asked.

"Haley. Campus police grabbed her at her boyfriend's dorm."

"Wait," I said, completely dumbfounded. "Haley's alive?"

He nodded.

I pointed behind him at the smoldering ruins. "Then who the hell did *that*?"

We had our first clue several hours later when we were back at the bureau. Several witnesses had stepped forward to suggest that they saw a woman in her late thirties wearing a uniform of some kind approach the strip mall on foot looking terribly distraught and wearing what looked to be a big backpack strapped to her chest. The minute she'd made it to the parking lot in front of a FedEx store, she'd ducked behind a car and they saw her trying to shimmy out of the backpack. In the next instant the witnesses were knocked flat by a terrible flash and an explosion. Sparks from the initial blast had caught the roof of the FedEx building on fire, and with all that paper inside, it'd become completely engulfed in under five minutes. The only good news was that all the employees and patrons had made it safely out the back of the store. No one but the bomber had been killed.

Cox had also confirmed that Banes's answering machine had recorded a warning from our unsub, and while questions and leads continued to pour in, I kept going back to the description of the woman.

She was described as between five feet five and five feet seven inches tall, 140 to 160 pounds, brown-haired, and wearing a maroon or brown uniform.

Something tickled the back of my mind and after having a brief chat with Candice, I carried one of the reports back to Brice's office, where he was talking with Gaston and one of the Homeland guys. "Excuse me," I said after knocking. "But I have a question."

Brice leaned back in his chair and waved his hand at me to proceed.

"Sir, did you ever talk with Debbie Nunez?"

Brice's brow furrowed. "Who?"

"The manager from the Jamba Juice. Did you ever get ahold of her?"

Brice blinked a few times. "Uh . . . no, Cooper. I never did. Why?"

"Has *anyone* heard from her?" I pressed.

Brice picked up his cell phone and scrolled through several screens of what I assumed were voice mails. "No. She never called me back."

I stretched out my arm holding the description of the victim to him. "Candice met Debbie the other day. She said she looked a lot like the description given of our bomber. We went back to talk to her yesterday at the shop, but one of the employees had said that Debbie wasn't there, and when we pressed for her whereabouts, I remember the employee saying that she thought Debbie must be in a meeting, but I don't remember that that was ever confirmed. Also, Haley mentioned that Buzz wanted Mimi to quit her job after they got married, but Debbie had already offered Mimi a promotion as assistant manager. I had the feeling that Mimi didn't like the idea of staying home barefoot and pregnant, and her job might have offered her some independence and freedom. A control freak like Buzz would've felt threatened by Mimi's promotion, and I'm betting he probably blamed Debbie for playing a role in his breakup with Mimi."

For several seconds, you could have heard a pin drop in that office. "Shit," Brice swore. "You mean to tell me we had the wrong girl in protective custody?"

I nodded, feeling almost physically sick over it. I was the one who hadn't put it together, and I'd been the one to set the protective detail on Haley because I'd been so sure that she was Buzz's next target.

Gaston held his hand out for the report and the Homeland guy leaned over to read it with him. Brice then pointed to me. "Take Fusco and Rodriguez over to Debbie's house and see what you can find out." I left his office before the expletives really began to fly.

Agent Rodriguez drove Candice and me to Debbie's house. The mood in the car was somber. Oscar had been pulled off any further protective detail for Haley, something I was pretty sure he was still smarting from. Her parents had insisted that she come home to their house and two APD officers had been assigned to stand guard out front. Two Homeland Security agents had also been quietly assigned to walk the block periodically and monitor the street to make sure Haley didn't leave and that nobody suspicious got too close.

Candice was also very sullen. I suspected she might be feeling personally responsible for not thinking to protect Debbie. I knew exactly how she felt.

*How had we missed that?* I kept asking myself. And I knew with intuitive certainty that Debbie had been the latest victim in this madness.

We found Debbie's town house after twice passing it by.

Her home was a rather indistinctive place; nothing about it stood out or made it different from its neighbors to the right or to the left: just a brown, drab home without flowers or fanfare.

We walked to the door and rang the bell. It gonged hollowly and we waited even though not one of us expected the door to open. Oscar pressed the bell again just to be thorough, while Candice eyed the street. There were several cars parked out front—impossible to tell offhand which one might belong to Debbie.

I could tell that Oscar was about to turn away from the door, but I had an impulse. "Did you hear that?" I asked.

"What?" Candice and Oscar both asked.

"I swear I heard a cry for help coming from inside," I said, feigning concern.

The corner of Candice's mouth quirked, and she looked at Oscar expectantly. When he wavered, she added, "You know, I think I heard it too. Someone's clearly in distress in there."

But Oscar was playing it by the book. "We'll get a warrant," he said, pulling out his cell—about to call Brice, no doubt.

Candice made a derisive noise and bent down to tug up the corner of the welcome mat at our feet. She stood up triumphant with a key in her hand. "Fusco . . . ," Oscar warned, but Candice wasn't listening. She inserted the key, turned the handle, and called out, "Hello? Debbie? It's Candice Fusco. We talked the other day and we have reason to believe you may be in danger! If you're afraid for your life, don't call out. If you're fine, please shout to us!"

Rodriguez rolled his eyes, but both Candice and I ignored him, moving into the foyer to look around. In front of us was a set of stairs. Candice pulled out her gun and slowly made her way up them. I sensed no danger, so I went around the stairs to the living room, which looked to be furnished by Ikea, and poked around a little. Debbie had a landline, and it appeared she'd missed eight calls—all from the previous few days. I found a photo of her on the half wall leading to the kitchen. She was being hugged by an older gentleman—I assumed he was her dad—and her flat plastic image smiled out at me. Debbie was dead.

"Anything?" Candice's voice asked from the foyer.

I turned and held up the picture frame. "She's deceased."

Candice didn't say a word, but the look on her face said it all. Moving past me to the kitchen, she took up a paper towel and tried the handle on the back door. It was locked.

"Hey, guys!" we heard faintly. Rodriguez was calling to us from outside.

We moved quickly back out to the front porch and found Rodriguez pulling something out from under a white Honda. It was dirty and covered with leaves, but I was able to make out that it was one of those reusable cloth grocery bags, and it looked partially full.

Candice and I made our way over to Rodriguez and I bent low to look under the car. There was a smunched-looking loaf of bread there, and several unopened packages of Lean Cuisine.

"She was nabbed here," I said, immediately turning on my radar and picking up the scent of a struggle.

"Probably right after I talked to her Saturday afternoon," Candice said. "She mentioned to me that she had to get going because she wanted to hit the grocery store on the way home."

I pointed to the white Honda. "This her car?"

Rodriguez nodded and held up his phone showing a text from Agent Cox with the description of a vehicle registered to Debbie Nunez.

"Dammit," I swore. "We've got to find this son of a bitch."

"Let's knock on a few doors and see if anyone saw anything," Candice suggested.

Rodriguez pulled out a crumpled piece of paper from the bottom of the grocery bag. "Store receipt says that Nunez checked out at three seventeen p.m. October twenty-fourth."

"Saturday," Candice confirmed.

"Which means this Buzz guy was either stalking her by following her around town and looking for an opportunity, or was camped somewhere on this street, waiting for her to come home."

"It also means that he had her hidden away somewhere until this morning."

"Come on," Rodriguez said, putting the bag in his car. "We better talk to the neighbors."

We spent two hours walking up and down the street and talking to anybody who would answer the door. No one had seen anything unusual. Looking at the rows of townhomes, I suspected that was because the windows on nearly every home had the shutters drawn. Nobody looked outside anymore—they were too afraid of someone looking in.

We drove back to the bureau feeling pretty defeated. When we got there, we briefed Brice, Gaston, and the Homeland agent on what we'd found at Debbie Nunez's town house, and Rodriguez presented them with the receipt before he headed off to call the grocery store and find out if they had any security footage of Debbie purchasing her items. With any luck, there would be a suspicious-looking character in the background keeping an eye on her and we'd at least get an image we could put out to the press.

"What about phone records for Mimi?" I asked, so frustrated that at every turn we were meeting a dead end. "She had to have had a cell phone with texts and phone calls from this Buzz guy."

"We sent over the warrant late last night," Brice said. "It'll take those guys at least a week to get back to us with her records, and that's with an expedited request."

"I'll see what I can do to put some pressure on them," Gaston offered, making a note to himself.

Brice turned to me and Candice. "Tomorrow I want you two to canvass Mimi's old neighborhood and see if anyone remembers her and this guy she was seeing."

And then Brice seemed to catch himself, and he pointed to me. "Scratch that. Cooper, you're on wedding detail. Fusco and Rodriguez can handle it from here."

I shook my head vehemently. "Sir," I said, "I'm not walking down the aisle until Saturday. Plenty of time to work through a few more leads until then."

Brice and Gaston both eyed me with unmasked surprise. "You sure?" Brice asked.

"Positive," I told him. I wasn't going to be able to relax until that awful foreboding feeling I had for Dutch's safety left me, and so far, nothing in the ether had suggested that it was lessening.

"Suit yourself," he said, then pointed behind me. "But you can be the one to explain it to that guy. If he asks, I'm going to tell him I already tried to order you off this case."

I turned and saw Dutch standing just outside Brice's office, his expression impossible to read. I got up quickly and headed out to greet him. "Hey!" I said as brightly as I could muster. "You heard, huh?"

He nodded. "It's all over the news. Do they know who the victim is?"

"Debbie Nunez. She was the manager of the Jamba Juice where Mimi Greene worked."

Dutch sighed and ran a hand through his golden hair. "Damn," he said. "Candice just talked to her, right?"

"Saturday," I said. There was a pause; then I decided to jump in with both feet. "I think I'm going to work this case another few days."

Dutch's eyes locked with mine. "You're not even supposed to be working it now, Edgar."

I put a hand on the collar of his coat and tugged a little. "We're close to nabbing him, cowboy. And I can't leave it alone until he's caught."

"What if he's still at large by Saturday?"

I sighed and leaned in to put my forehead against his chest. "Can you give me until Friday?"

Dutch didn't say anything for several seconds and I waited him out. What could he say, after all? Finally I felt his arms wrap around me, and he kissed the top of my head. "Stay safe, okay?"

I hugged him, but that familiar awful feeling crept in between us, and I shut my eyes against it. "I will. I promise."

With one last squeeze Dutch backed up and said, "We're all moved in and Mom and Aunt Viv are unpacking the kitchen as we speak. You coming home?"

I swallowed hard. "Candice's place is closer, and with your family at the house, I worry that I'll feel too distracted."

Dutch's jaw tightened, but he didn't protest. "Okay," he said. "Then I guess I'll see you at the rehearsal dinner."

I nodded. "Definitely."

And then he was gone, and I felt like someone had just punched me in the gut.

# T-Minus 00:14:51

The news that Abby was running down a highway in her wedding dress with a bomb strapped to her chest hit M.J. like a punch in the gut. It was one thing to sense her friend in danger; it was a whole other thing to have it confirmed by a police report, and the visual gave new perspective to the terror Abby must be experiencing with no one around to help her and the love of her life too far away to get to her in time. At that moment, however, the spirit of Rita came rushing back into M.J.'s energy, insisting—actually shouting—that she go to Margo immediately. The moment M.J. had a clear look at Margo, she understood why—the woman was pushing at a paramedic and trying to pull off the oxygen mask strapped to her face.

"Ma'am!" one of the medics said sternly. "Leave the mask in place! Your heart is showing signs of strain and we need to get you to the hospital."

Margo shoved at him again, but then her gaze fell on M.J. and she waved her over urgently.

Behind her, M.J. could hear the helicopter circling low, looking for a place to land. She imagined Dutch and Candice would be whisked off to try to save Abby at any moment, but she couldn't worry about that now. For the moment all she cared about was getting to Margo so that Rita would stop filling her head with shouts and demands to go to her friend.

"You!" Margo called, pointing to M.J. "Come here!"

M.J. was just a few feet away when she heard Candice yell, "Holliday! We need you!" But M.J. didn't turn around. Rita was being far too insistent.

At last she stood next to the gurney, which was half in the ambulance, half out. "What is it?" she asked Margo, and the moment she said that, Rita's voice subsided and her mind was once again free of noise.

"I . . . remembered . . . his . . . name . . . ," Margo wheezed.

"M.J.!" Candice yelled from behind her. "Get over here now! We need you!"

"Ma'am!" the paramedic snapped. "Please stand aside! We need to take this woman to the hospital!"

M.J. didn't even look at him. Instead she gripped Margo's hand and said, "Tell me, Margo. Tell me who came to the shop that day and scared Rita."

*"Holliday!"* Candice yelled one final time.

"His . . . name . . . was . . . ," Margo gasped.

M.J. nodded. "Yes? What was it, Margo?"

"Hey!" Candice snapped, at the same time that M.J. felt a cold hand clamp down hard on her shoulder. "Come on, M.J.! The chopper's waiting and we'll need you!"

M.J. tightened her grip on Margo's hand. Every second counted now, but she couldn't lose her cool. "Tell me his name, Margo!" she pleaded desperately.

"Buslawski . . . with a *B*. I remember . . . 'cause it was Polish . . . like my mom's family."

Behind her, M.J. heard Candice gasp. "Oh . . . my . . . *God*!" M.J. turned to face her and Candice's mouth was a round oval of shock. "I *know* him!"

Before M.J. could ask her how, Candice had gripped her free hand and was pulling on her so she had no choice but to let go of Margo. Then they were both weaving and darting through the crowd and then onto the street, weaving and darting again around all the cars until they were in the clear and heading toward the end of the street at a mad dash. There M.J. could see Dutch, Gaston, Brice, and the chief being whipped by the wind created by the helicopter, which had just landed in the baseball field of the school across the street.

Candice let go of M.J.'s hand then so that they could both run faster, and when they got to the men who were waiting on them anxiously, Candice grabbed hold of Brice's lapels, sucked in a few breaths, and said, "Buslawski! He's the unsub!"

Dutch's face had drained of color at the mention of the name and he looked anxiously to the chopper. "He'll have a detonator," he said, his voice so choked with pain it was hard to listen to. "We have to get to her, and we have to get to him!"

Gaston waved at the chopper. "You four go! We'll work on getting him!"

In the next instant M.J. was in motion again, running toward the chopper, ducking low to avoid the blades—but she had a terrible sinking feeling that all their efforts wouldn't be in time to save Abby.

# Chapter Fourteen

Candice and I stayed late the night of the third bombing, working any lead we could think of, and all the while I couldn't shake the terrible sinking feeling that no matter what we did, it still wouldn't be enough. I felt so strongly that time was running out, and the danger that'd been swimming around my fiancé like a cunning shark was almost ready to move in for the kill.

In desperation I suggested to Candice that we hunt down classmates of Mimi's at the community college, just to see if she had ever mentioned her boyfriend to any of them. But after several calls, it was obvious that hardly anyone remembered Mimi let alone knew that she'd had a boyfriend.

The next day yielded no additional clues. We headed to Mimi's apartment complex and had a talk with the apartment manager, but again, the only thing she remembered about Mimi was that she'd dropped off her rent checks on time, and she'd been a quiet tenant up until she'd blown herself up. I doubted that the woman remembered Mimi at all, and had only looked in her records to see if Mimi Greene had paid her rent before turning on the gas and lighting the match.

The thing that Candice and I had both registered from the visit with the woman, though, was that she knew that Mimi had committed suicide. We wondered about that enough to track down the fire marshal who'd issued the arson report and have a chat with him. He remembered having a talk over the phone with some guy claiming to have been Mimi's fiancé. He said that the man had called him to inquire about the fire in her apartment, but he couldn't remember if the guy had even given his full name. We asked him to check through his calendar in the hope that he might've written it down, and he promised to get back to us if he either remembered it or found it on his calendar. We never heard from him.

At the end of another long day I headed back to the bureau with Candice and we took our carryout dinners into the conference room in search of a little peace and quiet, because the office was teeming with our agents, those from Homeland, and the police. The conference room, while empty of personnel, was littered with boxes and files, all involving the bombings. You couldn't turn on the news without hearing about the case, and most of Austin was petrified to go out because locals were convinced that the bombings were a terrorist cell at work.

With a weary sigh I sat down at the table and lifted the lid of my grilled shrimp dinner. Candice was making me eat light so that I'd fit easily into my wedding dress . . . if there was a wedding. Cat was so mad at me she was practically spitting fire, and she'd now tasked Jenny Makeanote to pin me down on the remaining last-minute details. There were half a dozen voice mails from the poor assistant, and at some point I knew I'd need to put her out of her misery and call her back.

We ate in moody silence for a bit. Candice and I were both frustrated with the lack of progress and not up for casual conversation. My gaze kept drifting to the clutter on the table. Nearby was a photo of someone who looked familiar to me. It was paper-clipped to a thin file. Curious, I pulled it closer and saw that the picture was the driver's license photo of the photographer I'd ratted on at the FedEx bombing scene. The photog's name was Simon Salisbury, and lifting the lid on the folder, I discovered he had a criminal record. Busted for drugs five years previously, he spent about six months in the county lockup. "What'cha got there?" Candice asked me.

I looked up. "This is the file on that photographer we caught snapping pictures yesterday at the crime scene."

"Anything interesting?"

"He has a record. Drugs. Spent a little time at county."

"How long ago?"

"Five years."

Candice tapped her fork with her index finger thoughtfully. "He owns his own business, right? The photography studio?"

"He does," I said, immediately knowing where she was going with that. "But he doesn't look much like the sketch Haley gave us." Haley had sat with an artist who'd drawn up a mock-up of the elusive Buzz. The sketch was pretty generic, showing a round-faced man with a thick neck and flat nose. He could have been anyone, really.

"Oh, that sketch is ridiculous," Candice scoffed. "It doesn't even look like a real person. I mean, it's so generic that it *could* be this dude," Candice said, leaning over to look at the photo.

My radar wasn't buying that theory, however. "I don't think it's him."

"No?"

I shook my head. "We should still run it by Haley to make doubly sure, but . . ." My voice trailed off.

"What?"

I closed the folder and stared at Simon's photo. I didn't like him. He seemed like a sort of weaselly character and his energy was suspicious—like he often skirted the line between right and wrong. "I'm not sure," I said. "But I feel like he's connected to all this somehow."

"Connected? You mean like he's connected to this Buzz guy?"

A small lightbulb went off in my mind. "Yes!" Turning to her excitedly, I said, "I think he knows who this Buzz guy is!"

Candice checked her watch, then pushed her partially eaten dinner aside and slid the folder out of my hands. She opened the flap and trailed her finger down the page, which was a list of general information collected by the agent who'd interviewed Simon. "Let's give him a call," Candice said, pulling the conference room phone close to her so that she could dial. She waited through the rings and then mouthed, "Voice mail." She left a message for Salisbury to call her, then hung up and gathered her purse and the file.

"Let's go to Haley's first, then see if Simon's home."

We met Haley in her living room with her parents sitting on either side of her protectively. We showed her the picture of Simon Salisbury, but her face showed no sign that she recognized him. "Who is he?" she asked.

"Someone who may know Buzz," Candice said casually. "Have you ever seen him before?"

Haley shook her head. "No. He looks creepy."

I hid a smirk. Haley was pretty sharp. "You're sure you've never seen him before?" I pressed. "He was never in the store with Buzz?"

Haley shook her head again. "Buzz always came in alone."

"Did he ever mention having a friend who owned a photography studio?"

Haley shook her head for a third time.

Still, I was convinced there was a connection. We thanked Haley and her parents for their time, then headed out in search of the photographer.

We went to the address listed on the info sheet, but there was no sign of either him or his car. We then headed over to the crime scene in case he'd decided to ignore the crime-scene tape and had entered his studio, but the entire strip mall was dark and quiet—the burned-out hull of the FedEx store still filling the air with an acrid smell.

"Where is this guy?" I wondered.

Candice yawned. It was going on nine o'clock and we'd already had a loooong couple of days. "Let's camp out at his house until ten and see if he comes home."

After stopping at a nearby Starbucks, we did just that, but the stakeout was fruitless. We waited until midnight and Simon never came home.

Calling it a night, we headed back to Candice's, finding Brice asleep on the couch, surrounded by files. Candice gently woke him and made sure my "bed" was free of clutter, then promised to help track down Simon with me the next day.

We had a slow start the next day, the three of us waking up exhausted and grumpy. I dug through my suitcase for something appropriate to wear, but I'd packed most of my business outfits and sent them on to the new house, so in the end I had to settle for jeans and a waist-length leather jacket. At least I had my black boots with me. Candice gave me a subtle once-over when she came out of her room, but she didn't comment. Still, I made sure to let her know that my business attire had been packed up.

She moved to the hall closet and retrieved a sharp-looking scarf. "Here," she said, winding it around my neck. "It'll dress you up a bit."

We made our way to Simon's and parked in front of his house, nibbling on pumpkin spice muffins and sipping more Starbucks coffee. The air was crisp and the sky was gloomy—perfect weather for Halloween, and decidedly imperfect for a wedding. It was like the universe was trying to tell me something.

Salisbury didn't show up at all, and around noon we decided to head back to the office to see if anything else had come up. Brice was in his office with Gaston and the chief of police along with a stern-looking man in a black suit and shiny gold tie. I assumed he was part of Homeland Security.

My phone buzzed. It was Cat. For once I took the call. "Abby," she began, in that voice that said, "I will kill you if you say no. . . ."

"Hi, Cat," I said, trying to muster up that same enthusiasm that I'd been lacking for weeks.

"I need to take your final measurements, and you have yet to sit with the hairstylist! The makeup artist also needs to settle on a palette for you, and if I know you, you have yet to get yourself a manicure and pedicure. *And* I need you to pick out which headpiece you're going to wear. You keep putting all these things off, and you're making me so stressed-out!"

Cat's voice broke with emotion and I felt myself stiffen. I knew I drove her crazy, but I hadn't realized I was actually making her break down. "I can come right over," I told her.

Candice turned her head to look at me, her brow raised.

Cat sniffled. "I need Candice too. She has to go through a dry run with the stylist and makeup artist."

"We're on our way," I said, reaching for Candice's arm. Her eyes widened and she began to shake her head, so I clamped my hand firmly on to her elbow. "We'll see you in fifteen minutes."

We arrived at Cat's offices and were met at the elevator by Jenny. She was holding a basket and when we stepped off the elevator, she pushed the basket forward and said, "Mrs. Cooper-Masters would like you to place your cell phones in here."

Candice laughed. Not nicely. Sort of evilly. That worried me. "Of course!" I said, immediately dumping my phone into the basket.

Candice crossed her arms in a move that said, "I double-dog-dare you to take away my phone."

Jenny gulped, but the young woman held her ground, continuing to hold the basket out expectantly.

I nudged Candice with my shoulder. "Come on, Cassidy. It's only for an hour or two."

"What if there's a break in the case?" she said.

"Then there are a hundred agents and police who can act on it."

Candice took in a deep breath and let it out slow, all the while glaring hard at Jenny Makeanote. Still, Cat's assistant stood her ground, and I gave her huge props for that. Maybe she didn't know that Candice had a black belt in judo. And maybe she didn't know that my partner had also trained with the merchant marines. And maybe she didn't know that Candice's hands were registered with the FBI as lethal weapons.

. . . Okay, so I made that last part up, but seriously, Candice wasn't someone you stood up to if you knew how formidable (deadly) she could be. And yet, Candice at last handed over her phone, and when she did, I saw the slightest hint of approval in her eyes for little Miss Makeanote.

We walked to the back of the suite, and this time I was definitely convinced that Cat had hired more people. She was building up her Austin office really quickly. Too quickly for my taste. I loved Cat, but I loved to love her at a distance . . . say, the distance between Austin and Boston.

The minute we walked through the door of the conference room, we were pretty much assaulted. There was the hairstylist, dress stylist, seamstress, makeup artist, manicurist, aesthetician, and of course my sister acting like the ringmaster at Ringling Bros.

She deftly issued orders, talked on the phone, and constantly checked the weather reports for the weekend—which held a small ray of hope. "We might get a bit of clearing skies by midafternoon," she said. "Which means we'll want to photograph you and Dutch after the ceremony rather than before. You might be a little late to the reception, but a good wedding photo is worth making the guests wait a bit."

Cat kept us for the entire day. At one point, Candice and I simply glanced at each other across the room and dissolved into laughter. We were both so tired, anxious, and worried about solving the case that Cat and her circus were actually the perfect ridiculous distraction.

Around six o'clock Cat released us, and Jenny returned our phones. We both immediately checked our screens—not a single message for either of us. Candice called Brice from the car and put him on speaker. He sounded worn down to the nub. "We've still got a big fat nothing," he said. "Unless you count the four hundred phone calls that've poured into the tip line in the past two hours."

"Whoa!" I said. "Four *hundred* tips? What the freak?"

"APD released Haley's sketch to the local news, hoping it'd generate a lead. I fought hard against the idea, because that damn sketch looks more like Charlie Brown than a real person."

I glanced at the clock. The six o'clock news would just be airing, which meant another round of calls was about to roll in.

"Did you want us to come there and field calls?" Candice asked. I held in a groan. There was nothing worse than fielding calls from a tip line. The vast majority of them were a complete waste of time.

"Nah," Brice said. "You two were working some other lead, right?"

"Simon Salisbury," Candice reminded him. "Abs thinks there's a connection between him and the unsub."

"Yeah? Do you think the bomb was really meant for Salisbury and his studio?"

I blinked. I hadn't connected that very important dot, but hearing Brice say it out loud confirmed it in my gut. "Yes," I said. "Yes, I think that's exactly who the target was."

"Our explosives expert says that the device strapped to Debbie didn't go off early. He says the timer ran out and she was trying to get out of the harness when it detonated."

"Any footage from security cameras?" I asked hopefully.

"None," Brice said. "The cameras that would've caught anything were connected to the FedEx store and it burned to the ground."

"Has the coroner confirmed that it was Debbie?" I asked next.

"About an hour ago. It took a while to track down her next of kin and her dentist." Brice then changed tacks again and asked, "Have you already talked to Salisbury?"

"Not yet," Candice said, without going into detail about how we'd spent our afternoon. "We've been running by his house, but nobody's home."

"Okay, well, keep on that," Brice said, sounding distracted. "On line three?" we heard him say. "Okay, tell him I'll be right there. Babe, I gotta go. The director's on the other line."

We clicked off with Brice and headed back over to Salisbury's place. The house was dark and leaves were beginning to pile up in front of his door from the large red oak on his front lawn. There was no garage, just a carport, and no car in sight of the house either on the street or in the carport. "Where the hell could he be?" Candice asked, opening his file again to skim the pages.

"My guess is that he's gone into hiding. I mean a guy with a record like that . . . the last thing he needs is for the FBI to start poking around in his life."

"Or he's hiding because he knows that he was really the target," she countered.

I nodded. "Exactly. We have to find him, Candice. This unsub's gotta know he missed his target. Salisbury could still be in danger."

Candice closed the file and set it down. Then she reclined her seat a little and laid her head tiredly against the headrest. "We'll wait here a while, and if he doesn't show, then I'll call his parole officer in the morning and see if there's someplace else Salisbury goes in his off time."

"Like where?"

Candice shrugged. "A girlfriend's or a relative's. Or a buddy's house."

We sat in silence for a while, but something kept niggling at me. I picked up the file and clicked on the overhead light to read it. "The question I have is, why?"

"Why what?"

"Why Salisbury? I mean, what connection would he have to Mimi?"

"What connection did the beauty shop have to her? Or the dress shop at the mall for that matter?" Candice said, laying her head back and closing her eyes.

I tapped the back of the folder with my finger and the answer suddenly came to me. At almost the exact same moment, I saw Candice sit straight up and turn to me. "Wedding vendors!"

I nodded. "Yes!"

Candice turned her head to look out the front window again. "Do you think Buzz picked them randomly? Or do you think that he picked them because they were the ones he used for his own wedding?"

I sighed. Besides Buzz himself, there were only four people who could've answered that, and three of them were dead. "Since we can't ask Mimi, Rita Watson, or Carly Threadgill, the only person left who can tell us is Salisbury."

Candice nodded. "We gotta find him," she said, moving her seat back to upright again, and looking more alert than I'd seen her all night.

All that alert energy was to no avail, however. By ten thirty, with no sign of Salisbury we called it a night. On the way home, Candice called Brice and put him on speakerphone. We let him in on our theory. He said he'd try to get a warrant in the morning and send Cox and Rodriguez over to Salisbury's studio to look through the photographer's customer records. He then asked us if we needed help finding Salisbury, and I knew that Candice wasn't going to just hand over our lead to him. "We got it, babe," she said sweetly. "You guys have your hands full working all those tips. If we don't find Salisbury by the end of the day tomorrow, we'll ask for help."

I took a long shower when we got back to Candice's, wanting very much to clean the ugly feeling of this case off me. When I emerged, Candice held up a bowl of ice cream and pointed to my phone. "Dutch called," she said. "And I dished you out some comfort food."

I smiled and took a seat on the couch next to her, going first for the phone. I listened to Dutch's sweet message, wishing me a good night's sleep and hoping that I wasn't working too hard.

"You okay?" Candice asked when I wiped at my eyes.

"Fine," I told her, clearing my throat. "Thanks." Candice rubbed my arm sympathetically and it helped to have her company and her understanding.

I tried calling Dutch back, but the phone went straight to voice mail. It was well past eleven; he'd obviously gone to sleep. I drowned my sorrows in the Ben & Jerry's my BFF had dished out for me, and a short time later was fast asleep.

I woke up the next morning to the smell of coffee and toast. "Morning," Brice said when I sat up.

"Hey, there, boss man." Brice looked terrible. Like, haggard and gray from lack of sleep and stress. I could only imagine the tremendous pressure he must be under from his own bosses and the community at large to solve this case. "What time did you get in?"

Brice lifted his wrist, only to see it bare, so he turned to look at the clock on the microwave. "About three hours ago."

"Yikes. I think you need to go back to bed."

"No time for that," he said, taking a sip of his coffee only to make a face and stare into his mug. "Damn."

"What?"

Brice lifted the lid of the coffeemaker. "I forgot to put the grounds in."

I pressed my lips together to keep from chuckling and got up to help him with the coffee. When I came around the counter, I noticed that the toast was a bit crispy too, and by crispy I mean black and burnt.

I pointed to the couch. "Sit. I'll make your coffee and a decent breakfast."

Brice nodded dully and shuffled over to the kitchen table. While I was chopping up some veggies to put in his omelet, he nodded off. Candice came out of the bedroom, looking pretty exhausted herself. "How long's he been like that?" she asked, pouring herself a cup of joe.

"You mean asleep-asleep? Or just asleep on his feet? 'Cause if you're talking the former, about ten minutes. If you're talking the latter—at least the past three days."

Candice sighed and moved to the couch to retrieve the afghan I'd slept with. She fitted it around Brice's shoulders and kissed him sweetly on the cheek. "Thank God he'll be forced to take tomorrow off."

I was distracted with the vegetables, which might explain why I replied with, "Why? What's tomorrow?"

I didn't hear her answer, so I picked my head up to look at her. She was staring at me with a bit of bewildered alarm. "Your *wedding*."

I felt my cheeks heat. "Oh! Yeah . . ." I laughed and tried to make a joke of it. "I was just testing you."

Candice came to the kitchen counter and pulled up a bar-stool. "You okay?"

I was gently tossing garlic, peppers, spinach, and mush-rooms into a hot pan. "Sure. Why?"

"You don't sound so keen on this idea of getting married."

I felt my shoulders stiffen. "Well, of course I am!" I made sure to keep my face averted from her. "I mean, tomorrow I'll become Mrs. Dutch Rivers! Who wouldn't want that?"

Several seconds went by before Candice spoke again. "Abs?"

"Yeah?"

"Why're you crying?"

I hadn't realized she'd heard my sniffles. "I'm not."

"Abs . . ."

"It's fine! Everything's fine!"

"Sundance . . ."

"Please, Candice?"

I heard her sigh, but she didn't continue to press it, and I discreetly wiped my eyes and concentrated on making Brice the best damn omelet ever created.

Candice woke him when it was time to eat, and while she and Brice sat at the table, I made two more omelets for her and me. Brice left just as I was plating my own breakfast, thanking me for the coffee and eggs and promising to see me later at the restaurant.

I'd forgotten about the rehearsal dinner. Doing my best to hide my worry from Candice, I tucked into my meal, but I wasn't really hungry. She in turn pretended to ignore my distress and talked about our agenda for the day. "I need to go to our office," she said. "I want to dig into Salisbury's life a little and see if he's got any relatives living in the area."

"You think he might be hiding out somewhere close?"

"I do. I think, if he isn't legally keeping his nose clean, then he'll be looking for a way to stay close to his drug clients, especially with his studio shut down."

"How long do you think the strip mall will be off-limits to the store owners?"

"They'll probably release the crime scene late today, after Cox and Rodriguez have a chance to look through Salisbury's records," Candice said.

"And who knows when Salisbury will show up to open his shop again?" I said. "I mean, even if there is a customer record on file in Salisbury's studio, would we know who to look for, since Buzz is simply a nickname?"

Candice sighed. "That's why you and I have to track him down today, Abs."

I nodded. "Let's hope we can find him, Candice, because he could be the last hope we have of trying to find this unsub."

"I did have another thought that I wanted to go through with you," she said.

"What?"

"Well, I keep wondering about Banes. Why would our unsub contact him of all people?"

"When we interviewed him, he swore he didn't recognize the voice on his answering machine."

"Yes. But the voice could have been disguised in some way. I mean, you heard it, Abs. The unsub could have used a program on his phone to disguise his voice."

"There's an app for that?"

"There is. In fact there're a couple."

I made a face. "Figures."

"Anyway, I called Banes's nurse this morning," she continued. "You were right about him. He did have a stroke, a pretty massive one too. His condition is grave, he's in a coma, and his nurse doesn't think he's got a lot of time, so there's no way to interview him. I want to dig around in his case files and see if there's a connection to Mimi."

My brow lifted. "I hadn't thought of him having a connection to her."

"There might be none, but I thought it'd be worth checking on just to rule it out."

I nodded. "Good idea. We'll run as many leads down today as we can before time runs out." I felt a shudder go through me, and goose bumps formed along my arms.

Candice cocked her head. "You okay, Sundance?"

I stood up. "Fine. But I better hit the shower and get ready."

Candice and I arrived at our office a little after eight thirty, and she got right to work searching through Salisbury's info for a relative nearby where he might be hiding out.

I straightened up my own side of the suite for a bit, but started to feel a little helpless. Also, I missed Dutch terribly after not seeing much of him in the past five days. Thinking up a pretty good excuse, I called him. "Morning, dollface," he said with a gravelly voice.

"You're still in bed?" I was surprised. Between us, Dutch was usually the early riser.

"The brothers took me out last night for an impromptu bachelor party."

"Ah. How was it?"

Dutch yawned. "It was terrible. But don't tell them that. I spent most of the night missing you."

I squeezed the receiver. "I know, cowboy. Me too."

"You're gonna stay away tonight again, huh?"

I opened my mouth to tell him to hell with tradition, that I'd be home in the next hour, but what came out was, "Yeah. Don't want to tempt fate by seeing you before the wedding on our special day."

Dutch yawned again. "Well, at least you're mine at the rehearsal dinner tonight."

I smiled. Yes. At least there was that. "Listen, I actually called to see if you could give me the name of that detective from APD who's been your little buddy lately." Dutch had been quasi-mentoring a young rookie from APD who thought FBI special agent Dutch Rivers walked on water.

"Gavin?"

"Uh . . . yeah. Him."

"Gavin Spivey. You want his direct line at APD?"

"Please?"

Dutch gave it to me and we chatted for a little longer before promising to see each other later. I then pushed all melancholy and troubled thoughts out of my head and dialed Detective Spivey's number. The phone was answered by a woman. "Grayson," she said in a voice full of authority.

"Uh . . . hello?" I was confused. Had I misdialed?

"This is Detective Grayson," she replied. "How can I help you?"

"Oh, I'm so sorry. I'm looking for Detective Spivey."

"He's off today," she told me. "And I'm covering his desk. Is there something I can help you with?"

I hesitated. I was hoping that I could talk Spivey into looking up any record associated with Mimi Greene that might link her to Jed Banes. I was pretty sure the young rookie detective would do it if he thought that the request had come through Dutch, but the fact that he was off that day put a bit of a monkey wrench into things.

"Ma'am?" Detective Grayson said. "You still there?"

I made a snap decision. She had the energy of someone

you could trust, so trust her I did. I identified myself and told
her that I was a civilian consultant with the FBI investigating
a few leads connected to the bombing cases, and said that I
was running down a lead on a possible connection between
Mary or "Mimi" Greene and the retired detective Jed Banes.

"That old bastard's involved in this?" Grayson said, but
there was a touch of humor in her question.

"You know Banes?"

"I do, although I haven't seen him in a while. He got a bad
rep and in my opinion a bad rap for some bullshit that went
down a few years ago. But he always looked out for me, so I
guess you could say I'm partial to the old geezer."

"Did you know he's currently in the hospital?" I asked.

"In the hospital?" she repeated. "Is he sick?"

"My partner and I went to see him last week and he wasn't
well. Emphysema, I think. When we came back to reinter-
view him, we found him unconscious and in a really bad way.
He's had a stroke and he's now in a coma and isn't expected
to live much longer."

Grayson was quiet for a time. "Well, damn," she whispered. "The poor old geezer . . ." There was a little pause,
then, "You say you're trying to run down a lead between him
and someone else?"

I could hear her fingers clicking on a keyboard. "Mary
Greene," I told her. "But she went by Mimi. I doubt there's a
connection, but we just want to make sure that we've covered
all our—"

"Here it is," Grayson interrupted. "Banes filed a report on
a Mary Greene about a year ago. Looks like she had made
some sort of comment to a friend about wanting to harm
herself, and Banes was working some overtime out on patrol
when the friend contacted police. Banes responded to the
call, checked on the girl, talked with her for an hour or two,
and determined that the threat wasn't imminent. The report
also shows that he followed up with her two days later to
check and see that she was okay, and to drop off the name
and address of a local support group. He says here that
Greene was distraught over a breakup with her fiancé."

I was sitting forward on my chair, holding my breath,

while Detective Grayson spoke. When she finished, I said, "Is there anything else in the report?"

"Nope. It ends there."

Holy freakballs. We'd just closed the loop, but with Banes in a coma, we were helpless to get any more information out of him. He'd talked to Mary at length. He had to know something about her fiancé—this elusive "Buzz."

"Does it say in there who called in the report to APD?" I asked.

"No," Grayson said. "It says an anonymous male caller phoned it in and that he refused to give his name, saying only that he'd received a disturbing e-mail from a friend of his named Mary Greene, and then he gave her address before hanging up."

My skin tingled. I had a feeling that Buzz had been the "friend."

"Can you send me a copy of that report, Detective Grayson?" I asked.

"Not without a formal request from the FBI."

"Yes, of course. I'll have my boss call you. Will you be at this number for a bit?"

"I'll wait on the call, Miss Cooper."

I thanked her profusely, hung up, and did a quick hobble step into Candice's office. After filling her in, we both called Brice, who promised to call Grayson. "It explains why this Buzz guy may have called Banes," I said to Candice after we'd hung up with Brice. "He was the only person in this whole chain of people who took the time to try to help Mimi."

Candice tapped her finger to her lips. "But why call him at all?" she wondered aloud. "I mean, if Buzz thought Banes had tried to help Mimi, then why call him to taunt him with the threat of an explosion going off in two hours?"

I felt I knew the answer. "Because Buzz is creating a ritual. He was the one who originally called APD to report that Mimi might harm herself, and Banes responded to that first call."

"How do you know that?" Candice asked me.

"It's a gut feeling," I told her, knowing deep down that I was right. "I bet he got Mimi's e-mail, sensed she was feeling depressed and guilty, and maybe there was even something in there about wanting to die, so he called nine-one-one. We know that Buzz has a history of keeping close tabs on the women he's been abducting—I bet he was watching Mimi's apartment that night after he called, and I bet he tracked down which officer responded to the call."

My partner still looked doubtful.

"Buzz is repeating history, Candice," I pressed. "He's eulogizing Mimi by repeating certain things that led up to her taking her own life. The two hours on the timers of the bombs represent the two hours he waited for Mimi at the altar. The women he's choosing are all connected to her. The venues he forces them to go to are all wedding vendors they may have used for their own wedding. The call to Banes is just another part of that narrative."

Candice sat quietly for a moment, taking all that in. At last she nodded. "We have to find Salisbury," she said. "If Buzz knows the photographer is one of the few people that can identify him, he may try to kill him again."

"Any ideas where to look?" I asked, already sensing she'd come up with a lead.

She held up a piece of paper. "Salisbury's younger sister lives on the east side of town."

"What're we waiting for?" I asked, already turning to head back to my office for my purse and Fast Freddy.

We arrived at a low ranch home with burnt-orange shutters and white trim about twenty minutes later, and the moment Candice put the car into park, we knew we'd hit pay dirt.

In the driveway was a silver Ford F-150 with the license tag PHOTOG. "Well, hello, Mr. Salisbury," Candice whispered with a satisfied smirk.

We got out and approached the front door just as it opened and out stepped the elusive photographer. He seemed truly startled to see us coming up the front walk, and I saw him tuck a duffel bag behind him protectively. "Hey, Simon," Candice called breezily.

"Who're you?" he asked, his eyes darting warily between us.

"You don't recognize me?" I asked. "Aw, Simon, and here I thought we shared something special the other day."

He squinted at me. And then he glared hard. "You're the bitch that had me put in that cop car and taken in for questioning."

I smiled and placed a hand over my heart. "Guilty as charged."

"This is harassment—," he began, but Candice cut him off.

"Relax, buddy. We just want to ask you about this guy." Candice pulled out the rather generic sketch of Buzz and presented it to Salisbury.

He glanced at it before lifting his gaze back to us, but then I saw his eyes flicker to the sketch again and the tiniest hint of recognition appeared on his face. "Don't know him," he said quickly. Too quickly.

*Liar, liar, pants on fire . . .* , went a small voice inside my head. "Bullshit," I told him. "Who is he, Simon?"

Salisbury scowled at me, and I knew we'd never get him to cooperate. He was too mistrustful of authority. "I said I don't know him."

I balled my hands into fists. "Oh, cut the crap! Who the hell is he?"

Salisbury shook his head and adjusted the strap on his duffel bag. "I gotta be somewhere," he said, attempting to move past us.

Candice stepped in his path and held up the sketch again. "Why would this guy send a bomb to your doorstep, Simon?" she asked.

"I don't know what the hell you're talking about!" he snapped, working to move around her.

I stepped into his path too. "He's the guy that strapped a bomb to a woman and told her to go visit you, Simon," I said. "Why would he try to blow *you* up?"

Salisbury looked as if he was becoming increasingly uncomfortable. . . . Also . . . increasingly scared. "Get the hell out of my way!"

But we wouldn't. Every time he tried to move around us, we double-teamed to block him. Finally he moved to shove past Candice and she caught his duffel bag and pulled it right off his shoulder. "Ow!" she cried, pretending to fall to the ground with the bag. "Dude! You hit me with this bag!"

"Give that back to me!" he yelled, moving to grab the handle.

Candice swung out her leg and caught Salisbury midcalf. He went down hard and she was on top of him in an instant. "How dare you attempt to assault me!" she said, pulling his arms behind his back and securing them with her knee. Then she looked up at me and added, "Call for backup."

While I was on the phone with Brice, Candice pulled the duffel over to her and unzipped it. All the while Salisbury struggled to get up, but she had her knee jammed hard against his elbow, and every time he squirmed, the pressure threatened to dislocate his shoulder.

I was giving Brice the address when Candice unzipped the bag, and I saw her hand fly to her mouth. "Hey, hold on a sec," I told Brice. "Candice, what is it?"

Candice lifted her chin to me and I could see a look of utter horror and abject disgust on her face. She held open the bag and I saw that it was filled with photos. Photos of young girls wearing all sorts of S&M paraphernalia but otherwise naked. The youngest girl I saw couldn't have been older than ten. "Oh, you son of a bitch . . . ," I whispered.

"That's not my bag!" Salisbury shouted. "I was holding it for a friend!"

My stomach turned and I said to Brice, "We've got another problem. . . ."

Hours later we were still dealing with our encounter with Salisbury. Cox and Rodriguez had come up with bubkes. When they got the warrant early that morning, they'd noticed that the tape across the door of the photography studio had been tampered with, and when they went inside, they discovered Salisbury's computer was missing—along with all his customer files.

Salisbury himself had completely clammed up, and wasn't saying a word until his lawyer got there. We all knew we weren't going to get a peep out of him about our unsub until some sort of a deal had been made on the child pornography charges, but we were days away from assessing how many crimes Salisbury had committed, and special teams from both the FBI and APD had been dispatched to his home and photography studio in search of more child pornography evidence. In the attic and in a wall safe in the back of the studio, they found plenty. The bastard.

The sun was starting to set when Candice came to wrap an arm around my shoulders while I stared meanly through the mirrored glass at the slime bucket photographer. "Rodriguez just got word that Mimi's phone records will be available to us on Monday."

I glanced up at the clock. It read quarter after five. "Leave it to the phone company to take their time expediting critical evidence," I grumbled.

Candice squeezed my shoulders. "Yep. But what it really means is that it's finally time for you to set this aside, Sundance."

I squinted at her. "What do you mean?"

"You need to step away from this case and head off to the altar, honey. It's time to let it go and let us take care of it. With the phone records coming next week, we'll finally be able to put a name and a face to this Buzz by Monday afternoon. Tuesday at the latest."

I sighed and rested my head against her shoulder. Part of me wanted to continue to work the case until Buzz was brought in, while another part of me wanted only to walk away from it forever.

"Come on," Candice coaxed. "Let's get you dressed and to your rehearsal. Your sister will kill us if we're late."

The wedding rehearsal was only slightly better than a well-orchestrated disaster. Candice and I were late; Dutch, his brothers, and Milo had hit happy hour a little early (and were thus in giggly, slaphappy form); Brice had to skip the event because he was still hard at work on the bombing case; and Cat was making everyone wince through the use of her bullhorn.

Poor Jenny Makeanote looked harried and was scribbling so fast on her iPad that I thought she'd need to have her wrist checked for carpal tunnel later, and to cap it all off, the minister arrived coughing and wheezing and in full chest cold mode. His voice would never hold up through the ceremony the next day, but he gave his best effort, and after only eleven practice run-throughs, Cat let us go, but she didn't look at all happy.

She approached me gripping her bullhorn with fire in her eyes. "We have a problem."

"Only one?" I asked, maybe a *weensy* bit too sarcastically.

Cat glared hard at me and raised the bullhorn. *"I'm not in the mood, Abby!"*

I winced— man, that thing was loud.

Candice came to my side in a show of support. "Hey, Cat," she said. "Everything okay?"

Cat shoved a clipboard at me but replied to Candice. "No!" she yelled (thankfully without the use of the bullhorn). "They're predicting rain tomorrow and twenty-five-mile-an-hour wind gusts! We might have to move the ceremony inside, which means no butterflies, swans, or cupids!"

In that moment I'd never prayed so hard for rain in my whole life.

But Cat continued. "Also, I hear that some of the guests have been leaving messages on Abby's voice mail. I have *no* idea who's coming and who's not!"

Cat looked like she was close to having a meltdown. She'd been shouldering all of the stress of the wedding for me and I started to feel really guilty—especially since my cell indicated I had something like twenty-two voice mails on it that I hadn't bothered listening to. "Okay, honey," I said to her. "I'll check it over. And don't worry about the ceremony. Inside, outside—what does it matter?"

Cat looked at me with such fury that I took a step back. "It. Matters."

Candice and I were quick to nod. "Yes, of course it does," I said. "Sorry. I think I've got the prewedding jitters and stuff is just coming out of my mouth all willy-nilly—"

"Sundance," Candice interrupted.

"Yeah?"

"Shut it."

"Okay."

Candice and I both pushed big old smiles onto our faces and squared our shoulders like good little soldiers.

Cat's glare intensified, and then her gaze dropped to the guest list in my hands like she expected me to get right on it . . . and I wasn't about to do that because it sounded like a real pain in the keister and why not just let the guests come or not come on their own?

Candice lifted the clipboard out of my hand and surveyed the guest list. "I'll help Abby with this, Cat," she promised, which was Candice-speak for "I'll tell you what you want to hear if only you'll cut us some slack, Cat."

Cat's glare diminished to a simple scowl before she raised her hand and snapped her fingers. Jenny Makeanote was at her side in a hot second, and with one nod from Cat, Jenny was off again, hurrying into the reception tent only to rush right back out holding two garment bags, which she gave to Cat, who in turn handed one each to us. "Here are your dresses. The limo will be at Candice's condo at eight thirty a.m. and the driver will take you anywhere you'd like for breakfast, but you'll need to be here promptly at ten a.m. I've assigned you the two dressing rooms on the ground floor. Abby, you'll have the one at the back of the corridor straight off the main hall. Candice, yours is the second-to-last door on the left of that corridor. I have hair and makeup scheduled for both of you at ten thirty and eleven—there was some mix-up with the schedule, so you'll each be getting makeup before hair. Please don't put on your gowns until after you've had your hair and makeup applied. Abby, Jenny will be available if you need someone to help you dress."

I felt my face flush. She was starting to sound a bit too much like my mother for my taste. "I'll be fine, Cat, thanks."

"The ceremony is at three, right?" Candice said.

"Yes. *Promptly* at three. If the rain holds off, then we'll do the ceremony first and most of the pictures second, but, Abby, the photographer will want to get some photos of you prior to the ceremony, so be ready for him no later than two o'clock."

"Are Dutch, Milo, and Brice getting ready here?" I asked,

glancing at my fiancé, who was still laughing and joking with Milo and his brothers.

"No. They're having breakfast together along with Dutch's brothers, his mom, and his aunt. Then everyone will be driven here, where Dottie and Vivian will be given the upstairs dressing rooms, and the boys will be given full run of the guesthouse."

"Guesthouse? What guesthouse?"

Cat rolled her eyes. "The one right over there." I looked to where Cat was pointing and saw a modest-sized cottage on the other side of the lawn about fifty yards away.

"I've also secured the newlywed suite for the two of you for tomorrow night."

"Newlywed suite?"

Cat's scowl deepened. "If you'd come here and taken the tour like I told you to eight hundred times, you'd know that there is a romantic cottage up that cliff and tucked into those woods."

I again looked to where she was pointing and very faintly I could just make out the outline of a stone cottage way up the bluff overlooking the lawn we were standing on. Holding up my cane, I asked, "How the heck am I supposed to get up there?" There was clearly no road up to the cottage, and with my cane and bad hips there was no way I could hike up the side of a steep bluff.

Cat pointed to her left at the woods that flanked that portion of the lawn. "If you go to the left of the driveway out front, there's a little footpath that leads to a gondola made for two that takes you up to the cottage."

"A *gondola*?" Was she kidding?

"It's perfectly safe, Abby," Cat said.

"I've been up in it many times," Jenny Makeanote assured me. "It's actually a beautiful ride through the trees."

I wasn't convinced until Cat said, "I thought you'd be excited to have a little cottage to yourselves up in the hills where no one can get to you. I mean, with Dutch's brothers staying at your house . . ." She let the last part of that sentence trail off, and after thinking about it, and all the practical jokes Mike, Chris, and Paul might pull on us, I pushed that well-practiced smile onto my lips and nodded like a happy-faced bobblehead. "Awesome! What's a wedding night of bliss without a gondola ride?"

Cat narrowed her eyes at me. She could sense fake enthusiasm a gondola ride away. "*Any*way," she continued, "as I said, you'll need to be dressed and ready by two. The photographer swears that with such a small wedding party he can get all the pictures he needs in an hour, and the rest during and after the ceremony. Which reminds me, Jenny Makeanote, I need to sign the checks for the photographer, caterer, and baker tonight so that you can deliver them promptly when they arrive here tomorrow."

A tiny thread of a thought floated up from the back of my mind, but at that moment Cat raised her bullhorn again and yelled, "Let's go, people! We have the rehearsal dinner to get to! And Milo, please make sure the Rivers boys aren't driving, okay?"

Just like that, whatever thought had been about to surface evaporated and I was whisked off to a celebratory dinner, wishing the whole time that Dutch and I could sneak away and avoid the next day entirely.

I woke up on the day of my wedding feeling terrible. It might have been that I'd been sleeping on a lumpy couch for five days. Or it could have been that I'd had several glasses of red wine the night before. Or it could have been that I'd had a restless and fitful night's sleep, never really falling into more than a doze.

Mostly, though, it was probably because I didn't want to show up to my own wedding.

I sat up blearily and listened. The clock on the far wall said it was half past five, but no stirring sounds came from Brice and Candice's room. They appeared to be sleeping in.

I felt too restless to stay put, so I stood up, got dressed, left Candice a note in case she woke up and wondered where I was, and headed out.

I spent some time in my favorite coffee shop. It was nice and quiet on a Saturday morning, but after a while I felt too anxious and troubled to stay there too.

Getting in my car, I drove over to the new house. Several cars were parked in our driveway, but I didn't pull in. Instead I sat at the top of the drive, staring at our new beautiful home, and simply couldn't shake the ominous feeling I had that today was going to be awful.

Tears welled in my eyes for no reason I could identify, but I was helpless to stop them. I just felt sad. Terribly, terribly sad. And the more I tried to rationalize it as simply being overwhelmed by the wedding and the case I'd been working, the more the melancholy seemed to settle into my bones.

Finally I drove off and just meandered around the winding roads for an hour or two. I didn't know what to do, and I didn't know that I could talk to either Candice or Dutch about what I was feeling without them thinking the wrong thing.

Around then I got a text from Candice asking where I was. Remembering the limo and our plans for breakfast, I texted her an apology and told her to go ahead without me. I'd meet her at the venue. She immediately called my phone, but I didn't pick up. I couldn't talk to her without completely losing it and all I wanted was a little time to myself to try to pull it together.

I drove south to a park I knew and pulled into a space near a man-made lake and just stared out the window for a while. But my emotions wouldn't settle and the more I tried to figure out what the heck was going on with me, the more the answer seemed to elude me. I tried to think happy thoughts, that in just a few hours Dutch and I would be man and wife. I knew the idea should've made me happy, but it was as if some kind of a barrier had gone up inside me, and any thoughts about marrying Dutch only filled me with dread. In fact, the thought of walking down that aisle in a few hours made me almost physically ill.

Still, because so many people expected me to show up and smile like a good little bride, I eventually left the park and made my way over to the manor house, where I sat until nine, when the manager came out to let me in. She showed me to the room I'd been assigned, and then left me to go answer the doorbell. I saw that my gown had been placed on a hook next to a full-length mirror (after handing us our dresses the night before, Cat had thought better of it, and she'd grabbed them back and had them kept here).

I moved over to my dress and ran my hand down the beautiful silk. And then I burst into tears.

After having a good cry, I blew my nose, dried my eyes, and tried to find a distraction. Moving to the window, I focused on the wedding preparations. The day was gloomy, but the cold front that was supposed to sweep through Austin and bring rain and strong winds hadn't arrived yet. In fact, there seemed to be small holes in the clouds where some rays of the sun were managing to get through.

Meanwhile, out on the lawn there was a flurry of activity—chairs were being set out, flowers were being arranged, a red carpet was being unrolled. Everyone was working hard, but I could see them all periodically give the sky a wary glance.

Cat and her bullhorn hadn't yet arrived, but I knew she'd be here soon. In her place was Jenny Makeanote, who was talking to a man wearing Wellies with several pet carriers in tow. It seemed we were going to have swans after all. She handed him an envelope, then made a check mark on her clipboard before moving off to hand another envelope to a woman in a white apron I recognized from one of the meetings with Cat. She'd been the caterer, I thought.

With a sigh I moved away from the window and began checking out the digs. They were nice. There was a bottle of champagne chilling on a side table, along with a saran-wrapped fruit plate containing white grapes, pears, and sliced cheese. Nothing that might stain a wedding gown, I noticed.

There was also a photo album on the bureau, and curiously I opened it. Inside were the wedding photos of all the brides and grooms that had gotten married at the lovely estate.

As I was mindlessly flipping through the album, that tiny thread of a thought that I'd had in the back of my mind from the night before finally surfaced and bloomed so fully that I gasped. It had mingled with the image of Jenny handing envelopes to the swan handler and the caterer. "Checks!" I gasped.

"He would have written them all checks or put down a deposit using a credit card!"

If I was right and Buzz had used Rita's salon, Carly Thread-gill's bridal store, and Simon Salisbury's photography studio for his own wedding, then he would have put down some sort of deposit and made a payment. We already had Carly's and Rita's financial statements—that'd been part of the initial investigation into the bombs at their shops—and I was certain that we'd already collected Simon's bank statement records; that'd be useful in helping nail him as a dealer in child pornography. It would take only a few minutes for one of the agents to sort through the deposits in Rita's, Carly's, and Simon's accounts for a name that was consistent on all three statements. I was certain Buzz's name would pop up.

Whirling around, I ran to the bed where I'd thrown my purse and pawed through it to find my cell. Hauling it out, I was thumbing through my contacts list when there was a loud knock on the door and Cat sashayed in, holding tightly to her bullhorn and Jenny Makeanote close on her heels, along with Kendra, the makeup artist Cat had hired, who was carrying several small makeup bags.

"Who're you calling?" Cat demanded right away.

At first I ignored her. I was way too excited about what I'd just figured out, but Cat was clearly out of patience with me because quick as a feline she was in front of me, pulling the phone out of my hands.

"Hey!" I yelled at her. "Give that back! I have to call Gaston!"

"Who's Gaston?" Cat demanded, moving the phone behind her and out of my reach.

"He's my boss, Cat, and I *really* have to call him! It's important! I have a solid lead he *has* to follow up on!"

Cat squinted at me like she thought I was crazy. "Abby," she said crisply, "this is your *wedding day*! You're not calling *anybody*."

"Fine. Then let me just call Brice really quick. . . ." I made another grab for my phone, but Cat was too fast for me.

"No!" she yelled, twisting away and handing the phone to

Jenny Makeanote, who took it and dashed out of the room like a running back with a football at the Super Bowl.

I wanted to swat my sister. "Fine. Then I need to talk to Candice, Cat."

Cat shook her head, all the while continuing to look at me like I was a nut. "Candice isn't here yet, and I'm not letting you talk to her even when she does arrive. You are *not* working today; do you hear me? And you are *not* sending any of our FBI wedding guests or the groomsman on some wild-goose chase to hunt down some silly lead. You're always chasing a lead, Abby. That's your number one excuse, actually." Cat then adopted a tone a few octaves higher than her own, which I supposed was some kind of imitation of me. "Oh, Cat, I can't help out with all the gazillion things that need to get done for *my* wedding because I'm chasing a lead! Oh, Cat, Candice and I have to run out on you because we have a lead! Oh, look, the wind just blew in a *new lead* and now I'm going to do my disappearing act and *drive you crazy!*"

My eyes bugged. She had the crazy part down. "This is important, Cat."

My sister only glared at me. "So is this wedding, Abby. Whatever this *new lead* of yours is, it can wait a few hours."

I balled my hands into fists and started to protest again, but Cat wasn't hearing any of it. Instead, she held up her hand to me before turning to the woman carrying the makeup cases, and said, "Kendra, you remember my sister, Abby? She's impossible. Still, you have an hour to make her into a gorgeous bride. She will ask to borrow your phone. If I discover you've lent it to her, and it results in any of our guests dodging this ceremony, I will sue you into the ground. Do we have an understanding?"

The makeup artist paled; then she dug her phone out of her jacket pocket and handed it to my sister. "I don't need it while I work."

Cat took it, narrowed her eyes at me one last time, then headed to the door, tossing a "Good luck" to the makeup artist as she exited.

The door closed firmly behind my sister. I thought about

chasing after her, but Cat could enlist an army of support with one swipe of her AmEx no-limit credit card.

Kendra the makeup artist smiled nervously at me. My mind spun with options. Just as I settled on one, there was a knock at the door. Kendra opened it for me and Jenny Makeanote was there. "Hi, sorry, Abby. A messenger just dropped this off for you. He said it was from Mr. Rivers and that he wanted you to read it before the ceremony."

In her hand was a creamy envelope. Kendra took it and handed it to me. For a minute I was too distracted to think about plans of escape. Opening the envelope, I found a sweet card inside with a puppy on the cover. Opening the card, I immediately recognized Dutch's tight script and read:

*Hey, dollface,*
*I know things are a little insane right now, but if you have time to meet me at the new house, come by. I've sent everyone out for a few hours and I have a surprise for you.*

*Love you—always,*
*Dutch*

I was a bit shocked by the message and turned the card over to see if there was more, but there wasn't. And then I had the boldest thought of all. If Dutch was alone at the house, then maybe after I got through calling in my lead to Brice, I could talk to my fiancé and convince him to ditch the ceremony and run away with me. I knew that Cat would be absolutely furious, and Dutch's family too, but deep down I just didn't think that I could go through with this whole Cirque du Ceremony. Dutch loved me. He'd listen. He'd do it for me if it was important enough. I just knew it.

"Miss Cooper?" Kendra asked.

I jumped a little, realizing Kendra was still in the room and looking at me expectantly. I doubted she'd let me leave without alerting Cat. Smiling brightly at her (man, my smile was getting a good workout these days!) I said, "Let me just go to the bathroom and you can have at me."

Kendra seemed to relax and she returned my smile. I almost felt sorry for her. "No problem! I'll get my stuff set out. Take your time."

I headed to the bathroom, making sure to take my cane, the note, and my purse with me. I then moved immediately to the window, which was thankfully on the outer side wall of the house, out of view of the wedding crew, and pulled it open slowly, careful not to let it squeak. Then I pushed out the screen and hoisted myself up and out, landing a bit indelicately on the soft grass. Squatting down low, I snuck around the house to the driveway. Looking around, I waited until the coast was clear, and then I hurried to my car; ducking into it, I started the engine with a pounding heart and raced out of the drive. I didn't relax until I'd made it to the highway, but the thrill of escaping the ceremony was amazing. Deep down I knew I'd never go back there. As I drove, one thought prevailed—I had to get to Dutch.

Our house wasn't far from the venue, only about ten minutes, and I pulled into the driveway and saw there were no familiar cars there, but oddly, there was a white van. I wondered if Dutch's surprise involved a cargo van.

I was so intent to see him that I ignored the small tingle of warning my radar sent off, and parked at the bottom of the drive, shuffling quickly to the back door, which led straight into the laundry room. I turned the handle, finding it unlocked, and stepped across the threshold calling out to Dutch. Almost immediately the fumes hit me and I wobbled on my already unsteady feet. Where was my cane? Oh, yeah, it was in the car. I'd been so anxious to see Dutch that I'd left it behind. But what was in the house that was making me so dizzy? I blinked and tried to hold on to the washing machine to steady myself, but my hand missed it and I sat down hard on the floor, my head swimming so badly that I thought I was going to be sick.

My chin dropped forward and I saw stars, my vision was clouded by an encroaching darkness, and I heard myself call out to Dutch again, but my own voice sounded dull and lifeless to my ears. And then a figure stepped forward from the darkness of the hallway. But it wasn't Dutch. Whoever it was, he wore a gas mask. I could hear the sound of his breathing filling my ears with a haunting sound.

"Wha . . . wha . . . Why?" I asked, even as I felt my head loll back toward the tile floor. A sharp pain at the back of my head told me I was now flat on my back and as I stared up, my already clouded vision was filled with the sight of that man in the mask standing over me. And then I was falling down, down, down, and I saw nothing more.

# T-Minus 00:10:32

M.J. felt totally discombobulated flying through the air in a helicopter, which was nothing like riding in an airplane. Closing her eyes to fight the motion sickness, she squeezed the bar at the top of the chopper even more tightly. After a few minutes of flying blind, however, she decided it was probably better to keep her eyes open, but avoid looking down.

In the seat facing her was Dutch, his gaze trained on the ground visible through the small window next to him. His face was hard and his jaw clenched, and there was a large welt at the top of his forehead where he'd hit the ground after being Tased, but his eyes were intense and focused. M.J. didn't know how he was holding it together, because if the tables were turned and word came in that her boyfriend, Heath, was strapped to a bomb that could go off at any second, she'd have a complete meltdown.

Sitting next to Dutch was Candice; her lovely bridesmaid's dress now torn and dirty, her knees were both scuffed, and the paleness that'd marked her complexion earlier had returned. She held tightly to Dutch's hand while tears rolled down her cheeks. M.J. knew exactly how she felt—the situation seemed hopeless.

Before entering the chopper, she'd learned that Abby had

been seen heading down a road close to the wedding venue. How she'd gotten there from the house, she could only guess, and M.J. didn't know if Abby was trying to make her way to the estate or was trying to avoid it. M.J. suspected that she was probably out of her mind with fear, and she simply couldn't imagine what her friend might be going through.

The chopper made a sudden sharp sweeping turn and M.J. held her breath and fought the lurch in her stomach. "Put it down!" Dutch shouted, his body leaning forward as he stared out the window. M.J. knew he'd just spotted his fiancée.

Overcoming her fear, M.J. leaned forward too, and she caught a glimpse of a figure in white moving raggedly along the side of a railing acting as a barrier to the edge of a cliff.

The helicopter turned in another tight circle, but the pilot called over his shoulder that there wasn't a good place to land.

*"Put it down on the road!"* Dutch shouted. *"Now!"*

Still the pilot hesitated until Brice, who was sitting in the front seat, motioned firmly for him to do it.

M.J. swallowed hard as the chopper began to lower toward the ground. She knew that if a car approached and didn't see the helicopter in time, there could be terrible consequences, but as she looked through both windows, she didn't see any cars coming. And then with a hard bump they were down.

Dutch was out of the chopper in an instant, and Candice was right behind him.

M.J. got out quickly too, looking everywhere for Abby. She wasn't sure why she'd been brought along in the chopper, but she felt certain that Candice had been right to insist on her coming. Still, one look toward the other side of the road told her how desperate their situation was. Abby was perhaps fifty yards away from them, and she was gripping the side of the railing desperately. The poor thing was draped in the torn remnants of a wedding gown, covered in dirt, grass stains, and blood. Around her chest was a terrible sight—a metal cage encased her torso secured by half a dozen padlocks, and in the center of the cage was a digital clock and several black tubes that looked like dynamite.

Abby herself was covered in cuts, scrapes, and bruises, her hair a tangled mess and her face stained with tears and dirt. She was shouting at Dutch and holding up her hands as if to stop him from coming closer. M.J. was too far away and the chopper was too loud for her to hear what Abby was saying, but her body language was clearly begging Dutch and Candice not to approach her.

Still, Dutch moved steadily forward, but just as he was within reach of her, Abby did something most desperate. She swung a leg over the side of the railing, and for a moment, M.J. thought she was going to jump into the ravine below.

Dutch took three running steps and lunged—reaching her hand, he grabbed it tightly and refused to let go. Instinctively, M.J. moved closer, in spite of the danger of the bomb strapped to Abby's chest.

Candice was much closer to Abby and Dutch, and when she was about ten yards away, Dutch put up his own hand and told her to stop. Abby cried out to Candice then, and M.J. faintly heard her say, "He's at the wedding! Candice, he's at the estate waiting for me!"

M.J. felt a hand on her back and beside her Brice shouted to Candice, who immediately turned around and raced back toward them, waving to the chopper pilot, who looked as if he was ready to sweep into the air again. Before she knew it, Brice and Candice were back in the chopper and it was lifting off and whisking them away.

For a brief few seconds, it was once again quiet except for the sounds of Abby sobbing, begging Dutch to get away from her before the bomb went off. And then the air was filled with the approaching sounds of sirens.

# Chapter Fifteen

As I sat on the edge of the bed in the lovely cottage above the estate, staring at my abductor, I thought about begging. In fact, I was fully prepared to slide down to my knees and plead to him for mercy. But one look at the triumph in his eyes told me he wasn't the merciful type.

And that caused me to burst into tears. Great big sobs rose in my throat and I was helpless to stop them. "Why?" I blubbered. "Why, Russ? You *know* me. I had nothing to do with Mimi's suicide. I never even met her."

Russ Buslawski—my oh-so-friendly and oh-so-helpful exterminator, who'd solved my scorpion problem and the cricket infestation at our new home—got up from the chair and came over to stand in front of me. "Don't you see, Abby?" he said in a gentle voice that sickened me. "It's destiny."

I shook my head and more tears slid down my cheeks. "*How* is killing me destiny?"

Russ sighed, as if he were truly sorry that I didn't understand. "In the beginning I wasn't going to involve you at all. I was going to let Haley be the last one, but then I found out that you were working the case, and you were also getting married, and you took Haley out of my reach. Remember?"

And I did remember. I remembered looking at her in the Jamba Juice store and feeling that her life was in danger and that we had to protect her. I'd been the one to talk Brice into putting her into protective custody. I realized that Russ had meant to kill both women who worked there. He'd gone after Debbie first, but he'd planned on murdering Haley too.

"I was so mad at you," Russ said to me. "You kept ruining all my plans, and I almost killed you and your friend Candice when you two were staking out Salisbury's place, but then I had this thought. This amazing thought that maybe you kept getting in my way because you were supposed to. You were supposed to become a part of this. It was a like a big sign, you know?"

I shook my head. I wanted him to see that this was insane, that he was talking like a madman, but madmen don't know they're talking crazy. They believe in the logic of random circumstances as if they were a personal road map to carry out their twisted agendas.

"Mimi was sending me a sign through you, Abby. She wanted my last statement to involve you because she wanted me to pick an actual bride. It was supposed to be you all along. It's fate."

I bit back the bile forming in the back of my throat. "Mimi wouldn't have wanted this," I said to him.

Russ shook his head like he felt bad that I didn't get it. "She would've understood," he told me. "She wouldn't have wanted them to get away with it in the end. She said so in her e-mail. They all drove her to it, you know. Mimi found out I couldn't get my money back from that beauty shop, or the photographer, and she was sick over it. She'd never showed up to get her hair done, and she'd tried to take her dress back, but the owner wouldn't give her a refund. She sent it to me, you know, because she said she couldn't bear to keep it in her closet anymore. I'd paid for the whole wedding, and Mimi felt so bad. Hell, even the photographer wouldn't return any of my money even though he'd only taken a few shots at the church.

"Mimi said she felt responsible for hurting me both emotionally and financially, and she didn't know how she could live with herself. She said she wanted to die. And it was 'cause of them. 'Cause of her sister, who told her she was a loser, and her friends, who told her she shouldn't marry me. They wanted her to break up with me and work all their extra late-night shifts at the Jamba Juice, the selfish bitches. No one would listen to her. But I listened to her. I listened and I knew she was in trouble, and I tried to take her away from all that, but they poisoned her against me and told her to cut me out of her life. Even that student therapist told Mimi not to talk to me. And she just felt worse and worse and worse until she couldn't take it anymore."

"Russ," I whispered, desperate to get through to him. "Mimi killed herself because she was a troubled young girl who felt overwhelmed and couldn't see herself ever feeling better. She was obviously clinically depressed and that was no one's fault. That was just a function of brain chemistry coupled with a tragic set of circumstances. Mimi wouldn't have wanted you to do any of this."

Russ's eyes narrowed. "Well, it's too late, 'cause it's already done, Abby."

I bit my lip. "Russ," I tried again. "I know you don't want to do this. I know that you reached out to Jed Banes hoping that he'd figure it out and stop you—"

"I didn't want anybody to stop me," Russ snapped. "I just wanted you guys to figure out why. I was doing this out of revenge for all the mean girls out there. All the people who hurt people like Mimi, who don't deserve to die like she did."

My lip quivered. "And I deserve it, Russ? I deserve to die like Mimi?"

Russ's mouth became a thin line, and I started to hope that he might be having second thoughts. But then his eyes darkened again and he said, "Maybe your bomb will send the right message. Maybe then they'll finally get it."

I knew then that my fate was sealed. Swallowing hard, I whispered, "What happens now?"

Russ moved toward the door where a tuxedo was hanging on the doorframe. Pausing to take it down, he then reached into his jacket pocket and pulled out an envelope I recognized. "Now I'm going to your wedding. I'll be sitting in the front row, waiting for you."

I shook my head. If he thought for one second I'd go there

and put everyone I loved in danger, he was even crazier than I thought.

"Oh, you'll come," he assured me. "If you don't, I'll kill your fiancé." My breath caught. I knew he wouldn't hesitate to kill Dutch. Then Russ reached back into his pocket and pulled out what looked like a small TV remote control. "But to make even more sure that you'll come, I'll make you a deal. If you get to the aisle before the clock runs out, I'll tell you the code to stop the clock. But if you reach out to anybody for help, I'll detonate the bomb." Russ wiggled the remote wickedly and I now knew exactly how he'd gotten the other girls to comply with his directive. He'd promised to deactivate the bomb if they did as he said. Their only hopes had been in reaching the destination he picked for them in time. Little did Taylor, Michelle, or Debbie know that Russ never intended to let them live beyond the two hours he'd put on the clock.

And he seemed to think that I didn't know either. He looked to be counting on my having even a small ray of hope that he'd be true to his word and let me and Dutch and the rest of the wedding party live. It was so awful I wanted to fly at him and beat him bloody, but that remote in his hand kept me frozen in place. There was a red button on it that I knew represented instantaneous death, and while I had two hours, I knew I might still create my own ray of hope.

"I won't make it easy for you," Russ added, slinging the tuxedo over his shoulder. "Debbie almost got out of her harness, so I made that cage special for you. You'll never get out of it, so I wouldn't waste any time trying. There's no phone here, so don't waste any of your time left looking for one. You'll need every minute just to make it down the hill, because I'm going to go down in the gondola, and then I'm going to dismantle it. You'll have to make it to the estate on your own, but I've left you your cane and I'm pretty sure that if you're motivated enough, you can get down the bluff in time. Just don't fall. That timer's a little sensitive."

With that, Russ turned and left me without a backward glance.

The second he was out of the cottage, I got to my feet and grabbed Fast Freddy. There was no way in hell I was going to play his game, and I had to believe that I could make it down that hillside in time to warn Dutch.

I knew that Russ was going to be true to his word about one thing: If he didn't see me or hear the bomb go off within that two-hour period, he'd kill my fiancé. Shuffling to the door, I stood on the front porch, watching the gondola slide squeakily down the wire and disappear into the trees.

There was a small patch of land around the cottage that was fairly level, but beyond that, the terrain was steep, and filled with foliage. Getting down the side of that bluff with two bum hips, an oversized wedding dress, and a bomb strapped to my chest suddenly seemed utterly impossible.

I gripped the doorframe and had to take several deep breaths because I could feel myself starting to panic. I knew I had to make it down that hillside, but there was no way I was going anywhere near the estate. I'd never put Dutch, my friends, and family in danger like that, and I knew that Russ fully intended to detonate the bomb the moment he saw me.

Instead, I had to make it down to the road leading to the estate. There was a gas station not far from there, and they had to have a phone. All I needed was a few extra minutes. If I could get to that phone, then I could warn Dutch before I died. I could also tell him how sorry I was that I'd spent the last few days of my life hiding myself away from him. I'd explain that I hadn't understood my own intuitive feelings. I knew I'd presented a danger to him, but I hadn't imagined this. It all made sense now, but if I died before telling Dutch, he'd forever think that I'd pulled away from him because I'd had cold feet.

When I could breathe again, I closed my eyes and whispered, "Please, crew of mine, help me!" For a moment I felt nothing but my own panic, and then, almost like a tiny miracle I felt my spirit guides surround me and fill my chest with courage. I opened my eyes and in my mind's eye I literally heard them say, *Look to your left.* It was then that I noticed a very faint trail leading off to the side of the cabin. With trembling limbs I stepped carefully off the porch and onto the path, gripping my cane tightly.

The path was true, but I was not. I slipped and slid so many times that I lost count, and each time I felt my heart would burst with fear, afraid the jolt from hitting the ground would set off the bomb, but mercifully, it never went off.

I was careful each time I fell to always take the blow on my rear or my hip. The wedding dress severely hampered my pace; it was so big that I kept tripping on it, and I cursed it over and over, but there was no way to get it off with the metal cage wrapped around my torso. That also greatly hampered me, and it chafed against my skin until it was raw and bloody.

Yet my crew kept urging me on, pushing me to breathe and carry on. As long as they were with me, I knew deep down that I could do it. I kept my focus on putting one step in front of the other, and tried very hard not to look at the digital readout of the clock, but at intervals I caught myself peeking, and that mounting fear built and built as the minutes ticked down. At last, with about fifteen minutes to spare, I spotted the road, and began to sob again as I hurried along it toward the gas station.

Cars passed me and honked, and one car pulled over down the street and a woman got out. She took one look at me and I shouted at her to get back in her car and drive away. I didn't want to take the risk that the bomb might take out an innocent bystander.

The gas station would present a horrific choice. How could I warn the people inside to get out so that I could go in and use the phone? The answer came to me as the station came within sight. There was a man pumping gas right there. I shouted at him to go inside and tell everyone to get out. He looked at me like I was crazy, but then I pointed to my chest and he pulled out the pump from his car, rushed to the driver's side, got in, and took off.

I was so out of breath and so upset that I'd blown it that I almost didn't notice when the clerk came out to shout at the back of the car. "You!" I yelled at him. "Get out of here!"

He turned to me, and his expression mirrored that of the

driver who'd just sped away, but I pointed to the bomb and begged him to leave and he took off too as fast as he could run.

Keeping clear of the pumps, I ran inside the station and behind the counter. I called Dutch's phone, but there was no answer and it went to voice mail. I closed my eyes and cried bitter tears as his husky rich baritone came to my ear. "This is Special Agent Rivers. Leave me a detailed message at the beep."

"Dutch!" I cried. "Oh, God! Listen to me. I'm not sure if Cat took your phone too, but if you get this message, you have to leave the ceremony immediately! He got to me, baby. Russ Buslawski, our exterminator. He's the unsub, and he's going to kill you. He's already killed me. I'm going to call the police now, but before I go, I just want you to know how much I loved you. With my whole, whole heart I loved you. You were the best thing that ever happened to me, and I always knew that. More than anything in the whole world I wanted to be your wife and take care of you like you always took care of me. Please watch over Eggy and Tuttle for me. Tell Candice, Cat, and Brice that I loved them too. I'll never be far away from you, cowboy. I promise."

I hung up sobbing so hard I could barely breathe. And then I heard the sound of a helicopter approaching. Intuitively, I knew it was for me, and I also had another intuitive thought—Dutch was on that chopper.

Rushing out of the gas station, I hurried down the road away from the pumps. The wind from the blades of the chopper was kicking up so much dust and debris that it was hard to see, but somehow I managed to spy the railing at the side of the road. I had to keep Dutch away from me. I didn't know how much time was left on the timer, or whether Russ was close enough to me to detonate it, as I knew he would if he suspected I wasn't still working my way down the hillside.

And then I had hold of the railing and I turned to see Dutch getting out of the chopper. I felt such a well of sadness and hope all at the same time. He wasn't at the ceremony. He might still live. But then he came toward me and I knew this was exactly the moment I'd been dreading for the past two weeks. This was why every time he got close to me, I'd felt a horrible sense of foreboding. *"Stop!"* I screamed. But he kept coming. In desperation I pulled one leg up over the railing. Looking down, I saw that it was about a fifty-foot drop to the rocky terrain below.

*"Abby, don't!"* Dutch shouted.

I took a deep breath. Could I let go? Could I be brave enough to fall to my death?

I tried to steel myself, tried to convince myself that it would be so quick that it wasn't likely to hurt much, but I wasn't fast enough. Before I knew it, Dutch had hold of my arm. *"Let go!"* I screamed. "Get away from me, Dutch! *Get away!*"

But he wouldn't let go. Instead he hauled me back over the side and gripped both of my wrists tightly.

As I was struggling with him, I saw Candice. She was also approaching. *"Candice, stop!"* I screamed.

She listened, and the look on her face broke my heart. "Tell me how to help!" she cried.

For a moment her question threw me. Didn't she know I was quite beyond help? But then, a thought came to my mind. It was clear and sound and I knew it was from my crew. *Tell her to bring him here,* they said. "It's Russ Buslawski!" I shouted. "He's at the ceremony waiting for me to show up! But be careful, Candice! He's got the detonator!"

In an instant Candice was in motion, dashing back toward the chopper, and my focus was then back on Dutch. "Please!" I begged him, struggling to pull out of his grip. I'd throw myself over the side of the cliff if only to protect him. "Dutch, *please* get back!"

To my shock and horror Dutch responded by pulling out a set of handcuffs from his pocket. Gripping my forearm tightly, he slapped one cuff onto my wrist, and the other onto his own. *"Noooooooooooo!"* I screamed, pounding on his chest, so angry and afraid at the same time. "Why?" I demanded through my tears. "Dutch, *why?*"

"Till death do us part, Edgar," he replied, his own eyes misting.

I stopped fighting him. "But you'll die," I sobbed. "Don't you get it? You'll die!"

"Abs," he said gently, wrapping me into his arms. "Don't *you* get it? Without you I can't live."

I shook my head. "Not like this," I said to him. "You can't go like this!"

He just looked at me with such love and sympathy that it was hard to hold his gaze. "Abigail Cooper, there's something you don't know about me. Three and a half years ago, after you and I had shared a bowl of ice cream on your back porch, I called my mom and told her that I'd just had dessert with the woman I was going to marry. And you know what else? I think I knew the moment I laid eyes on you at the restaurant where we had our first date that you were the one for me. I might as well have married you back then. You are my one and only, sweethot, and I've never been more certain of anything in my life. I love you, Abby. I take you for my wife today, here and now, to love, honor, cherish, and occasionally call you out for swearing. I will be there for you to the end of my days, and if that day is today, well . . . then I'll go out with you wrapped in my arms, and that's better than the next fifty years without you."

"But—"

"But nothing, Edgar. I love you. So I do. I do, I do, I do."

I realized I was shaking from head to toe. It was all too much for me. I didn't want to be the cause of Dutch's murder, but I couldn't help feeling so glad, so relieved, so loved wrapped in his arms as the last moments of my life counted down. I was left speechless as Dutch wiped away my tears and kissed me so sweetly.

And then the chop, chop, chop of the helicopter was approaching again, and I looked up to see that we were literally surrounded by squad cars and black sedans. They were all about fifty yards away and the cops and agents who'd driven here were outside of their cars, eyeing us with a mixture of fear and trepidation. Instinctively, I also glanced at the clock on the bomb. Even upside down I could see that we had barely two minutes left to live.

# T-Minus 00:01:57

The chopper landed well away from Abby and Dutch, but close enough to M.J. so that she had a good view of who got out. She saw Brice and Candice and two other men in suits, and between them was a man of about thirty with a black eye, torn tuxedo, and victorious smile. His hands were secured behind his back and he had no chance of escape, but still, his smile widened when he saw Abby and Dutch. It made M.J. sick to her stomach to look at him. He had to be this Buslawski character they'd all been talking about.

Candice yanked on his arm and tugged him to the front of all the cars to face Abby and Dutch.

M.J. instinctively wound her way through the cars and police toward them, that intuitive sense that she stay close to Candice pushing her forward. "What's the code to deactivate the bomb!" Candice demanded.

Buslawski simply laughed.

M.J. walked forward; someone from the other side had just entered her energy. This was a new soul. And she felt strongly it was connected to the man who'd strapped Abby to a bomb.

"Candice, please!" Abby yelled from across the road as she pulled up her wrist to show that Dutch had handcuffed himself to her. "Please! Someone get Dutch out of these! Please! Save him!"

Dutch reacted by pushing Abby's hand down and pulling her close to him. He was willing to die with her and everyone there knew it.

"What's the code?!" Candice shouted again. This time she struck Buslawski so hard he doubled over. But then he lifted his head and actually laughed. "You'll never guess it," he sang. "And you only get one try!"

Candice raised her hand to strike him again, but at that moment M.J. rushed forward and yelled, "Wait!"

Candice's eyes darted to her, but her arm remained high, ready to strike.

M.J. bent down to look at the bomber in the eye. "Someone from the other side wants you to tell us the code," she said.

He merely snickered at her.

"I'm a medium," M.J. said quickly. "Someone with an *M* is trying to connect to you. She keeps saying it's me! It's mememememe!"

Buslawski's eyes narrowed. He didn't believe her for a second.

M.J. reached out to the woman with the *M* name. "Mary," she said to him. "Her name was Mary. She says that she's so disappointed in you. She never wanted this."

Buslawski turned away from her.

Candice struck him again. *"What's the code?!"*

M.J.'s jaw clenched. She wanted Candice to calm down, but she knew they were quickly running out of time.

"What's the timer say?" Brice called to Abby and Dutch as a large metal truck arrived with the words BOMB SQUAD on the side.

"It's too late," Dutch called back. "Less than a minute. You guys all get back!"

Around them people began to move away, but Candice stood there with Brice and M.J., who all refused to move.

Meanwhile Mary was practically yelling at M.J. to keep trying to talk to the bomber. "Mr. Buslawski," M.J. said, squatting down again to get right up into his face. "Mary says that she's the one who's responsible. She decided to take her own life, and nothing anyone else said or did contributed to it. She says please don't do this. Tell them the code!"

Buslawski remained unmoved.

In frustration M.J. stood. She had only seconds left to figure this out, she knew, and she reached out to Mary and begged her for a number that might have meant something to this man. *One,* she heard Mary say. *One, one, one, one, one, one!*

M.J. shook her head. She needed the other digits. Closing her eyes, she pleaded again, but Mary only continued to shout the number one, and then, in desperation she filled M.J.'s mind with the image of a wedding cake. And then she showed her M.J.'s symbol for suicide—a noose.

"Fusco! Harrison!" shouted a voice full of authority. "Grab that girl and the unsub and get back!"

A hand landed on her shoulder and M.J. shrugged it off. She knew Mary was giving her all the clues to the code, but she wasn't the one that was going to be able to put it together. She needed help, so she lifted her chin and shouted at Abby and Dutch. "The code is connected to a wedding, but not this one, and it's also connected to a suicide! I think one of the digits is a one!"

Abby reacted by gasping. "Ohmigod! I know the code!"

# Chapter Sixteen

**T-Minus 00:00:08**

"What is it?" Dutch said, bending down in front of me to focus on the keypad of the bomb. *"Abby, what's the code?"*

"Eleven, eleven, eleven!" I shouted, and I looked at Russ, whose triumphant smile evaporated. Mimi had killed herself at eleven eleven on the eleventh, and died a month after abandoning Russ at the altar, which would have been the eleventh of November 2011. I prayed that I was right and then I prayed that Dutch's shaking fingers could type the date in fast enough.

He began to tap at the keypad and I gripped his free hand tightly. At the last second I closed my eyes tight and whispered, *"Please!"*

At my chest there was a little *ping* and then . . . nothing.

Nothing at all happened. For several more seconds Dutch and I stood together, squeezing hands and waiting, but then there was a sound that began to fill the air. The sound was clapping. I opened my eyes. Everyone—all the cops, the FBI agents, Candice, M.J., and even the chopper pilot—was clapping, and then they were cheering, and then they were all shouting and giving each other high fives.

Barely able to take it all in, I looked down and saw that the face of the clock had stopped with two seconds on the timer. Two seconds. My knees wobbled and I nearly went down, but

Dutch caught me and held me close. "We did it, dollface!" he said. "Holy shit, we did it!"

I sobbed with relief and when I could support myself again, I looked to the crowd, searching. . . .

At last I found M.J. She was crying too. We exchanged a look and I knew that I would be grateful to M. J. Holliday for the rest of my life. And I planned to live a very long life as the wife of Special Agent Dutch Rivers.

The bomb squad had me out of the metal harness in about twenty minutes; it probably would've taken less time, but Dutch refused to remove the handcuffs until after they'd safely deposited the bomb in the metal truck.

And then, from down the street came a limo, and out of it stepped my sister, who looked like a complete wreck. She seemed rattled not only by what'd happened—or nearly happened—to me, but also by what'd apparently happened to her.

She was disheveled and just a complete mess from head to toe. There were butterflies still flapping in her hair, crescent-shaped bite marks on her legs, and in her hand she carried a broken arrow from one of the cupids' bows.

I had a feeling that Cirque du Ceremony may have perhaps gotten a little away from her. Still, she was so happy to see I was alive and, except for some cuts and bruises, okay, she barely mentioned the havoc the swans, butterflies, and rebellious little people had caused.

"Well, the minister has gone home with a hundred and two fever," she announced as I was being patched up by the paramedics. "But a few of the guests are still at the estate. We might be able to find someone to get the two of you hitched."

"Who's still at the estate?" I asked.

"Dave and his wife," Cat replied, picking at a swan feather clinging to her stocking.

"Dammit," I swore. I'd missed her again.

"We're *not* getting hitched today," Dutch said firmly.

Cat eyed him moodily. "I can't go through this whole wedding plan again, Dutch," she said.

"You won't have to," he said, taking my hand and kissing it, but what he meant by that, he wouldn't elaborate on.

Later that night Dutch and I were at our new home in the

master bedroom resting comfortably on our new beautiful bed when the doorbell rang. One of Dutch's brothers answered the door and Dutch and I heard Gaston's voice in the foyer. "You don't have to see him," Dutch said to me. He'd been doing a great job of keeping everybody else at arm's length while I recovered emotionally from our ordeal.

Truth be told, I was more worried about the big lump on his forehead. He had yet to tell me all that'd happened to *him* that day, and Candice had vowed to tell me only after I'd had some rest.

"It's cool," I told Dutch when a knock on our bedroom door alerted us that Gaston was waiting to be seen.

Dutch let him in, and the director smiled as he entered. I noticed he was no longer formally dressed, but he still looked dignified in a black sweater and matching slacks. "Sorry to disturb you," he said. "But I wanted to let you know that Russ Buslawski has made a full confession."

I sat up to hear what the director had to say. Dutch came to sit next to me, and he took up my hand and we listened without interrupting the director as he told us that in Russ's apartment they'd found a suicide note, where he'd confessed to being responsible for all the bombs. He'd planned all along to detonate the bomb the moment I came down the aisle, and he probably meant to die in the blast.

His note and his confession, Gaston said, were something of a manifesto, where he claimed that the bombs were his revenge against those who'd driven his fiancée to kill herself. He'd wanted the bombs to be a message to the general public to be kinder to one another, which I thought was crazy twisted.

"Russ managed to easily gain access to Michelle's apartment by posing as the exterminator. And he did the same at Taylor's apartment when Taylor and her roommate were off to class. He rigged the latches, then waited for a time when the girls were alone to abduct them."

"He couldn't have done that with Debbie Nunez," I said. "She would've recognized him."

"Yes, that's why he had to risk taking her on the street."

"How did he get the girls to go to their targets?" Dutch asked.

"He told them that he'd be watching them every step of the way, and if they didn't do as he said, he'd set off the bomb remotely." It was exactly as I'd suspected, I thought. "He wanted them to suffer," Gaston continued, "so he set each girl up with an obstacle course of sorts. Making them find their way out of wooded areas, he gave them a route to each of the locales that would be difficult physically and also keep them out of the view of anyone who might notice they were strapped to a bomb."

Gaston then focused on me. "You were the biggest challenge Russ faced. He said that when he found Dutch's note on your car, he thought it was something of a miracle. He knew how to lure you to your own house after everyone else had left, and he filled it with the same gas he uses when he tents a home for termites. It works on the central nervous system and, in large quantities, quickly knocks humans unconscious. Russ knew you'd fought your way out of difficult circumstances before, and he told us he didn't want to underestimate your ability to fight him, so he decided the gas would kill two birds with one stone by knocking you out, and anyone who immediately came looking for you."

I rubbed my forehead. "No wonder I still have a headache."

"Yes, well, it could have been worse. Miss Fusco is home in bed, where I hope she'll stay for the next day or two, and your best man, Rivers, was just released from the hospital."

Dutch squeezed my hand. "Remind me to call Milo before we leave tomorrow, babe," he said.

I nodded but then turned my attention back to Gaston. "Did he say how he got into my house in the first place?" I asked.

"Yes. Apparently he made a copy of the key your construction manager gave him."

I blinked and in an instant I remembered meeting Dave the night my landscaper came by to check out the damaged urns. He'd lifted a key out from underneath a paint can, and I realized that Dave had gone to meet his wife for happy hour the night before and hadn't met Russ at the house. He'd just left him a key under the paint can. "Dave . . . ," I growled.

"Hmm?" Dutch asked.

Not wanting to get Dave in trouble, I shook my head. "Nothing. Sorry, Director. You were saying?"

Gaston shrugged and turned for the door. "That's really all there is to tell, Abigail." But then he paused and turned back to us. "Oh, except for this," he said. Reaching into his pocket, he pulled out two airline tickets. "Agent Frost wanted me to give these to you and wish you congratulations."

I stood up and held out my hand for the tickets. "We're not married, Director."

"Yet," he said, and then he and Dutch exchanged a knowing look before he was gone.

I turned to my fiancé. "What're you up to?"

"You'll see," he said cryptically. "You'll see."


A few days later, I donned my beautiful silk slip wedding dress and took up the small bouquet of lotus flowers a young girl in a sarong had brought me earlier. I then walked out of the thatched bungalow set just off a beautiful white sand beach on the coast of Bali and made my way down a winding path lit by the tranquil rays of the setting sun. Inhaling the perfume of tropical flowers set all along the path, I sighed contentedly at the serenade of the tide coming in and going out along the beach.

After one final turn I came out to a stone walkway, at the end of which stood my fiancé, looking more radiantly handsome than I could ever remember. Dutch was dressed in a white linen shirt that set off his tanned skin and midnight blue eyes, which lifted when they saw me. I watched him gasp, and then place a hand over his heart, and it filled me with such sweeping emotion that he was so moved by the sight of me. I walked without my cane, steady and sure toward him, my gaze locked with his. When I reached him, he took my hand, tucking it into the fold of his arm, and with a cabana boy, the flower girl, and the hotel manager as the only witnesses, Dutch and I were finally married. It was the most beautiful wedding ceremony ever. And absolutely perfect.

Excerpt from FA...

332

went straight to voice mai...
doesn't count when you...
only to get the sam...
Candice's call. T...
I tried a t...
straight t...
or it b...
be...

My eyes popped open just after three a.m. I'm not sure what woke me except that I had a bad feeling the second I sat up in bed and looked around. My hubby, Dutch, was sleeping peacefully next to me, the sound of his light snoring filling the room.

Instinctively I reached for my cell phone, which was face-down on the nightstand and turned to silent. I always mute my phone before I go to bed because anyone calling after eleven p.m. usually has only bad news to share, and in recent months I've had all I can handle in the bad news department.

Focusing on the phone's display, I saw that my best friend and business partner, Candice Fusco, had just called—and she'd left a message. I pressed play and held the phone to my ear.

"Abby!" the voice mail began, and the urgency in her voice made my back stiffen. "You have to trust me. It's not how it looks."

It's been my experience that *nothing* good ever starts with those words.

Immediately I paused the message and called Candice. It

. "Shit!" I whispered (swearing whisper), and tried calling her again, e result. I looked at the time stamp of hree oh four a.m. It was now three oh six. rd time to reach her and again the phone went voice mail. Either Candice's phone was turned off ad lost its charge, because otherwise it would've rung ore clicking over.

"Where are you?" I muttered, tapping the phone to go back to that paused voice mail. "You have to trust me," I heard the message repeat. "It's not how it looks. But it's gonna look bad, Sundance. Real bad. Listen carefully, and whatever you do, don't share this voice mail with anybody. This is for your ears only. I need you to go to the office the second you get this and do something for me. In the back of my closet is a wall safe. The combination is Sammy's birthday—you remember it, don't you?"

Sammy was Samantha Dubois. She was Candice's older sister, who, tragically, had lost her life in a fatal car crash just outside Las Vegas when Candice was in her teens. Candice had been in the passenger seat at the time of the accident and had nearly died too. She'd pulled through after spending several months in the hospital. I couldn't imagine how difficult that time must've been for her, but I knew it still affected her deeply, because my best friend almost never talked about the accident. Still, I'd see the deep emotional wound appear in Candice's eyes twice a year on two specific dates: August 5th—Sam's birthday—and June 17th, the date of Sam's death.

I also knew that in years past Candice had kept a Nevada driver's license with her photo but her sister's information on it. As Candice was a private investigator by trade, she'd confessed to me that the fake ID came in handy on occasion, and it actually had come in very handy on one particular occasion that I could remember.

"Inside the safe you'll find a file," Candice went on, and it was then that I noticed her breathing had ticked up—as if she'd started running. "Take the file and hide it. Don't show it or share it with *anyone*, Abby. No. One. Not even Dutch or Brice. I'll be in touch when I can."

The cryptic message ended there. I replayed it and held the phone tightly, as if I could squeeze more information out of Candice's voice mail. And then I got out of bed and looked around the room, trying to figure out what to do.

After a few seconds I did what comes naturally to me. I flipped on my intuitive switch and tried to home in on Candice's energy.

I'm a professional psychic by trade. I have my own steady business of personal clients, and Candice and I work private investigation cases together. We work so well together that we've nicknamed each other after Butch Cassidy and the Sundance Kid. I'm Sundance, and, as there's nothing butch about Candice, she's just Cassidy. When I'm not working a case with Candice, or busy with my own clients, I also sideline as a psychic for the FBI—although my official title at the bureau is "FBI civilian profiler."

Kinda makes it sound like I have a fancy degree in psychology, doesn't it? For the record, I majored in poli-sci, and there wasn't much fancy about it. As long as nobody asks too many questions when they read my official ID, the Feds are happy.

My husband works for the bureau too. So does Candice's.

Brice Harrison, Candice's husband, is my boss at the bureau. Brice and Candice were married last month, when they eloped to Las Vegas and stayed there for a week and a half on their honeymoon. I wasn't invited to the wedding, but then, nobody else was either. I guess it's only fair, as Candice wasn't exactly present for my wedding to Dutch. And it was probably a little bit my fault that she hadn't gotten married locally. My sister, who'd attempted to orchestrate my wedding extravaganza, was still looking to exercise her wedding planner muscles on someone. The rest of us were just looking to exorcise my sister. She'd been like a woman possessed ever since Dutch and I had gotten engaged, and our wedding had hardly turned out like she'd planned (and planned, and *planned*!).

Still, it would've been nice to watch Candice and Brice exchange their vows. I'm pretty sure she thought the same about Dutch and me, which is why I pretended to be thrilled when she had called me from Sin City to let me know they'd eloped.

I think Candice knew I was a little hurt, but the weird thing is that ever since she got back from Vegas, she's been different.

Candice has always been a pretty cool cucumber—it's rare to see her lose her composure—but when she came back from her honeymoon, it's like someone turned the temperature of that cool demeanor down another few notches. She's become a little more withdrawn, and a little more—I don't know—*secretive*?

It's not anything I can put my finger on, but lately she hasn't been as open with me about what's going on in that highly intelligent mind of hers. I've been chalking it up to the fact that she and Brice have been busy house hunting and easing into their married lives. But deep down, no matter how I've been trying to rationalize it, I've been worried about her. And my radar has certainly pinged with a sense of urgency every time Candice and I have hung out. I kept thinking a big case must be coming our way that just hadn't appeared yet, but now, in light of the voice mail I'd just listened to, I knew I'd completely misinterpreted the signal.

"Abs?" I heard Dutch whisper as I fished around on the floor for my slippers.

"Go back to sleep," I told him. The last thing I needed was for Dutch to get involved in whatever this was before I had a chance to figure it out.

The light on his side of the bed clicked on. "What's wrong?"

I hid my phone behind my back and adopted what I hoped was an innocent smile. "Nothing, sweetie. I couldn't sleep, so I'm just gonna go downstairs and watch some TV."

Dutch rubbed his face and yawned. "Is there any cheesecake left?"

"No," I lied, willing him to roll over and go back to sleep.

Dutch blinked. "You ate six pieces between yesterday and today?"

My smile got bigger and more forced. "Yes. It was too tempting to resist."

Dutch focused on me, his eyes narrowing. Instantly I could tell he knew that (a) I was a liar, liar, pants on fire, and (b) I was hiding something.

"Abs," he said, his gaze traveling to the hand holding my phone behind my back. "What's up?"

"Nothing."

He sighed heavily. "So it's bad, whatever it is."

I opened my mouth to insist that there was nothing wrong when Dutch's phone rang. He glanced at it, then looked back at me as if to say, "I knew you were hiding something."

Heat tinged my cheeks, but I held my ground and motioned with my free hand for him to answer his phone.

"Brice," he said as he picked up the call, and a shiver went down my spine. I knew Brice was calling about Candice, and if Brice was calling Dutch at three a.m. about Candice, whatever was going on was as bad as bad gets.

If I needed any confirmation, the expression on Dutch's face said it all. As he listened, he visibly paled and then his jaw clenched before he said, "When?" followed by "Where?"

I shoved on my slippers and eased out of the room. Rounding the hallway into our beautiful new kitchen, I didn't even bother to click on the lights. I just navigated the darkness the best I could, muttering the occasional "Dammit!" (swearing doesn't count when you bump into furniture in the dark) and making my way toward the counter with the little copper dish that held my car keys.

"Abby?" I heard Dutch call from the bedroom.

I ignored him and hustled to the door leading to the garage, so thankful that I didn't require the use of a cane anymore. I'd had a nasty accident eighteen months before that'd nearly permanently crippled me, but with a whole lot of physical therapy (and maybe some tough love from Candice when I didn't push myself to get off the cane), I'd finally gotten the full use of my legs back.

"Abs?" I heard Dutch call again as I slipped out the door, closing it as quietly as I could behind me. I tapped the button for the garage door opener, then hurried to the car, tucking inside my shiny new SUV with my pulse racing. If Dutch discovered that I was slipping away, he'd grill me for details, and I felt intuitively that I had to get to the office and retrieve that file for Candice because time wasn't on my side.

I backed out of the garage and closed the door, hoping that

Dutch wouldn't see me leaving before the door closed. My hubby had coated the garage door with enough silicone to make a Slip 'N Slide look sticky. Dutch liked that it barely made a sound as it moved up and down, and at the moment I was really glad he'd used two spray cans of the stuff on the gears. It'd give me a few extra seconds before he gave chase, and I knew he'd give chase because that's just how Dutch rolled when it came to me.

Crouched over the steering wheel, I navigated the dark neighborhood streets, for once ignoring the beauty and quiet of our lovely suburban Austin community, and drove to the office I shared with Candice. My phone rang through the SUV's Bluetooth a couple of times, but I ignored the calls from my husband, focusing instead on getting to the office as quickly as I could.

Once I was within sight of the building, I circled the block, hoping to spot Candice's yellow Porsche nearby, but there was no sign of it. I parked in the alley between two buildings a couple of blocks down from the office, guided by my intuition, which was sending me lots of "Danger, Will Robinson! Danger!" signals, and, after looking around the all but deserted streets, I got out and trotted toward our building.

Along the way, I paused once or twice to listen and look, every nerve tingling with trepidation, and at last made it to the front door. I peered through the glass, looking around, but the place was so dark that I couldn't see anything inside.

It took me a minute to fish around my key ring for the right key—no way was I going to risk using a light to find the key—and when I finally had it, the sweat from my palms made fitting it into the lock tricky.

At last I gained entrance and practically ran to the elevator, pressing the button a dozen times until the elevator doors opened. After selecting the fourth floor, I pressed the DOOR CLOSE button another dozen times, then tapped my foot anxiously as the elevator climbed its way up. "Should've taken the stairs," I muttered.

The second the doors opened, I squeezed through and rushed down the hallway to our suite. The corridor was dimly lit—the main lights wouldn't come on for another two hours or so. Still, it was enough light to see by and I had no trouble getting in the door this time. The first thing I did was call out Candice's name on the slim hope that she was there, hiding. I felt my phone vibrate in my back pocket and I took it out to look at the display.

It was Dutch. Again. Trying to reach me for the sixth time.

I clicked the call over to voice mail and called out again. "Candice? Honey, it's me. Are you here?"

There was no reply and the office was eerily silent. The hair on the back of my neck stood up on end and goose pimples lined my arms. I realized I was alone and vulnerable.

Turning back toward the door, I checked to make sure it was locked, then squared my shoulders and got on with it.

Candice and I have shared the suite of three private offices and one central lobby for nearly two years. We had had a similar setup even before that when we both lived in Michigan. The arrangement of sharing space together worked really well for us.

Like me, Candice had her own set of private clients—the easy adultery cases or background-check stuff—and she and I tackled the more difficult missing persons and such cases together. It was a wonderful partnership, as we each brought something different to the investigation process. Candice had a wealth of PI experience, smarts, and a handy assortment of deadly weapons. I had my intuition, my sunny disposition, and a cache of colorful expletives I'd been saving just in case of emergency.

Candice's office was just to the right of the front door, and my two smaller offices were to the left. Anxious to follow my best friend's instructions and get the hello, Dolly outta there before anyone was the wiser, I headed to the right of the tiny lobby and found Candice's door closed. I tried the handle, but it was locked. "Son of a bitch!" (Swearing doesn't count when your best friend doesn't tell you she locked her office door and you need to get a secret file from the back of her closet before the poop hits the fan.)

Standing back from the door, I thought for a second, then remembered that I had a spare key to her office hidden somewhere in my desk drawer. We'd exchanged keys just in case of an emergency right after we'd signed the lease, but I hadn't seen the key since I'd moved in.

Grumbling to myself, I moved back through the lobby to my office and over to the desk. Once there, I risked turning on the little lamp at the edge of my blotter and began rummaging around in the drawers when I felt that same prickly tension creep up my spine again.

I stopped rummaging and turned off the desk lamp, listening for any sound that might suggest I wasn't alone. The seconds ticked by without incident, but instead of feeling less anxious, I began to feel even more nervous.

Turning around, I moved to the window and peered outside, and that's when I saw a patrol car ease its way down the street. "Shit!" I hissed. (Swearing doesn't count when you're creeping around in the middle of the night and you think the cops may be about to rain on your parade.)

As my heart rate ticked up, I swiveled back to the desk and used my phone to shed some light on the drawer, frantically pushing at all the odds and ends I'd shoved into my desk over the past two years. And then, miracle of miracles, I found the key. "Eureka!"

Clutching it to my chest, I hurried out of my office and back over to Candice's door. The key slid easily into the lock and I let myself in, then tapped at my phone to listen to her message again. ". . . In the back of my closet is a wall safe. . . ." I paused the message and moved to the small closet to the right of the desk, pulling open the door. Candice had a large filing cabinet in the closet, which took up almost the entire space and would neatly conceal anything behind it. Still, seeing it there was enough to make me groan. "*Really*, Candice?" With a sigh I pulled at the back edge of the filing cabinet, but it was extremely heavy, and trying to twist it out of the way was much harder than it looked.

It took me a minute or two of pulling, twisting, and shoving to get the cabinet to turn sideways so that I could wedge myself inside the closet and have a look behind it. I saw the wall safe midway down, just like Candice had said. What struck me, though, was that when we'd first looked at the space two years earlier, I was certain there'd been no safe inside this closet. Candice must've had it put in without telling me.

Why she'd done that, I couldn't guess, but it bothered me because I was Candice's BFF and we weren't supposed to keep secrets from each other.

Still, my radar was telling me I didn't have a lot of time to dwell on such things, so I hunkered down and stared at the dial. Putting the phone back to my ear, I listened to the next part of the message again. "The combination is Sammy's birthday—you remember it, don't you?"

"August fifth," I muttered, but then my breath caught. I didn't know the year. "Crap, Candice! What year was your sister born?"

In desperation I tried calling Candice's cell again, but now, instead of going straight to voice mail, a recorded voice told me that the voice mailbox was full. I had a feeling Brice might have been responsible for filling it up, because if Candice wasn't taking my calls, I doubted she was taking Brice's calls either. That could only mean she was in *serious* trouble.

Frustrated, I stared at the dial for a few seconds until I realized I could probably come up with the answer on my own. I started to spin the wheel toward the digits I did know—eight, five—then talked the problem of the remaining digits out loud. "Sam was four years older than Candice and Candice was fifteen at the time of the accident, so that would have been in nineteen ninety-five, I think. . . . Ninety-five minus nineteen equals seventy-six. So, right again to nineteen, then left to seventy-six."

Just as the dial landed on that number, I heard a noise from somewhere in the building. I froze and strained my ears to hear more. Faintly I could just make out the sounds of activity in the building and my pulse quickened yet again as my radar sent a little ping of warning. Crossing my fingers, I pulled at the handle to the safe and it popped open. "Thank God!" I gasped, and shone the light of my phone into the interior. There in the safe was a fat wad of cash, one of Candice's spare handguns, and a manila file without a label to indicate what it might contain. I snatched the file and the cash. "Leave the gun, take the casholi," I whispered, thinking that if Candice contacted me, she'd probably need the money. Then I closed the safe door and spun the dial to lock it.

Standing up again, I wedged myself back out of the closet and shoved the filing cabinet with my shoulder. Under the fuel of adrenaline, the cabinet moved back into place without nearly the trouble it'd caused me a few minutes earlier. I then closed the closet door and hustled back out of Candice's office.

Risking a few extra seconds to lock her door again, I made sure to keep the key close, tucking it into my pocket before darting to the small window in the lobby overlooking the street. There were two patrol cars parked at the curb.

I didn't even pause to utter an expletive; instead I whirled around and ran for our front door. Putting my ear to it, I listened, but didn't hear anyone out in the hallway, so I undid the lock and eased the door open a crack. Putting my eye to the crack, I peered out and that's when I heard the faint ping of the elevator. "Time to go," I whispered, ducking out into the hallway. I paused only long enough to reach back and lock the handle on the door before closing it softly, then dashed off in the opposite direction from the elevators. There was a maintenance elevator at the rear of the building and I didn't slow down until I'd reached it. I thought of using the stairs, but the door triggered the fire alarm, and I rather liked the fact that no one knew I was here in the building . . . yet.

As I waited for the service elevator, I could hear voices back down the hallway, and I knew the cops had made it to our office. I wasn't totally convinced yet that they were looking for Candice, but I had a bad feeling all the way around and the last thing I wanted was to get caught up in some hot mess before I even had a chance to figure out what kind of trouble I was about to be swept up into.